RELIGIOUS WARS

BRADLEY HALL

This is for all the people who are very close to me and have helped me get through hard times, inspired me to make this book, and, most of all, helped me with this book.

Those people are my mom Myra Hall, my twin sister Cayley Hall, my older sister Mya Hall, Mya's girlfriend Claire Denney, my best friend Alexzander Johnson, my grandpa Dominick Massett, his friend, Helen Coutant, and finally, the person that helped me make my dream to publish a book come true, Zoe Howard.

Contents

INTRODUCTION TO THE MAIN CHARACTER

In the state of Kansas, in Great Bend, lived a boy named Ren Claude, the son of an American father named David Claude and a Chinese mother named Shanna Claude. Ren was in his early twenties. He was born on March 23, 1997, was exactly six feet tall, weighed one hundred and eighty-five pounds, and had lived in Great Bend his whole life.

Ren was in college at Barton County Community Junior College, trying to get a scholarship to become a doctor because his mother and father were doctors themselves for many years. When Ren was a little kid, he wanted to become a doctor just like his parents. But currently, he was working in a library (called the Barton Library) near his school.

Ren was living by himself in his school's apartment complex, and he had many friends, but some of them didn't know he was a huge nerd. He loved anime and comics—like anything from Funimation and Shonen Jump shows.

Now, it sounded like he had a good life; however, soon it would all be about to change.

THE BEGINNING

June 11, 5:40 PM. Ren was in his room reading a Naruto manga on his bed to kill some time. He had finished all of his homework and done all of his chores around his apartment. He was relaxing for a while until his phone started ringing. Ren sighed, put a bookmark in his manga, and put the manga down on his bed to answer the phone.

"Hello? This is Ren."

Ren heard a familiar voice from his phone. It was a woman that worked at the library with him.

"Hi, Ren. Sorry for calling you on your day off, but that health book you ordered—it's finally here."

"Really?!"

"Yeah. We are about to close, but I'll just keep the library open until you come and get it. Just for you, Ren."

When she finished, she couldn't hear Ren. In excitement, he had just hung up without telling her because he had been waiting for this book for weeks and he wanted to get it as soon as he could. Ren quickly grabbed his jacket, wallet, phone, and keys.

Ren left his apartment as fast as he could to get on his bike. He had a car and he wanted to get there fast, but today felt good so he wanted to ride his bike instead. He left as fast as he could to go to the library. But little did he know that he hadn't locked his door or shut it hard enough, so the door was open, just a little bit—a little crack.

It took Ren one hour to get to the library, get his book, talk to his friends there, and ride home. When he came back, it was slowly becoming night and he couldn't wait to read his book. Ren quickly parked his bike to the side and opened his door, without realizing he hadn't locked it, and turned on his lights.

When Ren raised his head up, what he saw were two men right in front of him stealing everything he had. The two men and Ren stared at each other. No one was moving an inch. It was like prey that had noticed a predator was near and was about to pounce on him if he made the wrong move.

Ren was scared. He had no idea what to do in this situation. So his feet slowly moved back to the door, trying to leave his apartment. But without warning, he heard a loud creak behind him and when he tried to turn around, he was knocked out by a third person with a crowbar, making a good CRACK in Ren's skull.

This is where the real story begins.

WELCOME TO HELL

Loud, painful screaming could be heard in the background. Ren was too tired to speak, so he thought, "W-where am I? What is this? Are those people screaming? Why is it so hot, and why can't I move?"

He finally opened his eyes. He was in a cage that looked like it was made of flesh, with four big fires on each corner to provide light in the flesh-covered room, and when Ren looked through the bars from his door there were people—hundreds, maybe even thousands of people—being tortured by these hideous and, for some reason, cool-looking monsters.

Ren looked around desperately to find an exit, but saw chains wrapped around his arms, legs, torso, and neck, which explained why he couldn't move. But he noticed something about these chains—for some reason, they were not hot at all. They were actually ice cold even though there was fire everywhere. Ren tried to struggle free from the chains but to no avail.

Then Ren stopped shaking. He heard footsteps. But these footsteps were loud and were getting closer. Ren tried even harder to break free. But everything he was doing was just making the chains tighter. So Ren stopped to catch his breath until he heard his cage door opening.

Two creatures walked through the cage door. One of them shut it behind them. One of the creatures looked just like a humanoid goat—a goat that was standing on two legs, but instead of hooves, it had hands and feet, and it had a nice six-pack, and of course a goat head. But the other one was covered with sad and angry faces all over its body with its real face red and upside down. One of them had a board with a list of people's names. The goat one asked for Ren's name in surprisingly good English that Ren could actually understand, but Ren was too scared to speak.

Both creatures sighed in annoyance, so the multi-faced one decided to walk toward Ren and put its hand on Ren's head. Every eye on its face closed, and then it started to mumble. Ren couldn't understand what it was saying. It had to be its own language or a language Ren never learned in school.

Then a red flame engulfed both Ren's head and the creature's multi-faced hand.

Ren screamed, "AAAAAAAAAA!!!" His head felt like someone was putting a fire poker inside his brain. But, in actuality, the creature was reading Ren's mind.

It said, with multiple voices, "Ren Claude. That's his name."

The goat creature went through the papers. "Huh. I don't have any Ren Claude."

"What are you talking about? That's impossible. Every soul that comes here has his or her name on our paperwork," the multi-faced creature said.

"Look, see for yourself. His name is not on here. This has never happened before. Ever. Which means only one thing: he is not supposed to be here. He was supposed to go to heaven."

They were both shocked, trying to figure out what was going on.

Then the goat creature asked, "What did you do before you died to be here?"

But Ren didn't answer the question. He instead said, "WHERE AM I AND WHAT THE HELL ARE YOU TWO?!"

Both creatures suddenly started to laugh, and the multi-faced one said, "You are in hell, my friend, and we are demons."

Ren didn't believe what he had heard at first, but what he was seeing had to be real. There was no doubt about it—the pain from the chains, the heat, the fact that he didn't feel sick or delirious. Ren tried to remember how he got there, or, to be more exact, how he died, but he couldn't remember.

Ren hesitantly asked the two demons, "How did I die?"

They told Ren with a smile, "You got hit by a crowbar, which cracked your skull open."

After they told Ren, the goat demon said, "But teasing you aside, you are not supposed to be here. You weren't supposed to die like that and you weren't supposed to die this young. My paperwork says that you were supposed to go to heaven and die when you hit ninety-six years old from your heart giving out."

After that useful information, the goat demon left, saying, "I'm going to see what is happening here."

The other one decided to read Ren's mind again to see what he did that was so bad that he got sent to hell. It lasted for hours—hours of Ren's mind feeling like it was being melted—until the goat demon finally returned with a shocked face.

He said, "You didn't do anything wrong to be sent here, but someone in heaven ordered your reaper to send you to hell."

Ren said, "What are you talking about?!" His voice was tired and scrappy from his mind being melted.

"It's what I just said—someone in heaven told your reaper to send you to hell," the goat demon said.

"Who did?" Ren asked.

"I don't know, but it had to be a high-class angel. They have the power to boss reapers around. But," he said with a change of tone, "it doesn't matter anymore. We got our answer and you are in hell now and we can do whatever we want to you."

Both demons started to laugh very evilly. One of them summoned a tray for the ground. Ren didn't know who did it because he wasn't paying attention. But he could see various tools. There were multiple different types of blades that were rusted from blood. They didn't look sharp but that was the point—to make it more painful. Ren could also see hammers, pliers, and some other tools that he didn't know what they were used for.

Ren screamed in pain as the demons began to torture him. "NOO AAAAAAAA!!!"

Two hundred years had passed since Ren had been sent to hell, but in the living world, only two years had gone by. Ren was still in his cage, but he now had torn clothes and many, many scars all over his body. Ren's mind was slowly going insane because of all the physical and mental torture that he had been going though over the many years that had passed. But Ren's mind was not fully broken; he still knew where he was and who he was.

Then the goat demon walked in his cage with tools and said, "Hello, Ren. Are you ready for your daily torture?"

Ren's eyes widened. Ren was scared as the demon walked toward him with a rusty spoon in his hands. He was probably going to scoop out Ren's eyes again.

All that Ren could think was, "No, no, no more, please no more, I can't take it anymore. Why am I here? I don't deserve this, I swear to God— No, God. Oh God, you did this to me, God, you don't give a shit about me. If you did, you would have already taken me out of this fucking place, I—I swear to Go— No, to me—I'll kill that fucking angel and anyone who fucking did this to me. I swear I'll fucking kill them all!"

Then, out of nowhere, Ren's body started to glow red and change. The first thing that changed was Ren's head. It turned into a black cobra's head with both front sides of the hood that had one big red eye. He also grew two Polygonal ram horns, with no spiral, pointing down. His torso and arms became more muscular, scaly, and very white. He grew dragon-like wings and his fingertips looked like the tip of a blade, as did the tips of his toes. He grew a black snake tail, his legs looked like bat legs, and finally on the left side of his chest, there appeared the number 2000.

After the transformation was finished, the chains that were wrapped around Ren let him go and he fell to the ground, gasping for air.

The goat demon turned away from Ren, walked toward the door, and said, "Follow me."

Ren was still trying to get his breathing under control, but he managed to say, "Why?"

The goat demon said coldly, "Just follow me."

Ren had no idea what the demon was trying to pull but, for some reason, Ren's instincts were telling him to follow the demon. So Ren got up and started to walk with him. When he left his cage, the outside surprisingly looked different from when he was inside the cage. When he was inside, all he could see were tortured souls, but now it looked like a medieval hallway with many doors. As they both started to walk down the hallway, Ren could still see all the tortured souls, but they were in cages—the same cages that Ren had been in—and they just kept saying, "Please help me—someone help—no more—HELP—God, please forgive me—oh God, oh God—God please forgive me..."

Ren couldn't look at them. He closed his eyes in disgust and pity.

Ren quietly whispered to himself, saying, "I'm sorry, but I can't help you. I wish I could." A single tear came out of his right eye.

They walked for quite some time until they finally met their destination. The goat demon said, "Go inside." Ren looked at the demon, then at the door multiple times.

Ren finally walked to the door. The door looked too normal. It was just a brown door. Ren finally opened the door and walked inside. There was an office inside. It had red walls with a fancy carpet, and the walls had multiple pictures of tortured souls, but the pictures actually looked like art from an art museum. In front of Ren was another demon. He was a good-looking person, but he had black wings, spiral horns, and extremely red eyes that, if they looked at someone for a long time, would catch them on fire. He also had long black hair, claws, a red suit, and the number 75 on the left side of his chest. Even though he was wearing a suit, Ren could clearly see the number through the suit.

The demon said, "Ah, a visitor. Come sit down." He spoke like a businessman.

Ren slowly walked toward the demon. Ren didn't know why he was walking super slow; it was like his body was telling him to not move forward, as if danger lay ahead, but he kept walking until he was in front of a wooden chair. He slowly and quietly sat down.

The demon said, "Hello, there. My name is Astaroth. I'm the ruler of this world. Sorry for having you here when you just got your new form, but it's tradition for a new demon to meet his or her superior."

Ren didn't say or think anything. He was distracted by this demon's overwhelming demonic power.

Astaroth placed his chin on his hands, which were clamped together, and said, "I bet you have a lot of questions for me. So let me hear them and let me answer them, but first—here, have some tea. You look thirsty."

Ren was actually very thirsty. He hadn't drunk anything decent in years. So all he did was nod. Astaroth poured some tea in a clear glass cup that he got out of his desk and handed it to Ren. As Ren picked up the cup and started to drink the tea, he thought to himself, "Is this guy really a demon? He's really not that scary. He is pretty nice."

But even though Ren's mind was thinking that, his body was sweating and scared because he could sense Astaroth's huge demonic power and strength. Ren tried to stay calm, and said, "Your name is Astaroth and you are the ruler of hell?"

Astaroth smiled and said, "Well, yes and no. I'm the ruler of this hell, but hell is—how to put this—one huge dimension with many other little dimensions connected to it. To explain more clearly, that number on your chest is your ranking. It ranks you based on your skills, strength, intelligence, speed, durability, etc. when you first become a demon."

Ren was drinking some more tea when Astaroth was telling him all of this new information but then Ren asked another question.

"Wait, so does that mean I can rule over a dimension, or is it not that easy?"

Astaroth laughed a little bit and said, "Sorry, but only the demons with the numbers 200 and less get their own dimension, aka their own world, to rule over with their own demon army, and so this dimension is a hell that I rule."

Ren thought, "Figures." He surprisingly seemed to understand what Astaroth was saying, but one thing didn't make sense, so he asked, "Why only the demons with the number 200 or less? Why do they get their own dimension and army?"

Astaroth smiled and said, "Because those are the deadliest demons in hell—according to heaven, that is. They are so strong that heaven put a spell on hell: any demon that automatically has the numbers below 200 is fully stuck in hell, which means they can't leave hell or possess any humans."

"And you're number 75. That means you're the 75th strongest demon in hell?"

"Yes, I am the 75th strongest demon in hell. That is very impressive, but I'm nothing compared to the demon kings."

Ren's eyes widened. "Demon kings?"

"Yes, the demons with the numbers 10 and below are obviously the top strongest demons in hell. They also get their own world, obviously, but with no tortured souls except for one, but that doesn't matter right now because they are so great that they don't need to torture souls. And it is said that the top ten can even take an archangel head on."

Ren couldn't believe what he was hearing. Demon kings! They could take on an archangel? Ren didn't know that much about religion but knew that the archangels were the first angels ever created by God himself. So they had to be very powerful. But, yet again, another question appeared in Ren's head.

"If 1 through 10 are called the demon kings, then what are the demons with the numbers 11 through 200 called? What are you called?"

"We are called the demon generals."

Ren put his right hand on his chin and said quietly, "I see. So the top ten are the kings—the most powerful. 11 through 200 are generals—still really powerful, but they are the subordinates to the kings. And demons with a number above 200 are the soldiers."

As more and more questions were answered and Ren spent more time talking to Astaroth, he was finally starting to not be scared of Astaroth. In fact, Ren was enjoying the conversation because he felt like he was in an anime or a book, because he was a subject of Astaroth and Astaroth was his ruler.

Suddenly, Astaroth got a call from the phone on his desk. He answered it. Apparently, they had old phones in hell—so old that Ren couldn't tell what year it was made.

Astaroth picked up the phone and with a professional tone, said, "Yes, yes, I understand. Okay, I'll do just that."

Astaroth hung up and put both of his hands together.

He sighed. "Well, it was going to happen but I wasn't expecting this early.

Ren, you need to go to our top blacksmith to get your weapon."

Ren was confused for many reasons. One, hell had a blacksmith? Two, how did the person that just called know Ren was with Astaroth? And three, Ren needed a weapon?

Astaroth started talking, jolting Ren out of his thoughts to tell him how to get to the blacksmith. "Go straight to my red door with the skull handle that is behind you. All you have to do is to say where you want to go, wait for the skull eyes to glow, then stop glowing, and then open the door and go inside."

Ren thought, "Red door? Isn't his door brown?" Ren turned around to look at the door and to his surprise, the door was red, not brown. It must have had two different looks on either side.

Ren turned back around. "Okay." He stood up, turned around, walked to where Astaroth told him, and said, "Take me to hell's blacksmith."

The door handles did indeed start to glow and Ren waited for it to stop. It only glowed for three seconds before it stopped. Ren took a deep breath and walked through the door. The hallway on the other side of the door was almost pitch black, but both sides of the stone walls had multiple torches going down the hall, illuminating it.

"Geez, going from one dimension to the other is a really long walk."

Ren walked for quite some time through the dark hallway, lost in thought.

He thought, "I can't believe this is happening to me. I was once a college student trying to get his degree to become a doctor. But now I'm a demon in hell, a subordinate to a demon general, and I'm going to get a weapon from hell's blacksmith. All of this is just happening too fast. It's like a writer trying to skip the intro just to get to the good stuff."

But before Ren knew it, he was already on the other side of the hallway and the door was right in front of his face. He tried to raise his arm, but it wouldn't budge. He looked down at his arm and tried to move it. Still no good. Ren took several deep breaths to calm his nerves. He had already met a demon general. This guy had to be another one, right? Right? So Ren took his final breath and finally moved his right arm and opened the door.

The world that Ren had just walked into looked like a very old medieval town in the daytime. There were old houses, cobblestone roads, no trees any-where, and light poles on the roads, but instead of light bulbs on the top, there were bowls with sticks in it to feed the fire lighting them when it turned dark. When he shut the door behind him and stared at the town, the first thing he thought was, "Where is the blacksmith's shop?"

To Ren, any of the buildings could be it because all of the houses looked alike. They were two stories and made of carved rock (for the walls), logs to keep everything in place, and bound together with the help of clay. They had some windows, very thick old doors, and finally the roofs were made of straw and sticks. So to his eyes, they all looked the same, even though they could all have different purposes.

Ren then saw something walking towards him in the middle of the houses on the cobblestone streets. It wasn't a person and it looked too small for a demon. So what was it?

As the creature reached him, Ren could finally tell what it was. It was a dog. A Doberman dog, but this dog was rotting very bad (which explained the bad smell), and it had tiny blue flames surrounding its body. The dog started to sniff Ren's leg, probably to identify who Ren was. He seemed to pass the dog's sniff test, so the dog turned around and started to walk ahead. Ren had no idea what to do, but he thought the dog wanted him to follow it, so that's what he did. They walked for only two minutes, until Ren saw a building that looked like a blacksmith shop. The dog sat at the entrance and Ren walked inside.

Inside, were souls chained up on the walls, but they were not making a sound. Ren walked up to one of them and noticed that this soul didn't have his tongue or any of his teeth. Ren looked around and noticed that none of the souls had teeth or tongues. Ren also noticed weapons everywhere, but they looked very glowing with purple and black colors and looked like very thick glass. It kind of reminded him of something, but Ren couldn't put his finger on it. Then Ren turned a little more and found a demon working on something.

He had a human skull head, no eyes, spiral horns, six black crow wings, a long red demon tail, and a suit. He turned his head and said, "Ren, I presume. I told Astaroth to send you to here to get your weapon. My name is Azazel, hell's greatest blacksmith." As he turned around, Ren could see the left side of his chest. The number 10 was there, showing through his suit. Ren was shocked that he was one of the top 10 strongest demons—a demon king that Astaroth had just told him about.

Azazel walked up to Ren and put his hand on Ren's shoulder. "I know I'm very intimidating, but really, I'm a nice guy. Just don't piss me off, okay?"

Ren was shaking profusely but managed to nod. He was trying to calm down but could feel the humongous power difference between both of them. It felt like an entire bridge was on top of him.

Azazel took his hand off of Ren's shoulder and said, "If you don't mind, Ren, can you tell me: what is your fighting style?" Ren had no idea what he was talking about, so Azazel explained. "To get a weapon from me, I need to know what fighting style you have so I can give you a weapon that is perfect for you."

But once again, Ren didn't know what fighting style he had.

Azazel sighed. "Fine, if you won't tell me, then show me. Fight me."

"Huh?"

"What, did I stutter? I said fight me so I can give you your weapon."

Ren raised his arms in front of Azazel, waving them side to side, and said, "Whoa, whoa, hold on just a second! Everything is happening way too fast! I don't know who you think I am, but I'm just learning all of this! I literally just found out how hell works, that hell has a ranking system, there are demon generals and kings, and now you want me to fight you? A demon king, are you fucking stupid, you'll kill me!"

Ren was gasping for air. It seemed like the moment Azazel brought up that Ren had to fight him really was the last straw. Azazel just stood there, shocked that Ren just yelled at a demon king.

Then Azazel did something that Ren wasn't expecting. Azazel started to laugh. Pretty loud actually. "I'm sorry, I was not expecting that. See, most demons when I bring up the 'you have to fight me' thing, they always beg me not to or try to run. This is a new one. AH HA HA!!"

Ren was speechless. He had no idea what to say. He just yelled at him—a demon king—and he was laughing? It was not a fake laugh or a weak laugh; it was a real, genuine laugh.

Azazel finally started to calm down, put his hand back on Ren's shoulder, and said, "Ah-ha. Look, I'll be holding way back during our fight. I'll be entirely on the defensive, and trust me, you won't die, I promise."

Ren said nervously, "Oh, really? And why won't I die from our fight?"

Azazel took a deep breath to breathe normally. He had laughed a little too hard at Ren's question. "Because one of the few ways—and I mean few ways—to kill a demon is with a weapon that is 100% made in heaven or hell."

Ren raised one of his eyebrows. "100% made in hell? Few ways to kill a demon?"

"Yes. Since you'll need to know this anyway, listen up."

Ren looked at Azazel straight in the eyes—or, eye sockets, because Ren didn't know if demons could die because they were already dead. So this information was very important and Ren needed to know it.

Azazel grabbed a chair that was nearby, sat on it, and began his speech. "Okay, listen. There are things that CAN kill a demon, but they are very few and can also kill an angel."

Ren thought, "Angels?!"

"The most common way is with the weapons from the demons and angels. The reason why it has to be 100% made in hell is because in hell, the weapons are made of pure sin. But as for the angels, their weapons are made of pure grace. If either weapon is even 1% or .01 or point however many more zeros, that isn't 100% made of sin from hell or grace from heaven, so it won't kill us or them."

Ren seemed to understand what Azazel was talking about, and it also seemed that he had calmed down, knowing that Azazel wouldn't use any weapons that he made on Ren to fight him. Ren wanted to ask more questions, but coming from the look Azazel was giving him, he clearly didn't want to be asked any more questions. What Azazel wanted was to fight Ren so he could give him his weapon.

Ren's legs started to shake and his mouth was moving, but no words were coming out. But luckily for him, Azazel could tell what he was trying to say.

"Good. I'm glad you're ready to fight me."

Ren's legs stopped shaking, probably because his legs knew that he had done it now.

Azazel got off the chair, picked it up, and put it back where it originally was. Azazel started to walk around his shop, trying to find something.

Azazel muttered to himself, "Now, where did I put it? It has to be around here—Ah, found it." Azazel reached over a table that was covered in blood and guts. When he got what he was looking for, he moved away from the table, holding something long. "Okay, Ren. Let's go outside and get things started."

Ren looked down at Azazel's right hand to see what he had. It was a very long, probably six-footlong, bronze-colored stick. But Ren had seen plenty of nerdy stuff and knew that was not a stick: it was a staff.

Ren and Azazel both left the shop. Outside, they had more room to move.

Then Azazel just started to fly up slowly and said, "Come on, Ren, let's fight in the air."

Ren looked up and watched Azazel fly up in the air until he stopped. He must have gotten to the spot that he wanted. Ren looked at his wings, then back to Azazel. He took a big breath and started to flap his wings. It only took a second, but he was off the ground. He was completely baffled. He had just gotten his wings and this was his first time flying with them. It should have been very difficult, but it felt normal. He didn't struggle to fly; it was like he had been flying his whole life. It just felt natural. Ren flew all the way up until he was face to face with Azazel again.

"Okay, Ren, let's finally get started." Azazel put both hands on the staff and pointed it at Ren.

Ren said, "I guess, but remember I've never been in a fight, so I have no idea how this should go!"

Azazel didn't respond. He just wanted to fight. Ren raised his hands up, his right hand closer to his chest and his left far away from his chest. He looked like a boxer. He took a deep breath and flew toward Azazel with amazing speed. When Ren got close enough, he spun around with his right leg out, trying to go for a spin kick. His foot hit Azazel's staff, making a clinking sound, as though it was made of metal, even though it looked like it was made of rocks.

But Ren was not done yet. He moved back far enough that he could use his foot to grab the staff. With his foot in place, he pulled himself close and swung at Azazel with his blade-looking claws. Azazel smiled and moved his two top wings to block both of Ren's arms without even struggling. So Ren swung his tail to the left, trying to whip Azazel's left hip. But Ren didn't come close to Azazel's hip because he grabbed Ren's tail with his right hand. But that was what Ren was hoping for. Without Azazel realizing it, Ren's left leg, his last free limb, was moving up for an uppercut. Ren moved his leg at the same time he moved his tail, but this attack actually hit. It hit Azazel's chin. Something made a loud cracking sound, followed by a painful scream.

Ren screamed with all his might. "AAAAAA!!"

It was Ren's foot.

Azazel was shocked that Ren actually got a hit. He spread every limb that was holding Ren's limbs back, sending Ren back, then he grabbed Ren by the wing and tossed him down to the ground. He sent Ren down, breaking the sound barrier and making Ren crash into an old house. Azazel smiled because he immediately knew what weapon would fit Ren's style perfectly.

Azazel slowly flew down to the house Ren crashed into, then said happily, "Okay, Ren, I got all I needed, so let's give you your weapons. Ren?"

Ren didn't respond because he was not conscious. The impact knocked him out. Two minutes passed, and Ren felt something cold hitting him. He got up from the shock of how cold it was.

Azazel said, "Sorry for knocking you out. I thought I tossed you pretty gently, but I guess not."

Ren thought in annoyance, "That was gently?"

Ren looked all over himself and saw that Azazel had tossed water on him. He looked around and noticed he was back inside the blacksmith shop. He looked over his shoulder to see Azazel was crouched down in front of a chest.

Azazel said, "Aha, found it! Ren, come here. I have your weapons."

Ren, struggling, said, "Okay, sure." He got up from the chair he was sitting on and started to walk toward Azazel, but stopped to look at his left foot and thought, "Wasn't it broken? And why isn't my body hurting?"

Azazel asked, "Is something the matter?!"

"No, it's nothing."

Azazel stood up, holding four wrist blades that looked like something that the Predator would use. He helped Ren put them on. Two were for Ren's hands and two were for his feet, but as soon as they were on, they just disappeared.

Ren was very confused, but luckily Azazel explained.

"It's okay, they do that. To summon them back all you have to do is picture them on you, and to make them go away you have to picture yourself without them.

Ren nodded, then closed his eyes. He pictured himself with them. A purple aura surrounded his hands and feet and they reappeared. Ren smiled, then pictured himself without them and, surely enough, they vanished.

Ren said, "Thank you."

"Anytime." For a demon who could kill Ren with just one finger, he was actually a nice guy.

"I have to ask: why these weapons?"

Azazel smiled, crossed his arms together, and said, "Well, when we were fighting, you used all four of your limbs. If it's to overwhelm your opponent, distract your opponent, or trap your opponent in one spot, it's simple but effective. And I can tell every limb on your body is very strong. With these blades, you'll have a longer reach, and it will make your opponent use their weapon to block, not their body parts." His tone was smooth and satisfied with his answer. Ren thought Azazel might like him.

Ren was amazed, shocked, and scared of everything that was happening to him. Within the past couple of hours, just after transforming into a demon, he'd learned so much, like how hell worked and how the demons were ranked, and now he had weapons. All of this had been bothering him, but he was finally enjoying it.

Out of curiosity, Ren asked, "Hey, Azazel, you said these weapons are the common way to kill an angel and demon, right?"

"Yes."

"Well, what are the other ways of killing an angel and demon? As a demon myself, I should know what can kill me or even really hurt me."

Azazel smiled and thought to himself, "This kid is a smart one."

"Okay, you want to know the other ways to kill an angel and demon. So listen carefully because I'm not going to repeat myself, okay? Here are the ways that can kill demons in order:

"One. A weapon that is entirely made from heaven or hell, like I told you before.

"Two. The powers of an angel, demon, or on a very rare occasion, other gods. We demons all have three powers in common: One. We can all teleport. If you use this right with your weapon, you can kill or injure a lot of your enemies. However, it's very hard to teleport in the middle of a battle, so be careful. Two. We all have telekinesis. We can all move things with our minds, but it has to be in our line of vision and with this move, you can easily kill weak opponents, but if the opponent is stronger or as strong as you, it might not work on them. If you're smart, and if you really want to beat someone stronger, then you have to weaken them first. The angels also have telekinesis, can teleport, and have weapons that can literally do the same thing as our weapons, but they're just made differently. But these are the only similarities. The next ways are different.

"Three. Demons can shoot hellfire which is hotter than all colors of human fire except for white fire. Well, it kind of depends on how strong the demon is. Some demons' fire can be hotter than white fire, but I digress. Anyway, the only way to extinguish these fires is water from heaven itself, which is what all angels have, because you know—hell, demons, fire; heaven, angels, water. And the fire can also be put out by the fire caster.

"Four. Every angel or demon has another power which is unique to each one. I won't tell you what yours is because someone else will.

"And finally, five. Any item that has been touched by God himself, like the stick of Moses, can kill us. And yes, I know I said only pure items from heaven and hell can kill an angel or demon, but God is a cheater and a hack, so he can bypass these rules. And that's it. That's everything that can kill an angel or a demon."

To Ren, those were a lot of things to remember, and he thought he got all of it, but still had questions. "Those are all the things that can kill us, but what about things that can really hurt us? Like, is there something out there that can injure us, but can't kill us?"

Azazel sighed this time. He was pretty annoyed at this point. "Jeez, kid, you really want to know everything. Okay, fine. Well, there are the standard things like salt, holy water, cross, and the hawthorns from the hawthorn tree. Those are toxic to us because they were used in Jesus Christ's crucifixion and that's it."

"Wait, what about iron?"

Azazel tilted his head slightly. "First, iron really works on ghosts and polter-geists, but for us, it only feels like minor burns. You won't even notice it if the iron isn't touching you for that long.

"So is that all?"

"Yes, that's all."

"Thanks for telling me all of this information. I'm grateful. Now, if we are done here, I'm going to leave, if you don't mind."

"Well, you can leave from my place, but there is still one thing you have to do before you go and do whatever you want."

"What do I have to know?" Ren sounded like a bratty teenage girl.

"Before you go, you have to see our true rulers of hell: our gods Satan and Lucifer. They also want to meet you. This is the last tradition thing you have to do."

Ren felt like his heart had just left his chest. "Wait, you mean literally Satan and Lucifer? And they are not the same person?"

"No, but that is what everyone thinks when I mention them. this is what they actually are: Lucifer is a fallen angel, which I don't need to explain. You should already know his story. Lucifer created Satan as the first created demon in history and made him face God to show him that Lucifer created something stronger than his father, and also to show him that he was a better God, but we all know how that went. Satan failed at killing God and so Satan and Lucifer became the rulers of hell. And now they both want to see you."

After that conversation, Ren reluctantly agreed to go see Lucifer and Satan (even though he didn't really have a choice). Ren shook Azazel's hand, turned around, and walked toward the exit. Ren stopped to look at the dog that was still outside laying down. It must be a guard dog, or at least a good pet, for Azazel.

Ren's body started to shake again because if he was scared shitless just meeting Astaroth and Azazel, and sensing their power, then meeting Satan and Lucifer was not going to be fun at all. Ren turned his head to look at Azazel, who was leaning on a crafting desk, waiting for Ren to leave.

Ren said, "Thank you" to Azazel again. He walked away from Azazel's shop—all the way back to the door—and said, "Take me to Lucifer and Satan."

The door handles glowed red, then stopped. Ren opened the door and walked through. After a couple of minutes walking down the hallway in silence, Ren finally arrived at the other door. But this door was different. It wasn't like the other doors he had seen. It was pure white and had no handle. Ren pushed it open, revealing complete blackness. It was so black that it didn't look like it had a floor. Ren took his chances and took a step.

There was a floor, which was a relief. So he took a couple more steps forward, letting the door shut on its own behind him, and that was when he saw them. Two people sitting on huge seats in a pitch black room. Ren didn't know how he didn't see them when he walked in. Maybe they just appeared in front of him.

The one on the right looked like what everyone thought Satan looked like: a red, muscular, humanoid man with goat legs and a demonic tail, red scaly wings like a dragon, and devil horns. His face looked like pure evil, with razor sharp teeth that looked like they could eat through anything, and he had burning red eyes that looked hotter than any sun in the galaxy.

Lucifer, on the left, was a beautiful middle-aged man. He had elegant long blonde hair, twelve white angel wings behind him, and a long white robe. His face was artful, and his eyes were like gems. It seemed like hell didn't hurt him at all.

Ren took a couple more steps forward, getting closer and closer until his legs stopped on their own, indicating that was as far as he was going to go. Both Satan and Lucifer were huge giants. Ren could fully feel their power now; it was much stronger than Azazel's and Astaroth's power combined. It was so powerful that Ren felt like he was going to faint and be crushed. Both Lucifer and Satan noticed that he was going to faint, so they lowered their power enough that Ren wouldn't pass out.

It worked. They lowered it enough so that Ren didn't feel like he was going to pass out, but their power was still high enough to still show their dominance.

They both said at the same time, "Welcome. It's nice to see you, Ren Claude." Satan's voice was deep, but surprisingly smooth, while Lucifer's was surprisingly normal, as though anyone could have had that voice. Satan's voice would have been good in an opera.

As they stared at Ren with blank stares, Ren could tell that they were bored out of their minds, like they had done this so many times that they didn't care, if they even cared to begin with.

Ren gulped any spit left in his mouth and said calmly, "Thanks for having me here, but why did you summon me? I can tell that you don't do this for every newly-created demon, and I can also tell that you don't give a shit right now. So why?"

Lucifer said, "Well, well. What happened to all that fear? You were so scared of Astaroth and Azazel. Why not us?"

Ren said, "Well, I didn't know what was going on when I became a demon at first. But after Astaroth told me what I needed to know and Azazel gave me my weapons and more information and told me that I was supposed to meet you guys... I just don't care anymore." (But that was a big old lie; he still had so many questions left and was so very scared.)

Satan and Lucifer both just stared at each other and laughed very hard.

Satan said, "You really have some balls to lie to us. You do know that we can easily kill you? I think Azazel forgot to tell you that demons can die from..."

Ren interrupted Satan, surprising Satan, Lucifer, and himself. "No, he did tell me what can kill a demon."

Satan gave a little grin and said, "Well, never mind. Sorry, boy, we don't keep tabs on every conversation that every demon has, but I have a feeling Azazel didn't tell you one thing about yourself that's important."

Ren tilted his head in confusion and said, "What one thing about myself?"

"What is your own power?" Lucifer asked.

Ren looked back down and thought to himself, "Yeah, that's right—he did tell me every demon has a specific power. And didn't he say that someone else would tell me my power?" Ren looked back up at Lucifer and Satan, immediately concluding it was them.

"Yes, Azazel didn't tell me. So can one of you please tell me? I really do want to know."

Satan got out of his seat and started to walk toward Ren. Ren tried to stay calm. Satan was getting smaller in size as he walked, but his power stayed the same.

Satan stood in front of Ren, looking at him with his glowing red eyes. With a shocked look in his eyes and a smile on his face, Satan turned to Lucifer and said, "I think we have our guy to do our special mission." Lucifer rolled his eyes. Satan turned back around and asked Ren: "How do demons leave hell?"

All Ren could do was give Satan a confused look and say, "Possession, right?"

Satan said, "Yes. When a demon possesses someone, they can take control, but they can only use 45% of their true strength. While an angel possesses someone, they can use 50% of their strength, but for you—your strength is reversed. Instead of only 45% of your strength, you can use 55% of your strength because you don't have to possess anyone. You are a rare type of demon. You are a shapeshift demon."

"What?"

Satan replied with: "You don't need to possess anyone when you go to the world of the living. You transform into the form you had when you died—aka your old human form—or you can make yourself look older or younger."

Once again, all that Ren could say was, "What?"

Satan said, "Listen, Ren, we have a request for you to complete a task."

"What is it that you want me to do?"

"Start a war with heaven," Lucifer said.

Ren paused for a second to see if it was a joke, but Lucifer had a straight face.

Ren just lifted his head and gave them a simple, "No."

Lucifer got angry. "WHAT?!"

Ren said it again. "No."

"Why not?!"

"Well, let me guess. If we start a war with heaven, then all my friends, family, and many other innocent people will die. I may be a demon, but I'm not loyal to you or your cause."

Lucifer lifted his hand up off his chair and suddenly Ren's body started to feel like it was ten times—no a hundred times—heavier, and it felt like his bones and organs were being crushed. But Satan stopped Lucifer by looking him straight in the eye and shaking his head. Lucifer tsk-tsked and stopped whatever he was doing to Ren. He looked down with anger in his face.

Satan turned to look back at Ren and said, "So you won't help us because you don't want your friends, family, and innocents to get killed. How do you know that they will still love you? I know after you leave this room, you'll try to leave hell and you'll try to see them, but you do realize that you've been gone for two years up there after your death? They have finally accepted that you are dead. And you are just going to show up out of nowhere and say, 'Hi, Mom and Dad, I'm back'?"

Ren's eyes widened and he looked down in defeat. Satan was going to say something else until Ren smiled, looked back up, and said, "Yes, because I know them too well. When I explain myself, they will accept me for who and what I am. And before you say, 'What about the angel that did this to you?'—don't get me wrong, I still really want to kill that angel—I won't let my anger get the better of me. I have a second chance of living a normal life. I can go to the living world and just shapeshift to make it seem like I never died. I just have to stay away from churches and salt."

Satan looked a little angry with Ren's response, but that anger soon faded away. He turned away from Ren and started to walk back to his seat, growing back to his normal size.

"Fine, go to the door that brought you here and ask to go to the living world and teleport to your family."

"Thank you both."

Ren bowed his head, turned around, walked to the door, and told the door where he wanted to go. The door opened, and Ren left.

Satan said, "Hmm. Interesting kid, but for some reason, I think we might have forgotten to tell him something. Eh, I'm sure he will find out soon."

Lucifer looked at him. "Why are you letting him go and do what he wants?

All we needed to do was to tell him we know the angel that did this to him, and we do know who it is—we have spies in heaven. He would immediately join us if we told him."

"Don't worry, he'll come back to us and help with our goals, because even if his friends and family do accept him, I have a feeling that our friend from the sky might have something to say about that."

DESPAIR

Ren told the door to take him to his apartment complex. While Ren was walking down the hallway, he could feel his strength weakening. That was because he was going to the world of the living, and his power was being restricted by the law of God.

When Ren reached the other door, he took a deep breath and opened it. When he walked out, he was blinded for a second. When his vision fully adjusted to the light, he looked around and saw that he was in front of his old apartment complex.

Ren was shocked that he was back, and he really was back. He turned and saw a car. He ran over to look in its side mirror, and found that he looked just like he did when he was alive. He was even wearing the same clothes he had on the day he got killed. To fully make sure he was really back, he asked someone walking by what year it was. They told Ren the year and he was surprised that only two years did go by—only two.

He also realized that the person could actually see and talk to him, so he really did have a physical body. He tried to restrain his excitement, as he walked to the side of the apartment complex to make sure that no one could see him teleport. Ren closed his eyes and focused his mind. Azazel had said that to teleport, Ren had to imagine the person or place he wanted to teleport to. So Ren tried really hard to imagine his parents' house, then he snapped his fingers. He didn't feel like he moved at all, but when he opened his eyes, he discovered that he was in front of his parents' house. All he thought was, "I hope they didn't move."

Ren could feel his heart beating super fast. Everything was going too fast again. He just standing there, nervous. He kept saying to himself, "What should I say?" He was just standing there, sweating bullets because of how scared he was. He was scared of how his parents were going to react.

He stood completely still in front of his parents' house for five minutes, and many people walked by him with the strangest looks, as though Ren was a weirdo or a drunk person. Surprisingly, no one asked Ren what he was doing. They just kept walking, minding their own business.

Ren finally mustered up enough courage, and he walked up to the front door and knocked. There was no going back now. A few seconds later, someone opened the door. It was Ren's mom Shanna.

Hello, who is it?" Her voice was the same as he remembered: sweet and soft.

When her eyes met Ren's, she stopped in her tracks and stared at him. Ren stared back, both not saying a word until Ren raised his hand and said, "Hi, Mom."

Shanna slammed the door and locked it.

Ren said, "Well, that wasn't the reaction I was expecting. I was expecting a scream of happiness or shock or something, not having the door shut in my face."

Ren tried again and knocked on the door. This time it was his father that opened it. He was going to apologize for his wife's rude behavior until he saw Ren and he realized why she acted like that. His eyes widened for a few seconds, then he cleared his throat and said, "Wow, um, sorry about my wife slamming the door on you, but you look just like our son that passed away."

Ren gulped and said, "Look, I know this looks and sounds crazy, but that's because I am your son."

Ren's father David stared at him blankly, but it didn't last long because that blank stare turned into an angry look and he said, "Okay, look. Whoever you are, that is not a funny joke. You see, my son died two years ago, so don't you ever say that again or we are going to have problems!"

Ren responded nervously, "I am your son. This is not a joke."

In a furious rage, David grabbed Ren, slammed him into the door, and screamed, "Look, whoever paid you to do this? It's not funny. This is cruel and sick, so leave, and don't you ever return or I'll call the cops."

Ren whispered to himself, "Yeah, like the cops can do anything to a demon." But then he took a deep breath, looked at his dad straight in the eye, and said, "Look, I know this is hard to believe, but I am your son and I can show you— both of you."

Ren could see his mom in the living room sporting an angry look too. She speed-walked up to Ren like she was ready to punch him and said, "Okay, prove it."

Ren's eyes wandered around, thinking really hard about how to prove that he was their son. Then he remembered something that only he and his mom knew about, but not his father. Ren said, "Okay, Mom—when I was eleven, you sold all of Dad's mint-condition baseball card collection so you could go to the salon. And the reason you sold Dad's baseball cards is because the salon was really expensive and you really wanted to go and you thought it was stupid for a grown man to have kids' trading cards and treat them with better care then some of the other things in the house. You told me to keep quiet when I found out or I'd be grounded."

Shanna's facial expression slowly changed from anger to shock and then to sadness because no one, and she meant no one, knew about that but her and Ren, so now she was starting to think that this man who showed up at her house that looked like her son might actually be her son. David loosened his grip, turned around to look at his wife, and said, "I knew I didn't lose them! I just knew it! I put so much time and money into those cards and you sold them just so you could go to the salon?! God damnit, woman, you owe me some new cards."

Then David tightened his grip again and looked back at Ren. "Okay, you might somehow know what my wife did, but I bet you can't do it again."

Ren smiled and said, "Dad, you know how you always come after Mom for smoking? You're always saying, 'You're a doctor, you should never smoke, you're a disgrace to be called a doctor,' and that always made Mom cry, but you smoke too, Dad. One time when I visited you at the hospital when I was fourteen, I asked a nurse where you were. The nurse said, 'He's out in the back smoking with his buddies.' I didn't believe it at first, but when I went to the back to see if it was true, you were smoking. And then you saw me and begged me not to tell my mother."

Shanna walked up, smacked the back of David's head in anger, and yelled at him for giving her shit about smoking while he had been doing it behind her back all along. Ren's dad could not say anything to get him out of this situation. Then, after two minutes of bickering, Ren's parents stopped talking to each other and looked at Ren in shock. Slowly tearing up, all they could say was "Ren!" And they both hugged him with pure happiness now that they knew it really was their son and that he was okay.

Moments later, after the huge hug fest, they let Ren go and asked him, "How are you okay? We saw your body, we were at your funeral, and we buried you."

Ren looked at them plainly and asked them to let him inside so he could explain everything. So they let him in, shut the door, and walked to the living room. They all sat on chairs and Ren began to explain everything. It took one hour for Ren to tell his parents everything. Well, Ren did not tell them everything, like how hell works, but he told them that he was sent to hell by an angel and that he was now a demon.

After Ren finished telling them the truth, his parent just sat there with confused and scared looks. They couldn't believe what they had just heard and were again questioning if he really was Ren. So Ren took a deep breath, got up, closed the window curtains, and said, "Look, I knew this was going to be you guys' reactions, so I'll show you. I'll transform into my true form to prove that I'm a demon. Just try to not pass out when I transform, okay?"

But Ren didn't know how to transform, so he thought really hard on how to do it and he figured that if he thought about his true body maybe that's how he could do it. He was standing there, concentrating really hard, and as he was doing that, the room's lights began to flicker, the temperature started to drop at an alarming rate, and a black and purple aura surrounded Ren.

Ren began to transform, but something was different about Ren's transformation: he still grew taller—about six foot, five inches—but he didn't get muscular—he was still skinny. Ren still grew his dragon-like wings, he still got his horns and his bat legs, and the tips of his fingers and toes were still the tips of blades, but his body didn't become scaly or white, he did not grow his tail, and his head did not turn into a cobra's head. Ren's head stayed the same except his hair grew a little longer. It grew past his shoulder blades, but his eyes and tongue were a snake's eyes and tongue, and Ren's number still showed up on the left side of his chest. As Ren finished transforming, he looked at himself and noticed the changes. Maybe because he only had half of his strength, he only looked half of his true form.

Ren looked at his parents. They were leaning back in their chairs and shaking so badly from how scared they were that the chairs they were sitting on looked like they were going to break from how tightly they were being squeezed. He knew this was going to be their reactions when he transformed, but actually seeing it hurt way more than he imagined.

He looked down, sad that his parents were now afraid of him. He said, "I know to you guys I'm scary, but trust me, I'm still me. Please believe me. I'm begging you, if you guys can't accept me, then no one else in our family will. Please." Ren was starting to tear up from the fact that maybe Satan was right and they wouldn't accept him.

But when Ren closed his eyes to cry, Shanna got up, walked to him, while still shaking, hugged him, and said, "Ren, we know it's you. We were just caught off guard, that's all. How did you think we were going to react to the news that our son is a demon, except from complete and utter shock?"

Then David also got up, and walked to him. He hugged him too, and said, "Look, son, even if you are a demon, we will still love you. I mean, you came here knowing that you were a demon and knowing that our reaction would be like this. And yet you still came to us, you trusted us, loved us that much that you left hell to come see us, and to tell us you still love us. And our answer is that we still love you. It's just going to take some getting used to that our son is a great and powerful demon."

Ren's face grew into a very big and happy smile. He slowly transformed back to his human form and was still crying with happiness. He kept saying, "Thank you, thank you so much, I love you guys so much," again and again while his parents were hugging him and crying as well because they had gotten their son back.

Several hours went by, during which Ren and his parents talked about what had changed during the past two years that Ren had missed. After they told him everything they could think of, Ren thought it was time for him to leave because it had already become dark outside, and he needed to find somewhere to sleep. Ren told his parents that tomorrow he would going tell another one of his family members, maybe his grandma and grandpa.

His parents told him he could stay the night, but Ren refused, saying that he noticed that when he was near them, he gave them a cold vibe. He thought to himself that it would be a chilly night for his parents if he stayed, so he was planning to sleep at a hotel because he could just teleport into the building and stay the night. Even though he knew he might give other people the chills, he thought it was better if they were strangers rather than his parents. And this way, he could try to practice controlling his power—a.k.a., trying to control the temperature around him without harming his parents.

Ren left his parents' house. He waved his hand and said, "Goodbye" to them one more time, and they did the same, but as Ren teleported away, he did not see or sense the people around the block.

Ren was in his hotel room, sitting on the floor with the lights off. He was focusing on how to control his powers, but after a half hour of trying, he accidentally fell asleep. He began having a nightmare of people breaking into his parents' house and walking into their bedroom with weapons. They were about to kill them, and when they struck at Ren's parents, he woke up, scared and sweaty.

Ren stood, still breathing heavily. He rubbed his forehead and could feel all the sweat that came off. He decided to go outside to get some fresh air and to cool off. As Ren was standing up, he stopped and noticed that something was off. He couldn't sense his parents anymore. Ever since he had first seen them again, he had been able to sense their souls, but now he couldn't.

Ren quickly snapped his fingers to teleport to his parents' house, and when he arrived, he noticed that the door was broken down. Before Ren could rush in, a man's voice behind him said coldly, "Don't bother. They are both dead."

Ren stopped and slowly turned around with a murderous look. "What did you say, you jackass?"

Ren couldn't see where the voice was coming from but he knew he was really close.

"As I said, you scum, they are both dead just like everyone else."

"Everyone else?!"

"Yes, everyone. All of your friends and family, and even their pets. They are all dead."

Ren screamed in fury, "WHAT?! WHY?!"

"Because they would have accepted you just like your parents did and we were told that if your parents accepted you, then everyone else that you know would, too, so they must die."

All Ren could say was, "Again, why?"

The man sighed and said, "Because we were given orders to do so, and pieces of shits like yourself should not find happiness because you are an abomination to this world."

As the man said that Ren began to transform to his half-demon form. "So it wasn't just you? There were others?"

As Ren finished asking his second question, he sensed something else. A second person from behind him came at him from the house with a giant glowing hammer. It looked like a weapon from hell but it was a blueish white and the person's eyes were glowing and had big white bird wings. Ren jumped out of the way just in the nick of time, and the hammer crushed half of Ren's dad's 2018 Mustang.

From their appearance and from what Ren was sensing, he immediately knew what this guy was. Everything was now making a whole lot of sense—why they targeted the people Ren cared about, why they thought Ren was an abomination to them, and why they had wings—they were angels.

Ren looked at the other one that came out behind the car from across the street. He also sported his weapon: a chain with a pointed tip that was wrapped around his right arm. His eyes began to glow and grew white bird wings.

Ren said, "So you guys only look like that when you bring out your weapons, and since I've seen you guys, and I know what an angel feels..." Ren didn't finish his sentence. Something about these two seemed familiar—really familiar.

With a big smile on his face, one of the angels said, "What do you remember?"

Ren's eyes widened because he did know those guys. These two were the same guys that broke into his apartment and killed him. So they were angels all along. Ren summoned his weapons on his hands and feet.

The angels both sensed that Ren was super, super angry, but then it quickly vanished and he became surprisingly calm, so one of them asked, "May I ask: how are you so calm? I'm sensing hardly any rage in you even though we are the reason that your friends and parents are dead. And, not to mention, we are the ones that got you killed."

"If I am going to fight you and win, I need to stay calm, since this is my first fight to the death. Before we start and before I kill you, I want to know what your names are."

The one with the chain said, "I am Adriel."

The other with the hammer said, "I'm Dumah."

"Good. Now then—fucking die!"

The fight commenced.

Ren ran toward one of the angels and slammed his blade on the big hammer that Dumah had, which sent a shock wave that cracked the concrete they were standing on and made all the car alarms go off.

Dumah said, "Humph, Adriel!"

Adriel yelled, "Right!"

Adriel flew up to get some distance and snapped his fingers, sending an invisible barrier around the entire town.

Ren said, "What did you two just do?!"

Dumah said, "Don't worry. This barrier just makes all the humans in this town stay asleep. We don't want any interference, do we?"

Ren nodded in agreement. Then while still in the air, Adriel swung his right arm, which sent his chain straight at Ren. Ren could hear the chain rattling, and that noise was getting closer. Ren put a lot of strength in his right arm, which was still connected to Dumah's hammer, to push Dumah away so he could dodge the oncoming attack. It almost completely worked. Ren did push Dumah away with great force; it sent him flying into a car. Ren stepped forward to dodge the attack, but the chain did hit him; not anything vital, but it hit right through his left wing.

Ren grunted in pain, but it didn't hurt that much. Being a demon, he had a decent pain tolerance. Ren turned and cut the chain that was still through his wing and flew up as fast as he could to reach Adriel. Ren almost made it, but then he sensed Dumah flying up behind him. Just before Dumah's hammer hit him, he spun around Dumah, completely dodging his sneak attack.

Dumah stopped and turned around to see Ren. And when he did, he didn't see Ren, but instead saw a huge pillar of hellfire coming straight at him and hitting him.

Adriel cried, "Dumah!!"

Adriel swung his chain again toward Ren, but Ren saw that coming a mile away, so he moved to the side, dodging it, and grabbed the chain. It was burning his hands, but he sucked it up. Adriel came flying toward him, and without much time to react, with one big swing, Ren closed-lined Adriel and sent him flying straight down to the ground. He crashed into the road, making a huge hole. Ren saw Dumah had fallen down, covered in smoke, also where Adriel was. But even though Ren was winning, he felt that something wasn't right.

He thought, "No, this is too easy. If angels are as powerful as demons, then why is this fight one-sided?"

In the newly-created hole, Adriel stood up, looking up at Ren and brushing some dust off his shoulder. He looked like he didn't take any damage. In fact, he didn't look damaged at all. Not even a scratch. Dumah also stood up and swatted away the smoke that was around him, also showing no signs of being hurt.

Dumah said, "Hmm. He's pretty good for a freshly-transformed demon."

Adriel said, "Yeah, he is. I guess we should take this fight seriously or he might actually kill us."

"Yeah, if I didn't spin my hammer around to make a shield, that fire attack would have killed me."

Adriel said sarcastically, "Aaa, being honest?"

"Well, yeah, I'm an angel. Lying is for the weak. Okay, ready?"

"Yeah!"

Both angels spread their wings and jumped up, making the hole bigger, and flew straight for Ren. Ren cracked his neck, indicating that he was ready too, and flew down toward them. From afar, it looked like one missile in the air was about to hit two other missiles. When they got close enough, Ren moved both of his arms forward so they would be in front of him. He looked like a demonic Superman.

Before they collided, Adriel sent his chain flying to his right side, away from Ren. Ren looked to his left in confusion, but quickly looked straight ahead again since he was really close to the angels. But that was a mistake, because the chain quickly turned around and was headed straight for Ren's left side. Ren saw the attack coming, so he swung his left arm to hit the chain away. But the chain moved away from his hand and started to wrap around his arm. It was like a snake trying to constrict Ren's arm.

Before he tried to break the chain, he thrust his right arm and shot hellfire big enough to block Dumah and Adriel's vision. It worked. Dumah and Adriel shot holy water to block the upcoming attack, sending steam everywhere. Ren quickly tried to grab the chain and try to break it off, but the chain started to wrap around Ren's other arm. It was not long before both of Ren's arms were tied up.

Adriel yelled, "NOW!"

Ren turned his gaze away from his arms to look straight ahead, and what he saw was Dumah coming out of the steam cloud, right in front of Ren. His hammer was inches away from Ren's stomach. With a split-second right before the hammer hit him, two things happened. One: the chain that tied Ren's arms loosened up. And two: Ren flicked his head up, activating his telekinesis to slow down the impact of the hammer.

The hammer hit Ren directly and sent Ren flying back downward, straight into a house, completely destroying it and anyone that was in it. Ren was laying down, grunting for a second, but he quickly swatted away any broken house pieces off of him. He struggled to stand up, holding his stomach where the hammer hit. Before Ren could check to see how bad it was, Dumah appeared in front of him. With a raised right arm, Ren blocked the swing from Dumah, which sent Ren flying again, but this time up in the air.

CRACK!!

Ren grunted from the pain of his right arm being broken from the hit. It hurt, but luckily, once again, Ren had a decent pain tolerance. Ren saw Dumah flying toward him from below and also noticed Adriel coming at him from above. These two just wouldn't let Ren catch a breath, now. They were really taking this fight seriously.

Then he had an idea. He swung his right arm straight down, which made Adriel stop for a split second. Then he was sent flying down really fast, passing Ren and heading straight toward Dumah. He hit him and sent both of them flying down. Ren smiled, happy to get a second to breathe. But that smile faded away because Ren noticed something.

"Hey, wait—wasn't this arm broken?" Then Ren noticed another thing. "And why doesn't my stomach hurt at all? In fact, it's not even bruised at all!"

Ren's eyes widened like they were about to pop out, and a big smile appeared on his face. The Grinch's smile had nothing on Ren's smile.

"No way! I have regeneration! A really powerful one too. It wasn't even ten seconds ago when my arm got broken and it's healed! Same goes for my stomach wound! Wait!"

Ren turned to look at his wing and noticed that the hole that Adriel gave him was gone too. Ren was overwhelmed with joy. He really did feel like an anime monster, but his face changed from happy to serious in an instant because he thought of something.

Ren said, "If demons have regeneration, then angels have regeneration too. Theirs is probably as good as ours."

Ren felt something wrapping around his leg.

Adriel said, "Good you figured that out, you amateur!"

Adriel pulled as hard as he could, sending Ren closer to him. Ren quickly shot his hellfire at the chain to break free. The chain snapped and Ren was loose. He flapped his wings harder to get his balance back while also swinging his right arm with all his might, blocking Dumah's sneak attack.

Dumah smiled and said, "Now!"

Adriel appeared behind Ren and whipped his chain straight at Ren. The chain hit him and cut deeply into his back. Before he could yell in pain, Dumah raised his hammer and brought it down on him. Luckily, Ren raised both arms to block it but it dislocated both of his shoulders. Once again, Ren was flying down, straight to the road.

As Ren was falling, he was trying to think of a plan.

Ren thought, "This isn't good. I can't do anything now! All I can do is block! I know I'm stronger than these two but they have more battle experience then I do and it's two versus one. And what makes matters worse is that I can tell that they are getting cocky because they are winning, which is pissing me off!"

Ren slammed down on the pavement, making yet another hole in the road. The two angels slowly flew toward Ren with smirks on their faces. They descended for a good bit until they stopped, thinking that was a good distance. They both flapped their wings, blowing away the smoke to see Ren.

Ren was barely on his hands and knees and he was shaking crazily—so crazily that if a little gust of wind hit him, he might fall over. Ren slowly tried to crawl away, showing that he was in a lot of pain. Both of the angels were pleased at the sight of Ren crawling away from them. He turned his head to look at them with pure fear in his eyes.

Then SNAP! And Ren teleported away.

There was silence in the air. Both angels looked in shock and slapped their heads with their hands. They had forgotten Ren could teleport back to hell whenever he felt like.

Adriel said, "Damn. We were so enjoying the fight that we forgot he can teleport."

Dumah laughed a little bit and said, "Haha, yeah, but that's because he was making the fight so enjoyable that we thought he was going to fight until he dies. I guess not."

Dumah landed in the hole that Ren crashed into and said, "Well, let's fix the damage before the sun comes up."

Adriel didn't say anything because he was lost in his thoughts. He thought, "It doesn't make sense. Even though Ren was losing, he was holding his own pretty well, and not to mention that his regeneration was still working really well too. We didn't do that much damage to him, did we? Did he really teleport back to hell? Or did he just..."

Adriel sensed something, something fast. And it was coming straight for Dumah, who was distracted.

Adriel tried to get Dumah's attention. "YOU IDIOT, STAY FOCUSED!! REN DIDN'T ACTUALLY—"

But it was too late. When Dumah looked up at Adriel, Ren appeared in front of him, cutting his throat open, which squirted blood all over Ren's face. Dumah's entire body combusted into black flames. It first started with Dumah's eyes, nose, ears, and mouth, but shortly, his entire body was covered in flames. Within only a couple seconds, Dumah, an angel of God, was reduced to nothing but ash. But before Dumah burned, his blood that was on Ren's face disintegrated.

Ren thought, "Huh, it disintegrated? Is that part of the regeneration or was it because I killed him? Hmm, no matter. I'll ask Astaroth later. So right now, let's finish Adriel off."

Ren ran right through the ashes that once were Dumah and kneed Adriel in the face. He felt something break. It was probably Adriel's nose. From Adriel's expression, he couldn't believe what just happened.

What Adriel was thinking that had been distracting him from Ren was: "This can't be happening. An angel died? DIED?! That hasn't happened since the Yahweh incident."

Before Adriel pulled himself together, Ren grabbed him by the neck and said, "Okay, now that your friend is dead, I can take you on with ease because I'm sure you noticed that even when you had your boyfriend, you guys couldn't kill me. And you guys were trying really hard." Ren's tone was demonic and angry.

Adriel noticed that too. Even with Dumah's help, they couldn't kill Ren easily. And now Adriel was alone with Ren! Adriel wrapped his chain around his hand to make a fist and lunged at Ren's arm, hitting it. Ren let go from the shock and pain. Adriel turned and flew away with such great speed that he shattered every house and car windows that was within a one-mile radius. Adriel raised his right hand in front of him. He was about to snap his fingers to teleport away from Ren and go home to heaven to regroup. But before Adriel snapped his finger, he felt a huge amount of pain coming from his back.

What happened was Ren had flown to him so fast that he didn't have time to react, and because of that, Ren cut off Adriel's wings. But Ren was not finished. He stabbed Adriel right through his shoulder and began to spin around. He was quickly gaining speed as he was spinning. And when Ren was gaining speed, Adriel could feel the g-force pulling him away.

Since his shoulder was still connected to Ren's blade, he could feel his shoulder being ripped apart until his shoulder couldn't take the g-force any longer and it was ripped off of his own body. Adriel was sent crashing down, straight toward a playground. The impact destroyed it.

Adriel was laying on the ground, badly hurt. As he was laying there, his body regenerated a new shoulder. Adriel tried to get up, but for some reason, he couldn't. There wasn't anything on him, so he immediately knew that this was Ren's doing. Ren landed a couple feet away from Adriel and looked down at him like a predator sizing up a wounded animal it was about to kill.

Ren used his telekinesis to lift the wounded angel off the ground and floated him closer toward Ren. Adriel didn't even try to struggle anymore. He knew that he couldn't break free in his state. Ren brought him closer and closer to finish the job, but as he was about to kill him, Adriel started to laugh.

Ren said, "What's so funny? You are about to die. Is there something you really want to say?"

Adriel smiled and said, "I'm laughing because you try so hard to beat me and Dumah so, so hard. But guess what? We are just foot soldiers—common foot soldiers. There are so many angels out there in heaven that are so much stronger than we are, so don't take this fight with so much pride."

Adriel looked and saw Ren's face; it was expressionless. Did Ren even care?

Ren said, "Whatever. I knew you guys were weak, but guess what? I still won, didn't I? A win is still a win. And thanks to you two, I'm a little more experienced fighting angels now. But now that I think of it, before I kill you, I want to know one thing. Can I bring everyone you killed back to life?"

Adriel started to laugh again and said, "No. If a human is killed by an angel's weapon, they are stuck in heaven forever unless an angel more powerful than the angel that killed them can bring them back to life. Good luck finding an angel from heaven to help YOU! Have fun being alone forever. HA HA HA!!"

Ren thrust his blade right through Adriel's heart, killing him. Adriel burst into flames like Dumah and Ren threw his burning corpse to the side. He was now standing completely still on a destroyed playground with a burning angel corpse next to him. Ren slowly transformed back to his human form and fell on his hands and knees, scratching the ground. He began to cry. Knowing that Adriel wasn't lying, Ren could truly no longer see his friends and family ever again.

As Ren was crying his eyes out, he suddenly went into a rampage. He transformed back into his half-demon from and destroyed the entire playground, even more than it already was, with his bare hands. He just destroyed everything that survived the battle— slides, swings, everything.

After a couple minutes, he finally calmed down. He looked up with an angry, demonic look, tears still running down his face, and said, "Okay, you motherfuckers up in the sky, you really like to make me suffer, don't you? First you fuckers sent me to hell even though I didn't do a Goddamn thing to be sent to hell for, and now you killed everyone I love just because I'm a fucking demon?! Okay, fine. Go right ahead. Make me miserable, but while you guys do that, I'll kill every single last one of you. There will be no angels left when I'm done!"

RELIGIOUS WAR BEGINS

Still in the playground where Ren killed the two angels, Ren was slowly regaining his breath. He was still on his hands and knees because he actually did take a lot of damage. He must go back to hell to rest for a bit, but he could sense people were walking toward him.

The barrier that kept the people asleep must have vanished when Ren killed the caster. And thanks to his temper tantrum in the park, he must have woken up all the people that were close by and made them check out what was making all that noise.

Everyone was breathless at what they were seeing. A humanoid, bat-looking creature on its hands and knees was in front of them all with a cold look that could freeze anyone solid if they made eye contact.

Instead of running away like a smart person would do, everyone there took out their phones and started to record him. Even though they might die, it was worth it just to get famous on YouTube or on their social media or on the news. But Ren ain't got time for this, so he snapped his fingers and teleported back to hell.

Ren walked down the dark hallway until he reached a red door. He said something very quietly, but the door heard him and the handle glowed red. Ren opened it. On the other side was Astaroth's office. Astaroth was doing some paperwork on his desk. He stopped and lifted his head up.

"Well, well. Look who's back. I thought you were not going to come back to us?"

Ren walked through the door, shut it, and slowly walked toward Astaroth.

When he entered the room, he was in his half-demon form, but now that he was in hell again, he transformed into his full demon form automatically.

"Well, yeah. I wasn't planning on coming back here."

Astaroth gave Ren a little smile and said, "Really? So I assume everything was going well?"

"Oh, yeah, everything was going as planned. If you want to know, my parents did accept me for what I am and everything was going smoothly except for one little thing."

"And what is this one thing? Please, do tell."

Ren said, "Well, this little thing is, and try to keep up with me—" Ren inhaled and started to yell, "ANGELS CAME DOWN FROM HEAVEN AND LITERALLY KILLED ALL OF MY FUCKING FRIENDS AND FAMILY, EVEN THEIR PETS, FOR SOME REASON, JUST BECAUSE I'M A FUCKING DEMON, JUST BE-CAUSE EVERYONE THAT I KNOW WILL HAVE ACCEPTED ME FOR WHAT I AM. SO IN RETURN I KILLED TWO OF THE LITTLE SHITS THAT TOOK MY PARENTS AWAY FROM ME!!!" Ren was gasping for air.

Astaroth's facial expression was pure shock. He took a second to process what Ren just told him and said, "So angels killed your parents, friends, and even their pets just because they would accept you."

Ren, exhausted from screaming, said, "Yes."

"And in response to that, you killed two of them? I don't think you knew this, but that hasn't happened in thousands of years, so congratulations, Ren, you deserve it."

"Thanks, I guess, but can you do something for me."

Astaroth raised an eyebrow. "What would that be?"

Ren said, "I need to talk with Satan and Lucifer so I can start a war with the angels."

There was a pause.

But then Astaroth got a smile on his face and said, "I see. I will try, but I will have to schedule that appointment for tomorrow."

"Why?!"

"Because look at you. You are badly injured and exhausted. If you meet them now, with their power levels, you'll just pass out. So just go to your chambers and rest up, and you'll visit them tomorrow. We still have time in hell, so go to sleep and rest."

"I have my own chambers?"

"Yes. Every demon has their own chambers. I don't need to tell you how to get to your chambers. I'm pretty sure you already know how to get there."

Ren was furious that Astaroth wanted him to wait, but it couldn't be helped, and plus, Ren thought a nap did sound good right about now. So Ren agreed and was about to leave but he turned around and said, "Before I leave, I do have a question."

Astaroth sighed and said, "Fine, just ask me and go. I still have a lot of work to finish."

Ren walked toward a chair, sat down, and said, "Okay. First is—how does our regeneration work? Azazel, Satan, Lucifer, and you forgot to tell me that demons and angels have it, so I had to figure it out in my battle."

Astaroth said, "I see. I can't believe they, and I, actually forgot to tell you that."

Ren said sarcastically, "I know, right?!"

"Well, what do you know about the regeneration that you have during the fight?"

Ren put a finger on his lips and said, "Well, whenever I got injured with a blunt weapon or got stabbed, the moment that the weapon was not connected to my flesh anymore, the wound immediately healed up. And I don't know if that is a part of the regeneration or not, but when the blood leaves the body, it instantly disintegrates."

"Hmmm, okay. You've got the basics but there is more to it, so get ready because this is going to be complicated."

Ren nodded and placed his head on his hands.

Astaroth said, "Okay, what you said is accurate, and yes, the blood disintegrating is a part of the regeneration. But your blood isn't the only thing that disintegrates when it leaves your body. Let's say a limb or a piece of flesh is removed from your body. It also immediately disintegrates. Even if we use ice magic to freeze it so it won't disintegrate, it still does, just leaving a hollow hole in the ice. And how it works is this: you know regeneration is just a rapid cell-splitting increase to heal the wound of the host, right? But with us demons, it's more than that. You know demons are mostly or entirely made of sins—as the Bible says, demons are sins incarnate. Well, the sins in us, most accurately, the sins that want more, like greed, lust, and gluttony, increased the cell-splitting to an unimaginable scale because they want more cells as like everything else that those sins want. But not too bad that it would hurt us. And the sins that are in us that make the blood and flesh disintegrate when it leaves our body. That's the sin of wrath at work because it's so mad at the fact it's not with the host anymore that it burns the flesh into nothing. For an example, let's say you got shot by a tank shell point blank range at your face. Your face might get blown up in multiple chunks of meat. Well, it kind of counts on how strong you are, but let's say it does do that. All the flesh and blood left your body will disappear and you'll get a new head immediately, but it's still going to hurt. However, that doesn't mean you're invincible. Even there, there is a way to slow down the regeneration."

Ren took a big gulp and said, "What can slow it down?"

"A weapon made from heaven or hell, telekinesis from an angel or demon, the water from heaven and fire from hell, and or the powers of the angel or demon."

Ren got a cold chill down his spine. He now wanted to end this conversation, but he had to know or he might die in his next fight. He let Astaroth keep talking.

"Okay, Ren, let's start with the weapons first since they're the most common and since you didn't know about the regeneration. I bet Azazel didn't tell you that the weapons have powers."

Ren looked down and shook his head in embarrassment.

Astaroth sighed and said, "I swear that man is getting lazier by the second. Okay, Ren. The weapons do actually have three abilities. So listen VERY carefully. The first ability the weapons have is that they can cut, stab, break, or smash anything that is either made of flesh or is a soul. The weapons can bypass their skin and flesh durability. The reason I'm saying this is because there are angels, demons, and monsters that have skin that is many times more durable than steel. But the weapons can ignore their durability and damage them like it was normal human flesh. But if your opponent has, like, armor, an invisible barrier, or it doesn't have flesh or a soul like a golem, then to cut through any of those, it feeds on the angels' or demons' strength to damage them."

When Astaroth finished explaining the first ability of the weapons, Ren put his hand on his head because it felt like it was on fire. That was a lot of information and that was just one ability—Ren still had to hear two more.

Astaroth continued, "Now, the second ability targets the regeneration, which is what you wanted to know. You see, when the weapons deal damage to a creature that has regeneration—and I would like to point out that no creature has the same regeneration unless it's from the same class of species, so angels, demons, vampires, werewolves, etc., all have regeneration but they are all completely different types—the weapons still slow down every single different regeneration because it's still regeneration. How it does it is by leaving a little bit of sin or grace in the host. Now, with only a couple of small hits, the regeneration wouldn't slow down, but if the small hits are consistent, or the hits are big and consistent, then the sin or grace in them will keep increasing within the body. Soon the regeneration will drastically slow down or stop completely. Now it is temporary, the sin or grace that is inside you or your enemy will fade away in time. Which brings me to the last ability.

"If the weapons hit an insta-kill spot like the brain, heart, decapitation, etc., the weapons somehow nullify the creatures' regeneration and even their immortality. And nobody knows how or why the weapons can do it. Not me, Azazel, Satan, Lucifer, any demon, or angel knows why. It literally doesn't matter what regeneration you have and it doesn't matter what immortality you have—these weapons can kill ANYTHING if it hits an insta-kill spot. And those are all the abilities that the weapons have.

"Now, I know I still have to talk about the heaven water and hellfire but I'm tired so to say it in simple terms—the hellfire can burn anything in the living world and the stronger the demon, the hotter the flames. As for the holy water, if the water is super-compressed, then the water can cut or smash anything in the living world, and just like the weapons, the fire and water have the same abilities as the weapons. And that's finally everything you need to know, Ren."

When Astaroth stopped talking, Ren leaned back on the chair, looked up at the ceiling, and rubbed all the sweat from his forehead because that was a lot of information.

Yet, he was happy because he knew he had such power in his hands, and with it, he had the advantage in any fight. But he also knew that he shouldn't be cocky because, in the great words of Lao Tzu, "There is no greater danger than underestimating your opponent."

Ren said, "Thank you for telling me all of this. I do appreciate it."

Astaroth just nodded.

Ren got off of the chair and walked to the door and said, "Take me to my quarters."

The handle glowed and Ren opened the door and left. As Ren was walking through the hallway, he stopped to look at his fist. He remembered the angels that he killed with his own hands, and with pure rage, Ren smashed his hand on the wall, making a huge hole. It slowly rebuilt itself.

"You just wait, you white-winged bitches. I'm coming for you."

Ren reached the other door and opened it. When he fully opened the door, he couldn't believe what he was seeing. It was the living room from the apartment he used to live in.

Ren walked inside and could see everything. The living room, kitchen, and the bathroom. Ren ran to a door and opened it; it was his old room, but the room didn't have any of his posters of anime or any of his manga or comics, only his furniture, which was funny because he also only noticed furniture in the other rooms. He had photos of his family and plants, but the rooms didn't have those, so it looked like Ren had to get some from the living world for his new/old room.

After a good night's sleep, Ren woke up in his human form. He stretched. Ren took his covers off, walked to his bedroom door, opened it, and walked to his kitchen to make some coffee and breakfast. He ate, then he immediately left to go to see Satan and Lucifer.

Ren walked to the door and said, "Take me to Satan and Lucifer." He opened the door and left.

Ren walked down the hall while transforming into his true demon form and has a serious look on his snake face. He opened up the door and walked in. It was still the pitch black room with the two giants in the middle of the room.

Lucifer said, "So, you're back. Are you going to do what your masters tell you?"

"Yes and no."

Lucifer, with a confused look, said, "Yes and no. Please, do tell. This is interesting."

Ren said with a straight face, "I will start a war with heaven, but it's not for you guys or Astaroth or any other demon in hell. I'm doing it for me. So, I'm sorry. In the future, I won't be nice, respectful, or cooperative to you guys."

Lucifer smiled and started to laugh. "I'm—I'm starting to like you, Ren, and yes, that is a rare compliment from me, so take it."

Satan interrupted Lucifer's conversation with Ren and said, "Are you sure about this? If you do this, a lot of humans are going to die. A lot of innocent humans."

Ren stopped looking at Lucifer and Satan and looked down. He grabbed his left arm that was shaking. Actually his entire body slowly started to shake, probably from disgust or disappointment in himself.

But Ren looked up again and said, "Yes, I'm sure... WAIT a second, if we start this war, the entire world is involved, right?"

Satan said, "Well... Yes, the entire world is involved."

"Can I make a request, then?"

Lucifer said, "Aaa, sure. What is it?" He was interested in what Ren had to say.

Ren swallowed and said, "Good. Well, when and if we do start a war, can one country be left alone?"

Lucifer said, "A country?"

"Yes, a country."

Lucifer squinted his eyes at Ren and leaned forward and said, "What country is it?"

Ren said, "The country is Japan. The reason is because Japan is the main home for a lot of old and new manga creators, and technically new anime shows, and I don't want them to get killed, hurt, or possessed because I'm a nerd so I'll protect the homeland of all anime."

Lucifer and Satan had the stupidest looks on their faces—a look of "is this guy for real?"—but they could tell that Ren was serious, so Satan and Lucifer talked to each other.

Satan said, "Well, we can leave Japan alone. I don't think there are really that many seals there, and if he does succeed in starting this war it is the least we can do to make sure he stays loyal to our plans."

"Well, I guess, but isn't it a bit childish and selfish to leave an entire country alone just for some—what did he call it? Anime? Mangas? Like, he's fine with America being a battleground. The same country that he used to live in."

"Yeah, it is messed up that he is okay with his home country being destroyed. But I don't see the harm in it. Japan is a small country. Leaving it alone won't slow down the war."

Lucifer and Satan stopped talking to each other and turned back to Ren.

Satan said, "Okay. We agreed that we will leave Japan alone."

Lucifer said, "Yeah."

Ren said, "YES!!" with pure happiness and excitement.

Satan said, "Okay, since that is done and over with, let us begin by telling you how to start the war. And in order to tell you that, you must know what seals are."

"Seals?"

"Yes, seals. What the seals are, where they are, and how to break them."

"So it's just another teaching session from you, gramps."

Lucifer leaned forward, picked up a rock, and threw it at Ren. Ren's head exploded into many little pieces but they disintegrated and he regenerated a new head.

Ren yelled, "What the hell was that for?!"

Lucifer said, "How about a little bit more respect for the gramps?"

Ren thought, "Not going to happen."

Satan said, "Okay, are you two done now?! Let's start on what a seal is."

Ren said, "Okay, fine."

Satan said, "A seal is a solid item, and the item is literally a bone from Jesus Christ himself."

Ren took a step back in shock to hear that not only was Jesus actually a real person (because, to be honest, Ren didn't think he was real) but he was also shocked that they was HIS bones that Ren had to find and break.

Satan said, "Ren, do you know how many bones are in a human body?"

"Well, yes. But it kind of counts on how old the body is. If it's a body before adulthood then it has 270 bones but if the body did hit adulthood then it's reduced to 206 and Jesus died when he hit thirty-three, right?"

"Yes, he did."

"Okay, so technically there are a total of 206 seals out there—one for each bone. Okay, seems simple enough. So we have to break all of them."

Lucifer said, "Well, not exactly. Lucky for us, we don't need to break all of them. We only need to break 66 of them."

Ren said, "Only 66?"

"Yes."

Ren said, "Wow, break 66 seals to release really powerful demons. It really turns Supernatural on this bitch."

Lucifer said, "Yes, we are the supernatural."

"No, it's a show called Supernatural. It's about—ah, never mind. You guys won't get it, so go on."

Satan said, "Now, to find the seals we already know where they are, your ruler—which, in your case, is Astaroth—will tell you which bone you are going to get and what church it's in and where that church is."

"Church?"

"Yes. Each and every bone of Jesus Christ was split and spread all around the world by the angels, because when Jesus died the angels knew that his bones were going to be the seals. So by God's orders, they separated them because we knew about them as well. We once tried to get them all to ourselves when Jesus died and was buried. Me and Lucifer sent a lot of demons to get the body, but at the time, we didn't know that God had brought Jesus back from the dead and given him immense power. So we couldn't touch him for many years. But it turns out Jesus did get brought back and he did get powers to be called a god, but he was not immortal. He WAS still mortal and, get this, he died from old age without anyone—or, should I say, any human—knowing about it. With his second death, we tried again to get the bones, and that's when the angels spread them. They went to 206 churches in the world, even the ones that were not Catholic Churches, and hid one of Jesus's bones in the statue that they pray in front of. Only a few humans know about it today, and that's only because the angels told a few humans who were worthy at the time, and it was passed down through generations of high priests. But it's like I said, only a few know about it and that number has dropped through time."

Ren said, "But something doesn't make sense. The angels spread his bones at Jesus's time. Some of, or most of, the churches back then then must not exist anymore, right?"

Lucifer said, "No. Whenever a church is not being used or has been torn down, the angels cast a spell so that the bone will teleport to a new church that is still being used. It's a simple spell, but it only activated, like I said, when the church is not being used anymore, and we know when and where it's going to teleport to so don't worry about it."

"Okay, so now that I know what a seal is and we already know where they are, how do we break one?"

Satan said, "Well, that's the tricky part. Technically, you already have one of the pieces to break a seal and that is hellfire. You need to burn the bone in hellfire with something else."

"Something else?"

"That something else is the most holy man on earth, a.k.a., the Pope. We need the Pope's blood. What happens is that you get the bone, spill the Pope's blood all over it, light it up with hellfire, and do this chant in Hebrew: ליבשבו סיחצנ חצנל ופרשיי סה ובש סוניהיגל וישכע לפנ רתויב שודקה סדאהו חישמה עושי תכיתח סוניהיג הזה הלעי הפיגמל לע רודכ ץראה. That means 'Jesus Christ and the most holy man have both fallen to hell, where they will burn for all eternity, and because of this, hell will rise and be a plague on the earth.'"

Ren thought, "Okay, I might have trouble saying that, but I will get it down if I keep repeating it in my head."

Satan said, "So, Ren, your mission is to go to the Pope's cathedral, kill him, and send his body to hell. The angels will not be able to retrieve his body from us, and we will get a syringe ready for you because you will also be going to break the first seal, which will start the war."

Ren said sarcastically, "Wow, my first mission is a really important one. No pressure, right?"

He was surprisingly calm—so calm that Lucifer and Satan were surprised. He was ready to go and break the first seal right away.

But Lucifer stopped him and said, "Before you go we also signed a demon with you, not as a bodyguard, but just in case you fail, he will try to kill the Pope or break the seal or both, because as you might know, the angels ain't going to let it be that easy for you."

Satan said, "Oh, yeah, before I forget, there is one more catch with this sealing process."

Ren sighed and said, "For fuck's sake, what now?!"

Satan, shocked, said, "Lower your tone, boy!"

"Sorry. So what is it?"

Satan said, "Whenever you break a seal, you won't be able to break another one during the same day. Or the next day. Only three day later."

Ren thought, "So after I break a seal, I have to wait three days to break another one? Okay, that sounds good for me."

Lucifer yelled, "MIGUEL, you may come in now!"

The door opened behind Ren and suddenly the room got really cold. As Ren turned around, he saw a demon walk in. It was a six-foot-tall skeleton that looked like it was made of diamonds, but it was not the cold atmosphere and the steam coming off of it—it had to be made of ice—and to top it off, its eyes were this blood red color. On his left side of his chest was the number 2222.

Miguel walked toward Ren until he was right next to him. He bowed his head and said, "Yes, my lord?"

Ren thought, "He's talking without moving his jaw? Hmm, so he can use telepathy of some sort. That's pretty cool, and for an ice skeleton, his voice is pretty deep."

Satan said, "You already know what your mission is, so you and Ren here are leaving immediately."

Miguel bowed his head again and turned to Ren and said, "Are you ready for this? I know that you are a newly-made demon, and before you say anything, yes, I know you have killed two angels. Every demon in hell knows. Which, by the way, nice work, but this is going to be way more difficult than those guys. Are you fully ready for this?"

Ren smiled. "Yes."

If Miguel had lips, he would be smiling too. Ren and Miguel nodded to each other and both walked to the door.

Ren said, "Take us to the Pope's Cathedral."

The door opened and they both went in. As they were walking to get to the other side, Miguel decided to strike up a conversation with Ren, most likely just to try to get to know him.

"So, Ren, if I'm not mistaken, you used to be alive two years ago, right?"

"Yeah, why do you ask?"

"Well, you see, I used to be alive too, but instead of two years ago when you used to be alive, it was ten years ago when I was alive. And plus, I heard you say something through the other side of the door. You brought up the show Supernatural. I'm just wondering, are you also a comic and anime nerd too? Because I am."

Ren turned his head and said, "YES I AM! But to make sure you are a fellow nerd like me, I'm going to ask you a question to see if you are telling the truth."

"Bring it on. I think I can answer it, but remember, I died ten years ago, so I'm not familiar with some new ones. I do try to keep tabs on some new ones if I have the time."

"Okay, who are the big three?"

"Naruto, One Piece, and Bleach are the big three."

Ren smiled and started to laugh in relief because he had finally met someone who was a nerd just like him, and he was a demon too. Ren was sure there were others, but most likely they were all still tortured souls. Ren and Miguel started to walk more slowly to talk and get to know each other better, and it seemed like they were having fun. They brought up who would win fights, shows to see if they knew them, and their own ideology.

They were really enjoying each other's company at first, but Miguel stopped walking and asked Ren, "Are you really going to do this? Are you really going to start a war with heaven—with the angels—for revenge? You do know you were once human too, and if you start this war a whole lot of innocent humans will die. I'm only asking you this because I want to know if you still have any humanity left in you, just like me."

Ren was a couple feet ahead of Miguel, because he didn't realize he had stopped, but when Miguel asked his question, Ren stopped too.

"Yes, I'm certain. I know a lot of innocent people will die, and I know I'm going to feel really guilty, but why do they get to have happy lives, when I, the same normal person as them, had to get sent to hell and get tortured for two hundred years—and now everyone I loved is dead—because of some douchebag of an angel that, for some reason, sent me to hell? This is the only way for me to get to him or her and kill them, so I'm sorry. But you know the old saying: you can't make an omelette without cracking a few eggs."

As Ren said that, there was a shift in the atmosphere; where it once was a happy atmosphere, now it was awkward. Both of them started to walk forward again without saying a word to each other. They walked until they finally made it to the other door and opened it. They were at the outskirts of the city square, where no humans could see Ren—Piazza San Giovanni in Florence, Italy.

Ren took the form he had when he first showed in the world: his half-demon form. He couldn't see Miguel anywhere so Ren screamed out his name twice. In no time, Miguel showed up right next to Ren in a human body that he had possessed.

Ren looked at the body and asked out of curiosity, "Why do you possess that body? From what I'm sensing, that's a dead corpse."

"Well, we demons can possess anybody, dead or alive, but we human demons prefer to possess a human that is close to what we used to look like when we were alive."

His body was a tall, muscular male body with a natural (undertone) skin color, with a long puffy soil patch beard and puffy hair in a ponytail.

Miguel continued, "And plus, this body is my body. Thanks to my supernatural ice powers, I was able to preserve it from decaying for these past ten years that I've been dead. However, even though it's not decaying on the outside, it still smells like it is, and the color of the skin does turn very pale. So I have to use a lot of makeup and deodorant to make my vessel look alive."

Ren pinched his nose and said, "So that's what I've been smelling?! Dude, if I may, you don't have to use that much deodorant, and plus, whatever kind you use, it's bad."

Ren transformed to his human form and both of them began to walk into the city to go to the cathedral. Every time they walked past a person, the person shivered like they had just felt a cold breeze. Ren was not doing that before when he was in the world of the living in his human form, so it must be because of Miguel, who was a skeleton that was made of ice in hell. So they walked for a good bit, past a lot of neat places that they wanted to check out, but they didn't have the time for sightseeing.

Finally, they were in front of the cathedral. Ren was overwhelmed. He could feel the power of how holy this place was and it was making him ill.

He said, "Okay, let's go in."

Ren walked forward and placed his hand on the door handle, but before he opened it, he noticed that Miguel was still at the bottom of the steps.

Ren said, "Why are you just standing there? Come on."

"I'm sorry, but I can't. Right now, there are a lot of humans in there, and if two demons walked right in, especially with our ranking, angels will immediately come down to attack us and get the Pope out of there. But if just one—you—just go in, all those humans would mask your presence. And second, the Pope will be preaching in there, which means I would most likely be in a lot of pain and get exorcized out of my host."

"But wait, wouldn't I get exorcized too?!"

Miguel shook his head. "Don't worry. Since you are not possessing anyone, the preaching won't hurt you that much. You might feel like you have a really upset stomach, though."

Ren turned to the cathedral and looked back at Miguel multiple times. He took a deep breath and said, "Okay, fine then. What are you going to do?"

"I'll be outside waiting to see if you fail or succeed, and I'll buy some coffee too, because I never had Italian coffee before. So good luck, and wait until everyone leaves the cathedral so they won't get in your way."

In truth, Miguel just didn't want Ren to kill any innocent humans when he went after the Pope. Ren just nodded, turned to the door, opened it, and walked in. The inside was so beautiful, he couldn't believe that he was inside the cathedral that the Pope was in right now. Everyone was sitting and listening to the Pope talk while Ren was in the background with his back to the wall and his arms crossed.

The Pope said, "Just as an earthly father cares deeply about his children, your Heavenly Father loves you and wants you to be happy. That doesn't mean your life will always be easy or joyful. Because he knows more than you do, God allows you to experience challenges to teach you important lessons..."

The Pope went on with his preaching. Ren listened for a while, until he started to shake and hold his stomach tightly because he was feeling stomach pains. It was worse than what Miguel said it would be, so Ren looked around to see if anyone could tell him where the bathrooms were. Ren spotted someone who was also just standing and listening, so he asked him where the bathrooms were and the person told him.

"Thanks."

Ren went to the bathroom as fast as he could to try to get as far away from the preaching so the stomach pains would be easier to handle. Ren found the bathrooms and went inside to an empty stall. He locked it and sat down. The stomach pains did ease up a bit, but he could still feel them, even though they were less painful than when he was out there.

Ren mumbled to himself, "This is going to get some getting used to, because I'm going to be fighting a lot of priests if I do succeed."

An hour went by and Ren was still in the bathroom trying to ease the stomach pains from the preaching. When the stomach pains were gone, that meant the Pope must have stopped. In fact, Ren couldn't hear him anymore. He got off the toilet and left the bathroom to check on what was going on. The people that were listening to the Pope were leaving the cathedral, but before they left, they were being blessed by the Pope. So Ren waited in a corner for every last person to leave the church. Only a couple of minutes passed before finally, the last person left the church.

Ren looked around the corner to see where the Pope was. He was at the altar, completely exhausted from the long day of preaching and blessing. It was really exhausting for a man at his age. It was already dusk outside. Ren was about to go and meet him until he noticed three young priests, who looked like they were between the ages of fifteen and eighteen, helping the Pope away from the altar.

The youngest priest boy said, "Your holiness, you did well today, but now it's time for you to go home, eat, and get ready for bed. Here. Let us help you get to your car and we'll clean up."

The Pope smiled and nodded his head in agreement. All four of them were slowly walking to leave the church, but Ren smiled and walked out of the corner where everyone could notice him.

The Pope said, "Young lad, everyone has already left. Did you forget something?"

Ren kept walking toward the Pope and the young priest, without saying a word, until he was only a few feet away from them. He said, "No, Father. I stayed behind because I need to confess all my sins so you can bless and forgive me. I was too nervous to come close to you with all those people around."

The Pope smiled and said, "It's okay, my son. I can do that. So what are your sins so I and God can forgive you?"

"Well, you see the sins that I'm talking about are like lying and stealing."

"That's it, my son." The Pope chuckled a little bit. "You don't have to be embarrassed about those sins. I get those all the time. But it is still okay, my son. You might have lied and stolen, but you are still young, and you telling me this shows that you want forgiveness, so I forgive you, my son, and our Father has forgiven you as well."

"Well, there is another thing."

"What is it?"

"Well, you see, I'm a demon." After he said that, he began to transform.

As he did, the temperature fell, and all the candle lights that were still lit went out and the electrical lights kept turning off and on until they were fully dead, only leaving light that came from outside.

As Ren finished transforming, all three priest boys were scared—so scared that they couldn't look away. It was so bad that one of the priest boys looked like he was about to pass out from the pure sin radiating from Ren. Ren saw all of the young priest boys cower in fear, but noticed that the Pope was not scared at all. He knew why Ren was here because it was one of many pieces of information the church gave when he became the Pope.

The Pope lifted his head up to look Ren in the eye and said, "Please, let these boys go. I know why you are here, so please don't take any of their lives. They are still young and have many things to do for this world and for themselves." Even his voice was calm.

The oldest priest boy opened his mouth, presumably about to say, "No, Father, you can't just stay with that demon!" but no words came out. Not a single sound.

Ren looked at the three boys again, watching all three of them try to be brave, but failing.

Ren, with a cold look and smile, said, "Okay, I'll spare them, as you say, but all of you leave before I change my mind."

The youngest priest boy said, "Your Holiness, please. We can't just leave you. You'll die from this demon."

The oldest priest boy looked at the younger one, shocked that he said the words that he wanted to say but couldn't say them earlier.

The Pope said, "It's okay, my son. It's fine. I've lived long enough for my age. But you—you're the next generation of priests that need to live and fight the forces of evil for me. Don't worry. I have a feeling that this thing won't leave this place alive." His voice was calming and heart-warming, like a soothing song you play to relax.

But even though what the Pope said was relaxing to the young priests, they refused to leave. It didn't take long for the Pope and the two of the priest boys to start arguing about leaving or not. As the Pope and two of the priest boys were having their argument, the third priest boy, the one that had been quiet this whole time, walked slowly back to a table that was behind all of them. On the table were some flowers, candles, and a golden cup with holy water in it. The boy quietly grabbed it without being spotted by Ren. Ren was not paying any attention to him; he was focusing on the Pope and the other two boys arguing with each other in amusement. But he was going to find out that was a big mistake.

The third priest boy tossed the cup at Ren. It hit him, sending holy water all over his skin. It started to burn him. He tumbled back in pain as smoke came from his body. While this was happening the third priest boy that threw the cup yelled at the other two to take His Holiness and get out of there while he tried to exorcise Ren. So the other two, without a word, grabbed the Pope by the arms and speed-walked to the closest exit door. As Ren stopped quivering in pain, he looked at the boy who was trying to exorcise him.

The third priest boy said, "O Father, the son, and the Holy Spirit. Please help me vanquish this evil creature and send him back to the underworld..."

But Ren started to laugh and said, "Sorry, but that doesn't work on me, little boy." Ren walked up to the little priest boy and rammed his hand right through the boy's chest and pulled out his heart. He crushed it and tossed it to the side.

The two other priests with the Pope were already at an exit when Ren killed their friend. One of them reached for the door handle and tried to open it but it wouldn't open! Ren was using his telekinesis to make the door shut tight, but they didn't know that, and before they knew it, Ren had one hand on each boy. He turned their heads backwards, breaking their necks so badly that the heads literally came off like screw. Both bodies fell right next to the Pope's feet, splashing blood all over the Pope.

The Pope couldn't believe what just happened. What he was seeing were these boys, these two—boys, no, all three boys that the Pope had known for many years and worked with— were dead at his feet.

Ren was now in front of the Pope, towering over this old man with his huge demon body. Ren looked down and said respectably, "Any last words, Your Holiness?"

"Yes. Your kind will never win because humans are strong. We have God on our side and we have each other."

That really bugged Ren. "Well, guess what? I was a human two years ago but one of your precious angels that you pray to send me to hell. And since you know why I'm here, you should also know angels are supposed to stop me. Oh wait. Look around you. No angel is coming to save you. If they were coming, wouldn't they be here by now? Wouldn't they have stopped me from killing those boys to begin with?"

The Pope's eyes widened in shock.

"God doesn't give a fuck about you or me, so please give it a rest and don't fight back."

Ren raised his hand over the Pope and slowly came closer to his face until he grabbed it. The Pope wasn't struggling; he was not even going to try. But he looked up to look at Ren's face one more time and what did he see? He saw a single tear coming out of Ren's face.

The Pope closed his eyes and had one more thought to himself, "I see now. You may be a demon but I can tell that you don't want to do this. You still have humanity inside of you but you are doing this because you have a reason, even though you will suffer in the end. So once again, I forgive you, my so—"

SNAP!!!

Ren snapped the Pope's neck. He held the lifeless body of the Pope in his hand. He gently knelt down to put his body on the ground.

"I'm sorry, Your Holiness, and to the other three boys. But this is the only way to get to that angel."

While he was knelling and was still staring at the Popes dead body. Ren ever so slowly moved his gaze away from the Pope and looked at his own hands.

"It's strange I just killed four innocent people and yet I don't feel that bad. I mean I feel something but it's so small that I don't really notes it if I don't focus on it. I guess that is just another perk for being a demon."

As Ren was about to teleport the Pope's body away, a huge light came from the ceiling, and five beautiful people with angel wings—two males and three females—fell down to confront Ren. All five of them had plain white shirts, pants, socks, and shoes. They all had blonde hair and blue eyes and faces such that all of them could have been movie stars.

When they landed, they all looked at the Pope with a shocked face and then looked at Ren. One of them said, "What have you done!?"

Ren ignored them. He snapped his fingers and teleported the Pope's body to hell without any resistance at all. He stood up and looked at the five angels. But he was confused. Why didn't any of them even move a finger when Ren teleported the Pope's body to hell? Wasn't that the whole point of them coming here?

One of the female angels said, "So, let's begin."

She raised her right hand and turned it so her palm was facing up. Then a small blue circle formed on her palm and something slowly came out. It was a scroll with a string tied to it. She cut the string with a fast swipe of her finger and opened the scroll. A white light exploded out of the paper. The bright light went far enough for the entire population of the city to see it, including Miguel, who was still outside the cathedral.

Miguel said, "So, it's started."

The people were shocked by what just happened. It didn't take them long to figure out that the light came from the cathedral. Some of the people who were curious enough walked to the cathedral. The closest person walked up the stairs and was about to open the door, but for some reason he couldn't open it up. He knew that the Pope had just finished his speech within the church. It hadn't been fifteen minutes since then. The door should have still been open just in case someone left something inside; they could come back to get it while the lesser priests cleaned up. So the person tried to open the door again and when it didn't open once more, he yelled to everyone else that the door was locked. A couple people decided to look through the window to see what was going on, but when they looked inside, there was no one there except for the three dead priest boys.

A person that spotted them fell back and yelled, "THREE PEOPLE ARE DEAD INSIDE!!!"

Everyone else that heard him ran to the windows to see if he was telling the truth. Almost everyone saw the bodies and it kickstarted a panic outside the church. Everyone was calling the police, the fire department—anyone, really—to find out what was going on. One person decided to try to open the door again. It didn't work. So in frustration he took a couple steps back and decided to ram the door open. But when he hit the door, he got repelled back a whole twenty feet. Nobody knew why or how. But all they knew something bad was going on.

Inside, Ren had his arms crossed over his head to protect his eyes from the blinding light that was coming out of the scroll.

Ren looked around and said, "What just happened?"

The first male angel said, "We just scanned this entire area to get an exact replica of the city to transport us to a different dimension that looks just like this place. That way, we don't have to hold back and worry about destroying the buildings and people around it."

Ren said, "Clever on your end—very clever indeed. I can assume that every angel has this dimension scroll?"

The second male angel said, "Yes."

Ren said, "Before we fight, can I ask for your names?"

The first angel said, "Sorry, but no, we don't tell our names to nobodies like you. Especially ones that are about to die."

Ren sighed in disappointment, but he should have expected that answer.

Ren formed his weapon. The five angels did the same. They all had the same weapon: a two-handed sword that a knight would use. Within a second, after they had all formed their weapons, Ren jumped at them to start the fight that would decide the fate of the world.

THE FIGHTS THAT DECIDE THE WORLD'S FATE

Ren swung his left arm at one of the female angels and swung his right arm at one of the male angels. They both blocked the strikes. They were holding Ren in place for the other two female angels to try to attack him from behind, but he sensed them coming, so he blocked them with the two weapons that were attached to his feet. The four angels smiled, thinking they had Ren stuck in place, so the fifth and final male angel that wasn't connected to Ren was coming down from above to stab Ren in the back. He sensed that attack coming, so he waited until the last second before the sword touched his back and then he used his telekinesis to adjust the sword of the fifth angel.

It worked. The male angel that was falling down hit the other male angel that was blocking Ren's right arm and knocked them back, while Ren, with his free arm, moved quickly toward the angel on his left side and shot hellfire at her. The angel quickly spawned holy water to block the fire, but the fire was so close that the pressure from the steam pushed the angel back quite a distance and she crashed into a lot of chairs.

With two free arms, Ren used his telekinesis again to slide the two swords that were still connected to him away from his legs, tumbling the two female angels forward. Then Ren did a backflip over the two stumbling angels to try to stab their heads. But as they were tumbling forward, they both used their wings to flap them around and block Ren's attack. But Ren was not done with his attack. He kicked one of them so hard that she didn't have time to react. Ren could feel a couple of the angel's ribs breaking as he sent her flying toward the female angel that had crashed into all those chairs.

The pure force of Ren's kick sent both angels flying out of the cathedral and into a store. While Ren was still in the kicking movement, all three remaining angels "the one female and the two male angels" in the church decided to attack Ren in three different directions. Unfortunately for the angels, Ren saw that attack from a mile away. So he used his wings to fly above all three of them, but they were not as dumb as he thought they were. Before their swords hit each other, all three slashed upward to release holy water in a slash motion.

Ren was still close to them so he couldn't get out of the way, and the attack hit him, cutting off his left wing, right arm, and cutting his nose in half. The three angels then flew up with great speed to stab and hopefully kill Ren while he was falling down, because he had just lost one of his wings and that lost wing was still regenerating back.

When Ren fully regenerated, he curled up into a ball, and, with a combination of hellfire and telekinesis, made a humongous fire dome around himself. The three angels crashed into the fire dome because they were moving so fast that none of them could stop themselves. They all got hit and got really burned. Ren, with no time to spare, left the fire dome, by making an opening with his telekinesis, dove down, roughly landed back on the floor, and used his telekinesis to pull the three badly-burned angels toward him, and was about to stab them. But as Ren pulled the angels down, the two female angels that were outside of the cathedral broke right through the walls. One was on Ren's right side and the other on his left.

They had waited outside for so long to try to catch Ren off guard, but unfortunately for those two angels, Ren knew that they were going to do that. So he put more power in his telekinesis on only two of the three angels that was still in the air—the one male angel on the far right and the one other male angel on the far left. Ren pulled his arms down so fast that he made the two angels crash into the two female angels that were going to hit him. The third final female angel that was still in the air and was still under Ren's telekinesis control smashed into the ground hard behind Ren.

With all five angels hurt and off balance, Ren had to quickly choose—which ones to go for and kill, because Ren knew their regeneration healed them unimaginably fast. So Ren quickly chose the two angels on his right side because they were in front of him and they were the closes. Ren flew toward them. As they fully healed themselves and regained their balance, they both turned toward Ren to keep on fighting, but before they knew it, Ren had stabbed both of them in the heart. One of them burst into flames is one of the male angels but the other angel that was stabbed one of the female angels grabbed the arm that was stabbing her.

This surprised Ren because he knew he hit her heart. The blade did hit her heart, but it was off to the side a little bit, so she had enough time to do something before she died. The reason she grabbed Ren's arm instead of trying to kill him was because the last male angel in their team was charging at Ren. His sword was covered in his holy water and was growing in size because he kept putting out more and more water so his attack would be really big and powerful. Ren, without thinking, turned around and used the angel that thought she was holding Ren in place as a meat shield. The male angel couldn't stop himself in time so he hit his already dying companion. A big pillar of water appeared out of the angel's sword, which went up, destroying the church's ceiling.

When the pillar of water disappeared, something was falling from the sky. It was Ren. Even though he had used that angel as a meat shield, he was still very close to the attack and the attack sucked him in, damaging him in the process. Ren fell into a building next to the cathedral. He was coughing up blood, and although every limb was broken, they healed in no time, like they were never damaged in the first place. Ren jumped out of the destroyed building with a serious look on his face. The three remaining angels flew out of the cathedral and had angry and disgusted looks on their faces.

One of the female angels said, "How is it that you are still alive? And not only that—you're winning! You're outnumbered!!"

"Well, if I'm being honest, you guys are weaker than the first two angels I fought. I can tell that you guys are all about overpowering the opponent with numbers than actual skill. Like, you guys keep using the same moves over and over again, attacking me at all angles. Don't get me wrong, it's a good strategy, but if you guys keep doing it, you can be predictable. I'm sorry to tell you that. And know you guys are down two men—well, one man and one woman. And not to mention you three are more hurt then I am so it's not going to end well for you guys. So just let me kill you and stop wasting my time. I got places to be."

The last male angel said, "You know what, you cocky son of a bitch, fuck it. I don't care anymore. You are worthy now to witness our true power."

"Oh, your true power? Okay, I'm going to have to say NO to that. What do you think this is? An anime fight? Where the hero or the villain just lets their opponents transform or reach to their full power? No. Fuck that." As Ren said that he charged at the last three angels.

But as Ren was charging, all three angels stood side by side and threw their swords down, slamming into the ground. Waterspouts immediately came from the ground and hit all three angels. Ren managed to stop himself before running into the water. He had a scared look on his face. He knew he couldn't stop them now.

Ren could see the three angels—or to be more specific, he could see the shadows within the water. The three angel shadows were fussing with each other. Ren could sense all their strengths combining and transforming.

But Ren wasn't having it. He shot a powerful hellfire blast at the waterspout and hit it, but it didn't do anything until a pressurized holy water blast the size of a gas truck came from the waterspout. Ren put his arms in front of him just in time to block the attack. The attack hit Ren dead on and sent him flying from where the cathedral was to literally the end of the city. Ren landed on the ground in lots of pain. He was down, but not out, so he slowly got up, badly injured. Luckily, it was still healing almost immediately, but he noticed that his regeneration was slowly slowing down.

Ren thought, "What?! My regeneration is weakened? They hardly got any hits on me back in the church, but because of that one massive attack. It hurt me that badly enough to slow down my regeneration?!"

Ren noticed something coming at him and then it landed in front of him. It was a silver-skinned Phoenix, but replace the fire with holy water and the water looked like miniature waterfalls all over its body.

The Phoenix said with a deep, scary voice, "You have our respect, demon. Not only did you managed to kill two of our group members, but you have the honor to see us in our true form. This is our true power. But as you can tell, this is only three-fifths of our true power, since you killed the other two pieces, so be honored because not that many demons get to see this form and live to tell the tale."

As Ren got into his battle position, which looked like a boxing pose, the Phoenix roared, which spawned more waterspouts surrounding Ren and the Phoenix within a one-mile radius. All the houses and trees that were near the waterspouts were being sucked up and ripped apart by the water pressure.

Even Ren felt like he was about to get sucked in and ripped apart. As he lifted his head up, the Phoenix charged at him, tackling him, but it wasn't done. The Phoenix bit Ren's legs and kept slamming him to the ground, over and over. His blood was flying everywhere. The same could be said about the dirt and rocks Ren was slamming into. He was literally about to pass out. As the Phoenix was slamming Ren to the ground, he could also still feel the air pressure trying to suck him away from the Phoenix and into the waterspout.

Suddenly the Phoenix stopped slamming Ren and lessened its grip. Maybe it was tired of rag-dolling him. As Ren noticed it, he regained consciousness and tried to attack its throat. It turned out that the Phoenix loosened its grip because it shot a water blast from its mouth, hitting Ren and launching him into a waterspout. When Ren went inside the spout, he was spinning and spinning around like a piece of debris in a tornado. He felt like he was about to be ripped apart and if he didn't think of something, he would be.

Ren opened his eyes slowly, but because the water was holy water, it really burned his eyes. But thanks to his regeneration and his high pain tolerance, Ren managed to open his eyes—not fully, but just enough to see. He looked around to see what he could do, but all he could see was the water turning clockwise. It seemed hopeless until Ren got an idea. He stretched out straight like he was a stick, hands clamped together, feet close together, and his wings wrapped around his torso. He started to spin.

He was spinning the same direction as the waterspout, and while he was doing that, Ren was getting more and more speed from the spout to his spin. He became like a drill, and when he thought he had enough speed to his spin, he swung his head back to use his telekinesis to get him out of the spout. Luckily, it worked. He left the waterspout and was headed toward the Phoenix, who had been standing and watching Ren the entire time. The Phoenix was shocked that Ren got out and knew that it didn't have time to get out of the way. So it shot a water blast with all its might. It hit Ren, but he started to drill through it.

But don't get the wrong idea. Ren could still feel the water hitting his hands, and it felt like he was pressing his hands against concrete, the pressure was so strong. But it wasn't long before he drilled through the water, went inside the Phoenix's mouth, drilled through its organs, and came out at the tip of its tail. Ren crashed into the ground. From the looks of it, both of Ren's arms were broken. The bones were sticking out and Ren had broken his spine so badly that his head was touching his feet. But he was still alive.

The Phoenix fell, slamming the ground and sending blood everywhere. Ren stood back up, showing he was not done yet. Ren's wounds were still healing pretty quickly, but not as quickly as when he first started the fight. Ren walked to the Phoenix and was completely shocked that somehow it was not dead. It was still alive, but lots of blood was coming out of the mouth and tail.

It tried with whatever strength it had left to talk. "H-how-how...did you know...where I was...? You were spinning so fast that...you shouldn't be able to see...me?"

Ren said, "I'm amazed that you can even talk. That's cool and disturbing at the same time. Well, to answer your question, even though I could not see you, I could still sense where you were. I've got to admit, being able to sense my opponent's whereabouts is very handy and you standing still also really helped. And also speaking of handy—" Ren lifted up his right arm, extended the blades, and stabbed the Phoenix in the head, killing it once and for all.

After Ren killed the Phoenix and after the Phoenix burst into flames and turned into ash, something happened—the entire city that was in front of him was slowly disappearing in front of his very eyes, and, not only that, but the very spot Ren was standing on was also disappointing until there was nothing but an empty white void. The void started to crack and shatter.

Ren knew where he was.

He was back in the cathedral. He knew he was back because the three dead priests' bodies were here. They were not in the other dimension, and the cathedral was not damaged. But to really confirm that he was back, Ren looked out a window. He could see people surrounding the church. Ren also noticed something else.

"Is it still dusk?"

He turned his head around to look for a clock. Ren couldn't believe it; only five minutes had gone by in the real world even though his fight had lasted a whole lot longer than five minutes in the dimension. Ren felt like he was about to collapse from all the damage he took from those angels, but he managed to keep his balance and walk to the statue. He lifted his hand up, slashed it opened with his claws, and there was indeed a bone in it—more precisely, the pelvic (hip bone) was in it. Ren grabbed it, put it on the altar, lifted his left hand up so a spiral fire spawned on his palm, and summoned a syringe with the Pope's blood in it.

Ren soaked the bone with the blood and lit it with hellfire before he did the chant that was told to him by Satan and Lucifer:

"סוקי הזה סוניהיגה ללגבו חצנל ופרשיי סתואש סוניהיגל ולפנ רתויב שודקה סדאהו חישמה עושי המדאה לע הכמ היהיו."

As Ren finished the chant, the fire grew five times its size and a kinetic force exploded from the burning bone, sending Ren flying back. He hadn't been prepared for that. When the fire stopped burning the bone, it only left burn marks, no ash to be seen.

The world started to change.

The people that were outside the cathedral were in a panic because of the bodies until the shockwave that came out of the fire hit them all, knocking them on their butts. Before a single person had even asked what just happened, something caught their attention. The entire city, the entire country, and the entire planet was literally being covered in black thunder clouds, and fast winds started to pick up. The winds were so strong that people were being pushed back, and finally, the ground in every cemetery and graveyard around the world began to crack until huge holes opened up to release pretty much every demon with the ranking of 201 and higher. They sprouted out of hell to possess or walk or fly in the world of the living.

These demons had already begun to eat, kidnap, kill, and rape people and do whatever they wanted on earth, while other demons was to try to find and break more seals. Hell's army had been unleashed on the world. However, as that was happening, the black clouds turned white and white balls were falling down to earth like meteorites. That was because the angels were coming down to earth to stop the demons. So Ren's wish did come true—the angels did come down to the living world, and maybe one of those angels was the angel that had sent him to hell. The demons and angels were now at war with each other and everyone was a part of it.

As all that was happening, Ren walked out of the cathedral, transforming back to his human form, and saw all the people running and screaming. While every house was shaking and cracking, glass breaking and falling down on the side-walk, somehow no one was beneath where the glass was falling, so no one got hurt. Ren went to find Miguel, but he was nowhere to be seen so he stopped, closed his eyes, and tried to sense where he was. It turned out that Miguel was on the outside of the city, so Ren teleported to his location. With a single snap of his fingers, Ren teleported to where Miguel was. He was just standing there watching as demons rose from hell and angels fell from heaven to go to war with each other.

Miguel was watching it with a disgusted look on his face. He turned around to look at Ren and asked, "Are you happy? Are you happy about what you have done?"

All Ren said was, "Yes."

Miguel looked down, took a deep breath looked back at Ren, and said, "So how many angels were sent to kill you?"

"Five. They were good but they didn't have any outstanding fighting style. They were weak." Then Ren whispered to himself, "Until they transformed." Hopefully Miguel didn't hear him.

Miguel said with a hint of sarcasm, "So you let five weaklings kick the shit out of you?"

"Shut up. That's the demon side talking in me, but there is something that is bothering me, though."

Miguel, with a confused look, asked, "What is it?"

"Well, you guys said that the angels wanted to make sure that this would never happen. Like me killing the Pope and starting the apocalypse, right?"

"Yeah, and your point is?"

"Well, first, why did they send only five angels, especially those five that were not really that strong, since they were going for numbers rather than strength. Like, if that's their plan, why didn't they send a whole lot more angels? And most importantly, why were they late? They were so late that I had already killed the Pope. And what's more is that they were not very shocked—like, their eyes were wide open, but the way they spoke was as if they knew that they were going to be late. So what happened?"

"I don't know. I wasn't there, so I don't think I nor any other demon in hell will know, so just forget about it and let's go back to hell and give our report to Astaroth."

Ren nodded his head and walked in front of Miguel. He was about to teleport, but then Miguel summoned a long dagger and tried to stab Ren in the back. Ren, thinking quickly, grabbed his arm and swung Miguel through a building.

There was silence for a couple of seconds until Miguel jumped out of the building, stood up, and said, "You knew I was going to attack you?!"

Ren replied with a disappointed voice, "Yeah."

"How did you figure out I was going to attack you?"

"Well, two things. One, with that look of disgust on your face, I can tell you were not happy with what's happening. And second, when we were walking through the hallway, you kept asking me if I still had humanity, saying I should not do this, and wondering why was I going to bring humans into my revenge? So I could tell you were on their side. But I was thinking you were going to attack me in the hallway or when I walked into the cathedral, but I guess that you thought that the angels were going to kill me, so you don't have to. But it didn't turn out that way. So what are you going to do? Kill me or forget what you tried to do to me?"

"I'm sorry, but I have to kill you. If I let you stay alive, you might be the demon that breaks the most seals, and I can't have that."

"You do realize that if you fight me and kill me, you'll be a traitor to hell and Astaroth...no, Satan and Lucifer. They will send someone to kill you."

"Yes, I am well aware of my situation right now, but I'm willing to take the risk, because I'll join the angels and with me killing you, it will persuade the angels enough that they may not kill me."

"I see that. Too bad because I kind of like you, man. I thought we were going to be friends."

"As did I, but that's not possible right now."

As these two were done with their conversation, Ren immediately transformed while charging at Miguel, but Miguel lifted his arms up and summoned two small shields on each arm to block Ren's attack. He used his telekinesis to push Ren a couple feet back, then waved his hand and shot out a strong gust of cold wind at Ren. Ren couldn't move out of the way fast enough, so the cold wind hit him. But instead of freezing his entire body, it froze his feet to the ground and huge chunks of ice started forming on top of body.

Then Miguel stopped his attack. The ice balls stopped getting bigger. Ren didn't know why at first but then realized. The ice balls were too heavy, so they were slowly falling off, tearing off huge chunks of flesh that were connected to the ice. As Ren was screaming in pain, Miguel ran toward Ren with two daggers. Ren couldn't move his arm because two big ice balls were weighing his arms down and his feet were frozen to the ground. So Ren used his telekinesis to move Miguel's attack slightly down to hit the ice balls that were weighing his arms down.

It worked. Miguel hit the ice, then Ren swung his arms to hit Miguel's face but Miguel used the shields to block them. Then Ren, while his blades were still making contact with Miguel's shield, shot hellfire at Miguel, burning him and sending him flying toward the same building again. Then Ren, with the free time he had, tried to fly up to get some distance. It worked, but Ren lost all of the flesh on both of his bottom feet, meaning the bones were visible as he flew up. He was breathing really heavily because he was already weakened from his fight with the angels, so he was not at 100% right now, while Miguel hadn't taken any damage until now. He was pretty much at 100%.

As Ren was flying up, Miguel sent an ice wind attack up to hit Ren in the air. As that was happening, Miguel was also summoning an ice pillar beneath his feet to try to reach Ren in the air because he couldn't fly. Ren had enough. He shot a fire wall to cover himself from the cold wind and melted the ice balls that were forming on his body again. It worked. It was melting the ice, but even though the ice was melting, it was not melting them fast enough, so the ice balls were still heavy enough to tear his flesh.

On the outside of the fire dome that Ren had made, Miguel was not stopping; he was still moving toward Ren. Miguel swung his arms, his left to the left side and the right to the right side, to open Ren's fire dome. The dome opened, and in less than a second, Miguel was right in front of Ren. He swung his daggers at Ren, but Ren once again used his telekinesis to slightly move the daggers away from hitting any vital spots, but Miguel knew Ren was going to do that. His real target was Ren's wings.

As Miguel's arms moved away from hitting a vital spot, he moved his daggers slightly so they were pointing at Ren's wings. Two sharp icicles formed in front of the daggers—one for each dagger—and then Miguel cut Ren's wings in half. Ren started to fall to the ground, shaking in pain. His regeneration was almost gone because he had taken too much damage, so his wounds were healing really, really slowly.

CRASH!!!

Ren crashed on the ground like a meteorite crashing to earth.

Miguel was slowly making ice stairs from his ice pillar so he could walk to Ren, knowing he had won this fight. He said, "You thought you knew everything that I was planning from the start, didn't you? But guess what? You didn't because there was another reason why I let you live and fight the angels. And that's because you are a higher rank than me, so therefore you are stronger than me, but you aren't that much higher than me. But it's still higher so I couldn't take the risk of fighting you with your full strength, so I let the angels fight you—to kill you or really wound you. And that's another thing that I have over you: I have more battle experience than you, so I'm cleverer than you."

As Miguel said this, he was walking toward Ren. Ren was crawling away, finally fully healed with a scared look on his face, knowing that he might actually die. Miguel caught up to Ren and was now in front of him.

Miguel grabbed Ren by the throat, lifted him up, and said, "I'm sorry, Ren, that it has to be like this. I really did hope that we could be friends. So any last words?"

Ren and mumbled, "Yeah." Then Ren opened his mouth and a huge fire blast came out and hit Miguel's face, taking off all of it.

Miguel let Ren go to stumble back, then Ren, with smoke coming out of his mouth, ran toward Miguel and slashed his face in two, killing him. Ren fell back, in pain and exhausted. His mouth was so burned that his tongue and teeth were blackened. It was like that because Ren couldn't breathe fire. When he was in his fire dome, Ren knew that he was going to lose if the fight stayed the same, so he thought of a plan to catch Miguel off guard.

What Ren did was he use his telekinesis to put some of the fire in his mouth, condensing it to make it stronger, and when Ren opened his mouth, it burst out like a flamethrower. So Ren was laying on the ground, slowly going unconscious while looking at Miguel's body burning into ash. As Ren was fully laying on the ground, two people showed up next to him. One of them said, "Good work, Ren. You can rest easy now. We will take you back to hell." But Ren didn't hear them because had had fallen unconscious.

Ren woke up a couple hours later in his room, covered in sweat and in his human form. Ren looked around, trying to remember what had happened. Ren took the covers off of him and got up to get something to drink. But he noticed a letter on his door. It said, "Ren, meet Astaroth when you wake up."

Ren crumbled up the paper and tossed it into his trash can and left his room to see Astaroth without a second thought.

Ren opened the door in his demon form and walked into Astaroth's room. Astaroth said, "Ah, so you are awake. Now that's good. How was your nap?"

"Good, but how did I get back to hell? I thought I passed out in the living world?"

"You did, but some of my troops that were freed by you breaking the first seal saw your battle with Miguel—which, by the way, good job killing that traitor—and they brought you back. It's good that they did because they sensed some angels that were coming to finish you off. But luckily, they sent you back to hell. Your wounds were bad, but not too bad, so we didn't have to send you to our hospital—and before you ask, yes, hell does have a hospital. So we just let you rest, let your regeneration come back, and let it heal you."

"Thank you," Ren said, and looked at his hands.

Ren realized that there was no going back, that he had just jumped into an ocean full of sharks, and he had to fight to survive. He wasn't sure whether he regretted doing this or not. Ren lifted his head up and said, "Besides the one seal I broke, were any other seals broken when I was asleep?"

"Well, yes. Only one other, so two total have been broken."

"What? Why? Only one? How many hours have passed since I was out?"

"Only two hours."

"So then why? I killed a total of five angels for the first seal, so then why are they having so much trouble?!"

"Ren, you must know that not every demon is going to try to break a seal. Some of them don't see any reason to even try because they think and/or know they are not strong enough to take on an angel. Because unlike demons, who mostly just fuck around in hell, angels have a strong military force. And few of our demons have any real battle experience with anything—angel, demon, or human. And they are very arrogant because they know that pretty much nothing can kill them. But we do have an army; it's much smaller than what heaven has, but we still have one, and these demons are loyal to our goal, and you are one of them."

Ren nodded his head, stood up, and said, "What seal do you want me to break next?"

MANY FIGHTS TO COME, PART I

It was Ren's day off because he broke a seal four days ago. He could break a seal today, but today was his day off, so he was sitting down near his desk writing in his journal in his human form.

It's been almost three weeks since I broke the first seal in the living world, and so far, everything is as it said in the Bible; almost every town and city has been destroyed by demons rising from hell, and now they are everywhere in the world. The same can be said about the angels. So far, we have broken a total of nine seals since this started. I broke four of the seals by myself. That makes me the demon that has broken the most seals so far.

So far, the only seals that I have broken are the seals that Astaroth asked me to break. I really am a soldier for him. The reason that we only broke nine in two weeks is because we are outnumbered. Not only did most of the angels come from heaven to try to stop us, but pretty much every human that is still alive or that is not being possessed by a demon is on their side. However, we do have some humans on our side—all of the heretics—which is not very many, but take what you can get, I suppose. And another thing that I found out, which I should have already guessed, is that monsters exist. Like vampires and werewolves. That was a shock to me, to be honest, but I should have figured they were real since, I'm a demon. Surprisingly, I haven't fought any monsters yet besides angels. I don't know why, but I couldn't care less. It's less trouble for me when I'm in the living world.

Anyhoo, the monsters in this war, for the most part, are doing what they can do for themselves, whether it's killing or eating as many humans as possible, since the human population has drastically gone down. By the end of this war, they might be extinct.

But I have heard rumors that some monsters only go for humans that were or are being possessed because it's a rare delicacy for a monster to eat a human that is possessed by an angel or demon. I guess we add extra flavor in the blood or flesh or something.

There is another thing that I found out about the monsters, and that is that they are joining sides. I originally thought they were just doing whatever they wanted, but it turns out that most of the monsters are choosing a side to fight for. Like we do have some vampire soldiers, but they are like our foot soldiers to see what and how many enemies are in the church. The reason is for them to see is there any traps that are made for demons or if there are any surprise attacks. The demons don't care if they die, so long as they do what they are told.

Me, personally, I don't like to use the monsters as decoys. I know they are monsters, but I would feel guilty sending them to their deaths. So I told Astaroth that I didn't want any monster with me when I'm doing a mission. He surprisingly accepted my request. Now the last thing I have to say is that it turns out Satan and Lucifer did keep their promise to me if I started this war. Japan literally doesn't have any demons in it—hell, it's not even damaged at all compared to everywhere else in the world.

The people living there still have normal lives for the most part because it turns out hell released some sea monsters in their ocean, so anyone trying to enter the country for salvation will be attacked. But anyone trying to leave the country, like people leaving to join the war, the monsters won't attack them. They will just let them go. I don't know why but I don't really care as long as the mangas keep on being produced, which they are. Then I'm happy. So that's it. I'll come back later.

Ren closed his journal and leaned back on his chair, thinking only one thing: "Would I really find the angel that did this to me? Because I don't know who did it and I don't even know what he or she even looks like. I have no clues. That angel might even be dead by now from some random demon. I would be happy if that happened, but I would also be disappointed that I didn't kill it. Because if the angel died, that would be awesome, but I was hoping that I would kill it. Oh well, I'll find that angel someday."

Ren's cell phone rang. He picked it up. It was Astaroth.

"Come to my office. We need to talk." Click.

Ren sighed. "Well, so much for my day off." He transformed back to his demon form and walked to his door. "Take me to Astaroth's office." He left.

Ren opened the door to see Astaroth, and was surprised to see Azazel there too.

Azazel said, "Ah, Ren, it's been a while. How have you been? Want some tea?"

"Azazel, nice to see you too. And no thanks, I'm good."

Azazel said, "Okay," and kept drinking his tea.

Ren walked to an open chair, sat down, and said, "Okay, what is so important that you had to call me during my day off? Does it have to do with a seal?"

Astaroth said, "Yes, and we want you to break a seal."

Ren sighed, but his sigh was a mixture of disappointment and realization. "Okay, fine. I was getting bored anyway. But I have to ask: is it a specific seal that you want me to break or do you just want me just to get another random seal?"

"It's a specific one, but I'll let Azazel tell you, since that seal was supposed to be his target—or, so-to-speak, the men that he assigned's target."

Azazel looked at Ren and Ren could see embarrassment on his face. "See, so far I've lost three demons from that seal, but it was by no means from an angel. Oh no—it was by humans. That's what I've been told by the spy I sent to watch the third demon I sent to try to break the seal. I wanted to see what was going on. It turns out that humans set up traps inside the church, and from what he heard and saw, they changed the traps after every demon they captured. And yes, I said captured. They wrapped the possessed bodies with iron chains that were covered with salt, tied them up, and took them to an underground tunnel to most likely give them to the angels to get information. So that's the reason I'm here. I don't want to lose any more of my men. It's not because I care about them—not in the slightest—it's because I just don't want to lose any more to some mere humans, so I want to see you in action against some humans, since I haven't seen you fight yet."

Ren said, "I see. So let me get this straight: instead of sending another one of your demons and giving it this information, which it would most likely use to succeed, you want me to do it because you haven't seen me in a fight yet."

"Yes, that's correct," He was acting like it was the most normal thing to ask.

Ren put his hand on top of his head and shook his head slowly, like he had a headache. "Okay, fine. I'll do it. So where is this church?"

Astaroth said, "The church is in a town called Afton in Wyoming. Here is a picture of what it looks like." Astaroth handed Ren a picture and said, "Go now. There will be someone waiting for you to give you more information about that church."

Ren nodded his head, stood up, walked to the door, and said, "Take me to the church in Afton, Wyoming." Then Ren opened up the door and left without saying a word to Astaroth or Azazel.

A red door with skull handles suddenly appeared in front of the church in Afton, Wyoming. The door opened and Ren walked out in his human form. As he had finally arrived at the church, the door vanished behind him. Ren could sense someone behind him and it was no human, angel, or demon, so it had to be some other monster that Ren didn't know about. Ren turned around, transformed, and said, "Come out! I know you are there!"

The person that walked toward Ren from the shadows was a teenage boy with messy blonde hair and blue eyes. He was pretty skinny.

Ren said, "Who and what are you?"

"My name is Hermès. I'm a Greek god. You might know me. I'm pretty well known."

Ren said, "Hermès, as in the messenger of the Greek gods?!"

Hermès said, "Yes. So you do know of me. That's great. Very few humans still remember me, or, if they do, most of them would know me from that Hercules movie, which is a good movie. But anyway, as you can figure, I'm the spy."

"Wait, you're our spy? Why? You are not a demon or a human that became a heretic, or even a common monster. You're a Greek god. Why are you doing such a dirty job?"

"Well, I have my reasons. You see, I'm—what do you call it? A forgotten god. No one will pray to me, give me gifts in front of my statues, or give me any human sacrifices, which is why I look so skinny. I haven't eaten in a while. Well, to be more precise, a couple thousand years, but luckily, I won't die from starvation. But that didn't answer your question, did it? Well, you see, thanks to the war you started, the angels and demons will take any advantage possible, which is where I come in. The angels and demons don't like other gods because they see us as lesser beings—not to the same extent as humans, but close enough. But in my case, they want me because I'm fast and sneaky. I sneak into places where no angel or demon can go, and report back what I witness."

"Okay, then what do you get out of it? I doubt you want money, fame or women or men or whatever you are into. It has to be something good to risk your life. So what is it?"

Hermès said, "You're right, I don't want any of that. What they give me are some of the souls that they have in hell. They give them to me and when they do, I use my powers to give the souls their physical bodies back without them knowing why and how. So then, when the souls think they are being freed from hell, I come in and eat them. And I've got to say, the souls from hell, as they leave hell—they get a spicy taste in their souls, which... I don't mind spicy food."

Ren looked at Hermès with a disgusted look because he was not expecting that type of answer at all. He shook his head to try to forget what he heard and said, "Okay, let's just get back to business. So what kind of information can you give me?"

"As you can sense, the only thing that's in that church to protect the seal are humans. But these humans are pretty clever because every time a demon comes in the church, they have a different trap ready for them. Apparently, they don't use the same trap twice, so they change the trap a little bit or they use an entirely new trap."

"I see. If I had to guess, I'd say all of the traps have salt in them so they can trap the demons. Am I correct?"

"Yes. And what's more, if the demon is a weakling, they send it some place else. Either to an angel or to the government to get experimented on. And that's all I can give you. Like I said, they never use the same trap twice."

Ren said, "I see." He turned his head to look at the church. "Okay, thanks for the information. I guess I'll see ya later."

"Wait, Ren. If you don't get captured, can I ask you for something in return for the information I gave you?"

"Sure. What is it?"

Hermès said, "Well, I know you will kill all the humans in that church, but can you leave one for me? I would like a female." When he finished he gave Ren a smirk.

"No, I will not give you a human female, or any human in there."

Hermès, shocked, said, "Huh, why? Aren't you a demon?

Ren immediately said, "Because of two reasons. One, I know what you are going to do with that women. You are either going to eater her like what you told me or even worse you are going to rape that women and I'm not going to let you do either of those. So if their is a women in that church I'm going to give her a painless death like everyone else if they get in my way. And two, I may be a demon and I may be the one that started this war, but deep down, I still have some humanity in me left. So I'll not give you any humans."

Hermès smiled, turned around, and just walked away, waving his hand at Ren to say goodbye. He didn't seem disappointed about Ren's answer. In fact, he kind of respected Ren because of his answer. Ren watched him walk way, then turned toward the church and walked inside.

Ren was looking around to try to see any people around, but he couldn't. He sighed and said, "You all know I can sense you, so stop hiding and come out. I'll kill you, but it will be painless, I promise!"

For a short while, there was no response, but as Ren walked closer to the statue that had the seal, a person stood up from behind a chair. The person was now in front of Ren with a scared look on his face.

Ren said, "Well, looks like someone has some courage. So will you try to stop me or just stand there?"

He didn't get a response from the person, so he took a couple steps closer, and then the person finally said something.

"You just fucked up, demon!"

The person moved his entire body away from the chair with tremendous force, and as he did, two arrows—one on each side underneath the chairs that Ren was in between—fired the arrows that hit Ren's legs.

"AAAGH!!!"

As Ren fell in pain the guy yelled, "NOW!!"

The other people that were hiding let go of some rope, which dropped a bunch of salt that fell in a circle around Ren, trapping him. As the salt smoke slowly faded away, every person in the church walked toward Ren, surrounding him. On the ground in pain, he pulled both arrows out of his legs. He could see that the tips of the arrows were iron, covered with salt.

Ren thought, "So that's how the arrows penetrated through me." He dropped both arrows.

Ren got up from the ground and looked down at the guy who shot the two arrows at him. He could see two thin wires around his legs. Those wires must have been tied to the crossbows. And when he moved with that much force, the wires must have pulled the triggers. Ren looked around to see all the people around him. There were five of them—four men and one woman.

He said, "I see five of you, but I sense six, and since I'm in this salt trap I can't sense where you are anymore, so come on out."

A male priest, who looked like he was in his mid-sixties, came out from behind the statue with an annoying smile. He walked up to Ren and said, "You demons are so arrogant. You know that no matter how many times you try to take this seal, you keep falling for our traps. That's because you are so ignorant and so prideful of yourself that you think you can beat us humans because you are some almighty powerful demon. Well, you're wrong."

Ren listened to all the priest had to say while looking around to see if there was a way to get out of this trap and shut this guy up. Everyone noticed that Ren was doing that, so one of the guys behind him pulled out the crossbow he was carrying and shot Ren in the back. Ren tumbled toward the salt circle and hit the invisible wall, which pushed him back so he fell on his butt. And then the guy said, "Pay attention to the priest while he is talking to you, you disgusting demon!"

The priest said, "It's okay. You made your point, now come down, my son."

The guy said, "Sorry, father." He took a couple steps back to reload his crossbow.

Ren pulled the arrow out of his back and dropped it.

Then the priest said, "Now then, tell us, what is your name, demon?"

"My name is Ren. Ren Claude."

Everyone got a shocked look on their faces that quickly turned into angry faces. The only female in the church said, "So, you are the demon that started this entire war?!"

Ren smirked. "Well, a nobody knows who I am. I must be famous. Do you want my autograph?"

The people that surround Ren didn't like Ren's answer. So in a rage, everyone just started to shoot Ren with salt-covered arrows. But Ren spun around and caught every single one—two in his left hand and three in his right. While he was still spinning, he threw all the arrows back at each person's crossbow, breaking every single one by cutting the string. It all happened in the blink of an eye.

Ren said, "Are you done with all of your temper tantrums? Yes? Good. So now let's all behave like adults, okay?"

One of the guys said, "Fuck you, demon scum! The angels told everyone that you were the one that started this entire war just because you just don't like humans!"

The moment Ren heard what the man said, he suddenly started to laugh uncontrollably—even some tears came out of his eyes. "Oh, you poor things. You have no idea of the truth."

The priest, with curiosity, said, "The truth? What truth? Tell us?!"

"I didn't start this war because I hated humans. I started this war because an angel sent me to hell, and then when I left hell to see my family and friends, the angels came down and killed all of them just because they wanted me to be miserable." Ren's tone had slowly turned into anger.

The priest suddenly yelled at Ren: "That's a lie! An angel would never do such a thing to any human!!" This completely surprised everyone in the church. Everyone except Ren.

Ren said, "Well, I'm sorry to tell you, but an angel did do this to me, which means an angel is the cause of all of this."

Everyone, with humongous angry faces, ran to multiple huge buckets that were spread all around the church. The buckets were filled with water; more accurately, holy water. They each grabbed a big cup that was in the buckets, dunked it, and splashed Ren.

While Ren was squirming in pain from the holy water, the priest said, "LIES, all LIES! You demons are all the same—just liars! How dare you insult the great angels and lie to these good believers of God? REPENT! REPENT! I said RE-

PENT for all of your sins!!!!" His voice was getting louder and louder.

This went on for thirty seconds—just constant screaming from the priest, the five people throwing holy water at Ren, and Ren yelling from the pain until everyone stopped because they all got tired. Ren was smoking from the holy water. Ren said, "Okay, can I finally talk to an adult right now, because all I see are people having tantrums like little kids!" He was getting angry.

Everyone walked toward the priest saying, "Are you okay, Father?"

The priest looked up. "Sorry. I lost my composure there, but I'm okay now."

The priest dusted off his robes, coughed in his hand, and said, "So, now that we all got that out of our systems, let's decide on what we are going to do with this demon."

The person that tricked Ren said, "Well, since he is the demon that started this war and from what we can see on his chest, his rank in hell's army is pretty powerful, so let's call on the angel to kill him."

The priest said, "Yes, my son. Good idea."

As they said that, Ren was expecting everyone to pray for an angel to come, but the priest just pulled out a phone.

Ren, with a stupid look, said, "Really, are you serious? That's what you use to get an angel here? Not a prayer or a summoning ritual? A phone, really?"

Everyone ignored Ren because they also thought it was kind of lame to summon an angel by phone, too.

The priest called an angel to tell it that they got another one, so a second after he hung up, a person opened the door and walked in. Ren turned around to see if an angel had come. Yes. An angel had come.

The angel looked pretty plain. He was wearing a suit, but that was it. His hair was black and short and his face was nothing special. But everyone bowed down, even the priest.

The angel walked to the priest. "Thanks for capturing yet another demon."

The priest said, "It was nothing at all, lord angel."

The angel smiled. "As always, I'll give all of you extra years to live again."

The angel lifted his right hand up while his left hand went in his pocket. He pulled out a regular knife. With a quick motion, he cut his own palm. Blood was coming out, but for some reason, it was not disinteresting. Ren was trying to figure out why, when suddenly everyone, even the priest, ran to the angel and started to lick the bloody hand. That's when Ren could see that the angel's grace was surrounding the people and was indeed adding a couple more years to their lives.

Ren said, "So that is their reward? You give them extra years to live on this shithole that I created?"

The angel said, "Yes, but don't worry, we will win this war and defeat all you demons."

Ren rolled his eyes and said, "Riiight, sure, whatever."

The angel got a little annoyed by Ren's answer, so he changed the subject. "So anyway, it looks like it's my lucky day. I get to kill Ren, the most wanted demon and the demon that started this war. I'll be famous throughout heaven."

Ren said, "No, you will not."

"What do you mean, no?"

"As I said—no. I can tell that you did kill some demons, but I can tell the demons that you killed were the demons that these people already captured and give to you. And those demons were wrapped by salt-covered iron chains or was already trapped by a salt circle salt which either or makes them weak. So what I can tell is that you are a coward who is afraid to take a demon head-on because you've never fought one before. So you need these lovely people to do most of the dirty work and you take all the credit to tell everyone in heaven that you are some big shot. How about it? Am I correct?"

The angel crunched up his fist and ground his teeth, which meant Ren must have hit a nerve.

"Damn you! You will regret saying that now!" The angel summoned his weapon. It was a trident.

Ren started to laugh. "That's your weapon? A fucking trident? Oh my God, that's hilarious."

The angel got even more pissed off and charged at Ren to try to stab him, but Ren was hoping that he would lose his cool. As the trident went past through the salt wall, Ren stepped aside, grabbed the weapon, and pulled it to make the angel lose his footing and walk past the salt wall.

Ren grabbed the angel's face and slammed him to the floor, moving the salt away to make a path for an escape. Ren walked out of the salt and summoned his weapons. The angel got up and tried to attack Ren from behind but Ren nudged his head, using his telekinesis to move the trident away from him. Within a split-second, he lifted his left foot and cut the angel's throat, fully killing it.

Everyone couldn't believe that the mighty angel that they had worked for many days had died. It didn't take long for them to go into a panic and try to leave the church, but Ren deactivated his weapon and moved with great speed, killing everyone except the priest by chopping their heads off.

The priest collapsed in terror. "Why didn't you kill them with your weapon? Are we not good enough?"

"No, it's not that. I know that when a human is killed by a weapon from hell, it sends them to hell no matter how much good they did in their lifetime." And with a raise of his wing, he cut the priest in half vertically. The priest's blood and organs went everywhere.

Ren walked on the priest's organs to get to the statue. When he was in front of it, he cut it open. It was the right shoulder blade of Jesus. Ren grabbed it and proceeded with the ritual, and broke another seal.

Four days later, Ren walked into Astaroth's office. "Good morning, Astaroth."

Astaroth sighed in annoyance and said, "When will you call me Lord Astaroth? I am your master."

"Hmm, not going to happen. So what is my next seal?" Ren sat down on a chair.

Astaroth sighed again. "Your next seal is in the San Fernando church in Texas. And the bone is the lower jawbone."

"Damn, that's a big one, so I can expect some pretty powerful angels, right?"

"Yes. We even got some information on the two angels guarding that one. One is named Charoum and the other is Colopatiron. These two are something else, so be careful."

"I will. Is that everything?"

"Yes, that is all."

Ren stood up, bowed his head, and left Astaroth's office without saying anything.

Ren was so used to Astaroth's orders and how he explained them that it just felt like a regular workday for him. He walked through the dark hallway from one door to the other and appeared right next to the San Fernando church.

Something was off. Every building that Ren saw was completely damaged or destroyed, but for some reason the church didn't have a scratch on it. Ren could sense a huge amount of grace radiating from the church, which sickened Ren's stomach. Angels. They must be very powerful. But Ren sucked up the stomach pain and walked in the church to break this seal.

As expected, everything Ren saw was clean and not damaged, so this place really had not been touched by demons at all, and Ren was wondering, "If this church has not been touched by demon-kind, then how come Astaroth knows about the two angels that are guarding this place? I guess these two angels are well-known or... I guess we really do have spies in heaven."

As Ren was walking, light appeared from the ceiling and two people Slowly float down very gracefully. As an angel should. As that happened, Ren transformed. The two angels landed. One of them looked like a middle-aged male librarian with a suit, short brown hair, brown eyes, and glasses, while the other one just looked like a bodybuilder that you would see on the street working on construction sites, but he was also wearing a suit.

The first angel said, "Hello there, demon. My name is Charoum."

The second angel said, "And I'm Colopatiron, and since you transformed, we suppose you are Ren?"

"Yes, I am, and I have to say—you two so far are the most polite angels I have met."

Colopatiron said, "Yes, unlike the other angels that downplay and look down on demons, we try our very best to not to underestimate them."

Ren said, "I see, and because of that, you two are going to be a pain in my ass."

Charoum smiled. "Yes, we are, so let's begin."

Charoum pulled the scroll that scanned the entire town out of his pocket to send them to the other dimension. Ren let it happen because this was literally the only thing he let the angels do without trying to stop them. He would prefer not to let any humans that so happened to be near the area get involved during his fights with the angels.

Ren summoned his weapons and so did Colopatiron. His weapons were two small war hammers like the Vikings would use. But the other one just sat down and pulled out a regular violin—it wasn't his holy weapon, it was just a regular violin from the human world. And he pulled it from inside his suit. But Ren immediately knew what was going to happen.

Ren thought, "Oh no, the ones that look the most harmless are the most dangerous, especially when they use a harmless tool!" Ren rushed toward Charoum to kill him as fast as possible, but Colopatiron got in the way and slammed his hammers at Ren. Ren blocked them both, but Colopatiron was physically stronger, so he got pushed back so hard that he went through the wall of the church.

As Ren went through the wall, Colopatiron said, "Okay, are you ready?"

Charoum said, "Yes. So let's begin, shall we?" He started playing the violin.

Ren got up from the rubble saying, "Damn, those hammers are small, but they've got quite a punch to them."

As Ren got up, he could hear the violin being played. At first it sounded super relaxing, like he wanted to take a nap, but almost immediately Ren's ears started to hurt really badly—so badly that his ears and eyes started to bleed. So he could assume that this was the power of Charoum. Playing that violin was so painful to demons that it made the head hurt so much that their eyes and ears were completely useless from the pain and blood.

But as Ren was holding his ears in pain, Colopatiron charged at him, slamming one of his hammers on his chest and the other on his stomach. But luckily, Ren leapt back, so the damage was lessened—so lessened that it would not kill him, but it would still hurt a lot. Ren went flying again, but this time through a small building. As Ren was flying through the air like a bullet through a gun, Colopatiron teleported behind Ren to hit him again, but he used his wings as shields to block the hammer strikes.

Ren successfully blocked the attack, but both of his wings broke. He decided to use his fire to stop himself from being a bullet flying in the air again. He raised both of his arms and shot hellfire. It worked. He stopped moving, and as he stopped, his wounds immediately healed—all except for his head, which was still hurting so badly that his eyes and ears were still useless.

Ren thought, "What's going on? I have to be far enough away from the bastard's music range by now, so why can I still hear it?!" Ren yelled, "HA! Can you guys please explain to me through thoughts how your powers work? Like every cliché villain, when they are winning, because I'm at a total loss!!"

But that didn't work. Instead, Ren got yet another hammer attack from behind.

But before the hammer hit Ren, his head twitch and he dodged the attack, shocking Colopatiron.

Colopatiron thought, "How did he know I was coming to attack him? He can't see or hear me and his head hurts too much for him to focus or sense me, so how?"

Ren thought, "How did I know where he was coming from? I can't hear, see, or sense anything?"

Colopatiron said, "Maybe it was just a fluke, but just in case... Hey, Charoum, make your music more intense!"

"You got it!" Charoum played his violin more intensely, which indeed hurt Ren even more.

Ren held his head even tighter and yelled even louder in pain. "AAAAAAAAA!?!!"

Colopatiron said, "Okay, let's see if you can dodge me again this time."

Colopatiron shot a compressed water blast at Ren. It hit Ren dead-on with great force, sending him through even more buildings. When the holy water started to deteriorate, Ren rolled out of the holy water and flew up. He was really hurting from his body to his head, but he knew he was not dead yet and was still alive. He could find a way to win.

Ren stopped flying up, thinking he was high enough (even though he had no idea how high he was). Colopatiron shot a really powerful holy water blast at Ren and teleported behind him. The water blast that he shot was aiming for Ren's face. Colopatiron swung one of his hammers to hit the back of Ren's head. But Ren jolted his head up again and stopped flapping his wings to make him fall. As that happened, Colopatiron hit the water blast with such great force that, not only did the water explode around him, but it made a shock wave that cracked every building in the town.

Then Ren turned around to face Colopatiron and shot a big blast of hellfire in his direction. Colopatiron was still shaken from his hammer hitting his water blade that when he came to, it was too late. Ren's fire hit him, engulfing his entire body. However, it didn't kill him and it didn't last long. Colopatiron flew out of the fire, really burned for a short second, but immediately started to heal.

Colopatiron thought, "How, how can he tell where I am? This doesn't make any fucking sense. No demon we've faced has lasted this long, and not only that, he got a good hit on me. Does he have another ability or is it something else?"

Colopatiron stopped in the air and turned around to look at Ren while Ren landed, still holding his head in pain.

Colopatiron took a deep breath and mumbled to himself, "Okay, so how can he tell where I am? It's not from him sensing me and it's definitely not his eyes or ears. So what is it?! Wait! If it's not those then the only thing that he has left is..."

Ren was talking to himself, saying, "So I can smell him. Who knew demons—no, I—have a good sense of smell? And lucky for me, these angels give off a sweet scent. It's faint, but I can smell it. I guess I didn't notice it at first from my other fights because I was so focused on my other senses. Even though my head hurts, I can also still very faintly sense his presence. I can't tell where he is, but I know he's there."

Colopatiron looked at Ren with a raised eyebrow and said, "I think he forgot that since he can't hear, he is yelling while he is talking to himself, so that answers my question. Thanks, Ren. So he can smell me. Okay, now I know that I can remain calm and kill him NOW!"

Colopatiron came down with such great speed that he broke the sound barrier. Ren smiled, turned around, and raised both of his arms and literally took that entire attack, which destroyed every building that was around them within a one mile radius. Well, all buildings except for the church for some reason, and where they stood made a crater as deep as a three-story building.

As the crater was being made, Ren and Colopatiron were connected until Ren moved his arms into an upside down "V," which slid both of Colopatiron's hammers down and made Colopatiron lose his balance. He tried to flap his wings to escape, but his wings couldn't move.

Colopatiron was completely shocked at what happened, but at the same time, he knew what had happened. He thought, "I see so that's what he did. First, he knew I was physically stronger than he was, so when he knew I was close to him he used his telekinesis to hold his arms in place, knowing my attack would still hurt his arms. Second he use my momentum of my attack so I would slide off his arms when he moved them, making me lose my balance and to make sure I was not connected to him anymore. And third, the moment my weapons were not connected to him, he used his telekinesis to hold me down so I wouldn't fly away. He knew I would attack immediately when he yelled. Did I really underestimate him? He, a demon, actually out-smarted me. Hmph well-played, de— No, well-played, Ren." Colopatiron grew a smile on his face. Then he said, "Charoum, I'm sorry, but he won."

Ren made an X slash deep in Colopatiron's chest. The slash was so deep that it hit his heart, killing him. Colopatiron combusted. As Colopatiron was dying, Charoum sensed that his life force had vanished and stopped playing his violin for a couple seconds in shock that his comrade was dead.

Charoum had tears in his eyes. "Colopatiron, no!"

But he snapped out of it immediately because if Colopatiron had died, then Ren was still alive, so Charoum started playing again. But unfortunately, he got stabbed in the neck.

As Charoum was choking on his own blood, Ren said, "Maybe next time don't lose focus while in a battle. Oh, wait, there won't be a next time. Goodbye. And, by the way, your music sucks." And with that, Ren removed his blades from Charoum's throat, killing him in the process.

As Ren swung his blade to get the disintegrating blood off of his weapon, he turned his weapons off. Moments later, the dimension shattered and brought Ren back to the real world. While that was happening, Ren was still holding onto his head. All of his wounds had all healed up, but Ren still had a humongous headache from Charoum. But he would forget that sooner rather than later because, as the dimension finally brought him back to the real world, his chest started to burn out of nowhere.

Ren put both of his hands on his chest as anyone would if their chest started to hurt. Ren fell to his knees in pain. Then he opened his eyes and moved his hands away and noticed that his number was burning off. Ren didn't know why at first, but after it burned all the numbers off, it started to reform again, but with different numbers. The new numbers that formed on the left side of his chest were 1995. So that meant two things: one, Ren just got promoted because of how intense that fight was, and two, Ren just got stronger.

However, Ren couldn't tell at first if he got a little bit stronger or a lot stronger because he had suffered a lot of damage from that fight. That meant he would have to wait and get fully healed before he could notice the difference. So in the meantime, he walked to the statue and proceeded to break the seal. It worked. He walked out of the church with a victorious look on his face.

He stretched his arms and transformed back to his human form for a long hard day of working to raise Satan, Lucifer, and every demon with the number two hundred and less from hell. But the day had not ended. There was still enough light outside. Ren knew he couldn't break another seal for another four days and didn't want to go back to hell just yet.

Ren decide to walked for a while and noticed a flower store. He stared at it for a couple of seconds, then turned and walked toward the shop. He opened the door and went inside to see the flowers. What was inside wasn't surprising. Most of the flowers were dead—what a shocker—but a few of them were still alive somehow. So Ren grabbed all the living flowers that he liked and a vase that caught his eye as well. Before Ren left the store, he also grabbed two candles.

Ren opened up the door and was about to walk out. He turned and said, "Thanks for the stuff. Have a good rest of your day."

Because it turns out, a person was behind the counter trying to hide from Ren. As Ren walked outside with the stuff he got, he snapped his fingers and teleported away. He teleported to his parents' home. The home that they died in.

As Ren was staring at the house that started his journey, he was starting to get emotional—so emotional that he almost dropped the vase that was holding the flowers. Ren moved one of his arms to wipe some of the tears off his face and looked around at the environment around the house.

As usual, every building was badly damaged and the people that used to live in the area were nothing more than corpses that the crows were feeding on. Ren let out a quiet sigh and started to move forward, walking as slowly as he could. He had to walk for a full minute until he was finally in front of the broken door. He stopped and stared inside the empty house. Sweat and tears were falling down his face until his legs just moved on their own and walked inside his parents' house without noticing a camera moving on a light pole in front of the house.

A mysterious voice said, "Well, well, looks like we finally got our man." He grabbed a megaphone and said, "Everyone, he has finally shown himself, so get ready! We are moving out immediately!"

When Ren walked in, he saw the house all cracked up everywhere. It looked like it would come down on top of his head if he was not careful. It seemed like it had been looted. Most people would be mad, but Ren was not, because he knew that in an apocalyptic world, one has to get and do anything to survive.

Ren walked into the living room. He stopped and said very quietly and sadly, "This is where I told my parents everything."

He inhaled again and walked into the living room. He put the vase down on the living room table, put the candles next to it, and used his hellfire to light them. Ren sat down on the exact same chair that he told his parents that he was a demon.

Then Ren looked down at the floor and said, "Hi, Mom, hi, Dad, it's me, I'm back. I know it's been a while—a couple of weeks, to be exact. But I just...I just hope you guys are not watching me. The things I'm doing."

As Ren was talking, his face was starting to tear up and his face was turning red out of pure sadness. "I...I...I'm sorry. I'm so sorry it's because of me you guys are dead now, and not just you guys, but everyone—all my uncles, aunts, cousins, and even all my friends. All of you guys are dead and it's because of me." Ren had started to grab and pull his hair in sadness and anger. "And so I will make them pay. Every single one of them. I'll kill them all, not just because they sent me to hell, where I was tortured for two hundred years, and not just because they keep insulting me, but mostly because they took all of you guys away from me. And the reason wasn't even a good one. Just because I'm a demon and they think I should never be happy EVER!"

As Ren said that, his own power was illuminating and shaking the entire house. He noticed and calmed down.

"I don't know if you guys are watching me and if you guys want me to stop doing what I'm doing, but you need to know that I can't stop and I don't want to. Because, like I said, I want to make them pay."

Ren stopped talking and just sat there looking down at the floor with tears and snot still flowing down his face. He sat there for a good while—so long that the candles were halfway melted. He didn't make the fire that hot; he made it the normal fire temperature so they didn't burn so fast, but the candles were melting a little faster than normal. Ren's ears twitched and he opened his eyes in shock. Then—BOOM!—a bomb that was dropped from a fighter jet landed on Ren's parents' house and exploded it with Ren inside.

A soldier yelled, "Okay, everyone, hurry! Get into position! We have to surround the place. Hurry! Hurry! Move, move, move!"

A military army showed up out of nowhere and surrounded the destroyed house that Ren was in. Everyone got into position and aimed at the rubble, waiting for Ren to come out. Eventually, Ren did come out, already in his demon form, and he did not look happy.

Ren took a deep breath and said, "Okay, before I kill every single person here, I must ask—why are you people here and why did you drop a bomb on top of my old parents' house?!"

A soldier with a megaphone said, "We are a military force that was stationed out here this week. Waiting for you, Ren Claude—the demon that started this war."

"I see. So the angels even told everyone where my parents' house was, knowing I would come and visit it. Smart as ever, those glowing birds," Ren mumbled to himself. Louder, Ren said, "You said station for 'this week.' What does that mean?!"

The soldier said, "Every squad in the military spends a week stationed here, waiting for you to return to this area to try and capture you! So, if you please, stand down. You are surrounded. Everyone has salt covered bullets and will shoot if you make any move that signifies that you will be hostile!"

Ren just stood there, moving his head around and looking at every soldier around him.

Ren thought, "So what? I can see and sense that there are a total of a hundred soldiers surrounding me, and some more a little bit further back. They must be the backup. There are two tanks—one to my left side and one to my right side about a half a mile away, thinking that they can sneak attack me just because I can't see them."

Ren said, "Okay, listen up to what I have to say. If you have a family and if you don't want to die, then leave now. But I can tell that you fine gentlemen are not going to leave, and now that I think about it, you guys just destroyed my parents' house, so why would I let you guys leave alive?"

Without any warning, Ren lifted up both his arms, put them across from each other, and spread them away with great speed to shoot a humongous ring of fire at every soldier that surrounded him. They all burned to death.

It happened so fast that no one could even react to it; not even the people still at their stations who were watching knew what just happened. To them, one second there was a large group of people surrounding one person, and a second later they just disappeared, only leaving the one person that they surrounded.

Everyone was speechless at the sight of Ren just standing there with glowing red eyes as smoke rose from the ground and ashes fell from the sky. Ren turned his head left, then right, because he sensed that the two tanks had just fired their shells at him. With tremendous speed, Ren lifted his arms again and grabbed not one, but both shells and spun around and launched the two shells back at the tanks that fired them, destroying them both, along with the people inside.

As Ren stopped spinning, he looked up and saw five MIG-25 fighter jets flying toward him with great speed. All five fired their mounted mini guns at Ren. The bullets first hit the ground in front of him, which covered the area with smoke, then the bullets reached where he was. But because of the smoke, no one could tell if they hit Ren or not, so they waited for the smoke to clear away, since those bullets were also covered in salt. They figured that at least one should be inside Ren and paralyze Ren or greatly wound him. Then the smoke cleared away, but faster than expected—way faster, and the smoke didn't move on its own. It was like the smoke was pushed away. It turned out that the bullets that were shot at Ren were moving around him in a circle, like a bubble of bullets.

A fighter pilot said, "What? How and why are they spinning around that thing?"

The pilots couldn't see it, but Ren was twirling his right hand pointer finger, which meant he had used his telekinesis to catch all the bullets that would have hit him. When everyone was looking at him, he lifted up his right hand and thrust his entire arm forward, which shot all the bullets at the five jets with twice the speed that they were shot from the jets.

BOOM BOOM BOOM BOOM BOOM!!! All five jets exploded in the air. The pilots were killed.

Ren was twirling his hand around like it was tired and said to himself, "Man, those bullets did pack a punch, but unfortunately, I'm just better. So let's finish up with this warm-up exercise. I have to go back to hell to give my report to Astaroth before he nags at me for taking so long to come back."

Ren snapped his fingers to teleport. The people at the base lost sight of Ren.

The soldier, who must be the general, that was watching Ren said, "W... where did he go? Did he run away?"

Another soldier said, "I don't know, sir?!"

A third soldier said, "We don't see him anywhere on the radar."

"I don't know either, Sir, but I think he's right behind you," Ren said with a soldier tone.

The general turned around and saw Ren waving his hand at him with a smile. Then Ren shoved his hand through his chest and crushed his heart. When the other soldiers in the room saw Ren kill the general, they all pulled out their pistols and was about to shoot Ren. But Ren pulled his hand out of the generals chest and flew up, breaking the steel ceiling like it was nothing, and kept flying up until he was above the entire base. Ren moved his right arm so that it was pointing at the entire base. Everyone who saw Ren fly up began to shoot at him or run away. But it was too late for the soldiers that decided to run. Ren shot a big hellfire blast at the base, destroying it entirely and killing everyone in it.

Ren said sarcastically, "Thanks for the sparring match with my new power-up. It was really helpful." Then he looked at his hand. "So this is what it feels like going up a rank—and not just one rank, five ranks. I do feel a little bit more powerful than when I had the number 2000, and at first I didn't notice it, but now I do feel more powerful!" he added happily and excitedly.

Ren lifted his fingers up and snapped to teleport back to hell. But on the ground, a person walked out from the side of a building. Their entire body was covered in the shadows and they were wearing a cloak, but all that could be seen were its eyes, which were a very light blue color.

"Well, it looks like my creation is becoming more and more powerful after every battle, but he's still not powerful enough. I'll wait a little bit longer before I show myself to him."

A DIFFERENT TASK

R en was once again in his room in his human form, writing in his journal. *I can't believe one whole month in the living world has gone by since I broke the first seal and started this war. It feels longer than that. We've been making progress little by little—breaking the seals. We broke a total of eighteen seals so far, of which I broke a total of eight by myself. This means I still have the title of the most seals broken in hell, which also still makes me the most popular demon and makes Astaroth the most famous of all the other demon generals because I'm his soldier.*

Speaking of the other demons, the other demons that are also trying to break the seals are taking it seriously, but at the same time they are not taking it seriously. I've been noticing that these demons are making this war more like a competition then an actual war. Like, almost all of the demons are making bets to see how long the demon who broke a seal will last in this war. Like, if a demon bets on another demon that just broke a seal, and he thinks that demon won't last a week longer in the living world time, so the demon bets he'll die within a week. If that demon survives longer than the bet, then the betting demon loses, but if that demon does die, then the betting demon wins the price.

But what they are betting is not money. They are betting humans that they captured. Living humans. It doesn't matter what gender or age. I've seen them bet babies before. And whoever wins the bet and takes that poor human... the demon will either make them their food, sex toy, or just to torture them, because humans with still-living bodies make better screams, at least to them. It really sickens me that I'm helping these monsters, but I'm going to have to suck it up for a while longer.

Anyway, back to the betting thing—as you can guess. I have the most bets on me to see if I can survive this entire war. However, there is one other demon that has the second-most seals broken and has almost the same number of bets on them as me. They have a total of four, or maybe five, seals broken. I can't really remember. But here's the funny part—no one, and I mean no one, will tell me who this demon is. Every time I ask, they just give me no answer and start to laugh and say, "Really, you don't who?" It really just keeps pissing me off. So I just stopped asking because I gave up, but I've got a feeling I will find out who this demon is. Sometime soon.

Anyway, back to the war. The war has been brutal, and everyone is having huge casualties on both sides. Angels, demons, and every type of monster you can think of are dying left and right. But the humans have it the worst. They are being killed by demons, monsters, other humans, and yes, even angels. They are just getting killed whether they are being possessed or not. It really doesn't matter at this point. If you get in someone's way, you'll be dead.

And the absolute worst part is I know it's all my fault... These innocent people are suffering because of my selfish desire for revenge. I don't know how long I can take all this guilt. I think my desire for revenge is the only thing that is giving me the will to live. When I do finally get my revenge and kill that angel,. I think I'm gonna...

Ren suddenly just stopped writing. His hand was shaking so he slowly put the pencil down and he looked like he was about to cry. He slowly lowered his arm and just sat there, looking at his journal, completely motionless like a statue.

Ren stayed like that for a solid five minutes. Ren was going to shut his journal until his head jolted up and he quickly opened his journal again, like he almost forgot to write something down.

Oh, yeah, before I forget, there is one more interesting thing about the war. Lately I've been hearing about this angel that has stopped a lot of strong demons and these strong demons aren't even participating in this war their just doing their own thing and this angel has killed them. So that means this angel isn't even assign to a seal and is killing big shots in hell. And also about this angel that I heard it has stopped a lot of hells plans to give us an advantage over heaven AND the interesting part is that no one knows who this angel is, which means this angel has to be a human angel. Human angels don't have big names for them compared to the angels created by God. Those angels have been around for thousands or millions of years and are in multiple different kinds of Bibles, while the human angels are very few. Apparently, it's way harder for a human soul to become an angel than for a human soul to become a demon. The only thing that we know about this angel is that it's a guy.

For a second, I thought this was the angel that sent me to hell, but it's not. The angel that sent me to hell is apparently well known, but this angel is not. So my search still continues.

When Ren finished writing everything that came to his mind, he shut his journal, got up, and fell on top of his bed, arms spread and eyes closed.

He thought, "What to do now? I broke a seal yesterday so I'm off for the entire day. I don't feel like training. I went to Japan two days ago to buy any mangas that have been newly made or that I want. I don't feel like watching Netflix. So what am I supposed to do? I'm so bored! Who knew being a demon during a war would be this boring?"

Ren jumped up from his bed, put his hands in his pockets, and said, "I guess I'll go for a walk."

Even though he hated walking through hell, and seeing and hearing all the tortured souls, he was just so bored that he just needed something to do. So he walked to his door, opened it, and walked out. The door shut on its own behind him. He walked down the hallway, still in his human form. He just kept on walking and looking down so he didn't see the tortured souls, but he could still hear them saying, "Help me, just kill me, god help me, I'm sorry for everything I've done," and many other things.

But they were also saying to Ren, "How did you escape from your cell? Wait, come back! Free me, don't look away."

But they didn't know that Ren was a demon in human form. After Ren had been walking for a couple minutes, he finally looked up because he sensed two strong and one weak presences walking toward him. He stopped walking and lifted up his head. There were two demons walking toward him. One just looked like a giant gorilla and the other looked like a giant praying mantis but its legs were human legs and its skin was green like a mantis, but it was covered in human skin. The gorilla demon had something behind him...no, he was dragging something.

Ren squinted his eyes to see what it was, and sure enough, it was a human woman. That poor woman was being pulled by her long blonde hair. She had a badly torn red dress, her make up was all messed up, she had cuts everywhere, and she only had one high heel on her left foot. She was scratching and punching at the gorilla's hands but he must not have felt it.

She was screaming, "Stop! Let me go! No, no, no!! Someone help me! HELP!"

The mantis demon said, "Stop with all your screaming. We are going to give you a great time, and when we are done with you, you'll forget all the previous men you've been with. That is if you don't die from us putting it in you or how rough we are going to be."

They both started to laugh really hard, and then the gorilla demon saw Ren and said, "Huh, Ren, what are you doing here? We never—or any demon, in fact—see you walking through here."

Ren answered with a disgusted tone in his voice, "Well, I was bored so I decided to go for a walk. And from what I can see, you guys have caught a new toy."

The gorilla demon said, "Yeah, we captured her when we were up in the living world trying to break a seal, but then we saw this beautiful thing trying to hide from us so we said, 'What the hell, we don't have to break this seal, I'm sure someone else will.' So we captured her and here we are."

Ren then looked at the woman with a look of pity and thought to himself, "I'm sorry that this is happening to you."

The mantis demon said, "Hey, Ren, if you're bored, then come with us. The more the merrier."

"No, I would prefer to keep walking, but thanks for asking."

The gorilla demon teased, "Come on, don't be like that. Forget the walk and join us. We can tell you're a virgin."

Ren got a little annoyed and angry and said, "I said NO!"

The two demons looked at each other, then looked at Ren with a disappointed look and kept on walking while still dragging the poor woman with them. The woman screamed at Ren to help her, save her, please. But Ren did nothing. He just stood there, looking down and tightening his fists in anger and guilt. The reason why he didn't try to stop them, or simply kill them, was because they belonged to a different demon general's army, and from what they said, they were participating in the war. So if Ren killed them, or took what they said was theirs, then their general would find out, which would mean that Astorath would find out. Then Astaroth would punish Ren for something so small (aka, saving that woman) by torturing Ren for a couple of days and Ren didn't want that. Ren hated that he couldn't do anything to help people or that woman, but Ren really didn't want to get tortured.

But Ren kept saying to himself, "I may be a demon, but I will never rape or torture anyone because I despise that kind of stuff. I may be an outcast to the other demons, but I don't care as long as I still have some humanity and get my revenge. That's all I need."

Ren continued on his walk until he got a message from inside his head. It was Astaroth and he was using one of his mind magic tricks to talk to him.

"Ren, could you come to my office? I have something to talk to you about." He hung up without letting Ren say a word.

Ren sighed in annoyance but was also glad because now he might have something to do on his day off. He found the nearest door and asked to go to Astaroth's office and walked in. Astaroth was sitting in his chair as usual, but was also pouring some tea into two cups—one for him and one for Ren. Ren sat down in the open seat and grabbed his cup, blew on it, and started to drink.

It was good and hot and Ren asked, "What kind of tea is it?"

"Black tea. It's Russian."

Ren smiled and kept drinking while he asked, "So what do you want, Astaroth? I doubt it's just for me to try some tea and have a heart-to-heart."

Astaroth gave a small laugh and said, "No. I brought you here to do a little mission for me."

Ren put his cup down, leaned back on his chair, and said, "What is this mission?" He was all ready to go.

"We have intel that a couple of angels are meeting someone to get information from us."

"So you want me to listen to everything and report back to you. Is that right?"

"Yes, that is correct."

"You don't want me to just kill them?"

"No, don't kill them. Only kill them if they spot you and attack you."

"Okay, you know, the usual—tell me where, when, and what to do."

Astaroth smiled in amusement and said, "Okay, it's at your town where you died."

Ren thought, "Great Bend, huh?!"

"It's behind a library. If I'm not mistaken, that's the last place you went before you were killed, am I right?"

Ren grabbed his chair tightly and gave a quiet, "Yes."

"I see. Anyway, three angels are supposed to arrive behind the building at eight p.m. to meet whoever they are meeting. It's currently seven-thirty right now, so you have time. What you're going to do is to be on top of the building and listen to everything that's said and report back to me. Understood?"

"Yes, but wouldn't they sense me if I was there?"

"No."

Ren gave a very confused look.

Astaroth said, "Our top scientists have been working on a cloak to completely hide your sin so no angel can sense you. We have one right now, but it's still a prototype, so it's not complete."

As Astaroth was telling Ren this, he opened up his desk cabinet, pulled out the cloak, and tossed it to Ren. Ren caught it.

Ren said, "So what kind of flaws does it have?"

"If you take it off, it will disappear completely and it only has a two-hour time limit when you put it on, so only put it on when you arrive at the library, and this is a big one since it is just a proto type and you're the first to wear it on a mission there could be other flaws that we don't know."

Ren looked at the cloak and thought to himself, "So those are its flaws huh?"

"It's seven-forty-five now. Go, and if any of them see you, kill or run—it doesn't matter, just hear what they have to say."

Ren got up, bowed his head, and walked to the door.

It took Ren a second, but he said, "Take me to the Great Bend library in Kansas."

The door opened and Ren walked through. As he was walking down the dark hallway, he was hoping that the town where he lived wasn't that badly damaged. But Ren knew it would be. So Ren finally walked to the other end of the hallway, opened up the door, and walked out. He was right next to the library, still in his human form, to wait for the angels and the person that was supposed to give them information on hell's plans. So Ren was planning to be on top of the roof and watch and listen to the entire conversation.

As he was about to jump up, he stopped himself and just looked at the library. He even started to talk to himself, "It's funny. This was the last place I went to before I died. Just to get a stupid book, and now I'm here to spy on angels. Oh, how my life changed drastically." He laughed a little bit.

When Ren finished laughing, he remembered that he had to put on the cloak to hide his presence. He raised his right hand and a circle of fire appeared on the ground and summoned the cloak, just like how Ren summoned the syringe of the Pope's blood. He put the cloak on and jumped on top of the library to wait for a couple more minutes for the angels and the other person to show up.

About five minutes went by and Ren had not seen or sensed anyone, and at times like this, Ren really wished he had brought his phone to play some games but he's afraid that it will break. Then Ren sensed someone walking toward the library. He crawled to the other side and carefully looked down. A person, also wearing a cloak, was walking to the library. Ren couldn't see their face, and for some reason, he couldn't sense what they were anymore either. But Ren shrugged it off. He didn't need to sense it because it was right in front of him and maybe it would show its face later.

The person walked all the way around until they were completely behind the building. Then, less than a second after the mysterious person stopped walking, other people showed up. There were three of them, and once again, Ren could barely sense them. But barely wasn't completely, because he could sense a little bit of grace radiating from them, which meant they were the angels. They were also wearing cloaks. All three walked in front of the other person. They were only a few feet away from each other.

The angel in the middle removed the cloak's hood and revealed a beautiful young lady, probably in her early twenties, with long blonde hair and green eyes. Then the other two also removed their cloak hoods. The one on the left was a black girl with long gray dreadlocks and brown eyes who also looked like she was in her early twenties, and the one on the right was a white Asian girl with short brown hair that reached to her shoulders and blue eyes; she also looked like she was in her early twenties and she was the shortest one in the group. All three angels had the same taste in possessing young women, it seemed.

The blonde angel said, "So, did you bring what we want?"

The mysterious person said, "Yes, I have it right here."

Ren couldn't hear the person that still had its hood on after that. They were talking too quietly, but after a few seconds of hearing Ren could tell that it was a guy.

Ren saw him pull out a piece of paper and give it to the blonde angel.

She opened it and gave a pleasant smile.

The blonde angel said, "You'll get your reward later today, okay? I have to give this to my higher-ups."

Less than a second later, she, with the other two, teleported away.

Ren saw everything, but the meeting was short and quick. Ren didn't know what he was expecting, but he thought their conversation would last longer than it did. Ren also knew that piece of paper had information about the demon's plans and Ren did have a quick thought about jumping down and killing everyone. But he didn't do it, like something was holding him back from attacking. Ren knew he was stronger than those angels, but...

Then the hooded man gave a big sigh and sat down on top of a trash can that was right next to him. He removed his hood.

Ren could not believe it. The person that had given the angels a great deal of information about hell's plans was Hermès. Without a second thought, Ren jumped down in a rage. As he landed in front of Hermès, Hermès didn't even have time to react. Hell, he was looking down when Ren jumped off the library. And when he landed, all Hermès saw was some jeans, shoes, and a cloak. Then Ren grabbed Hermès by the neck and slammed him into the library's wall and cracked the entire thing, but it did not fall apart.

Hermès said, while breathing for air, "Well, it's good to see you again, Ren. But I can't say you feel the same way."

"Why did you do it?!"

"Sorry, but you are going to have to be a little bit more specific, buddy."

"Why did you betray hell!?"

"Betray?" He sounded actually confused.

"Yes, betray! You are hell's spy. You are supposed to work for us! Not the fucking angels!"

"I see. So no one told you?"

"Told me what?!"

"I'll tell you, but if you don't mind, let me go, please."

Ren took a deep breath, gave a long sigh, and let Hermès go. "Start talking."

Hermès coughed a bit, then said, "Sure. Well, you see. Yes, I am a spy for hell, but I am also a spy for heaven. I'm—what's the word I'm looking for?—a double agent, I guess. So see, I told you—I do these kinds of jobs because I'm starving and hell gives me souls right? So does heaven. Hell's souls are spicy like Mexican food, while heaven's souls are sweet like candy. So yeah, I work for both sides just so I can get something to eat and just to do something because I'm very bored."

"But some of these things just don't add up."

Hermès tilted his head. "What doesn't add up?"

"If hell knows that you are working for heaven as well then why aren't they sending demons to kill you? Same thing goes for heaven."

"Well, you see, I'm just too valuable."

"Valuable?"

"Yes, valuable. Because hell has spies in heaven, and heaven has spies in hell too. But they take forever to give them any useful information because they don't want to break their cover, while I don't give a shit if I'm caught because I'm just too fast. I wouldn't help them anymore, and that would be a huge blow to them even though they don't like asking me for help. I'm a forgotten god, so to them I'm lesser than a human."

Ren was listening to everything Hermès was saying, and it all made sense, at least during war. The other thing that made sense was why he didn't jump down and kill the angels and Hermès. It was because Ren's senses were telling him to not to attack Hermès because he would just be a casualty of his fight with the angels, and Ren would be in so much trouble if Ren killed him.

Hermès stood up, gave a deep stretch, and turned away from Ren. "Okay, I'm going home now. My job is done, but before I leave, I must tell you something."

"What?"

"Those three angels didn't actually leave."

"Huh?"

"Yeah. They just teleported far enough away so you couldn't sense them."

As Hermès spoke, two chains with a spike at the end stabbed through both of Ren's arms. The chains yanked Ren's arms back so he couldn't move. The angel to the right was the Asian angel and the one on the left was the black angel.

The blonde girl showed up right next to Hermès. "Thanks for distracting him, Hermès. You'll get even more of a reward."

"Thanks. It was nothing."

As the two were having their conversation, Ren was trying to break free but couldn't move. Hell, Ren couldn't even move any of his fingers. All he could move were his eyes.

The black angel said, "Don't even bother. Me and shorty over there have the same ability when we impale our enemy with our chains. Our grace will stop all of your brain transmission to your body as long as we keep pumping grace into you, which is not a problem. In other words—you'll be paralyzed."

Ren looked at Hermès with the most pitiful look on his face because he knew he couldn't do anything. He couldn't move, shoot fire, or even use his telekinesis. He was literally helpless.

Hermès noticed Ren was looking at him with "help me" eyes and said childishly, "Oh, sorry, man, but no can do. Remember what I said. If any side lays a finger on me, I will stop working for them. But don't worry, since you didn't know, I'll still work for hell but you will have to die and yes, before you ask, I do hold a grudge. When you slammed me into that wall, that hurt, so have fun dying and not being able to find the angel that did this to you."

The blonde-haired angel said, "Okay, are you done with your talking now? Get out of here. We don't want to give you any more souls."

Hermès said, "Fine. I'm leaving. Goodbye, Ren. It was nice to see you again."

Then, in the blink of an eye, Hermès was gone.

The blonde angel said, "So, now that's over—how about we get to the good part: killing you. And when we do this, the war will go a lot more smoothly on our side, and all three of us will be famous for killing the great Ren who started this war."

The blonde angel summoned her weapon. It was a plain, but long, rapier sword. She took two steps back and it looked like she was about to thrust her sword right through Ren's head and that was most likely that was what she was going to do.

Before she was about to kill Ren, Ren was panicking in his head: "No, no, this can't be it, it just can't, I haven't found and killed the angel that did this to me and to everyone I loved! But I can't do anything. I'm going to die. I'm actually going to die from these nobody angels."

The angel moved with great speed and was about to kill Ren. But suddenly she dropped her rapier and screamed in pain. It was a total shock for Ren and the other two angels. Because the reason why the blonde angel was screaming was because there was a knife deep in her right hand.

The Asian angel said, "What?! Where did the knife come from?!"

The black angel said, "How should I know?!"

The blonde angel pulled the knife out of her hand and tossed it to the side. Her hand immediately regenerated as she pulled the knife out, but her hand still hurt. She and the other two angels noticed that the knife had sin around it, which meant a demon had touched the knife. But they didn't sense any demons anywhere until—

"Sorry about that. I didn't think I threw the knife that hard, but since you guys are about to kill a friend of mine, I don't care." The voice sounded totally scary for the angels, but it sounded familiar to Ren even though he didn't know why.

All the angels were looking around and couldn't see where the voice was coming from until the short angel looked up and saw the person. The demon is on top of the library. For some reason, all three of them started to shake. Unfortunately, Ren couldn't see who it was, or even sense who it was for some reason, but he could tell it was a guy again from the voice. Ren also knew the three angels were pissing themselves in fear.

The man was wearing a striped red suit with a long leather trench coat with one combat knife in each hand, but he quickly put the knifes in his trench coat then he summoned a new weapon—two long Mongol swords. He spun them around, probably trying to look cool and fearsome. Then, in an instant, he wasn't on top of the library. Instead, he was on the ground behind Ren and, without any of the angels even noticing that he was now on the ground, he lifted his swords up and pointed them at the two angels that were paralyzing Ren.

He used his telekinesis to pull both angels toward him. His telekinesis was so strong that the two angels couldn't even struggle. A second later, the person stabbed both of them through the head. The bodies of the two angels fell to the ground, blood and brains splattering on the ground. The top half of their heads was missing. It was because the top half was still on the blades. When the two bodies burst into flames, the blonde angel was paralyzed in fear to see that her partners had just been killed.

He jumped toward her with both swords to his right side, about to cut her through. But she turned to her right side, holding her rapier firmly in her hands, hoping that she could block his attack. It worked. His blades stopped for a second, but they sliced through her rapier and he was still coming toward her. But she moved away from the slash at the last second. Before she could even think of her next move, he lifted both swords above his head and, in an instant, they disappeared and reformed into a big club. He slammed the club into the angel's skull, killing her. Blood and brains splattered, her eyeballs shot out, her hair went everywhere, and the force even made her bite her tongue off. She burst into flames.

Everything happened so fast that Ren couldn't even notice what the hell was happening. He didn't even notice that the chains that were stabbed in his arms had vanished and he had regenerated. The way he had seen it, the angels were about to kill him, and then a second later, all three of them were dead. Ren was lost for words; he just watched as the man was standing in front of him holding a club, watching as the angel burned into ashes in front of both of them.

Then Ren finally mustered the courage to talk and said, "Who are you?"

The person didn't turn around; he just said, sarcastically and playfully, like a child, "Oh, come on, Ren. I know you haven't seen me in a human body before, but how can you forget this power and my good looks?"

The man turned around, finally showing his face. He had a short black goatee, his hair slid all the way back (probably from his hair gel, which made his black hair shine), and he had crimson red eyes. Ren still did not know who the person was until he looked down at his chest to see his number. What Ren saw was shocking—so shocking that he rubbed his eyes and slapped himself. Because the number the demon had was the number ten.

"Azazel?"

"Yes, it's me."

Ren could not believe that this person was Azazel. Even though he could see the number ten on his chest, Azazel couldn't be here. It was just not possible.

Ren said, "Sorry, but you can't be Azazel. He is still bound in hell until all sixty-six seals have been broken. You have to be a fake."

As Ren said that, he got into a battle position and summoned his weapon while still in human form. He didn't transform because he didn't want to destroy the cloak. He'd transform if things got bad for him.

The man that said he was Azazel gave a big sigh and put his hands on his hips. "Okay, okay. If I show you that I'm really Azazel, will you calm down?"

"Yeah. If you show me, that is."

The person gave a big smile and then closed his eyes and tightened both of his fists. Ren had no idea what he was doing. He could feel that the air was getting denser, but he could still breathe normally.

"Okay, I powered up to a degree that will convince you that I'm really Azazel."

Ren still didn't believe him. Like, yeah, Ren could tell that the air got intense because of that man's power-up, but it wasn't bad enough to convince Ren, so he did not undo his battle position.

The person sighed again, then pointed at Ren and said, "I know. How about you take off that cloak?"

"What? Why?"

"Just do it. I get the feeling that if you take that off, you will believe me."

Ren still didn't trust him, but he guessed it wouldn't hurt and it didn't seem that this person wanted to fight, so Ren did take off the cloak. The exact moment Ren took off the cloak and put it down, the cloak disappeared just like Astaroth said it would. And out of nowhere, Ren sensed an enormous power radiating from the person in front of him. It hit him like a train; it was so sudden that Ren almost fell on his butt, but he grabbed a trash can that was right next to him. Ren was taking long breaths. A few moments later, he finally calmed down and got his breathing under control.

Ren smiled and said, "Well, so it is you, Azazel. I know no one has this kind of power but you."

Azazel said, "I told you it was me, but I can't blame you. This is the first time you've seen me possessing someone."

"Yeah, it is," Ren said, still in a shocked tone of voice.

Ren was glad that this person really was Azazel, but there were a couple of things that were bothering him.

"Hey, Azazel, can I ask a couple of questions, if you don't mind?"

"I don't see why not. We've got the entire day, so go right ahead."

Ren took a deep breath and exhaled. "So how come I didn't sense that it was you? Like, I feel like I would have known that it was you the moment you showed up, and when you powered up, especially since I'm really good at sensing other people's presences? Like, that's how I managed to win most of my fights."

Azazel put his right hand on his chin and said, "Well, it was the cloak you were wearing."

"Huh?"

"Well, you see, Astaroth did tell you that that cloak was the first prototype to hide a demon's presence when he or she puts it on, and he did tell you that it had some kinks to be worked out. So I have a feeling that one of the setbacks it has is that it turns off the person's sensory nerve, or greatly weakens it to the point that the person who is wearing it cannot sense anything."

Ren thought, "That makes sense, not only because I couldn't sense Azazel's presence, but it also makes sense why I didn't know that the person hiding his face was Hermès, or when the angels showed up that I only sense a little bit of grace, and when the angels left but didn't actually leave; they were just hiding to try to get the jump on me. That level of sneak attack wouldn't have worked on me. So it makes sense."

As Ren was thinking that, Azazel walked to where he killed the leader of the three angels and crouched down to pick up something. Ren looked at Azazel and saw that he had picked up a folded sheet of paper. He realized that was the paper that Hermès gave the angels.

"So what's on that piece of paper that was so important?"

"This paper has most of the information on the seals we are targeting and what demons are assigned to try to break them. It also says what that demon's powers are and what weapon it has. So if heaven got this, then they can get the perfect angel to defeat that demon. It's a good thing that today is the day that I'm here."

"That also reminds me—how are you here, anyway? It is said that the demons with a rank of 200 and up are still stuck in hell until the sixty-six seals are broken, so what the fuck?"

"See, that's the thing. I don't know either. What you said is true, but here's the thing: whenever a demon automatically gets the number of 200 and up, they can feel the spell holding them back, like a chain that keeps a dog in the backyard. But in this case, the strong and powerful demons are stuck in hell. But something unimaginable happened a couple of weeks ago when I woke up from a nap, I could feel that the spell that was cast on me had gotten extraordinarily weakened, like it hadn't completely disappeared, but I could possess a person for one full day. When the day is up, I get sent back to hell and I have to stay in hell for five world of the living days, to be exact. And when those five days are over, I can come back for one full day again. Then rinse and repeat."

"I see. So did Lucifer or Satan or any other powerful demon find a way to break or lessen the spell?"

Azazel rubbed his neck. "No, it wasn't anyone from hell, I know. I asked, but no one, not even Lucifer or Satan, has the power or knowledge to undo the spell. Not even the angels know how, not even the archangels. As you saw, the three angels had strong reactions when they saw me. You know the only way is to break the sixty-six seals."

Ren with the most confused face in the world said, "But wait—if it wasn't them or anyone in hell, then who? I know that no human or a random monster has the power to undo a spell from God himself, and you just said that not even the archangels have that power either, so who?"

"I don't know, Ren, I just don't know. It's just going to be one big mystery.

I know heaven is really going to try to figure it out, and hell will too. Only because they'll try to get more demon kings or generals to come out and break more seals."

Ren sat down on the trash can he had been leaning on with his arms crossed, trying to think of what was happening and trying to come up with an answer. Ren thought really hard, but he just couldn't think of an answer. Like, if demon generals, kings, Lucifer, Satan, or even any of the angels, including the archangels, couldn't undo the spell, besides the seals, then who?

Ren looked at Azazel and said, "You're really sure you don't know?"

Azazel shook his head. "I don't know, but all I do know is that we have an unexpected and unbelievably powerful ally that wants us to win."

Ren, with an uneasy feeling, said, "I guess, but it just doesn't feel right."

"I know, but we are just going to have to deal with it, okay?"

"Yeah. But still..." Ren looked to the side with an uneasy look.

Azazel walked toward Ren, put his hand on his shoulder, and said, "But, hey, it doesn't matter, because with me here, that means we automatically get a seal broken, and plus something else you might like."

"Huh. And what will that be, good sir?"

"Well, whenever I break a seal and when I have some time left, I go to a library or bookstore and get some—what do you call them—mangas?"

Ren was shocked but really happy. He stood up quickly and said, "Mangas. You mean the great Azazel, the blacksmith from hell, is reading mangas?"

Azazel was feeling uncomfortable by how excited and close Ren got, so he took a couple steps back and said, "Yeah. Well, ever since I met you, you're literally the biggest nerd I have ever seen. Like, literally, you ask our gods to leave a country alone just because that country is the home and creator of all things nerdy. So I just got curious and got my hands on some mangas and started to read them."

Ren, still with a happy face, backed up a bit because he knew he was making Azazel uncomfortable, and said, "So which ones and how many series are you reading?!"

"Well, just one series for right now. I want to finish it first before I move onto another series. I think, if I remember it correctly, it's called Naruto."

"Ah, good choice. That series is good for beginners such as yourself. So what do you think of it and how far in are you?"

"Well, I'm certainly enjoying it very much and I'm at...damn it, where am I at!? I'm halfway through volume twenty-two."

"Oh, I know what arc you are on. That is a fan favorite! And I know what fight is in that volume. I love that fight."

"Yeah, that's it, and like I said, I am really enjoying it so now I understand why you like this type of stuff. Anyway, I've got to go. I have to go break another seal before it hits one in the morning. So see ya later."

Both Azazel and Ren waved their hands goodbye, and then Azazel left, leaving Ren alone behind the library.

Ren smiled and walked away from the library with his hands in his pockets, and was talking to himself. "Well, so Azazel is the demon that has the second-highest number of seals broken. Right behind me, of course. But even though I'm happy that he is one of the demons that is helping to break the seals, it bugs me that we have no idea who freed him. And I didn't bring up the whole thing with me and Hermès because I've got a feeling he knows and he would just tell me to suck it up, so I will just have to avoid him now. It's funny—the more that this war is going on, the more mysteries just show up."

Ren stopped and when he lifted his head up, he noticed that he was surrounded by people wearing ragged clothing—most likely bandits.

The bandit said, "Hey, kid, where did you come from didn't you now this is our Trif."

"But even if I can't figure out all these mysteries, I will find that angel that did this to me." Then he smiled and transformed.

"W-w-what the fuck is that? Oh shit, it's a demon. Ru—"

Ren jumped and slaughtered every one of them.

HOW THINGS TURN OUT

In front of a church in a town called Watertown, South Dakota, someone was walking toward the church. That someone was Ren and he was in his human form. He is walking toward the church, noticing how badly damaged it was. There were holes and cracks everywhere, and it had multiple bloodstains with bodies near it. As he was looking at all the bodies, he just shrugged them away.

Dead bodies didn't bother him at all anymore. Dead bodies were pretty much everywhere, even when he saw one of the bodies was a little girl. Ren just walked around the dead bodies. Even though they were a common thing to Ren now, he will still never step on them. After he walked around every body and was in front of the church he put his hand on the door and opened it like it was nothing.

As the door opened, Ren thought about being in Astaroth's office and Astaroth telling Ren his mission to the church.

"Ren, I want you to go to this church in South Dakota in the town of Watertown. That's your next seal."

Astaroth put two pictures on the table. One was the town itself and the other was the church. Ren leaned over to look at the photos so that he could get a good summary of the place that he had to go and what it looked like.

Ren said, "Sure, but if I may ask, why this specific church? Because when you called me over and told me to go to this Watertown church, you had an uneasy tone in your voice."

"I see. So you noticed. I don't know if that's creepy or not?"

Ren raised an eyebrow and said, "Really, that's creepy, dude. We are demons. We are the champions of creepy."

"Don't call me 'dude' again. The reason why I feel uneasy is because we've lost two demons by this church, but they were not killed. They were captured and we have no idea who captured them."

Ren said angrily, "Really? No one knows who is capturing them? Where is Hermès?" Ren still had a grudge against Hermès.

"He is currently doing another job right now as we speak, so we don't know who is capturing these demons. All we know is that it is certainly not an angel because they don't take demons as hostages. So that should give you an adventure, because whoever they are, they can't kill you."

"Yes, but even if they can't kill me, I should still be careful."

Astaroth smiled and said, "Yes, exactly."

Ren opened the door in his demon form. He walked inside and saw that the inside of the church was in worse shape than it was outside. All the chairs were badly damaged. The stone floors were so cracked that Ren was stepping on pebbles and sharp rocks.

Ren looked left and right but didn't see anybody.

When Ren stopped looking for his enemies, he noticed that the statue had already been broken and the bone was gone.

Ren, in a sudden confused, but quiet tone, said, "What? The bone is gone? I thought the bone couldn't leave the church."

"It can't. Trust me, we tried."

Ren looked up and saw people hanging upside down, looking down at him. Then all of them fell down, surrounding him.

Ren looked at them and started to count—"One, two, three..."—and then he started to mumble to himself that the people surrounding him couldn't tell what he was saying.

Ren said, "Ah, so there are ten of you surrounding me. All of you look like a biker gang, and there is still one more up on the ceiling. Come on down! I can sense you guys now, so you can't hide from me!"

The last one finally fell down. As he landed, the floor that he landed on cracked underneath him. He stood. He was kind of short, maybe around five feet tall, he had a long white trench coat with small cuts all over it, and he also had a complete white suit, complete with a white tie, and with white shoes. His eyes were brown, he had very short curly hair, and his skin was black.

Ren said, "From how you are dressed, I can assume you are the boss, right?"

The person gave no answer. He just kept staring at Ren, but he did pull out a cigarette and lit it.

The person gave a big exhale of smoke and said, "From how you transformed and that number on your chest, you must be Ren, I assume?"

"Yes, I am, and from what I'm sensing, you and your goons here are not human or angel, so you must be a type of monster. Which is surprising, since you guys try to avoid me."

"Yes, we are not human or angel. We are something even better—we are vampires."

Ren thought, "Vampires. Huh. Interesting. I never thought I would ever fight one."

The boss vampire said, "And yes, it is true that most monsters do try to avoid you, since you can take on an entire military of humans and multiple angels at once, which is very impressive. But however—" He took another breath from his cigarette and exhaled. "—we are not some random vampires."

"Yeah, I can see that. Most monsters, I've heard, are very dirty—as dirty as humans. But you guys don't look dirty. In fact, you all seem kind of clean for the most part."

The boss vampire said, "Yes, that's because we are mercenaries that the government hires to take out certain people."

"Well, well, mercenary vampires. That's new. So how long has this been a thing?"

"It's been a thing for many years. If I remember correctly, I'd say it's been a thing for about two hundred years."

"Two hundred years, huh?"

As Ren and the boss vampire kept on talking, Ren was noticing that the other vampires were getting impatient. They wanted to fight Ren really badly.

Ren said, "I can see your team is running out of patience, so before we fight, I'd like to ask two more questions before we start killing each other."

"And what are these two questions?"

Ren said, "First, what is your name?"

The boss vampire said, "I don't have to tell you my real name, but I'll tell you my nickname. It is Alucard."

Ren, disappointed, said, "Wow, Alucard. What an original name for a vampire. So creative."

Alucard got a little annoyed by Ren's comment. "Yeah, yeah, I know it's not original, but shut up. I like it, okay?"

"Okay, then. My second question is: what do you get out of it? I doubt it's for money." Ren mumbled to himself, "But I can guess what it is."

Alucard said, "Well, yes and no. You see, when we finish a mission, we all do get money—like, lots of money—but we get two other things and they are: one, protection from people that hunt us, and two, they give us humans to feed on. Yes, it is just homeless people, and before you ask, no, the diseases that they have don't affect us. In fact, it gives them more flavor sometimes. But now, because of this war, they will give us any human. Poor, middle-class, and even some rich classes...anyone that isn't from the government itself."

Ren sent a disgusted look at Alucard and mumbled to himself, "Gosh, I hate the government. I bet they said it's all for the sake of humanity or some shit."

Alucard said, "Now, since you have no more questions—everyone, battle position and attack!"

As Alucard said that, every vampire surrounding Ren pulled out a military combat knife and attacked him.

Ren didn't look scared because he knew they couldn't kill him, and he thought that even though they were vampires, they couldn't cut him, because Ren once grabbed a tank shell with his bare hands with no damage to his hands—what could a knife do?

One of them jumped in front of Ren with a knife in one hand. Most likely he was aiming for Ren's head, but Ren lifted his right hand to block the oncoming attack.

Ren said, "Please, do you really think—"

Before Ren could even finish his sentence, he felt a sharp pain in his palm.

The knife actually stabbed through Ren's hand, but not only that, it also burned Ren's hand as well. He screamed in pain, and with his free hand, stabbed right through the vampire's stomach. Ren lifted his foot up and kicked the vampire away. The vampire fell to the ground with his organs coming out of the new hole.

Ren looked at his stabbed hand and thought, "God damn, this really hurts a lot. This ain't no normal knife."

Ren reached to grab the knife and was about to pull it out, but when he grabbed it, his hand was repelled by the handle.

Before Ren could even think of what just happened, the other vampires attacked him. But in the background, the vampire that had a hole in its stomach was acting weird. The organs were moving back inside the vampire's body and the hole was closing. It was closing slowly, but it was closing. When the hole was gone, the vampire gave a big gasp for air like it had just come to life. He jumped back on his two feet, grabbed another knife that was in his jacket, and charged again.

When the vampire charged back at him, Ren was dodging every knife attack that came his way. From the left, from the right, from behind, and in front—Ren was dodging everyone, all while the knife was still in his hand.

Ren thought, "These guys are good. They are better than any human I've fought, but they are not as good as angels."

As Ren was thinking to himself, one vampire decided to run the other direction and climb the wall to get on the ceiling. That vampire thought that Ren didn't know he was up there because the other vampires were distracting him. The vampire fell from the ceiling, trying to hit Ren, but Ren knew he was up there. Ren forcefully swung the stabbed arm, which sent all of the vampires that were surrounding him flying to the walls, and because of the force, the knife finally came out of Ren's hand. Ren quickly looked up and grabbed the vampire that was falling from the ceiling by the neck and slammed him on the floor.

The vampire's eyes widened in shock and pain. They were so wide, they looked like they were about to pop out. He was coughing up a lot of blood. Ren raised his left hand and finally summoned his weapon. He was about to slam it into the vampire's heart (even though Ren was thinking, "Why didn't I summon this earlier to block the knife that stabbed my hand?") until—

BANG BANG!!!!

Two gunshots suddenly rang out through the church, and the two bullets that were fired went through both of Ren's shoulders. Ren fell backwards from the impact of the bullets. The bullets also made Ren let go of the vampire he was holding, and so the vampire that was underneath Ren rolled back to get some distance from Ren. Ren got up and looked up at Alucard. He was holding two silver revolvers—one for each hand.

Ren smiled and said, "Well, now I can see how you guys can defeat demons now."

Alucard looked around to see how his comrades were doing. They were all trying to get up after Ren slammed all of them to the wall and were regenerating. But even though they were regenerating, being slammed into the walls really hurt them.

So Alucard knew he had to buy some time for them to get ready to fight again.

Alucard said, "Really, how do we?!"

"It's those knives and bullets you guys have. So tell me those knives and bullets aren't just made of steel, are they?"

"Once again, yes and no. Yes, they are made of steel, but they are also made from iron, gold, and silver. We even put some salt in it for extra support, just in case."

"Steel, iron, gold, silver, and salt. You pretty much made a weapon that can kill almost any monster."

Alucard did not respond to Ren's comment. All he did was give a small smile.

Ren looked around and noticed that every vampire had gotten back up and were ready for round two. Ren slapped his own forehead because he should have known that Alucard was buying time and he just let it happen.

Alucard said, "Okay, enough playing around. It's time for us to get this over with!"

Every vampire charged at Ren again. Ren lifted both of his arms and fire appeared in both hands. He was about to shoot his hellfire, but then Ren got shot by two more bullets and they hit his shoulder again. He flinched for a second, and then he saw all the vampires were only inches away from him. But then they all turned to the right and were running in a circle, cutting Ren up over and over again. He was grunting from the pain.

Ren couldn't take it anymore, so he jumped up to get out of the circle of knives. But the other vampires jumped too, less than a second after he did. But Ren knew they would do that so he pulled both of his arms and legs closer to his body. And as the vampires came closer to him, he stretched out all four limbs to try to stab at least four vampires with each limb. But as Ren stretched out, Alucard shot all four of Ren's limbs with perfect accuracy, knocking them away from hitting any vampire. As if that wasn't enough, every vampire stabbed Ren with their knives.

Ren fell to the ground with ten knives sticking out all over his body. The other vampires landed around him, looking at him and pulling more knives out of their leather jackets.

Alucard was looking at Ren's body from where he always was, but he couldn't see his entire body because his companions were in his line of vision.

One of the vampires walked toward Ren and said, "Did we get him?"

Ren smiled and said sarcastically, "I don't know. Let's see."

Then, when every vampire was shocked to see Ren was still conscious, Ren swung his right arm and sent a wave of hellfire at every vampire.

Every single one was burning in agony and screaming, "HELP ME, IT BURNS, AAAAAAAA, DAMN YOU!" They all fell to the ground as charcoal, and then ashes.

Ren slowly got up, and with all of his strength, used his telekinesis to pull every single knife out of his body. Ren walked slowly toward Alucard—with a serious look, but he was also in a lot of pain—as the knives fell to the floor, making a clanging sound.

Alucard said, "How—How—How are you still able to move with all those knives with iron and salt in you?!"

"Well, let's see. Iron is one of our weaknesses, but it just burns us, and buddy, I've been burned with much, much worse things than that when I was being tortured in hell. All of those other demons that complain about being burned by iron—they were pussies. As for the salt—well, salt is just an invisible wall that demons can't go through. Yes, it does really weaken us and repel our physical bodies. And if there's a lot of salt that surrounds us, it can nullify our powers, but just a handful doesn't turn off any of our powers. Unless..."

Alucard said, "Unless?"

"Unless one of those knives hits my brain or spine, which the salt and iron knife would have stopped my body from functioning, which, if you didn't notice, none of them hit those spots and I assume that's how you captured the other demons before me. From your expression, you guys didn't know that."

Alucard said, "No, we just assumed they passed out from the pain."

"Well, you're welcome."

"Duly noted."

When the two were done with their conversation, Ren was in front of Alucard.

Alucard smiled and dropped both of his revolvers to the ground. He opened his arms and said, "Okay, just do it. You killed all of my companions. I want to join them too."

Ren raised an eyebrow and took a few steps back. He was suspicious of Alucard, so he took even more steps back and raised his arm and pointed at him Alucard.

"Okay, you'll be with your companions."

At the tip of Ren's finger, a small ball of hellfire appeared. Ren was aiming at Alucard's head and was about to shoot.

BANG BANG!

Two gunshots were fired again, but this time it hit Ren's chest. Ren lowered his arm and placed his hand where the new bullet holes were. Ren looked down and saw that the two guns that Alucard dropped were pointing up at Ren, but nobody was handling them.

Alucard said, "Please. Did you think that demons and angels were the only ones that had telekinesis?"

In an instant, Alucard put both hands inside his trench coat, and without Ren noticing, ran with tremendous speed. Before Ren could react, Alucard was right in front of Ren. His arms came out of his jacket and uppercut Ren right in the jaw, making a disgusting snapping sound as Ren's jaw broke and his teeth went everywhere. Alucard did not hold back at all.

Ren stumbled backwards, but regained his balance with his jaw already regenerated. He saw Alucard's new weapons. In both hands, he had two brass knuckles with spikes and a blade at the bottom. Both revolvers were floating behind him.

Ren said, "I assume those new weapons you got are made of the same materials as your comrades' knives."

"Yes."

Alucard ran toward Ren, holding both weapons close to his chest while both revolvers were floating behind him. Ren swung both arms to clash with Alucard's weapons. When their weapons collided, sparks went everywhere and Ren used his telekinesis to pull Alucard close and grab his arms. He lifted his right leg to try to cut Alucard in the chest. But one of the revolvers fired at Ren's leg, hitting the blade, and repelling his kick. The other revolver shot Ren in the left hand, loosening his grip on Alucard. Alucard punched Ren right on the chest, making Ren fully let him go.

Ren rubbed his chest and said, "You are good, but those revolvers are almost out of bullets." Ren sounded confident until...

The revolvers' mags opened up.

Ren had no idea what was happening. But when he saw the revolvers drop the used bullets, his eyes just followed the bullets as they fell to the ground, and what he saw when his eyes looked straight was Alucard opening his jacket.

The inside of his jacket was covered in bullets. Each and every bullet was inside its own small pocket. Then the bullets came out of Alucard's jacket and flew in the revolver to fully reload it.

Ren thought, "So when his revolvers run out of bullets, he distracts me while the bullets come out of his jacket and reloads his guns using his own telekinesis. That's very smart."

Alucard ran toward Ren again with a barrage of punches, slashes, and shots. Not slowing down, he didn't want Ren to think of a plan. All Alucard wanted was Ren to only think about dodging or blocking.

It was working. Ren could only block or dodge. It was so bad that he couldn't counterattack. If Ren even tried to attack, Alucard blocked, dodged, or used his revolvers to shoot Ren's attacks away. Ren knew he had to get some distance between them or he might actually lose and be captured. Ren quickly raised his arms and tried to thrust them both forward, but Alucard jumped back to only dodge Ren's attack.

When Alucard landed, he rushed back at Ren. Ren, with his arms still forward in front of him, was about to shoot hellfire. But Alucard saw that attack coming, so he had his revolvers shoot at Ren's back hand. The force of the bullets was strong enough to force Ren's arm straight down, making Ren lose balance.

Alucard saw the opening he needed to stab Ren in the head. When he was right in front of the still-tumbling Ren, he raised up his knife and was about to stab Ren right in the skull. But he didn't see Ren smiling and didn't see that Ren had moved one of his fingers to point at Alucard and shoot hellfire at him. Alucard saw the fire coming from Ren's finger but it was at the last second. He moved to the left just a little bit and the fire missed his head, but it hit his right shoulder.

The string of fire went through Alucard's shoulder, leaving a pinball-sized hole. Alucard, in pain and in a state of panic, jumped far back from Ren, giving them both some room. Alucard was gasping for air, showing Ren that he was starting to get exhausted while Ren was not. Demons had really high stamina if their regeneration was not weakened. Alucard looked at his right shoulder to look at the wound.

Alucard thought, "Humph. For a small wound, it really hurts like hell. I guess that's hellfire for you."

The wound had started to heal. Alucard's look that showed exhaustion and pain slowly turned into a smile. It seemed that Alucard was enjoying the fight while Ren was trying to figure a way to win. Suddenly Ren's eyes widened and he smiled. Alucard looked at Ren with a serious look on his face.

Alucard thought, "What is he smiling about this time? I guess he has a plan. That's not good. I have to end this fight now. If I could just hit Ren's head or spine, then I could win, but he knows that's the two places I will go for. But I've got no other choices. I have to end this fight even though I am enjoying it a little bit too much."

Ren jumped toward Alucard, slamming his blades on Alucard's blades. The impact cracked the floor Alucard was standing on. Ren lifted up both of his legs while still in the air (he must be flying with his wing), then both of the revolvers aimed and shot again but Ren turned his head to see where the revolvers were before they shot.

When the bullets were moving toward Ren, he moved his left pointing finger then the bullets stopped literally centimeters before they hit Ren's skin. Ren then twirled his finger to used his telekinesis to turn the bullets around and shot them back toward the revolvers. Alucard noticed Ren's plan and was about to use his telekinesis to move his guns away, but Ren started to put more pressure on Alucard, making him focus on Ren rather than the bullets.

And it worked. The bullets, full force, went back into the guns, breaking them and making them useless to Alucard now. Alucard couldn't believe what had just happened, but he knew what happened.

Alucard thought, "Ren knew that I was running out of options and wanted to finish the fight. So he ran toward me and deliberately slammed his blades on mine and used his wings to stay in place, making me think he was just doing that to hold me still. Knowing that I would use his stillness as an opportunity, I shot my guns, which was what he was waiting for—to break them."

Alucard smiled and said, "Well played."

Ren lifted his legs up to attack. Alucard closed his eyes, knowing he was done for. Knowing there was no point in fighting now. Ren had won.

Without the guns, Alucard would only delay the inevitable. There was a clinking sound and Alucard opened his eyes to see that his brass knuckles were shattered into pieces by Ren's kick. Ren took a couple steps back to look at Alucard. Who fell on his knees.

Alucard said, "Why didn't you kill me? I was right open."

"Don't get the wrong idea, I do want to kill you, but I just thought of something better."

Alucard looked up with a confused look.

Ren said, "Tell me, do the mercenary vampires interfere with the demons that are trying to break a seal a lot?"

"Yes, we've interfered with your kind a lot because it's our job to stop you."

"Have you guys lost a lot of your kind?"

Alucard looked down and said, "Yes, we've lost so much."

Ren smiled and said, "Well, how about this? I can tell that you are the leader of the mercenary vampires—am I right?"

"Yes, I am the leader."

"So you and your companions don't ever mess with me or any demons again, and in return I'll ask Lucifer and Satan for the same thing. How about it? You won't lose any more of your kind to demons and we won't have to deal with vampires when we try to break a seal."

Alucard was shocked by what he was hearing, but he smiled and was started to laugh. "So that's why you want me alive. Okay, fine, that sounds good to me too, but what about the human food the government gives us?"

Ren said, "Sorry, can't help you, there but you guys will somehow manage, especially since you're their leader."

Alucard gave one more smile, then he got up, put both hands in his pockets, pulled out a bone that was inside his pocket, and dropped it beside Ren.

It was the kneecap.

Alucard walked past Ren while pulling out another cigarette and lighting it up.

Ren said, "Before you leave, can you tell me what your real name is?"

"It's Louis."

Louis walked out of the church doors without looking back.

Ren said, "Louis, huh. Well, Louis, let's hope we won't have to fight again."

Ren bent down, grabbed the bone, and started the ritual. Yet another seal had been broken.

MANY FIGHTS TO COME. PART II

A week had gone by since the agreement with the vampires and the demons. So far, both sides were holding up their end of the bargain. No mercenary vampires were interfering with the demons who were trying to break the seals and no demons were killing any of those vampires. Thanks to this deal, breaking the seals had gotten just a little bit easier... but not by that much.

Right next to a badly damaged bank, a fire-covered door appeared and was slowly opened. When the door fully opened, Ren walked out wearing his usual clothes in his human form. He lifted his right hand up to shield his eyes from the sunlight that was hitting him in the face. It was the middle of the day and the sun was up, but even though the sun was up, it was mostly covered by extremely black clouds from all the smoke from all the battles. Ren turned his head around, looking at his environment to see what was around him.

"So this is the little town of Rising Sun in Maryland. I have to say, everything seems to be normal—buildings destroyed or badly damaged, no signs of any life. The church is in front of me, and it's only a little bit damaged. Yep. Everything seems to be normal... but this is new."

Ren looked up to the light post. The light post that was in front of Ren had a hanging body, stripped naked, missing some flesh (probably from the crows), and on his chest was carved the word "HERETIC." Ren looked and saw every light post had hanging men and women of various ages. All had the word heretic carved on their chest. Ren looked down in disgust.

He looked back to the bodies, and said, "Even though I'm a demon now and

I have a mission to do, I can't leave them hanging like this. This is just wrong."

Ren took his time cutting everybody down and gently placing them in front of the church's door with their arms crossed and eyes closed (if they even still had eyes). Ren lifted his right hand and summoned hellfire and burned the bodies. He looked down at the burning bodies with a gaze full of sadness and pity. He just stood there, watching them burn, not looking away, moving an inch, or saying a word. He just stood there like a statue for a couple of minutes.

Ren finally spoke. "I'm sorry that this happened to all of you, but I'm also not sorry because this is the only way for me to find the angel that did this to me and my family and friends. So you all are just casualties for my revenge and I'm deeply sorry."

Ren was done talking to the burning bodies, but waited for a little bit longer until the bodies were turned into dust. When he couldn't see the shape of the bodies anymore, he swatted his hand to extinguish the fire. All the bodies were gone. They were all burned so badly that not even their ashes could be seen. Ren looked at the church, took a deep breath, exhaled, and walked inside.

Once inside, he stopped after he had taken a couple of steps. The door closed behind him and Ren put his left hand on his hip. He raised his right hand, three fingers pointing up.

"In three, two, one—angels."

As he said that, a bright white light appeared from the ceiling.

"I'm so used to this I can predict—"

But something was off. The two angels that came down were very different. They looked like human mannequins of both genders. They both had no hair, they were kind of muscular, their eyes were pure light blue, and they both had angel wings.

Ren was in shock at what he was seeing. They didn't look like angels, but from what he was sensing, they certainly were angels, and one was way taller than the other one. Ren could estimate that the tall one was around six feet tall and the other one was close to five feet tall. Then it clicked in his head: the reason they didn't look like the other past angels that Ren fought was because they were not possessing anyone. Ren was so used to seeing angels possessing people that he forgot those were not their real bodies.

Ren said, "So, if you two are not possessing anyone, then you guys are just like me. You two can shapeshift. Shapeshifting angels."

Neither of them said a word, but one of them lifted its left arm and summoned a scroll—the same type of scroll that would send them to a different dimension to fight. Ren did not even try to stop it; it was the only thing that Ren let the angels do. But in the meantime, he transformed into his demon form and was now ready to battle. The scroll opened and a large light flashed, covering the entire town. The scroll disappeared. They were already in a different dimension and the fight could begin.

The tall angel said, "Yes." Its voice sounded like a combination of a man and a woman's voice.

Ren didn't know what the angel meant. "Huh? Yes? Yes what?"

 "Yes ,we are shapeshifters. Just like you." The short angel also had the same voice as the tall one.

Ren said, "Oohh, I see. So, wait—if you guys are just like me, then does that mean your power isn't being restricted as much as the other angels?"

The short angel said, "No, it is true that these are our true bodies, but our power is still being restricted by 50%."

Ren said sarcastically, "So then what will you guys do to defeat me? Please do tell."

The tall angel said, "You'll see. When we transform, you won't be able to hurt us even if you want to."

Ren slowly lifted his hand up to touch his forehead. He shook his head back and forth and exhaled. "Okay. I think I know what you guys are going to shapeshift into."

The short angel said, "Really. What are we going to shapeshift into?"

"Come on, it's a cliché thing. You guys are going to turn into one of my family or friends that I deeply love or care about. And because you look, sound, and act just like them, I won't be able to bring myself to hurt you. But sorry, they won't work on me. I know that they are dead and you're not them, so sorry."

Both angels started to laugh loudly and the tall angel said, "No, sorry. Good guess, but wrong."

Ren, confused, said, "Huh, what? If you guys are not going to turn into what I just said, then what?"

The tall angel said, "Oh, you'll see. RIGHT now!"

Both angels flapped their wings and the feathers that were on their wings came off and started to surround them both.

Ren thought, "I know I should really stop this, but I am so curious as to what they will turn into. If it's not a family member or a friend, then what is it? I'm actually excited."

One of the angels started to talk from the giant cloud of feathers: "We knew that transforming into one of your family or friends won't work on you because you are a smart demon, but there is one thing you can't ever betray!"

"What are you talking about? What can't I betray?!"

Then Ren heard a different voice—a voice that sounded very familiar... "You can't betray the anime that you watch and love."

Ren's eyes opened so wide that they looked like they could've popped out of his head. "No, I can't! You wouldn't?!"

Another different voice came from the giant cloud of feathers. "Oh, yes, we did. We looked at your past and did our research on every anime and manga you have ever watched or read to the best that we could."

From inside the cloud of feathers, Ren could hear a chain shaking, and a cold breeze was hitting his face. Then the cloud of feathers stopped spinning and started to fall. It was at that moment Ren could see both of the angels and what they turned into.

The tall angel said, "As you can see, I have turned into Itsuki Kobayashi, replacement grim reaper."

The short angel said, "As for me, I turned into Ruca Kaneko, also from the same anime you really love."

Ren could not believe what he was seeing with his own two eyes.

Both of the angels said, "We turned into your number one favorite ship: Itsuca!"

Ren was sweating bullets at what he was seeing.

Ren thought, "I can't believe this! The tall angel turned into Itsuki after the first time skip. With his brown smooth hair that comes to his shoulders, red eyes that goes along with his handsome face, white skin, wearing his silver Shinigami Komoto, with the black belt, and his old fashion waraji sandals. The same could be said about the short angel that turned into Ruca. She has short white hair, white eyes that also goes along with her beautiful face, very pale skin, the same silver Shinigami Komoto, with the black belt, and the same waraji sandals.

"They look just like them, they sound just like the English dubbed voice actors, I bet they have the same powers as them, and they even have the same weapons: Itsuki's donki Jigoku no kiba (hells fang). Which was a crimson red long tachi katana, everything about this sword was a dark red. The blade , the handle, the X shaped guard, to its spiky short chain that was dangling from the end of the handle. While Ruca's chikoi Shiroi Yuki No Megami (white snow goddess). Was also a Long Tachi katana but it was an a very light blue and just like with Itsuki's sword everything about Ruca's sword was blue the blade, handle, and to the star shaped guard."

Angel Itsuki said, "Now then, you already know who these characters are and the situation you are in. So how about we get things—"

Before the angel could finish Ren interrupted him. "Wait, wait! Before we fight to the death, could you two do something for me? Please, it's an emergency!"

Both angels looked at each other, then back at Ren.

Angel Itsuki said, "Um, okay. What would that be?"

"Please, please—you two have to kiss!"

Angel Ruca, with a confused, shocked, and annoyed voice, said, "Excuse me? What did you just ask us to do?!"

Ren, who still sounded in a state of panic, said, "I know it sounds a little weird."

Angel Itsuki said, "A little weird? Sorry, but it's very weird. You just asked us, your enemies, to kiss each other. How does that not sound weird?"

"Yes, I know, but please just listen to me!"

Angel Itsuki looked at Angel Ruca and said, "Um, should we listen to what he has to say? I know we should be fighting right now, but..."

Angel Ruca said, "I think we should listen a little bit because from the face that he is giving us, I think he is being dead serious. And I really want to know why he wants us to kiss." She blushed a little.

Angel Itsuki said, "Yeah, same. I want to know too. Okay demon, go right ahead."

"Okay, great. You know you guys look, sound, have the weapons, and most likely the same powers as Itsuki and Ruca, right?"

Angel Ruca said, "Yeah, so what about it?"

"Well, you guys are literally the actual characters in real life, and I don't know if you guys know this, but at the end of the Shinigami series, Itsuki and Ruca didn't get together and because of it, the franchise lost a lot of fans and all the Itsuca fans, including myself. I was very sad. Like, come on, they could have been beautiful together. Like, they could've been happy."

In the background as Ren was talking, Angel Itsuki said, "Uh, Ren, Ren, REN!"

"Huh? Oh, sorry again. I got a little bit ahead of myself. Anyway, to make it short and simple, if you would kiss that would please so many people. Like, so many people."

Angel Itsuki, with a disturbed look on his face, said, "I don't know. First, how would these people even know about our kiss? There is literally no one around and we are in a different dimension!"

Ren said with a smile, "Oh, trust me. They will know."

Angel Itsuki looked at Ruca with a confused look and said, "Okay, then if we do kiss—I'm not saying we are going to!—what do we get out of it?"

Almost immediately, Ren said, "I'll let you two get one free hit on me while I'm standing still!"

Angel Ruca said, "What, are you serious? You do realize that those free hits might be the two killing blows?"

"Yes, I'm well aware, but it'll be so worth it. So please do it, please!"

Angel Itsuki said, "Um, what do you think? Because I'm at a total loss for words right now."

Angel Ruca said, "I know what you mean. We've never gotten a request like this before, but I think we should. No other angel would find out, since we are in this dimension. And look at his face. If we just do what he asks, we can really hurt the demons' progress of breaking the seals. And it is just one kiss."

Angel Itsuki crossed his arms and started to tap his foot.

His tapping slowly got faster and faster until he gave an annoyed grunt and said, "Okay, okay, I guess we will do it, but you'd better hold up your end of the bargain!"

Ren said, "Yes, yes, I will. Now go on and make it passionate."

Both angels looked at each other and gave a long sigh. They both turned completely to face each other. As the environment went silent, Itsuki was looking down at Ruca, trying to look straight into her eyes. But Ruca looked away in embarrassment, knowing what Itsuki was going to do. Then Itsuki walked closer to Ruca while she was still looking away, all embarrassed. When Itsuki was right in front of Ruca, he slammed his Jigoku No Kiba in the ground right next to him so he could have both of his hands. Itsuki took his left arm and wrapped it around Ruca's waist. The moment Kichiku did that Ruca looked straight at Itsuki and their eyes were looking at each other. Neither one could look away.

Itsuki lifted his right hand and put it on the back of Ruca's head. Then Itsuki, with a quiet and smooth tone, said Ruca's name and Ruca said Itsuki's name a second later. Ten Ruca closed her eyes and Itsuki's head came ever so close to Ruca's.

While this was happening, in the background, Ren was jumping up and down a lot and holding his hands tightly together, watching like a fanboy. Oh, who was he kidding? Ren was acting like a fangirl because he was making a high pitch "eeee" sound.

Itsuki's and Ruca's heads and lips were about to touch (they were an inch away), until...

Angel Itsuki, in an instant, grabbed his sword, said, "Tengoku No Katta (heaven cutter)!" and fired it. Angel Ruca lifted her right arm and said, "Superu 33

Kuroi hi (black fire)!"

Both attacks were fired at Ren, who was standing still. A huge explosion appeared, destroying all the buildings within a half-mile radius. Out of the huge mushroom cloud, Ren flew out. He was covered in scratches, but they all healed immediately.

Ren was moving his arms side to side as fast as he could while yelling, "Wait, wait! Stop! You two were so close! Please stop! You were like an inch away. Please do it over. DO IT OVER!"

The two angels jumped up and flew toward Ren.

Angel Itsuki started spinning to the left, while angel Ruca was spinning to the right. They both had their swords on them, so they were spinning like a saw blade, coming at Ren.

Ren lifted both arms and summoned his weapons to try to block the oncoming attacks. There was a CLINKING sound, which indicated that Ren did indeed block the two spinning slashing attacks. But he was spitting blood out of his mouth because he did block the swords, but he didn't block the two kicks that hit him in the stomach.

Ren went flying down, crashed into a house, and the house collapsed down on top of him. Then, without wasting a second, Angel Itsuki flew down with such great speed that he made a shock wave behind him that blew away the clouds.

Angel Itsuki said, "Stop playing dead! I know you are still in there! Tengoku No Katta!"

The angel shot another blast that blew up the house that was on top of Ren. Or so they thought, because it turned out Ren was not in the house anymore.

Angel Ruca said, "He's not there anymore! He's over there!" She lifted up her sword to point where Ren was.

Angel Itsuki said, "So, running away, huh?!"

Ren was flying away as fast as he could, right over the road, talking to himself "Damn it! I can't fight them. If I even hurt them, I can't call myself a Shinigami fan. Shit! What to do, what to do?!"

Ren looked over his right shoulder to see the two angels chasing after him. "Good. It appears I'm faster than they are so I can think of a way to—"

Then Angel Ruca suddenly disappeared. Ren's eyes widened, thinking, "Where did she go?" Then Ren sensed that she was right beside him. He lifted his left arm to block the slash attack. They clashed, and it caused a shock wave that flattened the trees around them.

Ren said, "Oh my god, you just used Supidosuteppu (speed step) on me! That is so cool."

As Ren finished, he suddenly felt a sharp pain on his back. He turned to see that Angel Itsuki had just slashed his back.

Ren said, "And now I just got cut from Jigoku No Kiba. This is the best day ever."

Angel Ruca was getting pissed off. She yelled, "Stop fanboying and fight us!"

She moved her sword slightly away from Ren's arm to stab him in the chest, and she did. Luckily, Ren used his telekinesis to move the sword to the right so that it missed his heart. He then used his telekinesis to push angel Ruca away. Unfortunately, it worked but she didn't get that far away.

Ren's blood splattered all over angel Ruca's sword, but the blood immediately disintegrated. Ren gave a small grunt and moved both of his arms—one pointing at angel Itsuki and the other at angel Ruca—and used his telekinesis again to push them away as far as he could. Both angels had the same thought and they both slammed their swords into the pavement to stay in place. But Ren flew up to get away from them.

Ren said, "They are right. I'm being too much of a fanboy to fight. Come on me—if you don't fight back, you'll die!"

Angel Itsuki jumped up to get to Ren. When they were only a couple of feet away, Ren raised both of his arms to block Angel Itsuki's attack. They were in the sky clashing with each other. Angel Itsuki was moving his arms as fast as he could, trying to slash and stab Ren, but Ren was blocking every attack that was coming at him.

Ren thought, "So they might look, sound, and have the same powers as them, but they are not as strong nor as fast. This is frustrating. I'm clearly stronger than them, but I just can't bring myself to hurt them. There has to be a way to win."

Angel Itsuki suddenly smiled, and with one spin, he slammed his sword on both of Ren's arms, which were covering his face. They were connected for a few seconds until Ren moved his arms to see where he had gone off to. Ren saw the angel flying away. He suddenly felt a cold chill and he knew why. He looked down and saw Angel Ruca directly beneath him.

Angel Rucio said, "Dance number one Shiroi Inseki (White Meteor)!" and a giant white circle appeared behind her.

Ren said, "Oh shit! Move, body, move!!" Ren moved as fast as he could. A huge ice pillar appeared in the sky.

Angel Itsuki landed right next to Angel Rucio and said, "Did you get him?"

Angel Rucio lifted up her left hand and pointed up right next to her pillar and said, "Well, yes, I hit him, but he is not in the ice. You can see him falling."

Then Angel Itsuki put his left hand over his eyes to try to see where Ren was falling and said, "Ooo, yeah, there he is. He is falling pretty fast. I wonder why?"

Ren said, "Damn, so that's Shiroi Inseki. It's so awesome that I just got hit by that. Man, it was so cold though, and to make matters worse for me it hit both of my wings and they both are gone. All that's left are two frozen stumps."

Ren lifted up his right fingers and shot hellfire at his two stumps to melt the ice. When the fire hit the ice it had already melted off and Ren's wings were regenerating back but it wasn't fast enough and he slammed on the ground with great force.

Ren said, "Ow, that kind of hurt."

He coughed up blood, but all the blood that was seeping out of him was disintegrating, and all of his broken bones were being healed. Ren looked forward and could see the two angels walking toward him with smiles on their faces.

Ren jumped up and said, "What are you two so happy about? We're back to square one."

Angel Itsuki said, "Really, I don't think we are, because this entire time you have been taking damage left and right while we haven't taken any damage at all."

"Yeah, I guess you're right, but it's only because you two have turned into my favorite ship. But I don't know, it could have been worse."

Angel Ruca said interestedly, "Really how so?"

"Well, the only thing that is worse for me to fight than my favorite ship is, in my own opinion, the top two sexiest girls in all of anime that I want to sleep with, but you guys have no idea who they are. Or you would have turned into them instead, so I'm in the clear."

Both angels started to laugh and Angel Itsuki said, "Sorry to disappoint you, but there is a way for us to find out."

Ren said, grinning, "And how is that?"

Both angels looked at each other and nodded. Then Angel Itsuki came at Ren with great speed, slamming his sword on Ren's claws. He just kept on attacking, trying to keep Ren's attention on him while Angel Ruca was behind him.

She slammed her sword into the ground, put both her hands together, and fell to her knees. It looked like she was praying. And she started to say, "סיהולא וה ילש סיביואה ומ עדימ לבקל יל רוזעל השקבב חוכ ונל ותנש לודגה." (It was Hebrew for "Oh great God that gave us power, please help me to get information from my enemies.") When she was done with her prayer, both of her hands were covered with very light blue-colored flames.

Angel Ruca leaped forward with great speed, and without grabbing her sword that was still in the ground, said, "Okay, I'm done. Move!"

When Angel Itsuki heard what his comrade said, he gave a smile like they just won. He turned his sword's sharp end so it was facing up and swung up with great force. Ren blocked it, of course, but that was a part of their plan.

The moment when Ren blocked Angel Itsuki's attack, the force was so great that it raised both of Ren's arms up above his head. Angel Itsuki did a backflip. All Ren could see was Angel Itsuki doing a backflip, but he realized what he was really doing. Angel Itsuki was moving out of the way so that Angel Ruca, who was beneath Angel Itsuki, could get closer.

When Ren realized this, it was too late. Angel Ruca slammed both her small hands on Ren's head. Then the blue flames that were covering her hand then covered Ren's entire head.

Ren screamed in pain, "AAAAAAAAA! GET OFF ME!"

It lasted for a while until Ren managed to get enough strength to swing his right arm. It made Angel Ruca let go and move away. Ren put his left hand on his face and the flames went out.

Ren, while gasping for air, said, "W-w-what did you just do to me? Those flames weren't even hot?"

Angel Ruca looked at Angel Itsuki and said with a smile, "I got it. Now, let's do it."

Angel Itsuki said with a smile, "Yes. Let's."

Both of them summoned their angel wings in a blink of an eye and were surrounded by their feathers again. So much that Ren could not see them anymore again.

Ren was looking at the cloud of feathers both angels were in, and then looked at the sword that Angel Ruca left. It suddenly started to turn into feathers. Then those feathers just went into the cloud of feathers to be a part of it. Ren didn't move a muscle. He just stood there, watching and letting the two angels transform.

Angel Itsuki's voice started to talk from within the cloud, but it was slowly changing. "I bet you are wondering what forms we are about to change into."

"Well, no. I know what you two are going to change into. Like, I literally gave you guys a hint on what to change into next."

Angel Itsuki got embarrassed because he forgot that Ren did give them a hint, but he continued to talk. "Well, shut up. We are trying to be intimidating here. But whatever. It's okay because we are done."

The feather that was twirling around them suddenly stopped and started to fall slowly. Ren went into a boxing stance with his dominant hand close to his chest and his other hand a little farther away. He took the same stance with his feet.

Ren could hear a voice from the falling feathers that started to speak. It sounded like a young woman's voice. "Well, why not introduce yourself?" And then an red staff, with white polka dots, and a pyromantic-shaped diamond on the top came out of the wall of falling feathers and swatted them all away.

Ren could clearly see them now and he couldn't believe what he was seeing.

The angel that was Ruca said, "Say hello to my new form. I was once Ruca from that Shinigami show, but now I'm Namina, from that pirate anime." And it was the Namina after the two-year time skip. She had dark skin, curly long red hair, tight camp jeans, red high-heeled boots, and a blue and black swirly bikini top.

The angel that was Itsuki said, "And don't forget the most beautiful woman in the world that can turn any man or woman to stone and is one of the four warlords of the oceans Hebi." And the angel had turned into Hebi with her very tight pink dress with flower patterns, silky smooth white hair that matched her shoulders, and silver snake earrings. Her beautiful face was perfect, and she wore white high heels, and yet she didn't have her snake with her.

Ren had a serious look on his face. He thought, "So they did turn into them, huh? And not only do they sound just like their English dub actors, but I assume they both have the same powers as them, so I'm pretty much facing the real Namina and Hebi."

Angel Namina said, with the biggest smirk on her face, "So now that we have turned into your top two favorite women in all of anime that you want to sleep with, I bet you won't even be able to even fight—no, defend—now."

Ren said, with a scared look, "So you think you guys won?"

Angel Habi said, "Yes, we do, my friend. When I placed my flaming hand on your head, I just read your mind and these two characters were the answers I got. So yeah, we won."

Ren then lowered both of his arms all the way down and was also looking down in a stance that looked like he was giving up.

Angel Namina raised her staff and said, "Don't worry, it will be quick."

But then Ren lifted his head up and gave them the scariest smile they had ever seen. They both widened their eyes in shock at the facial expression Ren was giving them. Then...

Ren disappeared and they could not see him anymore. And then they both suddenly felt an enormous pain in both of their gorgeous chests. They both saw blood flying in front of their eyes. They both looked down to see that Ren stabbed both of them in the back.

Angel Namina, while spitting out blood in pain, said, "B-b-but why? W-w-we just turned into..."

Ren said, "Yeah, I'm just going to stop you right there. You didn't turn into my two favorite female characters. In fact I actually hate these characters. Next time when you are about to read a demon's mind, don't forget we demons are the masters of lying. Now, I know you might say, 'but this spell even works on demons.' Well, you see, when I was alive, I was such a good liar that I even convinced myself that I was telling the truth. And me becoming a demon has given me a lying boost. So ya, next time... Oh, wait. There won't be a next time. Sorry and goodbye." And then both angels felt their chests get really hot and then two big fire blasts (one for each big-breasted chest) appeared, burning right through them.

Both Angel Namina and Angel Hebi had two big holes that once were their chests. Ren looked down with disappointment in his eyes and said, "You angels get so full of yourselves when you guys are winning—you know that? Like, seriously, why would I bring up the topic of my two favorite female characters when I'm losing in the first place? Simple. I had a plan and you idiots fell for it."

While Ren was saying all that, the dimension was slowly fading away and the two angels turned back into their original form and started to combust into flames and then into dust. When Ren was fully back in the world of the living and inside the church, Ren turned to see the bone on top of a table.

Ren walked toward the bone and picked it up. Suddenly, he dropped the bone and fell to his knees, holding himself. Ren looked back and forth, and side to side, with the most scared look on his face.

He said, "I just felt a disturbance in the anime community. Or, to be more specific, the Hebi and Namina fans are very pissed."

Ren got up and quickly grabbed the bone.

"Okay, let's get this seal broken and get the hell out of here."

He quickly did the ritual and broke the seal. When the ritual was finished, he grabbed himself again and said, "Okay, I have to get out of here. Angels and demons got nothing on angry anime nerds, especially the ones that think I'm a traitor to the community. Great—now they might think I'm not a true anime fan. Fucking perfect. Thanks, angels!" And with a snap of his fingers, Ren was gone.

A full week in the world of the living went by after Ren killed those two shapeshifting angels and broke yet another seal. Thanks to that seal being broken, the demons were now another step closer to their goal.

The demons had a total of thirty seals broken so far. They were almost half-way done, with Ren having broken a total of sixteen, which still made him the demon that had broken the most so far. But Azazel had broken ten; he was getting closer to Ren's total. The other four seals were broken by some other random demons.

But with all that, Ren hadn't broken another seal ever since he killed those two angels. He had been hiding in hell, in his room, throughout the entire week, and to make things worse, he had even refused a summoning from Astaroth. No one in hell knew why Ren was so scared.

In hell, there was a hallway filled with souls' screams of agony that could be heard from everywhere. The screams were coming from every jail cell, from the right side and the left side—human souls being tortured by demons and just going insane from the environment around them.

A demon that was covered entirely of sad and angry faces could be seen walking in the middle of the hallway, ignoring every screaming soul. But he had a distinct smile on his main face, which looked like it had third degree burns on it. It seemed he enjoyed all the screaming of the tortured souls; it was soothing to his many ears.

He walked to a red door with a skull for a handle and human spine that was wrapped around the entire edge of the door. The multi-faced demon asked the door to take him somewhere. The door handle skull eyes glowed red, then it stopped, indicating it was done. The demon turned the handle and opened it.

The room that he walked into looked like a regular room that had all the stuff that a teenager would live in: a computer, a big flat screen tv, a bed, anime posters everywhere, and a shelf that was pretty much covered with mangas.

The demon sighed and said, "Ren, I know you're in here. I can sense you and I know you're under the bed."

Ren stuck his head out from underneath his bed, showing that he was still in his human form (if he had been in his demon form, he wouldn't have been able to get under his bed).

Ren, like a frightened child, said, "Why are you here?"

The multi-faced demon said, "I'm here to get you out of your room and to bring you to Astaroth so he can give you the next seal to break."

Ren said, "No, forget it. I can't go back out there. There is still a disturbance in the anime community and they want my blood."

The multi-faced demon, with all of his faces showing a confused look, said, "A disturbance in the anime—? What the hell are you talking about?" The demon lifted up his right hand and covered his main face with it. "You know what?

It doesn't matter. Look, I was told by our Lord to finally bring you to him, okay? So please just get out from underneath your bed and come with me."

"No!" Ren pulled his head back under his bed.

The multi-faced demon said, "Oh my fucking god. You are just like a toddler refusing to do what his parents are telling him to do! Look, it's been a living world week. Just go see Astaroth, okay? Please? If I go back to him without you, I'm dead. Literally."

Ren put his head out again, looked down at the floor, then looked up at the demon and sighed. "Okay, fine, I'll get out of my bed to see Astaroth, but not because you said you might die by him."

The multi-faced demon "Not might—will die from him."

"Yeah, yeah. It's because you said it has been a week up there, so I suppose the community calmed down a little bit. And I am bored of hiding anyway, so okay." With that, Ren fully came out from under his bed, still in his human form.

The demon turned to face Ren's door, walked toward it, and said, "Take us to Astaroth's office." And the door handles' eyes glowed again, stopped, and the demon was going to open the door until...

The demon stopped and said nervously, "Oh, that reminds me. No hard feelings about me torturing you for two hundred years, right?"

Ren was surprised by what the demon just said.

He smiled, walked up to him, put his hand on his shoulder, and said, "No, no, it's all good. I'm over it now."

The multi-faced demon said, "Oh, really, well—"

"However, that doesn't make us friends. I'm just focusing all of my anger at the angel that did this to me. So when I do kill the angel? I'm coming for you. And I will not kill you but I will beat the ever-living shit out of you." And with a creepy smile and with his eyes closed, Ren tightened his grip on the demon's shoulder and crushed it, making its shoulder squirt blood everywhere.

Every face on the demon's body screamed in pain and he fell to the ground, holding his already-healed shoulder and looking at Ren with an angry but very scared look.

Ren said, "Don't forget to shut my door." And with that, Ren walked away, shutting the door behind him with the demon still in his room.

Click-click-click-click-click. Astaroth was typing on his computer, most likely finishing up his work, when Ren opened the door and let himself in.

Astaroth said, with a hint of annoyance, "Ren, come on in."

Ren walked into Astaroth's office and saw Astaroth sitting, clearly overworking, with a big cigar in his hand while drinking some tea.

Ren said, "Wow, Astaroth. Buddy, you look awful. What happened?"

Astaroth said, "First, we are not buddies, and second, all this paperwork is killing me. Like, I already had a lot of paperwork to do even before the war, but this war is making it a thousand times worse."

Ren thought, "I'm so glad I don't have to do that, but I do feel bad for him."

Ren sat down on a free seat. "So then, let's just jump right into this. What seal do you want me to break next?"

"Right, the seal. Okay, give me a second." Astaroth moved down to his left side and opened his drawer.

He pulled out a bottle of rum with a date saying 1869. He opened the bottle and took a big gulp. He looked at Ren and moved the bottle toward him. Ren lifted up both of his arms and said, "No, thank you. I don't drink."

Astaroth shrugged his shoulders, pulled the bottle away from Ren, and took another drink. He was already a little bit drunk. "Okay, fine. Let's begin, shall we?" He handed Ren some leftover tea that he still had and said, "The seal I want you to break next is in the country of Ethiopia. It's the Ethiopian church."

Ren lifted up his right hand and placed it on his chin. "The Ethiopian church, huh? I heard it's pretty famous because of the priests, scientists, and the local people that saved about five percent of the forest that surrounds the church, am I correct?"

"Yes. I sent a couple of demons to break the seal before you, two at two different times, these two demon had complete multiple other tasks for me without fail so I send them to break this seal thinking that they were ready, but they both died."

"So you want me to break yet another seal that other demons couldn't? I'm starting to feel like I'm just a janitor, cleaning up other demons' failures."

Astaroth gave a little laugh, drank some more rum, and said, "Yeah, maybe, but I must warn you, this one is different from the others." His tone went from a smooth drunken tone to a serious tone and a serious face.

Ren looked back, also with a serious and interested look, and said, "How so?"

"Well, you know whenever an angel shows up to stop the demon from breaking the seal, they send themselves and the demon to a different dimension to fight to the death, right?"

"Yeah."

"Well, from what I got from Hermès, this certain angel doesn't take itself and the demon to a different dimension. It just kills the demon within the real church."

Ren put his hand on his chin and said, "Really? So I guess this angel doesn't care about the safety of the church. As long as the seal is safe, nothing else matters."

Astaroth nodded, already showing that he was sobering up. "Yes. Another thing that is interesting is that neither the demons nor Hermès saw what this angel even looked like. But what little information I got from Hermès is when he was watching the second demon, when the demon got close to the seal, he screamed in pain as he kept getting these small holes appearing all over his body. Like the holes are the size of golf balls and they just kept showing up all over his body at random times. And we know it's an angel because the demon dies. And to fully confirm that it is an angel, Hermès can sense grace from the holes that keep appearing on the church's walls and ceiling, and these holes are the same size as the holes on the second demon."

Ren said, quietly talking to himself, "Hmm, the holes from the demon match up with holes from the church. Could it be?"

"Ren, Ren."

Ren jerked up and looked at Astaroth. "Sorry, I got lost in thought."

"Look, Ren. This one is risky. We don't have any real and helpful information on this angel. This time I'm going to say you don't have to take this one. There are other seals out there."

"No. This angel is a problem. We have to take care of it now. If not, then it's going to be a problem later, so I'll take care of it, but if somehow I fail, send Azazel. He could take it on. But for right now, I call dibs."

Astaroth smiled and shook his head. Ren quickly stood up, showing that he was actually excited for this fight. He turned toward the door and said, "Take me to the Ethiopian church." The door opened and Ren left Astaroth's office.

Ren walked down the dark hallway toward the other side where a red door was waiting for him. But while he was walking, he put his right hand on his chin and was mumbling to himself.

Ren was uneasy because of this mission. He was excited at first, but for the very first time he was having some doubts now. Could he really win against this angel? But Ren wouldn't back down. He came this far. Ren had to break this seal to be another step closer toward his main goal.

Then Ren was in front of the red door. He took a deep breath and said, "Okay, let's do this." With that, he opened the door.

It was nighttime when Ren walked out the door. He looked around his surroundings to see if he could see anyone. He looked to his left side, then his right, and then closed his eyes to try to sense anything around him but he couldn't sense anything. To his knowledge, he was all alone and that made him feel uneasy. He looked straight ahead to see the church that was right in front of him. It didn't look that much different than any other church he had seen. That's when Ren noticed it—all the holes that the church had. And it was not just at the front entrance of the church, it was all over and the holes did look like the size of golf balls.

Ren closed his eyes again to try to sense if anything was around him now, but still nothing. He opened his eyes, lifted both of his hands, cracked them, and opened the door. When the door fully opened, the moonlight shone through the newly-opened space, but it didn't matter because the moonlight was already slipping through all the holes in the church. When Ren got inside, it only took him a second to see a human rib bone just laying on a table in front of him, ready to be taken.

Ren didn't like that it was just out in the open, and more so that it was not in the statue. In fact, there was no statue to be seen anywhere. It was like this church didn't even have one.

Ren said, "Okay, if this angel is trying to psych me out, it's working." He transformed into his half demon form and carefully walked toward the bone.

So far, nothing had happened, but Ren was still on guard. But it didn't matter. Ren walked toward the bone with no trouble whatsoever.

"Huh, I guess this angel is just a no—"

SPLASH!!!

Ren's right hand exploded while trying to reach for the bone.

"AAAHHHHH!" Ren screamed as loud as he could from the pain and shock. The worst pain ever was getting hurt without even noticing it until it was too late.

All the way on the other side of the forest from the church Ren was in, and on top of the last tree, there was a girl, probably eighteen years old. She wore a white tank top, torn up jeans, black Nike shoes, a small black leather jacket that seemed to only cover her chest, a silver cross necklace, short green hair—but the hair in front of her head was covering her left eye (her eyes were a silver color, but they were in the form of a cross as well)—and finally, her weapon was a sniper.

Aruru said, "Ooohh, what do we have here? Looks like I just caught a big fish tonight. I hope he is as good as the other angels say he is, or this will be no fun."

Her tone was like a teenager who finally had something to do after a long boring day of nothing. She took aim again.

Ren's hand fully regenerated back to normal and he twirled it around, trying to get rid of what was left of the pain. He looked at the fresh new hole that the bullet made. Ren sighed and said, "As I thought, this angel is a sniper. Of all things, a goddamn sniper. I hate snipers. They're so annoying."

Ren took a deep breath and exhaled, but when he finished exhaling, he lifted up his right arm as fast as he could, pointing at the hole that the bullet came through, most likely trying to shoot hellfire where the angel was.

But the moment Ren fully pointed his right arm toward the hole, another bullet came through again, breaking the wooden wall and slamming into Ren's finger. The bullet went through the tip of Ren's finger, through his entire arm, and exited through his shoulder.

Ren screamed as loud as he could from the pain, but it was a distraction. As Ren was screaming, his wound fully healed like it never happened. Ren put his left hand behind his back which looked like he was trying to snap his fingers so he could teleport.

Ren thought, "If I can just snap my fingers and teleport out of this church and into the forest, hopefully I'll be in front of the angel, or at least be near it just enough so I can sense it, since it's been shooting from the same spot."

However, when Ren got his fingers in position and was ready to snap, another bullet came through the church again, but it was from a different side of the church. It hit Ren's fingers, which exploded into multiple little pieces of meat.

Ren said, "What? How did it know I was about to teleport and how did it get from one side of the church to the other?"

In the forest, Aruru started to talk to herself. "Don't even bother trying to teleport or run away. When I'm in this body, my bullets can move at 440,000 miles per hour and so can I. I've never met a demon who can move faster than my bullets, and since you can't even react to my bullets, you can't move that fast. So try to make this enjoyable." She sounded like a child that was just disappointed about something she was looking forward too.

Knowing he was running out of options, Ren looked at the bone on the table and started to run toward it as fast as his legs and wings could. However.

Crack-crack-crack-crack!

Both of Ren's legs and wings were shot off. Ren fell down on his face, and from the force of his speed, Ren slid all the way past the table where the bone was and hit the wall.

Ren shook his head to get some of the impact out of his body and lifted his right arm to try to shoot hellfire again but the angel just wouldn't let him do it. Another bullet came through the church, hitting Ren's shoulder. The impact tore off Ren's arm.

But he was not done yet. The moment his right arm got shot, he was planning to lift his left arm to try to do the same thing, but before he could even lift up his left arm, it was already getting a bullet through it.

Ren thought, "How? I only moved my left arm like a millimeter off the ground, and this angel already knew what I was going to do?! How am I supposed to beat this thing if I can't get near it, I can't sense it it's too far away, and I can't even smell were it is. Then again I didn't really trained to master or improve my sense of smell since it was only helpful during that one fight. And to make it worse, it keeps making sure I can't use my long-range attacks. What am I supposed to do?!"

Aruru said, "Okay, now it's time to really mess with him." Aruru took a deep breath and moved away from the spot she was at, fully disappearing.

Crack-crack-crack-crack!

Bullets came from every direction, either making new holes or coming through the holes that were already there. Either way, all of the bullets came through the church at the same time and all of them hit Ren. He fell to the ground, his arms, legs, wings, hip, horns, ears, and nose, shot off or turned into Swiss cheese.

All the wounds fully healed immediately, and all the blood that came out of his body disintegrated—as did all the flesh that came off.

Ren slammed his right hand on the ground, which made a huge hole, and said to himself very quietly, "I can't win, I just can't. This is impossible. It's just playing with me. It's hitting every non-vital spot on my body, making me live long enough to suffer until it gets bored and finishes me off. Typical angel, but I can't lose. I have to win. Come on brain—work! I've managed to think my way out of many hard fights, and I can do it again. I can do it for this one as well, but in the meantime, I have to make sure this angel doesn't get bored of me yet and kills me."

Ren looked up with an angry face and screamed, "COME ON, IS THAT THE BEST YOU CAN DO? STOP PLAYING WITH ME! I HATE WHEN YOU ANGELS DO THAT! JUST FIGHT ME FACE TO FACE!"

Aruru said, "Ah...one of my favorite parts of the hunt. They just lose control of their feelings and get super angry and sloppy. Now, I wonder what you will do, Ren." She gripped her sniper with excitement and fired again, hitting Ren in the ear.

Ren stumbled back and proceeded to run toward the bone.

Aruru said, "So all you can think about now is trying to finish your mission. I can respect that." With a smile, she shot again.

The bullet hit the wall—CRACK—and hit Ren on the hip. Ren fell down but got back up and just kept trying to get the bone while he was thinking of a way to win.

Ren thought, "Okay, I got it distracted. So how am I going to kill this angel? So, I know it's a sniper, and coming from the one attack where all those bullets came at the same time from different directions, it can move at the same speed as the bullets or slightly faster." (While Ren was thinking, he was being bombarded by bullets. That's when it hit him. No, not a bullet—an idea.) "Wait. Every time a bullet hits the wall before it hits me, I can hear it as the bullets are coming through the walls. I can hear it. But my reaction speed is still way too slow. So my sense of hearing is on par with it but my body just can't keep up."

Then a bullet went through Ren's nose and he fell to the ground, holding his face.

Ren thought, "Shit, I can't keep doing this. I'm running out of time and I can feel my regeneration is about to stop working. This is hopeless. Am I really going to die here?! Did I really start this war and make billions of people suffer just to get killed again?"

Ren closed his eyes, indicating that he had given up and was awaiting his death.

But then he had an idea. Ren thought, "Wait. My regeneration. Maybe, but it's too risky and I don't even know if it's possible or will even work, but I'm out of options and I have to do and try something."

Ren was laying on the ground because he kept getting bombarded by bullets. He got up, standing on his two feet. He looked to the ground and gave a sigh.

Aruru looked through her scope on her sniper, then looked away to rub her eyes and said, "What the...?" She looked through it again and said, "What's with the purple and black mist surrounding him? What's he up to?" There was pure curiosity on her face.

In the church Ren was still standing still with the purple and black mist surrounding him but Aruru was not just going to let Ren keep doing what he was doing, so she shot again. It went through the church's wall and was about to hit Ren straight in the head.

She was not taking any chances. Ren was doing something she had never seen before. She had to kill him now. But then, before it hit Ren, he moved his right wing to block it. The bullet hit the tip of the wing, but it was enough to slow it down so he could move his head ever so slightly, and the bullet missed.

Aruru smiled and gave a little giggle and said, "Well, looks like you predicted that one, but what about this one?" Aruru moved away from the spot where she was with great speed. And now she was on a different side of the forest, which meant she was at a different side of the church.

Aruru shot again. The bullet came through the wall, now on Ren's right side. It was about to hit Ren in the head again but then Ren moved his head and the bullet missed and just hit the floor.

Aruru lowered her sniper with complete shock on her face, but it was only for a second, and she smiled again.

"So you think you're clever, huh? You managed to block one and dodge one, but guess what? I'm done playing around. You're dead." She moved again and she shot not once, not twice, but three times.

All three came through the church. One was in front of Ren, aiming for his head. The other two came from both sides—one from the left and one from the right—and they were aimed at Ren's chest.

Aruru said, "You managed to get lucky and dodge the last one, but you can't dodge three coming at you at the same time."

Crack-crack-crack!

All three bullets hit something, but not Ren. They all hit the ground Ren. Ren had managed to dodge all three of them.

Aruru, with sweat coming down her forehead, said, "No. Impossible." She looked through her scope and she saw Ren turning toward her and for a second their eyes connected.

Aruru widened her eyes and said pretty loud, "He knows where I am."

Then, when Aruru lowered her sniper, she felt an enormous amount of pain coming from her chest and she knew why.

The moment she lowered her sniper, it blocked her vision and Ren was right in front of her, stabbing both of his weapons into her chest.

Aruru thought, "What—how—? I was out of his range where he could not possibly sense me. And he didn't teleport here. He ran here and I couldn't react to him! And his face? What's wrong with his face?!"

Ren said, exhausted, "So you were a female. Good to know and goodbye."

Ren finished her off by moving his weapons away from each other while still being in Aruru so she got torn in half, which fully killed her.

As Aruru's body burst into flames, the light from the fire hit Ren's face. It was covered in scratches, probably from when he slammed through the church's wall to get to where Aruru was. And from the firelight you could see Ren's eyes. One was white while the other was still its original color. Ren lifted his right hand to cover his left eye and looked down at his legs.

Ren thought, "I think both of my legs are severely cracked and I don't have regeneration anymore, so it looks like I'm flying to do the ritual."

Ren started to flap his wings as fast as he could. He turned so he was facing the church again and started to fly to it, all while looking back at the ash pile that was once an angel.

Ren finally made it to the church, Ren went inside. When he was in front of the bone, he summoned the syringe that had the Pope's blood, and started the ritual.

When the ritual was done, Ren could feel the victory of yet another seal broken. But he got tired of flapping his wings, so he stopped and landed on both of his feet. But they were so badly damaged that they both broke and he fell to the ground.

Ren didn't have the energy to scream in pain. That showed how tired he was.

Ren said, "So this is it. I'm going to die here by bleeding to death. Not the way I imagined I'd go out." Ren was slowly closing his eyes but he quickly opened them as fast as he could.

Ren, with his dying breath, said, "No, I can't die. I still haven't...found and killed that...a...that did this to me and everyone I care about. No, no, this isn't f......air." And then Ren closed his eyes and fell asleep.

In the middle of a white hallway with torches on both sides of the walls, giving light and on both sides, an angel wearing white robes, golden sandals, long white angel wings, blue eyes, and his golden hair in an undercut hair style was walking. The walls of the hallway had multiple different paintings and sculptures of various different artists that depicted heaven and angels.

This angel was walking toward a big plain white door that looked like the Romans would use. The angel walked toward the door until he was in front of it. He took a deep breath and opened it.

Inside was a room. One side of the room had a waterfall, the other side had a lava fall, and in the middle of the room was a white carpet with two chairs and a desk with a big leather chair facing the other direction. It was facing a window.

A voice came from the other side of the leather chair, his voice soothing. "What news do you have for me?"

The angel sat down on one of the open seats and said, "My lord, the angel

Aruru has been killed and the seal she was guarding has been broken."

"Really? Let me guess—it was Azazel. Because he is the only demon on earth right now that can beat her."

"I'm sorry, my Lord, but no, it wasn't Azazel."

"What? That's impossible! Then who killed her?"

The angel was hesitant, and he had a scared face, but then he got the courage to finally answer. "It was the demon that has broken the most seals . The human that you ordered to be sent to hell: Ren."

The lord angel got up from his chair in shock and excitement. The messenger angel could see his white suit and his very long silver dreadlocks that almost reached his butt.

The lord angel said, "Well, my creation somehow managed to beat Aruru, our best long range fighter. Tell me how."

The messenger angel bowed his head and answered without a second thought, "From the footage we got from their fight, Ren did something to himself that allowed him to move faster than Aruru's bullets, which can go—"

"Yeah, yeah, we all know how fast her bullets can go, but what is this something Ren did to himself?"

"Well, that's the thing. I don't know. In fact, no one who saw the footage knows what he did. But from what we can tell, he had to give up something or risk something to get this humongous power-up so he could win against Aruru."

The lord angel said, with a wave of his hand, "Hmm, I see. Okay, that's all I need to know."

The messenger angel stood up and bowed his head again, turned, and walked out the door.

The lord angel said, "Hmm, Ren, you are certainly becoming an interesting demon indeed." He sat back down and grabbed a glass of water that was on his desk. He took a big gulp and put the glass back on the table. "Okay, then. I guess it's time for me to get started on my plans."

THE AFTERMATH OF THE FIGHT

Ren thought, "What happened and why am I so comfortable? Did I die again? Is this what happens when angels and demons die? They go to a world of darkness? No, wait. I can hear something and feel something." Ren's body started to twitch and he slowly opened his eyes.

His vision was very blurry, but slowly becoming normal. When his vision fully returned, the first thing he saw was a white ceiling. That wasn't all; he could also hear a familiar voice.

"Hey, look. Ren's finally waking up!"

Ren could hear the voice coming from his right side, so he slowly moved his head and saw the two men—no, monsters—sitting.

The two monsters were Astaroth and Azazel.

Ren said in a very tired tone of voice, "Astaroth...Azazel...What happened and...where am I?"

Astaroth said, "Well, first: you won. You killed Aruru and broke yet another seal. And as for where, you are in hell's hospital. And yes, hell does have a hospital for demons who get badly injured when their regeneration is gone."

Ren looked down to see that he was laying on a hospital bed in his human form. "That explains why I am so comfortable."

Azazel asked, "So how do you feel, Ren?" He had a very convincing look of concern on his face.

Ren looked at the ceiling again and said with a voice that was slowly going back to normal, "Well, besides still feeling tired and a little bit numb, I'm okay. But could one of you bring me some water? I'm kind of thirsty."

Azazel smiled,(or gave somewhat a smile since his head is a skull), stood up, and left the room. Astaroth was still sitting, looking at Ren with a nervous and somewhat excited look on his face. Ren didn't know why he was making that face but he would find out really soon.

Azazel came back with a glass of water and handed it over. Ren grabbed it, but with his still weakened strength, he almost dropped the cup. He started to slowly drink it.

Astaroth said, "Okay, I'm sorry. I can't wait. I have to ask!" It was so sudden and loud that Ren started to cough from the water that was going down his throat.

Azazel said to Astaroth, "Geez, calm down. Look, I want to know too, but Ren just woke up and that was just too loud."

Astaroth said with a lot of excitement, "I know, but I can't help it. No matter how many times I watch the fight, I can't tell what he did to win."

Ren, rubbing some of the water and spit off his chin, said, "What are you talking about?"

Azazel said, "Look, I was hoping to wait a little bit longer before either one of us asked the question, but how did you win that fight with Aruru?"

Astaroth said, "Yeah, how did you? You couldn't do anything. You were helpless and she was toying around with you. But you did something that allowed you to win that neither I nor Azazel have ever seen before, so would you please explain what happened?"

Ren looked at them, then back to the ceiling, then back at them. He sighed and slowly moved so that he was sitting up.

Ren looked at them with still sleepy eyes. "It was my regeneration and my senses."

Both Azazel and Astaroth looked at each other and then looked back at Ren.

Astaroth said, "What about them?"

Ren said, "I got rid of them."

When Ren said that, it interested them even more. He started to explain. "Okay, let's start with my regeneration. So let me ask you guys this—how does our regeneration work?"

Astaroth lifted an eyebrow and said, "Well, for us demons, our regeneration works with three of our sins: lust, gluttony, and greed."

Ren said, "Correct, and what do those sins have in common?" Neither Azazel nor Astaroth answered, so Ren gave them an answer. "They all want stuff. It's true that lust only wants one thing, gluttony only wants food, and greed wants everything, but all three still want something and or everything for them."

Astaroth put both of his hands together and placed his chin on them with a look of interest while Azazel still had both of his hands on his lap, listening carefully to what Ren had to say.

Ren said, "I'm not going to lie. I didn't think it would work, or if it was even possible, but I was desperate and out of time. I knew my regeneration was compressed with those sins so I assume that they were taking in information and every detail of every bullet that was entering my body—how fast it was, its damage output, its durability, and so on. I assume they wanted all of that before they deactivated from the angel's grace."

Azazel interrupted Ren for clarification. "So you got rid of your regeneration? Those three sins forever?"

"Correct. I got rid of them because they should know how the bullet works, like I said before, and so they should also know how to beat it. So to make sure I got that information from my own sins, I had to get rid of them, meaning I got rid of my regeneration. Before you ask, no, there was no other way to get the information from my three sins because they are known to want and take, not give or share even if it's your own. So I got rid of them and the conclusion that they thought of, surged through my entire body, which made me stronger."

Astaroth said, "Okay, so how much of a power boost did you get?"

"Well, before I tell you about my power boost, I have to tell you about me getting rid of my senses."

Azazel said, "Right, Please, do tell."

"All of the information that I got from my own sins was incredible, and it sounded like another person was giving me the information in my own head, but it also told me that my body was too damaged and weak to get the power boost I needed. Because of that, I had to make more sacrifices for that power. And it suggested that I get rid of half of all of my senses. So without questioning it, I did. I got rid of my left ear so I couldn't hear from that ear, my right nose hole so I could not smell anything, my sense of taste was really weakened by half, so if I ate something I won't enjoy it as much as I used too, and same can be said about my sense of touch, but that one might have helped me because pain would be lessened. And finally, my left eye was blind."

But when Ren finished his sentence, he realized something and made an aggressive move and placed his right hand in front of his face. He was shaking and couldn't believe it. He could see with both of his eyes, and not only that—he could tell that all his senses were normal. But how?

Ren looked at Astaroth and Azazel, but they both shook their heads, indicating that they did not bring his senses back.

Ren, in shock and with a little bit of happiness, said, "But how?! I got rid of all of them and now they're back?! I wonder?" Ren lifted up his left hand, grew his claws and cut the palm of his right hand. It regenerated immediately and the blood also disintegrated immediately as well.

Astaroth smiled and said, "The reason you have all of them back is because hell has one incredible nurse."

Ren didn't understand at first, but out of nowhere, he could feel an enormous amount of sin coming toward him.

Ren thought, "What an overwhelming amount of sin! It's way more than Azazel and Astaroth combined! Is it Lucifer or Satan? No, it's huge, but it's not on their level. But it's close. But if it's not them, then who is it?"

Azazel smiled, stood up, turned toward where the sin was coming from, and said, "Ren, say hello to hell's greatest nurse, interrogator, the strongest demon in hell besides our two gods, and the leader of the ten demon kings." Azazel paused and opened the curtains. "Lilith."

Behind the curtain was an Asian girl, probably in her early twenties. She had blue eyes, short straight black hair, decent-sized breasts and ass, and she was wearing a 1980s nurse outfit, which fit really tight.

Ren's eyes widened so big that they looked like they would pop off because of how the nurse looked.

Ren thought, "Oh my god, this demon looks just like my type."

Lilith said with a smile, "That's because it is."

Ren thought, "Even her voice sounds so innocent. Is she really a demon? And what does she mean 'it is'? Did she read my thoughts?"

Astaroth said, "Lilith here is a succubus. She can transform into anything that is truly sexy to whomever sees her."

Ren said, "So that's not her true form?" He thought, "Even if it's not, please stay in that form."

Lilith said, "No, it's not. It's just one of many abilities that I have."

Ren looked at her with an interested look, "Many abilities. So you're saying that you have more?"

Lilith giggled and said, "Well, besides the standard and my own power that is unique to me, every succubus has the ability to change their form."

Ren put his right hand on his chin and mumbled, "I see. That's pretty handy both in battle and for having a good time."

When Ren was talking to himself, Astaroth looked at Lilith and said, "Okay, Lilith, why are you here? And could you please turn back into your true form, please?"

Lilith sighed. "Fine, fine. I just want my patient to be happy."

Lilith started to glow red and her appearance started to change. All of her clothes just disappeared and she was naked. Her hair turned a blood red color and got super long—it reached her butt—her breasts and butt got even bigger, she grew sharp fingernails which were black-colored, her eyes turned into white snake eyes, she grew four dragon-looking wings—two on her shoulder blades and the other two near her hip—and she was still naked; nothing was covering any of her lady parts. And finally, there was a number 1 on the left side of her chest.

"There. Are you happy now, Astaroth?"

Astaroth looked at Lilith with pure lust in his eyes and said a satisfied, "Yes."

Lilith sighed and looked away from Astaroth. She said to Ren, "I'm here because I sensed that Ren was awake and so I wanted to meet him now that he is awake."

Ren didn't say anything because he couldn't look away from Lilith's body.

Azazel coughed into his hand and said, "Anyway, can we continue with our conversation, Ren?"

"Huh? Oh, right, sorry. Um, where did I leave off?" Ren closed his eyes and scratched his head in embarrassment.

"You finished telling us about you getting rid of half of your senses and was about to tell us what kind of power you got."

"Oh, right, sorry. When I got rid of half of my senses, that was enough to start my power-up. But I knew that the angel would not just sit there and wait for me to get all powered up—this was not a stereotypical fight where the hero lets the villain transform. So I just put all of my power into my speed and my sensory nerve. And because I did that, the distance of how far I could sense was doubled, so I was perfectly able to sense from the church to the end of the forest where the angel was. And finally, my speed was something else."

Ren stopped on purpose to make everyone be on the edge of their seats.

Azazel said, "Well, don't stop. Tell us!"

"Well, the information that I got told me that the bullets moved at 440,000 miles per hour—literally twice the speed of lightning. Which was unbelievable, not only because my sins actually got that information, but also i fought someone that fast. So anyway I put most of my power into my speed and my top speed now is 450,000 miles per hour. I got an extra ten thousand mile more than the bullets and that's why she couldn't react to me. I was just too fast for her." He had a smirk on his face.

Lilith, Azazel, and Astaroth were very impressed, and Astaroth was about to say something, but Ren interrupted him.

Ren looked down in disappointment and said, "But what's the point of this speed, because yeah, sure, I got my regeneration back, but because my durability is still bad, every time I go that fast, I'll break or really damage my legs..."

Lilith interrupted Ren this time and said, "No, that won't happen."

Ren looked up with a confused look, but Lilith didn't mind and said, "You see, that's not entirely true. It's true your legs did break the first time you went that fast, but that's because you were in a fight and your regeneration was gone, but now you're not fighting. And since you have your regeneration and sense back, your body can now adapt to your speed."

Ren said, "I'm sorry, but I don't understand."

Lilith sighed in annoyance. "If you just let your body rest a little bit longer, your body's durability, strength, and the senses you got back will be at your current level. Just give it some time to adapt."

"Current level?"

Azazel said, "Look at your number."

Ren looked down to the left side of his chest to see his number and he couldn't believe what he was seeing."

Astaroth said, "Because of what you did, it really bumped you up, kid."

The number on Ren's chest had been 1995 but it was now 1250.

Lilith said, "Congratulations, you became the 1250 strongest demon in hell through an unorthodox way."

Ren couldn't believe it. He literally could not believe it. Just seeing that number was making him start to cry with happiness.

Astaroth said, "Come on, Ren, don't be a bitch. It is true that you're at that number, which is very impressive, but you're still way weaker than us."

Lilith slapped Astaroth on the back of the head and said with some anger in her voice, "Don't ruin the moment for him, even if it's true."

After a couple minutes of them just talking to make Ren feel better, Lilith said, "Okay, I have to go soon to treat my other patients, but before I go, I have to tell Ren something."

Ren, Astaroth, and Azazel looked at Lilith in silence because they all knew that this was probably going to be bad news for Ren.

Lilith pulled a seat up and sat down. She crossed her legs and said, "Look, Ren. I'm happy that you killed that angel and broke another seal, but I have to tell you this—if you do that strategy again, I won't heal you."

When Ren spoke next, he sounded like a little kid complaining about something he didn't understand. "But why? Because I did that, I got another seal, and I got an enormous power up."

Lilith said, "Yes, but the only reason that strategy worked is because Aruru loves to mess with her prey. If her personality had been a little bit different, you would have died. And not only that—at first, I didn't know how to heal you. You did something I had never seen before, and what I mean is you got rid of your sins of lust, gluttony, and greed. I've dealt with demons losing some senses before, but not like that. I almost gave up on you, which meant you would most likely be useless, until I thought of a way to cure you."

Ren said, with a scared and nervous tone because Lilith was looking at him with a serious and scary look, said, "And what would that be?"

Lilith said, "I had to ask for help from the literal embodiment of those three sins. Three of the ten demon kings. The demons with the ranks of 5, 6, and 8: greed, lust, and gluttony."

Ren stopped her and said, "Wait, you're telling me that the literal seven deadly sins are the majority of the ten demon kings?"

Azazel said, "Well, yeah. Didn't anyone tell you?"

Ren looked back at Azazel with a hint of annoyance and said, "No, nobody did!"

Lilith clapped her hands and said, "As I was saying, I had to ask them for help, and luckily they agreed. I have a feeling they would have declined if it was some other demon, but they knew that you had the most seals broken, so they said yes. And they had to pump those literal sins into you again to see if your regeneration came back. I had to cut you so many times to see if it came back. It lasted three whole hell days until finally it worked. And now I'm indebted to them and I don't want to be any more than I already am. So the point I'm making is: if you do it again, I won't help you. I'm not your mother. You have to take responsibility for your own actions. If you get injured by an enemy and if your regeneration was off from a mission, then fine. But if it's that way again, then I won't help you. Are we clear?"

Ren couldn't say anything. Was it because he was mad or was it because he was sad? Either way, all Ren did was nod.

Lilith smiled, got up, turned around, walked to the curtains, and opened them. But before she left, she said, "Oh, and, by the way, if you help us break all the seals, I would like you to come to my world and I'll give you a reward as thanks for releasing us." She turned her head, winked at Ren, and walked away.

Ren smiled but Astaroth looked at Ren and said, "Don't do it. Remember, she is a succubus. If you have sex with her, she will suck your soul out of you and you'll die. Yes, yet another power she has because she is a succubus. It works on anything that has a gender."

Ren gave a disappointed look, not just because of that, but because of something else entirely.

Both Azazel and Astaroth noticed and Astaroth said, "Hey, don't be bummed. Trust me, it does suck because I would also go to her world and—"

Ren interrupted Astaroth, not only because he didn't want to hear it but also because he had something to say. "I know she has a point for why she doesn't want me to do it again, but she also had to know that there was no other way for me to win. Like, I only have telekinesis and shoot hellfire. My shapeshifting powers don't help that much so I didn't have any other options."

Azazel put his hand on Ren's shoulder. Ren looked up to look Azazel in the eye sockets.

Azazel said, "No, you did have another power."

Ren slammed his head back on his pillow and said, "Oh my fucking God. I'm starting to get sick of you guys not telling me everything. Especially things that can help me win in a fight."

Astaroth said angrily, "Don't give us that attitude. Even if we did tell you, you couldn't use it at that time hell you still can't use it."

Ren looked at Astaroth. "What do you mean?"

Azazel used his telekinesis to hover his chair over toward Ren. He sat down and said, "Ren, this ability—you didn't have it yet. Demons can only get this ability when they hit the level 1000. It's called the Final Attack."

"Pffff, lame name."

Azazel sighed and continued, "The final attack is what it sounds like—you put literally all of your energy into one big fire blast, and the higher rank you are, the more destructive you are."

Ren got excited because this sounded just like he was talking to one of his old friends about who was more destructive for a crossover battle. "So what can the rank of 1000 can destroy at its level?"

Astaroth said, "Well, when a demon hits that rank it can only destroy, at best, a town."

"Hmm, so a town buster. It's not bad, not bad at all when i hit that level I'll take that destruction."

Azazel got Ren's attention again and said, "Every time you go up a rank, your final attack gets stronger and stronger."

Ren said, "Why do I have a feeling there's going to be a 'but.'"

Azazel said, "Yeah, you guessed correctly. Not only do you have to charge for this attack—so it'll take time—but there is also a cost when you use this technique—you'll be so exhausted that you'll go into a coma-like sleep. Luckily the amount of time stays the same no matter what level you are."

"And what would that be?"

"A full week if you have no damage."

Ren lifted an eyebrow. "No damage?"

"Yes. If you use this attack and you have taken no damage so far in the fight, you'll only go into one week of sleep. But if you took damage, and it counts how much damage you took before the attack, it will extend the period of time you'll be asleep. We once had a demon who was asleep for a whole year."

Ren swallowed loudly, not because of how long that one demon stayed asleep, but because Ren was scared of even using that attack now.

Then he thought of something. He exhaled and said, "Okay, since you just told me about the cost of the attack, now tell me who has the most destructive capability in history."

Azazel said, "Sure. But before we get to that, let's start with me. Because I'm a part of the ten demon kings but I am the weakest one." While Azazel said that, he slowly looked away and tightened his fist in anger.

Ren noticed but did not say anything and gave Azazel a couple seconds to himself.

Azazel lessened his fist and continued to talk. "Sorry about that. I get kind of angry when I think I'm the weakest."

Astaroth laughed a little bit and said, "Sheesh. If you feel that way about your rank, just imagine how I must feel."

Both Azazel and Astaroth looked at each other and began to chuckle. Then Ren coughed and said, "I think we are getting a little off topic. Please tell me how destructive you are, Azazel."

Azazel smiled and said, "Okay, my full destructive capability is that I can fully destroy all of Mexico plus Texas."

When Azazel said that, Ren jumped up with such great force that he almost fell off his bed, but luckily, he grabbed the other side of the bed and stopped himself. "Sorry about that. I wasn't expecting that—like God damn you can destroy all of that?"

Azazel said, "Yes, I know it sounds very impressive."

Ren thought, "Sounds impressive? It sounds impressive?! I'm not ready for the strongest ones."

Azazel said, "Now, there are only three beings in the entire world that have this destructive capability. And those people are Lucifer, Satan, and the first arch—no, the first angel ever created by God himself—Michael and the other two can destroy all of America, plus Canada."

Ren only gave a wide glance at Azazel, but he lifted up his hand and gave him a number one with his pointed finger, indicating to Azazel he was saying 'give me a minute.' Then Ren turned toward his left side and threw up all over the floor. Azazel, who was on the left side, jumped back in disgust and Astaroth laughed.

When Ren was done throwing up, he struggled to say, "Sorry, but that was too much to handle. Like, seriously, beings like them actually exist?"

Astaroth said, "Yep. They sure do."

So Ren sat up yet again and rubbed off some of the vomit that was on his mouth with his arm and said, "Well then, I've got three questions. I hope you can answer them."

Azazel knew Ren was talking to him, so in response he said, "Yes."

Ren nodded and began his questions: "Okay. One, how do you know that's their destructive capability because in the Bible it has no indication about that and the earth has no scars of that power?"

But when Ren asked the question, instead of Azazel, it was Astaroth that answered. "It's hell's many worlds."

Ren looked at Astaroth with a confused look like he didn't understand.

So Astaroth exhaled and said, "Remember, hell has multiple dimensions that are being ruled by us demon generals and kings, but we also have worlds for training as well. When hell was still being worked out to be the hell we have today, the demons weren't fully loyal to Lucifer and Satan so they called all of them to a world that was nothing but a wasteland and showed them their power. When they both used their Final Attack. The pure length and destruction that everyone saw was equivalent to America and Canada. And we all assume that Michael has that same power because he was equal in power with Lucifer when he banished him to hell."

Ren put a hand to his chin and thought to himself, "I see. So that's how. And coming from my first encounter with Lucifer and Satan, they don't seem like the type to train to get stronger. And from all the angels that I fought so far, it doesn't seem Michael would train either."

Ren put his hand down and began to ask his second question: "When you said all of America, I know you meant all the states that are connected, but what about Hawaii with all its islands and Alaska? They are states of America."

Azazel answered this question with a smile. "Bravo, Ren. You are the first demon to ask that. And well, yes. Hawaii, with all of its islands, are included, but not Alaska."

"Then why did you say, 'all of America' when it's clearly not all of America?"

Azazel scratched his bone cheeks and said, "Well, most people forget about those two states, so we didn't feel like we needed to say it or they assume we are including them."

Ren shook his head but he got it. He began his last question: "Okay, final question. You said the strongest beings—and you mentioned yours, Azazel—but what about the other archangels and the other demon kings?"

"Well, the rest of the five archangels all have the same destructive capability."

"And that would be?"

Azazel said, "They can destroy all of America and yes, it means with all of Hawaii but not Alaska and Canada."

Ren said, "I see. That's still very impressive. So let me guess—only Lilith has that kind of power in hell?"

Astaroth said, "No," with a serious look. He didn't seem to like that answer, but Ren didn't know why.

Azazel said, "The demons with the rank of four through two have that power."

Ren said, "What? Four to two? Then how powerful is Lilith?"

Astaroth said, "What about the demons nine through five?"

Ren said, "Ehe, I can guess how powerful they are because they would have to be more powerful than Azazel but not as powerful as the number four demon king."

But Azazel didn't say anything. Instead, he exhaled and pretended he didn't hear that and continued to answer Ren's question. "Lilith is the only being in our records of every demon and angel that we know of that has this power."

Ren was starting to sweat from the suspense because he really wanted to know.

"She can destroy all of America plus Mexico. She is hell's greatest demon hell has ever had and that is, of course, not including our gods."

Ren was amazed by all of what he was hearing—not only that beings like this actually exist. Ren only heard these topics in anime, comics, or video games. But he was actually meeting them and he could maybe be one of them.

Astaroth sat up and said, "Okay, that's enough talking for today. Let's give Ren some more rest. We can talk more when you're out of the hospital, okay?"

Ren nodded and both Azazel and Astaroth began to walk away. But while they were doing that, Ren was looking around and noticed something and screamed, "Wait!"

They both turned and said, "What!"

Ren said, "Where is a TV?"

They both said, "Huh?"

"I'm going to be here for a couple more days and I'm not going to be asleep for all of them, so where's my TV with an Xbox or PlayStation so I can play video games or watch YouTube or Netflix?"

They shook their heads and Azazel said, "You don't have one, but I'll bring your laptop later, okay?"

Ren puffed his cheeks like an anime character when they were upset. Both Astaroth and Azazel left the room where Ren was and left the hospital.

They walked through the dark hallway, quiet until Azazel said, "Are you sure we shouldn't tell what's happening right now in the war?"

Astaroth said, "You know as well as I do that we have our orders from our gods to not tell him yet."

Azazel said sadly, "I know, but the angel that did this to Ren has finally made his move. I feel like we should tell him who and what he is and what he is doing right now."

Astaroth stopped and turned toward Azazel. "Look, we can't tell Ren about him until he is fully healed, okay? And plus, even if we do tell him, he would just get mad and try to leave to go kill him in his condition right now."

Azazel said, "I know, but still." He looked back at the door.

Astaroth started to laugh really loudly and said, "You know, Azazel, you really have changed a lot. The old you wouldn't give a shit about a lesser demon. Hell, you didn't give a shit about me—you only like the other ten demon kings—but here we are, talking like friends."

Azazel also started to laugh a little bit and said, "Well, for all the years I have been a demon king, every demon I have ever met was scared of me or just kept kissing my ass to be on my good side. I was getting sick of it but Ren was different. He was scared of me at first, but as time went by, he wasn't anymore. In fact, he treated me like I was his equal even though we were not and he got me into anime." Throughout Azazel's spiel, he gave a somewhat looking smiling the entire time.

Then Azazel looked at Astaroth and said, "But what about you? You told me that you hate Ren but you showed up to see if he was okay, so you have changed as well."

"Well, unlike you, I like demons fearing me and kissing my ass. It gives me pleasure and power. But when I met Ren, he treated me like I was his equal. It really pissed me off—like, there was no respect in his tone every time we talked to each other. But I guess he just grew on me."

They both laughed and continued to walk until they reached the other side, but before one of them opened the door, one of them, most likely Astaroth, said,

"Let's just hope that the angel we think it is is not, because Ren has no chance against him."

He opened the door. They both walked through it and the door shut slowly.

THE BIG FIGHT

Ren woke up from his long nap a week later in hell. His body had finally recovered and Ren was ready for a fight with his new power. He got out of bed and stretched his entire body, with a lot of cracking in his joints, while still in his human form. While Ren was stretching, from the other side of his bed, Lilith was standing there holding a clipboard. She was in the Asian form that Ren found really attractive.

"Well, Ren, since now you're on your feet again, do you feel like your bones or muscles got weakened?"

Ren stopped stretching and turned toward Lilith. "No. Remember, demons are made of sins and sloth is one of them. Demons can't get weaker by being lazy."

Lilith just gave Ren a smile but didn't say anything else. She seemed satisfied with that answer.

When Ren was finally done cracking his bones, he said, "Thank you for taking care of me. I'll repay you by breaking more seals."

Lilith once again didn't say anything and just smiled.

Ren turned toward the curtains, walked toward them, opened them, said, "Thanks," one more time, and walked away.

Lilith, now alone, stopped her smiling and said to herself, "I hope you can, because what's going to happen next will change this entire war."

When Ren walked out of his curtains, he saw so many other white curtains. Some were probably empty and some might have pretty beaten up demons behind them. But Ren couldn't care less about that. So he looked, trying to see where the red door was. It was to his right side all the way down the hallway.

Ren started to walk there while thinking to himself, "It's been a while since I broke a seal. I hope I still have my title of the most seals broken. And I'm hoping we did make some progress. For some reason, Lilith, Astaroth, and Azazel wouldn't tell me anything about the war when they visited. They always changed the subject. That's usually not a good sign, but now I'm up and ready to go."

Ren was finally in front of the red door. He asked it to take him to Astaroth's office, the handle glowed red and Ren opened it and walked in.

After a long walk through the hallway in complete silence, Ren reached the other door. When he opened it, Ren was not expecting what he saw. As Ren walked into Astaroth's office, there was paperwork everywhere—on his desk, on the floor, and on the chairs. There were also empty bottles of alcohol everywhere.

Ren could not say anything because he was shocked by what he was seeing. Then he heard the door handle shake and it opened behind Ren. It was, of course, Astaroth, holding another bottle of whiskey. Astaroth stopped when he saw Ren standing there with a confused look on his face.

"Astaroth, what happened here and what happened to you? You look terrible."

Astaroth just walked past Ren to his desk and sat down. He used his telekinesis to move all the papers from his desk, chairs, and floor to the side of his walls, surprisingly very neatly. He waved his right hand for Ren to approach and sit down. Ren nodded and sat down in the now clean chair.

Astaroth took a sip of his whiskey and said, "Ren, this war has really been not good for us."

"What do you mean? What's happening out there? Please tell me and don't leave anything out!"

Astaroth put the bottle of whiskey down, rubbed his face, gave Ren a serious look, and said, "We are hardly getting any seals broken and we are having humongous casualties on our end. Even worse than usual."

"What? When?!"

"The day after your fight with Aruru."

Ren jumped up and said, "What's been going on since then? Why didn't you tell me?!"

"I'm telling you now, so calm down and sit back down and let me explain what's happening."

Ren begrudgingly sat down and listened.

Astaroth sighed, took a deep breath, and said, "It's an archangel. One of them made a move."

Ren, shocked, said, "What? An archangel! Are you serious?!"

Astaroth nodded. "Yes, an archangel, and this angel has an interesting plan."

Ren leaned closer to hear this plan better and to get more details.

"This angel called all the angels that were stationed to guard the seals to come back to heaven."

"Really, why?"

"So he could guard all the seals himself."

Ren didn't understand what he meant, but didn't interrupt him and let Astaroth keep talking.

Astaroth said, "Archangels are master spell castors. They know a wide variety of spells, some Lucifer knows and some that he doesn't. And this spell is new to him. What this angel did is send what's left of the seals that hadn't been broken a clone of himself to guard them. Now, these clones are—no, were—as strong as the real archangel, they only have one fourth of the original archangel's strength. I know that's small, but still, even with one fourth of an archangel's true strength, it is still far beyond any demon with the rank of 201 and up."

Astaroth stopped to get another sip of whiskey.

Ren said, "I see, but what about Azazel? Has he not been able to break any seals?"

Astaroth gave a big burp and said, "What are you talking about? Remember he is one of the ten demon kings. He is supposed to have the strength to fight a fully powered archangel, so those clones are nothing to him but since he can only show up to the world of the living so many times, we haven't been making that much progress."

Ren leaned back on his chair, thinking to himself about all this news. Then he asked, "Are the clones the reason we are having so many casualties?"

"Well, they did kill a lot of demons, but they are not the only reason. Remember the other angels that were supposed to guard the seals are not guarding them anymore, so what are they doing right now?"

Ren only shook his head, meaning he had no answer for Astaroth's question.

Astaroth said, "They are hunting down every demon on earth with the help of the other angels that weren't stationed to guard seals, and the humans are helping too. Not to mention the monsters. They are capturing and killing so many demons that our numbers are falling at an alarming rate."

Ren was looking down and thinking to himself, "That's right. Some demons have some other missions besides to break seals, and some demons don't care about the seals and are just going around doing whatever they want on earth."

Ren said, "I see. So what do you want me to do?"

Astaroth looked away from Ren for a second but he looked back at him and said, "That's up to you, but before you give me that answer, I have to tell you one more thing."

Ren raised an eyebrow and said, "What is it?"

Astaroth took a deep breath. "The archangel that cast the clone spell is also on earth guarding a seal in Washington, D.C.'s Saint Patrick's church."

"What? Then why hasn't Azazel gone and fought him?"

"Two reasons. One, it's much easier and more tactical to go for the weaker ones so he could break a seal. And two, he wants you to fight the archangel."

Ren was hesitant to even talk. He was shaking but he mustered up the courage to talk. "Me... Why me? I can't take on an archangel! Why would Azazel want me to do it?"

"Because we think—no, we know that this archangel is the angel that sent you to hell and killed all of your friends, and family, even the pets."

Ren's eyes widened for a second, then they went back to normal. Ren raised his head up slowly, inhaled, and exhaled from his nose very loudly. Then Ren jumped up from his chair with great force and slammed his hands on Astaroth's desk, cracking it.

Astaroth would have been mad at any other time, but he understood why Ren was so angry. Ren was shaking in pure frustration, but he moved his hands away from the desk, turned to look at the door, and said, frustration evident in his voice, "It's at the Washington, D.C., church, right?"

"Yes."

"I'm going, but before I leave, what is this archangel's name."

Astaroth didn't hesitate to answer that question. "One of the seven archangels, and the fourth son of god himself: Raphael."

Ren didn't say anything when he heard that. All he did was walk toward the door. "Take me to Washington, D.C., Saint Patrick's church." He left.

After Ren left Astaroth's office, Astaroth said, "Ren, I know you're very angry, but be careful. He is far beyond your league."

Ren was speed-walking toward the other end of the hallway, swinging both of his arms with great force. However, when he got closer and closer to the end of the hallway, Ren was slowing down with every step he took until he was in front of the red door.

Ren was so angry that he kept repeating in his mind, "Kill him, kill that bastard, kill that angel for everything he did."

But Ren's body wouldn't move. He was in front of the door. All he had to do was lift his right hand, open the door, and he would be in front of the church. But his body wouldn't respond.

Ren was very angry, but his fear was more powerful. His fear was telling him to "Stop and go back, this won't end well for you, start with one of the clones first."

But Ren couldn't do any of that. The person Ren was looking for so long was going to be right in front of him. He just couldn't ignore it and walk away. So Ren took the longest breath of his life and exhaled.

Ren closed his eyes and saw pictures in his mind of his family and friends with him all having fun—laughing, smiling, and crying together. Ren opened his eyes with a calm but serious look. Then Ren's arm finally started to move. He opened the door and walked out. The door shut behind him and it disappeared.

Ren was now in front of Saint Patrick's church. He looked left and right, and what was surprising was that the place Ren was at didn't look that bad compared to the other cities and towns he had been to. Of course, most of the building's windows were broken. The same thing could be said for the walls, but they were in okay condition considering the whole apocalypse thing.

Ren walked up the steps that were in front of the church and walked up to the front door. He could feel his heart beating really fast. He was scared, nervous, angry, and many other emotions were swirling inside him like a tornado. He didn't know if his emotions were going to destroy him or help him. But all he knew was that it was time to meet him. After one more loud exhale, Ren shook off any hesitation left. He transformed into his demon form and finally opened the door.

Ren walked in, looking around to see, hear, or sense anyone's presence. But so far—nothing. Ren could see the statue all the way on the other side of the church. Not a scratch on it. At least for now. Ren took another step forward toward the statue, and then he could feel it—an enormous amount of grace just appeared on top of him. It was so big that Ren felt like he was going to be crushed.

However Ren put on a smile and said, "You do have an enormous power, but it's not as bad as Lucifer, Satan, and Lilith."

A voice echoed through the church, "Hmm, you better watch what you say, boy, I would think. You don't want me to get angry, do you?" The voice sounded very annoyed at what Ren said.

Ren was moving his eyes around to try to see where the voice was coming from. He couldn't see anyone in front of him so he turned around to see if he was behind. But when he turned around, he heard a piano being played behind him.

Ren quickly turned again to see a black man with a white clean suit and long silver dreadlocks that reached to his seat. He was playing the piano. Ren had never heard someone play a piano so well and so beautifully before in his life.

But Ren had had enough and yelled at the man, "Turn around and face me!"

The man stopped playing and indeed turned for Ren. The man's facial structure was so perfect he looked like he came from a painting. Ren couldn't look away from him. Even when he spoke, it sounded like a beautiful instrument being played elegantly.

"So do you know who I am?"

Ren didn't say anything at first but then he shook his head and said, "Yes, I know who you are, Raphael."

Raphael gave a little smirk and crossed his arms and said, "You look like you have a lot of questions. I guess I could answer some, if you like? Before our fight, since I'm being so kind."

"Yes, I do. I want to know from you and you alone, and I want a straight answer, no bullshit. Are you the one that sent me to hell?"

Raphael didn't answer. He just stared at Ren. And that pissed Ren off even more.

So Ren asked again, but this time he yelled in fury, "Are you the one who sent me to hell?!"

Raphael didn't answer again for a couple seconds. But then he finally said something. It was short and quiet but Ren heard it. "Yes."

Ren spread his wings with such great force that he shattered every remaining glass window in the church.

"Before we get started, I have to know why? Why did you send me to hell and kill everyone I know and love?!"

Raphael put a finger to his perfect face and said, "Well, it's quite simple really." He stopped talking and gave Ren a cold look. "I was bored, that's all."

Ren's eyes were blank, his arms and wings fell, and he looked like he was going to collapse. All he could say was, "What?"

Raphael sighed, looked at Ren and said, "I was bored in heaven. Out of all the archangels, I'm the one that loves to fight. But it's forbidden for an archangel to fight another archangel in heaven or on earth, and all the other angels in heaven are too weak for me to fight. The same can be said about you demons. I was so bored, it felt like I was rotting away from how bored I was. Then I found you…"

Ren had heard enough. He spread his wings again and his arms in a threatening posture. With great force, a red aura appeared around Ren. It was massive and hot. Raphael looked around and could see that all the books, chairs, and everything else that was made of paper and wood caught on fire.

Then Ren shouted with a demonic voice and blood-red eyes, "ARE YOU SE-

RIOUS?! YOU SENT ME TO HELL AND KILLED EVERYONE I KNOW JUST BECAUSE YOU WERE FUCKING BORED!!!"

Raphael put one of his fingers in his ear and said, "Geez, can you be quiet? We are in a church, after all. And yes, that is literally what I just said. But technically the part about killing your family and friends… That is your fault."

"WHAT DID YOU JUST SAY?! WHY WAS IT MY FAULT?!"

"Well, when I sent you to hell, I was hoping you would immediately try to break the first seal and start this whole war so we could fight sooner. But unfortunately, you didn't have enough hate for me—you still had a lot of humanity in you. So thanks to the spies in hell, they told me you were going to the world of the living to see all of your family and friends to say, 'Hey, I'm okay and I'm going to try to live my life again.' So I sent my soldiers to kill them so you would hate me more… and here we are. They are dead because you still had humanity in you. So if you had tried to break the first seal when you became a demon, your friends and family would maybe still be alive. Maybe you would have sent them to Japan to keep them safe. But no, that didn't happen, and here we are."

When he heard all of that, Ren looked down. Raphael could not see his face, then Ren swung his right arm with great force and the entire wall that was behind him blew into millions of pieces.

The aura got even stronger and then it vanished. It went quiet for a while, then Raphael could hear something.

It sounded like a sizzling noise.

Raphael gave a big smile and said, "Ah, I see you're going up the ranks again. You know, I'm very jealous of you demons. We angels, humans, and monsters have to train to get stronger but you demons get stronger from training and from your sins. The stronger the sin you're showing, the stronger you get. In this case, it's your wrath."

When Raphael was talking to Ren, all Ren was doing was grunting from the burning pain from going up the ranking system. He put his right hand on his number, in pain.

Raphael was still talking: "So, I wonder what number you will get now. Coming from the damage you did to this church just from getting angry, I can say it's going to be high."

Then the sizzling stopped. Ren was still squeezing on his chest, blocking the numbers. Raphael was just standing there in silence. Then out of nowhere, Ren just leapt toward Raphael, with both of his weapons already formed on his hands with great speed.

Ren was in front of Raphael and was going to try to stab Raphael on both sides of his face, but before Ren's blades got close to him, Raphael grabbed both of his arms, sending shockwaves at the church and cracking it.

Raphael looked at Ren's chest and saw his new numbers. He had been at 1250 but was now at 1200.

Raphael started to laugh with excitement and said, "Okay, let's do this, but not here."

Ren replied, somehow back in his normal tone of voice, "Okay, where? In a different dimension?"

"No. Better." Raphael loosened his grip just on Ren's right arm then moved his head fast, indicating he was going to use his telekinesis. Ren's right arm went flying backwards, dislocating it. Then Raphael snapped his finger, teleporting him and Ren to somewhere else. Ren didn't focus on where Raphael teleported them to. He was still focused on Raphael.

Ren didn't care about his right arm being dislocated. His regeneration fixed it in no time. So Ren tried to stab him again, but Raphael kicked him in the stomach, sending him flying back. Ren used his wing to stop himself.

Now that Ren had some distance from Raphael, he could finally notice his environment around him. The first thing he noticed was the cold winds, and then he looked around and noticed a lot of mountains surrounding them.

Raphael said, "Welcome to Nepal, the home of the biggest mountain on earth: Mount Everest."

Ren looked to his left and could see Mount Everest.

Raphael said, "This will be our battleground, and since there are no humans, demons, angels, or any type of monsters around here for millions of miles—I made sure of that—there will be no interruption." With that, Raphael lifted his left arm to summon his weapon.

He summoned a double-edged Egyptian fan axe with strange markings all around it that Ren had never seen before. Ren curled his fingers into fists and raised them both into the stance of a boxer. The fight began.

Ren moved his right hand with great speed to shoot a big fire ball at Raphael. He shot another one with his left hand and then flapped his wings to follow the second fireball.

Raphael just shook his head in annoyance. He put his weapon on his right hand, with his free left hand, he raised it, and made it like a handgun.

"Bang bang." Two bits of water that were the shape and size of bullets shot from Raphael's fingertips.

The two water bullets hit both of Ren's fireballs that were coming toward Raphael, fully extinguishing them and spreading steam where they had been.

However, Ren was behind one of the fireballs, so he came out of the steam cloud and swung with his right hand, trying to cut Raphael's throat. Raphael blocked it with relative ease.

However, that didn't stop Ren.

When his right hand was connected to Raphael's weapon, Ren swung with his left hand. But Raphael, with his great strength, moved his weapon ever so slightly to block Ren's other arm.

Ren tried to stop Raphael with all his strength, but he couldn't. So Raphael stopped the other attack. But Ren was still not finished—he still had the weapons on both of his feet. So Ren raised both of his legs to slash Raphael from his groin to his head.

But once again, Raphael saw it coming a mile away, and he gave Ren a wink from his eye, which sent Ren flying away from him with great force. Ren stopped himself in mid-air before he slammed into a mountain.

Ren thought, "He used his telekinesis to throw me away! With that much force from a wink." Ren was getting angrier by the second.

Raphael smiled and moved his weapon so it was behind him and went into a fighting stance. He pointed at Ren and kept curling his finger at him, indicating that he wanted Ren to come on and keep attacking him. Ren obliged and came at Raphael.

Ren did a spin kick, but Raphael blocked it. He threw an upper cut at Raphael, but he blocked that too. Then Ren shot hellfire with his free arm at Raphael, but he dodged out of the way. Raphael just kept dodging, blocking, or shooting holy water at Ren's attacks. But Ren just kept attacking him, slash after slash, kick after kick, punch after punch, even throwing a couple of headbutts, but Raphael just blocked or dodged all of them with ease.

While they were fighting, every hit or block sent a huge shock wave around the area, shaking the snow in the mountains and causing a lot of avalanches. However, Ren had had enough of this and used his telekinesis to send Raphael flying only a couple feet back so Ren could take some steps back as well.

Surprisingly, it worked! Raphael went back a few feet and Ren flew back a few feet too. They were both not breathing heavily—they were not even sweating at all—but now they had gotten some distance from each other Ren said, "Stop messing around!"

Raphael teased, "What do you mean?"

"Don't play dumb. You haven't attacked me yet. Hell, when you are blocking my attacks, I can tell you aren't even trying at that either! You're just messing with me!"

Raphael sighed and said, "Sorry, sorry. I'm a bit rusty. I haven't fought in some time now, so let me stretch a bit." With his weapon still in his hands, he started to stretch.

Ren said, "Oh no, I'm not going to let you..."

Raphael swung his axe up when he was stretching, which sent an air slash toward Ren. It hit something. What it hit was the mountain that was behind Ren, completely splitting it in half.

But Ren didn't notice the mountain being cut in half behind him. He was focusing on what he could see with his right eye. In fact, he couldn't feel anything on his right side. All Ren could feel was a great deal a pain.

What happened was that the air slash literally cut Ren in half. His right half was falling toward the ground while the left side was still up in the air. A lot of blood, pieces of bones, and some of Ren's entrails were falling out of his body.

They all immediately disintegrated before any of it came close to hitting the ground and Ren fully regenerated. When his body fully regenerated back to normal, he was lost for words. The sheer amount of pain he felt just from an air slash that Raphael maybe did on purpose was too much for Ren to comprehend.

Raphael stopped stretching and looked at Ren with a shocked look. "WOW, sorry about that. I didn't mean to cut you and that mountain in half. That was an accident."

Ren widened his eyes so much that they looked like they would pop out.

Ren thought, "That was an accident? An accident?! Oh God!"

Raphael smiled and made his weapon vanish. "Okay, let's have some fun."

Ren gave him a scared look, knowing what was going to happen. He turned around and flew away. He was flying so fast that his sweat was coming off his body faster than his body could produce it. Then a hand grabbed Ren's shoulder, crushing it.

"Sorry. When I said let's have fun, I meant it." He turned Ren around and punched right through Ren's chest. Ren was spitting out blood on Raphael, but he didn't care. In fact, it seemed like he liked it.

Raphael quickly moved his hand out of Ren's chest and karate chopped Ren's forehead so hard that it split Ren's head into two. Both of Ren's eyeballs completely came out, blood and brains sprayed everywhere. Ren's body was falling but Ren's head and the hole in his chest regenerated back to normal in no time.

Ren screamed, "YOU SON OF A BITCH!!" and shot a huge pillar of hellfire at Raphael.

Ren saw it hit Raphael and he started to laugh, thinking he just killed or really hurt Raphael, but then Raphael said, "Hey, could you turn down the heat? I don't like it hot." He swatted the flames away with the back of his hand.

Ren said, "No way. That's impossible." He was shaking unbelievably. He never saw someone take a hellfire blast head on and not take any damage whatsoever. Was Raphael's grace that much more powerful than Ren's sin?

Then Ren knew he only had one thing left to try to kill, or at least hurt, Raphael. Ren landed on the ground gently, then quickly jumped up at Raphael with his top speed, trying to do an uppercut. Ren hit something. The shock wave made all the clouds around them disappear.

But what Ren thought was a hit wasn't a hit, it was a grab. Raphael grabbed Ren's attack at top speed.

Ren said, "No, that's not possible. How could you even see my attack coming? I was moving at 450,000 miles per hour."

Raphael shook his head slowly like he was getting rid of a headache and said, "Oh boy. Look, Ren, your speed is good and all, but it's nothing to an archangel's speed."

Raphael let go of Ren's arm.

Ren grabbed his arm and said, "What? How fast can you go?"

"Wait, you actually don't know? Let me guess: Astaroth and Azazel didn't tell you how fast archangels are."

Ren looked down in embarrassment and said quietly, like a kid being made fun of for something he didn't know, "No, I don't."

"Okay, I'll tell you. Let's see. I have to remember half of my power if being restricted right now, so... Actually, instead of telling you, let me ask you this: how fast is the speed of light?"

Ren gave a very quiet, "Nooo."

Even though it was quiet, Raphael gave a big smile indicating he heard Ren.

"Yes, the answer is 670 million miles per hour. But my speed is 680 million miles per hour. Ten million more than light."

Ren didn't say anything. In fact, Ren's face looked like it was going to come off.

"Well, my speed isn't the best, but it's not the worst either. I'm like in the middle compared to the other archangels. So I can't really complain. But that's enough talk. Let me give you a glimpse of my speed."

When Ren heard what Raphael just said he was going into a defensive possessing but—

CRASH!!!

Something hit the mountain behind Ren with great force.

Ren didn't see or hear it because what crashed into the mountain was Ren's skull.

Raphael moved so fast that Ren didn't even react. Ren's body still had the neck and lower jaw attached, but his lower jaw was missing some teeth.

Ren's head fully regenerated back, and when it did, Ren immediately tried to snap his fingers to try to teleport away, knowing that he couldn't win now.

"Hey, Ren, if you are going to teleport away, aren't you going to need this?"

Raphael lifted up his right arm and when he did that, Ren could see that Raphael had Ren's right hand in the snapping position. Ren looked at his arm to see that his hand was indeed missing.

Ren remained calm. He was going to try to teleport again with his left hand while looking at Raphael, but when he was looking at him—Raphael dropped Ren's arm and pointed at Ren with a bloody finger. Blood was squirting out from all over Ren's body. What happened was that Raphael moved and poked holes all over Ren's body with his finger without Ren even knowing he did that.

Ren fell from the sky and crashed on the ground, sending smoke everywhere.

Raphael said, "Well, it looks like we are done. Thanks, Ren, for somewhat entertaining me."

Then from within the smoke, two huge fireballs came out of the smoke, heading toward Raphael.

Raphael, annoyed, said, "Really, you don't know when to quit, do you?" So Raphael inhaled and blew the two fireballs away and the smoke where the two fireballs came from.

Raphael said, "Aa, I see. They were a distraction for you to get away. Nice move, Ren."

It was just like Raphael said: Ren was gone. He did use those fireballs as distractions so he could get away.

Raphael said, "Well, round one goes to me. Now then, let me fix all the mountains that we damaged for our next encounter."

Ren was in a dark hallway. He was slamming his fist on the ground, cracking and making a hole. That hole was getting bigger and bigger with every hit.

Ren was yelling, "Damn it, damn it! That wasn't a fight—it was just training for him! I can't beat him! Not with the power that I currently have! Power, power—I need more power. Astaroth!" Ren looked straight ahead and ran as fast as he could to reach the other side.

When Ren reached the other side and was in front of the red door, he yelled "Take me to Astaroth's office!"

The door handles glowed in front of him and Ren opened it.

Astaroth was just relaxing in his chair, listening to some old opera music while drinking some tea. It seemed Astaroth was taking a break from paperwork and was just trying to relax...until Ren opened his door with great speed and ran into his office. The air current that came behind Ren hit Astaroth and all of his neatly organized paperwork went flying everywhere.

Ren didn't even apologize. Hell, Astaroth thought Ren didn't notice because Ren was in a blood rage.

Ren grabbed Astaroth by the suit and pulled him closer. Ren stank of sweat, but once again, Ren didn't seem to notice his own stink. Ren was saying, "Power, I need more power, Astaroth, give me power."

In the midst of all this, Ren was transforming into his true demon form.

Astaroth rolled his red eyes and flicked his left wrist, which sent Ren flying and crashing into Astaroth's wall, holding him there.

Astaroth said calmly but angrily, "Calm down, Ren. Take a deep breath and ask me again."

Ren was trying to break free from Astaroth's telekinesis but Ren quickly gave up and listened to what Astaroth said. He took multiple deep breaths for a while. Then Ren said in his normal tone of voice, "Okay, okay, I've calmed down. You can let me go now. I'm sorry."

Astaroth nodded and let Ren go. Ren landed on his feet and was just standing there while Astaroth used his telekinesis to completely reorganize all his papers that went flying when Ren showed up.

Ren walked toward Astaroth's desk, pulled up a seat and sat down.

Astaroth sat as well and gave Ren a cup of hot tea. He said, "Okay, Ren. Drink that. It will calm your nerves and when you are done, ask me again what you want."

Ren just nodded and picked up the cup of tea, but the cup was shaking due to Ren's anger. He blew on the tea to cool it off so it wouldn't burn his lips. Then he, ever-so-slowly, took small sips to savor the flavor and because it was still a little hot.

When Ren decided he'd had enough sips, he put the cup down on his lap, took a deep breath, and said, "I want—no, I need—more power. I can guess you already know from my entrance earlier."

Astaroth said, "Yes, I know. But not just because of your entrance. I saw your fight as well."

Ren was not shocked. He sort of remembered Astaroth saying he kept track of all of his subordinates' actions. So Ren drank some more of his tea instead of saying anything. But out of nowhere, Astaroth just stood up and walked toward the door. Ren's eyes followed Astaroth's movements, trying to figure out what he was doing until Astaroth said, "Take us to Satan and Lucifer." The door handle glowed. Astaroth turned just his head and said, "If you want power, follow me."

Ren didn't say anything again. All he did was finish his tea, put the cup on Astaroth's desk, walked toward Astaroth, and shut the door behind him.

They were both walking in a dark hallway with a little light from the torches on the walls. All they were doing was walking. They were not talking to each other. In fact, they were so quiet that all they could hear was their own footsteps. Each and every step.

But Astaroth did turn his head to look at Ren. Astaroth clearly wanted to say something to Ren, but he could tell that Ren was not in a talking mood anymore. At least he didn't want to talk to Astaroth All Ren wanted was to talk to Satan and Lucifer.

After a couple more minutes of walking in silence, they both made it to the other side. Astaroth said, "My lords, we are entering," and opened the door.

They both walked in, and the door shut by itself behind Ren. When Ren and Astaroth fully saw Satan and Lucifer, Astaroth immediately fell on one knee and bowed his head, showing respect to his gods. But Ren didn't bow. Instead he crossed his arms with an impatient look on his face.

But luckily for Ren, Satan and Lucifer were already used to Ren's behavior toward them.

Lucifer said with a smirky attitude, "Aah, Ren, welcome. It's nice to see you. Tell me: how was that beat down that my little brother gave you?"

Ren did not answer. He only gave Lucifer a cool look and tightened his grip on his hands.

Lucifer liked the look that Ren was giving him so he kept teasing Ren. "What? Got nothing to say? Come on, you were asking for your ass to get kicked. Like, come on, what can a little shit like you can do to a—?"

Before Lucifer finished his sentence, Satan interrupted him. "Stop it, Lucifer. I know you don't care about all the wannabe angels out there. But I know you still care about the other archangels because they are your brothers. But remember, they are our enemies."

Lucifer just raised his shoulders and gave a little smirk. Lucifer knew his brothers were the enemies in this war, but he could not keep himself from teasing Ren.

Satan gave a little sigh, looked at Ren, and said, "Ren, what Lucifer said is true. You were reckless and impatient. You knew only me, Lucifer, and the ten demon kings can take on an archangel."

Ren looked down in embarrassment, like a kid being scolded by his parents. However, Satan was not done with the scolding.

Satan said, "Look. In normal circumstances we wouldn't care about you and your humiliation by Raphael. But you did start this war for us, and you still have the most seals broken, but Azazel is getting close. So we can't afford to lose you yet. So we will help you get more power."

Ren looked back up with a serious look on his face and, without looking away from Satan's eyes and without even blinking, asked, "How can I get this power?"

Lucifer instead said something. "Let me ask you a question first."

Ren turned his head to look at Lucifer with the same look that he gave Satan.

Lucifer said, "Tell me—what kind of demons exist in hell?"

Ren didn't understand at first, so he had to think about the question that Lucifer just asked him. He put his right hand on his snake chin and said, "Well, there are three kinds of demons. The first are the human demons, then created demons, and then fallen angel demons."

Lucifer gave a big old smile and said, "Correct! For you to get more power from us we must turn you into a different class of demon. To be more exact—a created demon."

Ren thought, "A created demon?!" He said, "How and why turn me into a created demon?"

Satan answered Ren's question this time. "It's because they have fewer restrictions and limitations."

Ren looked confused by Satan's answer so Satan kept on explaining.

"Humans have so many limitations when it comes to strength, knowledge, and power. When you became a demon, those limitations got removed, but compared to the other two classes of demons, there is now a new limit."

"I don't understand."

Satan said, "Okay, maybe those limitations didn't get removed. They got very weakened because, think about it—you killed so many angels but before your fight with Aruru, you didn't get stronger. Why is that?"

Ren's eyes widened in shock. Ren thought, "He's right! I fought so many strong angels before Aruru, but for some reason, I didn't get stronger. I stayed at 1995."

Satan said, "So you get it now? Even though you are a demon now, you were once human, and that's holding you back from getting stronger, unlike the created and fallen angels."

Ren said with a little smile, "I see. Okay, I understand, but now I'm going to be a created demon, so no more boundaries."

Lucifer said, "Now hold on. You do realize there is a risk or two for this to happen."

Ren sighed and stomped his foot on the ground like a kid about to go through a temper tantrum. "Of fucking course. What is it!?"

Satan moved his finger ever so slightly. Ren fell on both of his knees.

Ren said, "Ugh?!" He was in pain because it happened out of nowhere.

It was because Satan was using his telekinesis. Satan said, "Don't give us that tone, boy. We will help you, but tone it down."

Satan stopped using his telekinesis, so Ren was free, and he was slowly getting up, now thinking twice about what he should say.

Satan said, "Now then. Let's talk about the risks." Satan lifted up his hand and showed one finger, his pointer finger. "First, when we do the ritual to turn you into a created demon, there is a slight chance that you might—"

"Die," Ren interrupted.

Satan shook his head back and forth. But when he stopped, he spoke again. "No, you don't die. You go into a coma forever."

Ren was shocked by that answer—so shocked that he took a couple steps back, because going into a comatose state sounded worse than death. But then he stopped shaking and looked at Satan and said, with a raised eyebrow, "Really? A coma? Tell me this—how do you know that's going to happen?"

Lucifer said, "Because you aren't the first demon to ask for this power."

Ren didn't say anything. He felt stupid. He should have known that was going to be the answer.

Satan said, "Not including you, there were fifty demons that asked for more power, and we tried giving them the power."

"How many succeeded?"

Lucifer said, "Only three passed. The rest fell into a coma and we killed them because there was no cure and there was no point in wasting good resources on them."

Ren thought, "Even though it sounds cruel, like they just gave up on them, I guess it's more of a mercy to end their suffering." He gulped and said, "Okay, what's the second risk?"

Lucifer said, "Well, this risk doesn't count as a risk to—well, every other demon except you."

Ren didn't understand what Lucifer meant, but he was going to find out.

Satan said, "If the ritual is a success and you become a demon, then you will then see humans as lesser beings."

Ren's eyes once again widened. Then Satan said, "We all know you still see humans as equals, and you feel terrible for starting this war and making them all suffer. We know because of your humanity you won't eat, torture, or rape any humans; instead you give a disgusted look to any demon that does those things. You only kill humans if they get in your way. But if the ritual works, you might—or will—do all the things you despise."

Ren immediately said, "But if I lose my humanity, would that mean I will lose my reason for hating Raphael and I might not like anime anymore?"

Lucifer said, "Really? You're worried about not liking anime anymore? Sigh, no, you'll still like anime, and as for the other reason—no, you will see humans as inferior creators, but you'll still have your memories of all the good times with your friends and family. Yes, you might see them as inferior too, but those will be the only humans you'll still like and so your hatred for Raphael will get stronger because he took the only humans that you like away from you."

There was a long pause.

Satan said, "Well, Ren, do you still want to do it, knowing the risks? Decide."

Every eye looked toward Ren. Ren was shaking, trying to think of an answer while scratching his head. He had no idea what to do.

Ren thought, "What am I going to do? I'm not that scared about the coma thing but my humanity—is it really worth it? Is it worth becoming those other demons that I look down on for being disgusting creatures for what they do to humans just for revenge?"

While Ren was thinking really hard, he was scratching his head really hard too. He scratched so hard that his head was bleeding really bad. Then Ren, for some reason, remembered all the good times with his family and friends in every single detail, which put a smile on Ren's face. But then that smile slowly faded away and into a frown because Ren was now imagining all of his loved ones being brutally slaughtered by the angels—all because of Raphael. Raphael. Raphael. RAPHAEL!!!

"AAAAAHHHHH! NO, I NEED TO KILL RAPHAEL! HE HAS TO DIE!!"

Lucifer gave a creepy and big smile and said, "Good. Now, let's get things started."

Both Satan and Lucifer stood up. Satan said, "Ren, come closer."

Ren walked closer toward Satan and Lucifer.

Lucifer said, "Okay, stop. That's good enough. Satan and Astaroth, get into position."

Astaroth, who was still kneeling and hadn't said anything throughout the conversation, said, "Yes, my Lord," and moved with great speed to a certain spot.

Satan and Lucifer both got smaller until they were both Ren's height. Satan clapped his hands together and, with a quick movement, separated them. This made a shock wave that carved the ground all around Satan, Lucifer, Astaroth, and Ren.

What the carving looked like was a large triangle that was connecting Satan, Lucifer, and Astaroth. They were each on a separate point of the triangle, but the points were circles and they were standing in the center of them. Around the circle were the Roman numbers for a clock. The three of them had the numbers surrounding them, and finally there was a line in front of all three of them that led to the center of the triangle, where Ren was in the middle, in his own little circle.

Then all three of them started to talk in Hebrew. "וה שמש תרדהנ תדדועש ונתוא סונייקוא רדהנ שנותו ונל סוקמ להרוג איבי אויר. והו אדמה הלודג הנתנש ונל להתקייס. אוי אוקיינוס צללים. אנא עזרו ונל להעניק קינע דשל הז כוח עצרם כך שהיה יהיה מכת על האנושה." What it meant was, "O great sun that gives us shadows to hide. O great ocean that give us a place to kill our foes. And O great earth that lets us exist. Please help us grant this demon immense power so that he will be a plague on humanity."

Two chains came out of the ground right next to Ren. One stabbed Ren's left palm while the other did the same thing to his right. Then both were pulling Ren down so that he was on his knees.

Ren was grunting loudly but, in his mind, he kept saying, "This is nothing compared to when I was being tortured." Then a third chain came from behind him and wrapped around his mouth and went back into the ground, pulling Ren's head back a little bit because that chain was for Ren to bite on while he screamed in pain.

Then Satan, Lucifer, and Astaroth all opened their eyelids and Ren could see that they didn't have any eyes; it was like they never had them to begin with. All three of them lifted their left hands and, with their right hand, slit their wrists. The blood was not disintegrating—instead their blood was steaming. And when the blood hit the ground, it started to move toward Ren.

Ren could see the blood moving toward him while also feeling that the temperature was getting hotter. Ren realized that the blood was making the temperature super-hot, which explained why it was steaming.

Ren shook in fear, but he couldn't break free; the chains were just too tight. Then the blood finally hit him.

"MMMMMMMMMMMM!!" He screamed in pain. He felt like he was being touched by magma. Then the ground on which he was kneeling started to melt and he started to sink in.

He thought, "Why is only this spot being melted?" He realized that he was going to be in a little puddle of this magma blood. Ren was screaming so loud that every demon could hear him screaming. Ren's entire body sank in the puddle of blood and no one could hear him He were only a few bubbles and the blood started to glow bright red.

A full week in the world of the living, and a full week since Ren's fight with Raphael went by. The demons were not doing so well ever since Raphael used that spell to make clones of himself for every church. The only demon able to break a seal was Azazel, but he could only do that so many times with his time limit on the world of the living. While every other demon was being captured, exorcised, or killed, it was not going well for the demons at all. Every human and angel had a smile on their faces, knowing they were winning the war.

Well... every angel except one.

Raphael said, "Damn it!"

He was very angry. He was in his office sitting on his big leather chair listening to his water and lava falls and some soothing music.

So why was Raphael so angry? Well, as it turns out—

"Damn it! Forty-something years since this thing was invented and I've still only got two sides!" Raphael was playing with a Rubik's cube and he was getting mad that he couldn't solve it, like a kid.

"That's it! I'm done!" He slammed the cube on his table. "I will win someday. Ah, I'm so bored. No demon is coming into my church to fight me. And it's been a week since I fought Ren. I bet he is training or working up a strategy to try to kill me, I guess." Raphael's chair leaned back onto his desk and he put both of his hands on his face to rub off the sleepiness. "Maybe I'll go take a nap a—"

A red light appeared in his office from behind a wall, making a very loud and annoying noise. But that put a smile on Raphael's face.

"Ah. Someone has entered my church. And I get the feeling it's Ren." Raphael stood up from his chair in excitement and quickly snapped his finger to teleport himself to the church.

Inside the badly damaged church, Ren, in his demon form, was sitting on a bench, legs crossed and both arms behind the bench, waiting for Raphael. A bright white light appeared inside the church. Raphael slowly descended from the ceiling, trying to show how beautiful and majestic he was. But Ren was not having this shit, so he summoned his weapon, and immediately attacked Raphael.

Raphael said, "WHOA there!" He grabbed Ren's right arm and spun him around so fast that it looked like a mini tornado was about to form. "Ren, it's so good to see you too. I know you're really eager to fight, but, let me change the setting first."

Raphael snapped with his free hand while they were still spinning and teleported them back to Mount Everest. Raphael let him go, and the force made Ren fly away from Raphael, breaking the sound barrier, and Ren crashed into a mountain. Raphael summoned his wings and his Egyptian fan axe and slowly moved closer to where Ren was. Ren kicked the rubble that was around him, completely unscathed. He flew up so he could be face-to-face with Raphael.

Raphael and Ren were both flying in the air, not saying a word to each other. The only noises that they could hear were the cold winds and the animals howling at them—or, to be more precise, at Ren.

Raphael said, "Well, aren't you going to say something? And why are you blocking the number on your chest, and why are you looking down? What? You got promoted again? Show me." Raphael was very curious as to what Ren was about to say and or show.

Ren started to laugh uncontrollably. And then he said, "You want to know why I'm covering my number? This is the reason!" Ren moved his hand away. The number on Ren's chest completely shocked Raphael.

Ren's number was 1200 the last time they saw each other, but now it was 200. Ren had become a demon general.

"Not only that—I'm a demon general, but I'm not a human demon anymore. I'm a created demon now! I'm so much more powerful now than I was for our first fight! What do you have to say now, Raphael?!" The way Ren was talking sounded very sadistic and insane.

Raphael said, "Ren you—you—" He put his right hand on his face.

"What? Are you scared?"

"You couldn't be even more of a disappointment."

Ren fell silent. All of that insane laughter just vanished and all Ren could say was, "What?"

Raphael said, "It is true that you got much stronger than last time. And yes, I don't know how you became a created demon—probably from an intense spell from my disgraced older brother—but you are still no match against me."

Ren began to only see red and he started to grind his teeth. "SHUT UP!" He moved with great speed and clashed with Raphael. The shock waves were so great that they cut the tip of a mountain off.

Ren moved his hand up to grab Raphael's weapon to hold him in place. He then moved both of his legs up to cut Raphael. But Raphael blocked both incoming legs with his left arm. Ren thought he saw an opening, so with his left free arm, he raised it up, about to throw a punch.

Raphael, of course, moved his head out of the way of the punch. But Ren knew he was going to do that, so his arm moved counterclockwise so that his palm was facing Raphael's face. And with a quick motion, Ren opened his palm and shot Raphael in the face with a blast of hellfire, completely catching him off guard. But Ren knew that wouldn't be enough, so he opened his mouth and shot hellfire into Raphael's face as well. Ren must have learned how to shoot fire out of his mouth when he turned into a created demon.

Raphael said, "Stop it. I can't see." He let go of his weapon and moved his fist so fast that Ren couldn't react to it. His fist made contact with Ren's face, and the impact made his eyes pop out of his skull. It sent him flying back.

Ren's head fully healed and he spread his arms, legs, and wings apart to slow himself down. It was working for a little while until Ren felt a humongous pain on his stomach. It was Raphael kicking him with both of his feet with his arms crossed. Ren was sent down even faster and crashed into the ground. It shook the mountain right next to where he landed and caused an avalanche, but he got out of the way before it came close to hitting him.

Ren flew at Raphael with a sadistic look on his face. He swung to the left, he swung to the right—he just kept on attacking Raphael with a barrage of punches and kicks. After dodging for a while, Raphael had enough and moved his head to the left. Ren moved to the left with great speed. But Ren stopped himself from going any further.

Ren looked up toward Raphael and saw Raphael swing his axe to the side. Ren knew what was about to happen, so he put both arms up in front of himself to block the air slash that Raphael had just made. The mountain behind Ren got cut in half horizontally; the impact was so powerful that the top half that got cut off flew up a couple hundred feet until it fell back to the ground, hitting its bottom half and destroying itself entirely.

Ren was breathing heavily and said, "Ha, see? I didn't get cut in half this time. You only damaged my lungs and cut off both of my arms." With that, both of Ren's arms fell off his body.

But out of nowhere, Raphael said with a cold look, "Stop, just stop." He pinched his face.

"What did you say?"

"Look, the Ren I know and heard of doesn't rely on brute strength, powerful attacks, and a barrage of attacks. He is cunning, always trying to outsmart his enemies by using his environment around him, or by using his senses, which are surprisingly better than the average demon. But you—you are so angry at me that you blinded yourself." He almost sounded sincere.

Ren looked left to right with just his eyes closed and said, "Well, so what? Killing you is all that matters to me! And as you can see, you are trying harder than our last fight, and from the shock wave from my first attack that cut that mountain, I'm closer to your power."

Raphael gave the biggest sigh of his life and said, "I can't believe this. I sent you to hell, made you start this war, just for you to waste my time. And F.Y.I., I'm still not even close to my full power."

When Ren heard Raphael, he immediately screamed, "LIAR!"

Raphael closed his eyes and spread his arms and wings as far as they could go. Then out of nowhere a huge beam of light struck Raphael, covering him in light. It was so bright that Ren had to cover his eyes with his hands. When Ren realized the light was gone, he moved his hands away to see, and what he saw was something else entirely.

Raphael's entire body was covered in gold armor—even his weapon turned gold. The armor was smooth and perfectly symmetrical; it looked like the armor of a knight, but more graceful and elegant, like the type of armor an angel would wear. The light was bouncing off of the armor and bouncing off of the ice from the mountains, and with birds flying behind him, multiple rainbows behind him, and the enormous amount of power that was radiating from him, it felt like an entire country was on top of Ren.

Ren was at a loss for words. Even his mind was blank except for two words that kept being repeated: "beautiful" and "perfect." Ren looked down and slowly descended to the ground. When Ren finally touched the ground, he fell immediately to his knees.

Raphael appeared in front of Ren at this exact moment. He didn't say anything; he just walked toward Ren. With every step, there was no sound being produced. Even wearing a full suit of armor, it was silent. It was like a feather moving on the ground, not making a sound.

When Raphael reached Ren, he could see water hitting the ground, lots of water.

The water was tears and snot. Ren was crying.

Raphael said, "Don't do that. You are a powerful demon. Show some dignity before you die."

Ren didn't say anything. He was done. All of his anger and fighting spirit was gone. He was just awaiting the killing blow.

Raphael raised his axe. "Goodbye, Ren. You at least gave me some entertainment." And with that, Raphael swung his axe and decapitated Ren.

Ren's head rolled on the ground lifeless, and then light came from Ren's eyes, nose, mouth, ears, and the new hole on his neck. His entire body glowed a bright white, and the light burst all around. Then it stopped and Ren's body was burned black. The mountain breeze sent Ren's body into ashes, blowing away. Ren was dead.

It was completely dark, no light or noise anywhere—or, it used to be, because one by one, torches started to light out of nowhere. One, then two, then three—they kept lighting up in a circle until there were a total of ten torches that were lit in a circle. Five of the flames were crimson red like blood, and the other five flames were black like the darkness itself. And each flame had a demon in front of it.

Each demon was different from its looks to its height, but all of them were standing in front of the torches with their eyes closed (if they even had eyes) and hands behind their backs. While they were standing there, two voices overlapped each other and said a chant: "Oh please, the god of death, who is also known as the grim reaper, please, we offer you these ten demon souls as sacrifices. With all of their strength combined, it's equivalent to the demon we are trying to resurrect. Please accept these offerings so he might come back again."

The two voices that were overlapping each other were Satan and Lucifer. They were still in their giant bodies, but they both were kneeling. At first, there was nothing around the two demon gods to kneel for until a large figure that was covered with a badly damaged cloak appeared in the air.

The cloak was badly torn and very dusty, and if one looked up from underneath the cloak, there was nothing to see. Even trying to look inside the hood, there was nothing, until the cloak figure finally started to talk.

"I accept your offerings, but just this one time. Don't ever ask again." The voice was so cold and scary that it made Lucifer's right arm shake.

Then the cloaked figure raised his arms. The sleeves came back a little bit and two bony hands appeared. They both had multiple scratches and crimson red stains, and on the wrists were very old handcuffs that had been rusted throughout time.

The figure moved his right hand to grab his left hand's pinky and remove it. The figure crushed the finger into dust and spread it around so all ten of the demons could inhale in the dust.

The reaper said, "It is done. Farewell." With that, the figure disappeared like he was never there. Then—

"AAAAAAAAAAAAAAAAAAAAAAA!!!"

All of the demons started screaming in pain because the dust that they inhaled was melting their bodies into mush. It was like watching someone just drop a bowl of acid on you and you watching as your flesh melted away.

Satan and Lucifer just watched with no expression on their faces as their subordinates melted in front of their eyes, showing that they didn't care in the slightest. But then, as the demons melted, their blood and gore was going down a hill into a pit. Inside the pit was a purple rectangle crystal just floating in it. If you looked close enough, there was something inside the crystal that was oddly shaped.

When the demons had fully melted, all of their blood had fallen fully into the pit, covering the crystal with blood. Then the blood started to move around the crystal like a whirlpool. Then there were mini red waterspouts that, from afar, looked like tentacles. There were six in total.

Each and every one impaled the crystal and the figure that was inside it, and then the crystal shattered into multiple pieces. Thats when they could see what was inside of it. It was an arm. But not any arm. This arm had a weapon on it. The weapon looked like a metal claw. It was Ren's arm.

When the mini blood waterspout stopped impaling the arm, they moved away from the arm and fell back into the puddle of blood. The arm started twitch a little bit, then it started to twitch profusely. Until the arm started to regenerate to a full body again. Within a couple seconds, the arm had fully regenerated its entire body back.

The body fell into the puddle of blood. A huge splash appeared when the body fell. For a couple seconds, the body didn't come up, which made Satan and Lucifer a little worried that the spell didn't actually work, until...

"Gaaahhhaa!"

Ren was alive again. Well, as alive as a demon could be. Ren climbed out of the puddle of blood in his full demon form, still coughing, then he looked to the left, then right in total confusion, then asked, "How am I?"

Shortly, he got an answer: "We brought you back, you're welcome."

Ren looked up to see Lucifer and Satan.

Satan said, "But coming from your face, you don't look happy to be alive again."

Ren's facial expression was lifeless. His eyes looked like they were about to close for the last time. Even his voice had nothing to it.

"Why didn't you just let me stay dead?"

Lucifer seemed annoyed. "Well, it doesn't seem you are the slightest bit curious about how we brought you back. To answer your question like we told you, you are very important to our success in this war. So try to not die again because that spell wasn't free and it won't work a second time."

Ren looked down to see that his weapon was still activated and in a split second he moved his arm to try to kill himself. But his arm only got five inches off the ground. It looked like something invisible stopped Ren from killing himself, and that something was Satan, who used his telekinesis to stop Ren.

Satan said, "Didn't Lucifer just tell you if you die again, you won't come back? We didn't bring you back just so you could kill yourself!" Satan sounded really angry.

But Ren just replied with, "So what? Bringing me back was a mistake. You can see and tell. No. You both should have already known that I was going to be like this. I can't kill Raphael. I won't be able to reach his power anytime soon. So just let me kill myself because I won't be able to avenge everyone I ever loved!" Ren started to cry.

Satan and Lucifer could tell they were losing Ren with every passing second. Soon he would go insane from his depression. But then a door opened behind Ren and someone walked in, shutting the door in the process. Ren didn't need to turn around to see who it was because he could sense him.

Ren said, without turning to look, "Why are you here, Azazel?"

Azazel didn't say anything. He just walked toward Ren. Without warning, he grabbed Ren by the neck, lifted him up with ease, and slammed him on the ground with great force.

Ren coughed up blood in pain. But the blood immediately disintegrated and Ren was now laying in a Ren-sized hole.

Azazel picked up Ren again. "Just look at yourself. You're a wreck. Just because you lost to an angel that is stronger. Boo hoo. 'I lost so I can't avenge my family and friends'—grow up!"

Ren looked at Azazel and started to grind his teeth. "What did you just say? Hey, jackass. I don't think you realized, but they are the reason I fight! And why should I keep on fighting when I know it's impossible to avenge them! Huh? Tell me that?!" Ren was yelling at Azazel with pure rage, which was better than his emotionless tone from earlier.

Azazel let Ren go and said, "There is a way to catch up to Raphael."

"How? Please tell me. How can I reach him in power?!"

Azazel sighed and said, his words scalding, "Did you forget that there is another class of demon in hell that you might turn into?"

Ren didn't even flinch when he heard Azazel's question. All he said was, "Yeah, I know. So what? That won't help me, so what's the point? Me becoming a created demon did give me great power, but I still didn't reach Raphael. I doubt becoming a fallen angel would help."

It was no use. Ren was too depressed and angry to listen to anyone. So Azazel knelt on one knee and put a hand on his shoulder. "Ren, I know you're going through tough times. I can't say I've been there, but I can say this much: I do care about you. You are a dear friend to me, and not just me, but Astaroth as well, even though he won't show it."

Ren looked up at Azazel in shock at what he was hearing. Ren knew Azazel saw Ren as a friend, but he never expected to hear it from him in person because no demon ever showed their feelings to anyone unless it correlated with the sins. And Azazel was doing just that, even in front of his gods, knowing he might get made fun of by them.

Ren smiled and said, "Hmph, look at us. We look like a cheesy anime make up scene. When one character yells at the other character, some fists go around, and then they tell their true feelings to each other. If this was a book or show, many people would ship us right now." They both started to laugh.

A yawn in the background could be heard. They both stopped laughing and turned toward the noise.

It was, of course, Lucifer. He said, "Are you two done with your gayness and telling each other about your feelings? Because there is still a war going on right now and we need Ren to kill Raphael."

Azazel said, "Yes. Sorry my lord." He got back on his feet and bowed to Lucifer.

Ren also got on his feet and said, "Okay. So me turning into a fallen angel. It's just like me turning into a created demon, right?" Ren was talking back to Satan and Lucifer with a little more spunk than last time. But they could all still see in his eyes that he was still depressed and would still like to die.

Satan said, "Almost alike. The only similar things between this ritual and the last one are that it's going to hurt a lot, the chains that come out of the ground to hold you down, and you will be submerged in blood. But besides those, everything else is different. From the words, to the demons that need to give you their blood, to the risks."

"And what are the risks?"

Lucifer said, "Well, the last one puts you into a permanent coma. This one kills you, so hey, you get a win with either outcome—you get power or you die. It's a win-win for you." Lucifer was being sarcastic, but Ren did see it as a win-win. It even put a smile on his face.

"And how do you know it will kill me? Let me guess—the three demons that became created demons still wanted more power, so they asked to become fallen angel demons and they died. Does that sound about right?"

Satan gave a surprised laugh that sounded very sadistic and said, "Correct. You hit the nail on the head." Satan gave Ren a weak clap.

Lucifer said, "So then. Are we ready?"

Ren didn't say anything, he just nodded his head with confidence, which gave Lucifer a little smile.

Lucifer waved his hand to open the door. The door opened and Ren immediately fell to his hands and knees from the enormous number of sins he was sensing. When Ren tried to look up, he saw nine demons come in. Ren only knew one of them—Lilith. She waved at Ren and gave him a wink, but the other eight Ren had never seen before.

One looked like a completely regular muscular human male in his late twenties. He had a gorgeous puffy black beard that connected to his long smooth black hair. He wore pants, but besides that, he wore no shoes or shirt (he wouldn't be getting any customer service in any restaurants anytime soon) and he was covered in scars. He had a number two on the left side of his chest and red eyes.

The other seven were shadow-like people with various shapes, sizes, and numbers on their chests. But they all had red eyes. One was about the size of a sixteen-year-old girl, and she gave Ren a narrow look. That was probably Envy with the number nine.

The next was a really fat guy. Ren couldn't even tell if he had a neck. He was number eight. That was Gluttony.

The next was a regular-looking figure. Ren thought it was a male because it had no curves or breasts, but he could be wrong. This figure looked like it might fall over and take a good nap. Ren thought, "I sure could go for a nap right about now too." It had the number seven. That was Sloth.

Next was a very curved and busty woman with long hair and a big ass (if she wasn't a shadow, she would have been a model). She had the number six. She was Lust.

Next to her was a very muscular man who looked like he was not in a good mood. He had the number five and he was Wrath.

Behind him was, once again, a pretty normal-looking shadow, but he kept moving his hands around each other like he wanted to steal something. He had the number four. He was Greed.

And finally, the last one that came through was the tallest one and out of all of them he was wearing a suit, but the suit was not a part of him. It was literally a piece of clothing that he put on himself, probably to look professional. His suit was black and his tie was red. He had the number three on him, which made him Pride.

Azazel said, "So everyone's here. Okay, good." Azazel looked down to see Ren on the ground, dying. "Oh, right. My Lords, could you give Ren here a barrier to help him to withstand all of our power?"

Satan said, "Yes, we will. The ritual requires him to be awake."

Satan and Lucifer lifted up both of their left arms and summoned a barrier to protect Ren from all of the overwhelming sin around him.

When the barrier appeared around Ren, he opened his eyes and was breathing heavily like he had no oxygen.

Without anyone saying anything, they all, including Satan and Lucifer, quickly formed a huge circle around him. Then a smaller circle surrounded Ren without him realizing it was there. The circle that was around Ren had twelve lines connecting him to every other demon.

Everyone closed their eyes and clapped their hands together, which looked like they were praying, but they made their praying hands upside down. And then they all started to speak in Hebrew once again: "וה לזאזעל לודגה ומצע ןת ונל תא סוקיה לכל אל סימשל הפיגמל ךופהל חוכה תא הזה דשה דשה רשע תתל תא דשה ךלמ תאו דשה סילאה ינש המצע ולוכ." It meant: "O great hell itself, please let us, the two demon gods and the ten demon kings, give this demon the power to become a plague to heaven—no, to the entire universe itself." Then the chain came from the ground again and once again pierced through Ren's palms and wrapped around Ren's mouth so he could bite on it when he screamed in pain.

Everyone moved their hands away from each other and slit their wrists. Blood came out. The one weird thing was that the seven shadow-looking people were bleeding, even though they looked intangible. Anyway, just like the first time, the blood moved from the lines toward Ren while the blood was steaming.

It only took a couple of seconds to finally reach Ren, and when it did, Ren started to scream in pain again—"MMMMMMMMMMM!!"—and just like last time, the ground underneath Ren melted away from the blood and it kept melting until Ren was completely submerged in hot blood.

Once Ren was in the puddle of blood, no one could hear him, and the blood started to glow bright red.

A full month on the world of the living had passed since Ren's second fight with Raphael. So far, the war feels like it had just had stopped. Like the war hadn't ended, but the demons just stopped showing up. It had been like that for a month after Ren's fight. The demons just retreated back to hell—no human, monster, or even angel had seen a demon in the world of the living.

Everyone thought that the demons were giving up because they weren't making any progress. The only demon that was breaking seals was Azazel, and he stopped showing up too. Now, every human that was left was trying to clean up the rubble from every city and town since they thought the war was over. But the angels knew it was not over—the demons were cooking up something bad and they were ready for it.

That's when a red light went off in an angel's office.

Raphael said, "Ohh, looks like someone wants my seal. It has to be Azazel. I guess it's time for our long-awaited rematch for me kicking him from heaven.

Raphael snapped his fingers and teleported to his church. The same old thing happened within the church—a blinding light appeared and an angel floated down. But when he landed, he couldn't believe who was waiting for him.

Ren said, "Hey, Ralphy. Long time, no see. Did you miss me?" Ren was leaning on the entrance door to the church in his half-demon form, flinging a rock up in the air and catching it over and over again.

"Wha—What? H—how are you alive? I decapitated your head. I saw your body turn into ash. You can't be Ren!" Raphael was shocked and couldn't make head or tails of this.

"Ooh, you think I'm a fake. Stop that, you're going to make me cry."

Raphael thought, "No, from what I'm sensing he's a created demon." Raphael looked at Ren's chest. "He has the number 200 on the left side of his chest, and from his way of talking, there's no doubt about it. It is Ren. But how...?" Raphael stopped thinking in his head and gave a big sigh. "I see. So my stupid older brother did something to bring you back."

Ren smiled and dropped the rock and started to walk toward Raphael.

Raphael was also walking toward Ren while talking. "I don't know how Lucifer did the impossible to bring back a demon after he had been killed. But I'm going to kill you again." Raphael sounded excited—too excited. All he wanted now was to fight Ren to see if he'd gotten better.

Raphael summoned his weapon and Ren did the same. They both charged at each other and before the moment of their clash, Raphael teleported them both to their usual fighting spot.

They clashed and the final battle for these two had commenced.

As their weapons were connecting, sparks and electricity were coming off their weapons. Raphael had a distinct smile on his face of excitement and ecstasy.

Raphael quickly let his left hand go from his weapon and went for a punch, but Ren used his right pointer finger to activate his telekinesis to slightly move Raphael's punch out of the way. It worked, surprising Raphael. Then Ren, with his right hand, grabbed Raphael's left arm and started to swing him around and then let go, sending Raphael through a mountain.

Ren followed after Raphael, then ducked and the mountain that was behind him got cut in half.

Raphael said, "Good. You saw that one coming. I'm impressed!" With a punch, he sent a blast of holy water toward Ren.

Ren dodged the incoming attack; however, Raphael teleported behind Ren and swung his axe down, trying to cut Ren in half. But once again, Ren used his telekinesis to slightly move the axe. It still hit Ren but it only cut off Ren's right wing and arm.

At this point, Ren had already had a good, high pain tolerance from the angel's weapons.

But less than a second after Ren's wing and arm got completely cut off, Raphael elbowed Ren in the shoulder, dislocating it, which sent Ren flying down toward the ground. However, before Ren got even a foot away from Raphael, he used his free left leg to actually cut Raphael's left leg, and it was a pretty decent cut.

As Ren was falling, he managed to stop himself from crashing and quickly turned to see Raphael just standing there looking at his leg.

Raphael said with a grin, "Humph, not bad. You actually cut me and it was pretty deep too. How careless of me. I must have gotten too into the fight."

Ren didn't say anything. He slowly descended to the ground, without taking his eyes off of Raphael, until he finally hit the ground. Raphael raised his axe above his head with both hands and said, "But don't let that hit get to you. It was just a lucky hit!" And with that Raphael flew straight down, about to slam his axe on Ren to cut him in half.

Ren, on the other hand, just stood there and raised his right hand.

A big crash appeared where Ren was standing, dust surrounded Ren, and with the mountains' strong winds the dust was blown away very quickly. What was inside the dust cloud was shocking. Raphael's attack did hit but it didn't do any damage to Ren because Ren grabbed it with his right hand that he raised. Ren didn't grab the blade—he grabbed the handle that was attached to the blade.

Raphael was just floating above Ren, completely shocked that Ren just grabbed his mighty axe. And with Raphael completely in dumb shock, Ren quickly raised his left hand and managed to cut both of Raphael's hands.

Raphael quickly flew back to get some distance and to think for a moment.

Raphael thought, "Okay, calm down. You know exactly how Ren caught your attack. He used his telekinesis from his right hand to greatly slow down your attack to grab it. Because he knew if he did that, I would just be in too much shock to even move, so just calm down." Raphael closed his eyes and took a big deep breath.

Ren saw Raphael close his eyes, so he flew up to attack him.

Raphael smiled and moved his right hand to shoot compressed holy water at Ren, but before Raphael was about to shoot, there was a sharp pain in his right arm. Ren somehow just moved so fast that he caught Raphael off-guard and stabbed him in his arm.

Raphael screamed in pain—"AAAAA!"—because it had been a while since he'd had his entire arm stabbed. "You son of a bitch!" Raphael quickly moved his left arm and punched inside Ren's stomach.

Ren was losing lots of blood, but before the blood that left Ren's body could be disintegrated, Ren could feel that Raphael was about to shoot holy water from his left arm that was still inside Ren.

So Ren quickly put his left foot on Raphael, and with all of his strength and using his telekinesis, he managed to remove himself from Raphael's arm and dodge his attack. And in a quick second, Ren moved his right leg for a spin kick on Raphael's face.

Ren's kick hit Raphael in the face and Ren could feel Raphael's cheekbone cracking before he sent Raphael flying. Raphael crashed into a mountain. He went so deep Ren couldn't see him. But he could still hear him.

Raphael talked to Ren while he was inside the mountain. "I see now. It was a bit strange that a month went by and you didn't get stronger, that you stayed the same. I originally thought you were just going on a suicide battle, but I can see I was wrong. You did get stronger and that number on your chest is fake."

Raphael slowly came out of the mountain, dusting himself off, and he looked like he didn't take any damage.

Raphael looked directly at Ren and said, "You're using illusion magic to hide your true number, and you're purposely holding back to match that fake number when we are apart. But when we clashed, you only powered up that one limb to withstand me."

Ren gave Raphael a surprised look and said, "Wow, you figured it out. I'm impressed." Ren was clapping his hands. "Yeah, it's true. I got Astaroth to teach me a basic illusion spell. Don't get me wrong—I am not a master in magic. I just wanted to know that little spell to trick you. And to my surprise, it worked."

Raphael took a bow, saying "Thank you, you're too kind." Then he raised his head and said, "So then show me—what is your number now?"

Ren said with a smile, "How about you show me that armor of yours, then we'll talk."

"You know, it's funny. I know you're playing me, but okay."

Raphael moved so fast that he was suddenly in front of Ren, like he was right in front of him the whole time. Raphael took another deep breath and then the same beam of light hit him and the same scene was in front of Ren again—light bouncing off Raphael's golden armor and weapon, light bouncing off the ice from the mountains, animals singing, and multiple rainbows appearing behind him.

Raphael said, "I see you're not shaking this time. Good. Now show me your number."

Ren smiled and instead of giving Raphael what he wanted, Ren instead said, "Now hold on. Before I do that, I want to show you something cool as well."

Raphael tilted his helmet to the side in confusion. He knew he shouldn't let Ren do what he was about to do, but he did want to see what Ren was about to do.

Ren closed his eyes and started to do something. Huge black clouds appeared and started to swirl around Ren (it looked like a mini hurricane), then two big tornadoes appeared behind him, but these tornadoes were so strong that they were sucking up every animal, big or small. From small birds to a big snow leopard, they were all getting sucked in—the same was happening with snow, rocks, and trees. While that was happening, huge lightning bolts kept flashing around Ren until one hit him.

When it hit Ren, the little armor bits that were connecting to the blades started to expand until they covered Ren's entire body. And when it fully covered Ren's body, he looked like a completely different person.

His entire body was covered in armor, but the colors were black and purple.

And just like with Raphael's armor that looked too picture-perfect for an angel to wear, Ren's armor looked too picture-perfect for a demon to wear. It looked very sharp, and every joint of Ren's body had a little spike, but the final key difference was that the armor didn't take the form of Ren's half-demon form when he was in the world of the living, but the form of his full demonic body from hell (but without his tail). The two tornadoes stopped and disappeared, leaving falling debris of rock, wood, blood, and flesh. The lightning also stopped, but the dark clouds were still there.

If someone was there watching the fight they would be looking at a picture perfect image of an demon vs angel. Ren with his demonic armor on and dark swirling clouds above him. While across from him was Raphael wearing the most elegant and beautiful armor that has the light bouncing off of him making him glow and his surroundings has no clouds around just pure blue skies showing symbolizing how pure he is.

Raphael was gasping at what he was seeing "No way. You have full armor, too, but it is said the only demons in hell that get those are the ones with the number of 50 and up—the true elites. I'm going to guess that you are a part of the ten demon kings since you actually managed to cut me."

Ren gave a little chuckle. When he spoke, because of his armor, his voice sounded metallic and more demonic, "Hm, good guess, and I totally see why you might think that, but no, I'm not part of the ten demon kings." Ren moved his right hand over his number and said, "Release." He moved his hand away.

Ren had deactivated his spell and Raphael could see the numbers changing, but he only saw the number zero from the far side fading away. Then he realized. "Your true number is 20?!"

"Yes, I got it by transforming into a fallen angel."

Surprised, Raphael said, "Fallen angel?"

"Yes. You are dealing with the 20th strongest demon in hell—the fallen angel Ren Claude!"

Raphael put his right hand in front of his face and started to shake his head. Ren thought he was doing it because he couldn't believe Ren had gotten so powerful, but that wasn't the case at all. The reason Raphael was shaking his head was because he was once again disappointed with Ren.

Raphael heaved a sigh and said, "Ren, how many times do I have to goddamn tell you that only the top ten strongest demons can take on an archangel. It is true that you are very strong indeed, but you're still no match for—"

Raphael didn't even get to finish his sentence because Ren moved so fast that he was right in front of Raphael and he kicked him in his face, which sent him flying away, before he knew what hit him. Raphael spread his wings to try to stop himself. It worked. He stopped. Raphael looked up at Ren and started to move his head to the right, then to the left, to crack his neck. Some pops did come out and Raphael was satisfied.

Raphael said, "That was a good kick, Ren. That caught me completely off guard. I'll give you a round of applause for that." Raphael literally started to clap his hands and since he was wearing his armor, the claps were metallic.

Ren didn't say anything. Instead, he moved his left leg forward, his right leg behind him, his left arm forward, and his right arm closer to his chest. He was in a boxing stance, which showed that he was not playing around anymore. He was here to fight and to kill.

Raphael gave Ren a big old smile, but Raphael forgot that he was wearing a helmet and Ren couldn't see. So he got into his battle stance—his left foot forward, his right leg behind him. Both of his hands were on his axe, his right hand closer to the blade, and his left hand closer to his hip.

It was silent. Neither said a word. They were just staring at each other, waiting for the right moment. They were like that for twenty seconds until out of nowhere, they both moved at high speeds and clashed. They moved so fast that a normal person couldn't tell if they were still separated or whether they were right next to each other the whole time. The shock wave was so great that it cut every mountain's tips off for a one hundred mile radius.

They were still connecting with each other's blades, with such great force that electricity was coming off of them, and this electricity was so big that it was the size of actual lightning bolts from a lightning storm. Ren, with his free hand, moved with great speed to try to cut at Raphael's face. Raphael was distracted, so Ren saw it as an opening. But Raphael sensed the attack coming, so he moved his head away. Ren's attack didn't cut Raphael's actual face, but it did deeply cut his helmet.

Raphael nodded, which sent Ren flying down, and Raphael followed Ren in pursuit. When Raphael got close enough, he swung his axe to try to cut Ren from his hip. Ren saw the attack coming, so he used his telekinesis to move Raphael's attack slightly down so that it only cut both of his legs off. It did. Raphael's axe moved down and cut off both of Ren's legs, sending them flying away. But Ren was not done yet.

Ren shot hellfire at Raphael, hitting him directly. Raphael moved both of his arms in front of his face and chest to block the attack. He thought that this attack wouldn't do anything to him and wondered why he was blocking it in the first place. However, Raphael was grunting loudly from the flames. Not just because of the impact the fire brought, but it was really hot. Not hot enough to give him any serious burns, but enough to make his skin feel like it was on fire.

Raphael backhanded the fire away with his left hand, but Ren was right in front of Raphael and slashed at him with both arms from both sides. Raphael quickly punched Ren in the face, sending him back a couple of steps. There was a brief pause in the fighting.

Ren's helmet was badly cracked, but it was quickly repaired in less than a second. Ren turned his head to look at Raphael and saw him touching his chest in shock.

Raphael thought, "Did I really see that? Did I really feel that?" A flashback showed that before Raphael punched Ren away, Ren's attack did connect with Raphael's chest, and not only did it cut through his armor, but it also cut Raphael. The cut was as thin as a paper cut, but it stung a lot. Of course the cuts were gone, but Raphael could not believe it.

Raphael moved his hand away and looked at Ren and said, "Hmph. Looks like you're better than I thought. You actually cut me." Raphael raised his right arm to point at Ren. "But no more—I'm going to take this fight more seriously!"

When Raphael finished his little speech, Ren disappeared from Raphael's vision. Raphael's eyes widened within the helmet when he suddenly felt a really sharp pain coming from his right arm.

Raphael looked toward his arm and saw that Ren stabbed his arm with his blades.

Ren said, "Okay, then. I'm going to be serious too." He moved his pointer finger to point directly at Raphael's left chest.

Raphael realized what Ren was doing so he moved his arm out of Ren's blades and moved to the left. Pressurized hellfire came out of Ren's finger, a stream as thick as his finger. It was supposed to pierce through Raphael's heart, but it pierced Raphael's left shoulder instead. Raphael spun counterclockwise with his axe on his left hand, about to hit Ren in the face, but Ren blocked the attack with both blades from both arms.

Raphael wasn't done yet. He kept on spinning like a buzz saw, just continuing to hitting Ren's blades, sending sparks flying everywhere. Raphael's axe is slowly cut through Ren's blades until the blades couldn't take it anymore and broke.

When his blades broke Ren without a second to loose immediately moved his entire torso back and dodged the axe. It looked like he was doing limbo. But before he could react, Raphael stopped spinning with the axe and was now directly above him. And with a quick motion, Raphael slammed the blunt side of the axe onto Ren, cracking his armor. Some blood came out through his helmet, and the force sent Ren once again flying directly to the ground, hitting it with great force.

Raphael moved down to slash Ren again, but without realizing it, Ren was right next to him with a kick. Raphael took the surprise attack with full force and this time he was spitting blood through his helmet.

Raphael slammed into a mountain, completely destroying it. Ren raised his left arm and sent a huge hellfire blast at the destroyed mountain, completely burning it until it was nothing but ashes.

Raphael said, "Where are you aiming there, champ?!" His voice came from behind Ren.

When Ren turned around, Raphael shot a blast of holy water at Ren. Ren lifted up both arms to catch the attack, and he did, but the impact was so great that it was moving him back, while in the air, while cracking all of Ren's bones from the force itself. Raphael teleported behind Ren, ready to finish him off.

But Ren knew he would do that—that was an old trick. So Ren moved his head to the right and moved his left arm away from the holy water that he was holding in place. The water on the left side went past his head and hit Raphael directly, pushing him back. Ren turned out of the way from what was left of the holy water that he was holding back. It also hit Raphael, and then Ren teleported far away, behind him, and shot a huge fire blast at him.

Raphael turned his head and saw the attack coming but couldn't do anything about it. So the fire hit Raphael and he became sandwiched—on one side was Ren's hellfire and on the other side was his own holy water hitting him at the same time with great force.

Both attacks disappeared, creating a huge burst of steam. The steam cloud was so big that it was the size of a mountain. Then the steam was spinning around like a tornado and Ren could hear Raphael.

Raphael, while slinging his axe around like a fan getting rid of the steam, said, "Yes, this is what I call a proper fight between an angel and a demon! I'm feeling pain, my armor is getting damaged, I'm bleeding! This is a battle that I've been waiting for—no holds barred, fight to the death!" He swung his axe to the side and looked up to look at Ren. Ren was just flying up in the blue sky with no clouds, looking down at Raphael while Raphael was standing on the snowy, badly-damaged ground.

"Yes. I couldn't agree more, Raphael." He was excited, but not on the same level as Raphael.

Then they both moved and clashed again with their glowing eyes that could be seen through their helmets. And it faded to black.

Sixty hours later, Ren and Raphael were still fighting, the sound of metal clashing ringing across the landscape. It was nighttime and the stars were up. There were still no clouds to be seen. All of the snow had melted from all of the hellfire that Ren had been firing. And there were no more mountains anywhere—not even Mount Everest—because Ren and Raphael literally destroyed every mountain by crashing into it or by any other means.

They were still fighting with unimaginable speed, sending shock wave after shock wave with every hit until Ren kicked Raphael on his arm and they finally had some distance between them. Ren's armor was badly damaged; it was cracked everywhere and it was also missing some chunks. It looked so badly damaged that if you blew on it, the entire thing might crumble.

Raphael, on the other hand, didn't look any better. His armor was covered in deep cuts, scratches, and shallow stabs. All of his cuts were bleeding. Raphael looked like a tree that had been used for sword practice. Both were shaking from the pain, but neither of them were breathing heavily, indicating that they were not exhausted. Ren was still calm on the outside, and in his mind, he was determined to win.

Raphael looked calm on the outside but his mind was not...

Raphael thought, "This doesn't make any sense. Not only is he still alive, but he and I are equally matched! No, we're not. He is getting more hits on me than I can on him, so my regeneration is still good for way more hits but his regeneration is in better condition. How—How is this even possible? It is said that only the ten demon kings can take on an archangel, on so how the fuck is he wining?! Is his number still an illusion? No, he literally turned his illusion magic off, so how-how-hoW-hOW-HOW!"

Raphael shocked Ren because he screamed out of nowhere, "HOW ARE YOU WINNING? IT DOESN'T MAKE ANY FUCKING SENSE AT ALL!"

Ren smirked and said sarcastically and childishly, "What's wrong, Ralphy, are you getting triggered?"

Raphel said angrily, "Stop calling me Ralphy. That's not a good nickname! And don't dodge my question—tell me!"

Ren teased Raphael even more. "I don't know... Maybe you angels are just so pathetic and lazy that you think no demon can beat you, so you guys don't train at all. And because of that, the demons in hell were getting stronger. So maybe it is not the top ten that can take on an archangel—maybe now it's top twenty.

That's my theory."

Raphael was biting so hard because of what Ren just said that blood was coming out of his mouth. Then he started to laugh.

"Ah, ah, ah, is that so? You know what? I can test that theory for you," Raphael said psychotically.

Ren tilted his head and said, "How would you do that?"

Then Raphael flew up in the sky, deactivated his weapon that he was still holding, and raised his hand and started to shout: "I'm going to destroy America and let's see if you can stop me!"

Ren looked up and said, yelling so Raphael could hear him, "You do know you are pulling a cliché anime villain move when he is losing, right?!"

"Shut up! I don't even know what that is!"

Ren put his right hand on his chest and said, "What? You don't know what dragon ball is? That hurts more than any damage that you could ever do to me!"

"SHUT UP!" Raphael bent all five of his fingers to look like a claw and then these things, like blueish-white wires, came from each fingertip. They were really compressed holy water, and they came together and were forming a small ball that kept on growing until it was the size of a golf ball in Raphael's palm.

Ren smiled in his helmet and said, "Finally, he is doing it." He got into his stance.

Ren had his right leg in front, his left leg behind him, and both knees bent. He raised both arms up in the same claw position as Raphael's hand, and summoned red thin wires that came out of each fingertip. They were really compressed hellfire; they came together, and slowly grew into the size of a golf ball in both Ren's palms.

Raphael was still screaming, "Okay, you know what? Fuck America, fuck the humans, fuck the angels and demons, fuck the seals, and especially fuck you and die! Final attack!!"

The golf ball-sized holy water just grew and shot out of Raphael's palm. The blast was as big as Raphael himself—he was about six feet tall.

Ren fired his attack toward Raphael's in response.

Not even a second after they fired their attacks, the two blasts hit each other and became a stalemate... at least for a second. Raphael's holy water was slowly getting closer to Ren and it made Raphael really happy.

Raphael said in a victorious tone, "HA, see? What were you thinking?! Did you think your blast could stop mine?! I mean come on, I can destroy all of America and you, all you can destroy is the combined size of California and Texas. Impressive, but still nowhere near my level! Goodbye, Ren, it was nice to know ya!"

Ren could feel the pressure of Raphael's attack getting closer and closer. It felt like someone was slowly putting more and more cinderblocks on top of him. The ground Ren was standing on was cracking and he was sinking into the cracks because of the pressure. It was also cracking Ren's armor and then it started to crack Ren's blades, but for some reason when Ren saw his blades cracking, it put a smile on his hidden face and he said, "Finally. I don't have to do it myself."

Up in the sky, Raphael was not holding back at all. He was just flying there, maintaining his focus and energy in his hand which was still shooting. Until…

"AAAHHH!!!"

Raphael just started to scream in pain. The pain was coming from his hand, so without thinking he moved his hand away from the spot where he was firing, which stopped his final attack. Raphael looked at his hand to see what the problem was and what he saw was shocking. Through Raphael's right hand was one of Ren's blades.

When Ren noticed that Raphael stopped his attack, he pulled both of his arms back, which looked like he was thrusting, but in actuality, Ren pulled his Final Attack back into him so that he wouldn't pass out from the side effects of using the Final Attack. He did stumble a bit when he fully absorbed it back, but he knew there was no time to lose now.

Ren crouched down and jumped up with all his might, destroying the already badly damaged ground. Raphael didn't notice when Ren absorbed his Final Attack and when Ren jumped toward him, Raphael was focused on pulling Ren's blade out of his hand. It worked; he pulled it out, but it was too late for Raphael. He suddenly felt an even worse pain coming from his back. Raphael turned to see what it was and it was Ren cutting off both of Raphael's wings.

But Ren was not done yet. Ren had his arms crossed like an X right under Raphael's legs, and with one powerful flap of his wings, Ren flew up while moving his arms away from each other with great force. And when Ren did that, not only did he fully cut off both of Raphael's legs, but he also cut off both of his arms. Raphael had no legs, arms, or wings. He was just a floating—no, falling—torso.

Ren was still not done. He moved forward to do what looked like a front flip, but in actuality, Ren was about to kick Raphael on top of his head. It hit, and lots of blood came out of Raphael's helmet. Ren sent Raphael flying down to the ground. Raphael was going so fast that he literally caught on fire like a comet crashing to earth. Raphael crashed and left a big crater. He was on the ground, moaning from the pain while his arms, legs, and wings regenerated with great speed, but it took a total of thirty seconds for them to fully come back (that was a big deal for an archangel).

Raphael tried to crawl away but he couldn't—his body was sore—so he turned over to lay on his back to rest for a moment, completely forgetting about Ren. Ren fell from the sky, kneeing Raphael with both knees on his stomach and making the crater bigger. At that moment, Raphael only thought one thing: "Mistakes were made." He forgot about Ren and he paid the price.

When the smoke finally cleared, Ren was standing right next to Raphael. While Raphael took off his helmet and started to throw up from being kneed in the stomach, Ren walked toward him and kicked him while he was throwing up, sending him a couple feet away. Ren walked toward Raphael. He saw Ren coming toward him, so he tried to teleport away, but Ren saw that and swiped the air with his arm, sending an air slash and cutting off Raphael's fingers.

Raphael screamed, "AAAHHH?!!"

"Oh be quiet, you did that to me. Karma, bitch." Ren elbowed Raphael to the ground. Raphael's armor disappeared, leaving him with no more defenses.

Ren said coldly, "Well, I guess that's it. I've won your will to fight is gone and you die."

Instead of pleading for his life, he said, "How—how did you beat me? Please tell me. I have to know."

Ren chuckled a little and said, "So you want me to explain how I beat you and how awesome I am, villain monologue style."

Raphael said, "I don't know what style that is, but yes, tell me how you beat me?!" His voice became scratchy.

Ren moved around, all excited. "I don't know—well, okay fine, if you insist. But let's make sure you don't do anything while I'm talking." Ren flicked his wrist, which spread all four of Raphael's limbs as far apart as they could go, and moved Raphael's palms down so they were touching the ground to make sure he didn't shoot holy water at Ren. to finally finish his preparation, Ren jumped up and landed on all fours on top of Raphael.

Raphael said, "AAHH, come on!" The reason why Raphael was screaming was because when Ren landed on him, Ren stabbed all of his limbs with each blade to make sure Raphael didn't move.

Ren broke off all of his blades so that they were still inside of Raphael to hold him in place and make sure he didn't regenerate. Ren used his telekinesis to move a big boulder that happened to be close closer to him so he could sit on it. Ren sat, crossed his legs and put his hands together.

"Let's start with our stats. Let's start with the stats that show that you are superior." Ren sounded like a teacher about to teach an entire class. "You are way—and I mean way—physically stronger them me. The same can be said about your destructive capability. You are also more durable than me and still have more battle experience than me. Like, for god's sake, you fought and beat Azazel—the guy I mostly respect in hell."

Raphael said, "Wait, if I'm stronger than you, how did you—"

"Ah-ah-ah, I'm not done yet. You may have those stats on your side but I have superior reaction, senses, and, get this, speed."

"Speed? That's impossible. You can't be faster than me. I move faster than light."

"Yeah, yeah, I know, but listen—you will not believe how much faster I am than you. Okay, get this: your speed, if I remember correctly, is 680 million miles per hour, right?" Raphael just nodded. "Well..." Ren was snorting from laughter. "My speed is 680 million, 450 thousand miles per hour."

Raphael was speechless. His eyes and mouth were wide open.

Ren started to laugh loudly. "It's so funny the speed that you made fun of me for at our first fight is the speed that out-blitzed you. That is poetic, don't you agree? But surprisingly, even though I was that much faster than you, you actually managed to somewhat keep up with me. You archangels are something else entirely."

Raphael closed his eyes in disappointment but he slowly opened them again and said, "But that's not all, right?"

Ren stopped laughing and got more serious again. "Yes, there's more. So let's start with something that you, for some reason, haven't noticed yet." Raphael tried to tilt his head in confusion at what he hadn't noticed yet.

Ren said, "Why haven't my blades in your limbs faded away by now?"

Raphael quickly raised his head up to look at his limbs and Ren was right—they were still there.

Raphael thought, "He's right. A demon's and angel's weapons only go away if they deactivate it, the weapon is too far away from the wielded so the weapon disappears on its own, or if the weapon breaks off; after a short period of time it will also disappear. So why isn't it going away?" And that's when Raphael saw it: a red string touching at the end of each blade going straight back toward its source—Ren.

Ren said, "So you finally noticed it, huh. I used this same move on you when our Final Attacks collided. This string, which is pumping my sin through the string and into the broken-off blades, makes the blades think they are still at-tached to me. This allows me to move the broken blade to wherever I want it to go. Of course, the string is very fragile and even the weakest angel in heaven can cut it with no effort. If you want to know, this is the move I used to stab your hand while you were in the air."

Raphael cut Ren off again. "But that doesn't make any sense. How did you know where I was and where my hand was for your blade to stab? My blast was as tall and wide as me, so it had to be covering my entire body. You couldn't see me."

Ren sighed. "Raphael, did you already forget? Remember, I have superior senses than you. It is true that your Final Attack did block my vision from seeing you. But before you fired it you were up in the air for a long period of time to charge and insult me. That gave me enough time to see where you were, calculate the distance between you and me, and calculate how long your arms are and when you extended them to fire your attack."

"Y—you actually calculate all of that?"

"Yeah, I'm really good at math, but there is another reason. During our second fight, you said I wasn't being myself, that I wasn't being tactical. And you know what? You were right. My rage blinded me. I was a completely different person. So when I fully achieved my new form—fallen angel form—and number, I stayed in hell and to train to get used to my new body and make up a strategy to defeat you. That's how I managed to create my string thing and to absorb my Final Attack back into me so the side effect wouldn't hit me when I try to kill you. Man, I don't know how many times I failed in trying to absorb my Final Attack back into me. Like, I must have fallen asleep like five times or more. But don't get me wrong—it took me months of nonstop training to master those."

"So wait—this whole time you weren't trying to kill me with all of those stabs and cuts—you were waiting for me to use your final attack so you could use your new moves on me?"

Ren shook his head. "No, no. I really was trying to kill you with those cuts and stabs, it was just that I was ready for you when you used that move."

Raphael was silent. He was amazed by Ren. He had wanted to fight Ren with everything he had, and he did, but Ren just outsmarted him.

Ren said, "However, my new moves, stats, and rank wouldn't have really mattered if it weren't for one thing."

Raphael was silent because he wanted to know what the one thing was.

"Your personality, Raphael. If it was slightly different, I would have lost again." Raphael didn't know what Ren meant by that. Ren continued, "When people make verses videos, they always forget about personality, thinking it doesn't matter, but it does. Even though I have better stats than you, if you weren't so battle hungry, playful when we were clashing, and if you had managed to keep your cool and not lose your temper about how I was beating you, you would have won, hands down."

Raphael didn't say anything. He slowly closed his eyes in shame because Ren was right. If he had stayed calm and didn't snap, he would have won.

Ren slowly got up and walked toward Raphael and said, "Okay, story time is over. It's time for you to die."

Raphael opened his eyes and said, "Wait! Please don't kill me! You don't know the consequences of killing an archangel!"

Ren was silent and kept walking closer.

Raphael said, "I— I'll return all of my angels that are in my army to heaven. Neither you nor any other demon will see them again, so please spare me."

Ren was silent again. He raised his weapon up and lowered it with great speed for the killing blow.

Raphael said, "Someone told me about you." He had his eyes closed but he opened them when he felt no pain from anywhere, or at least any new pain.

Ren said, "What did you just say?"

"I didn't actually know you even existed. Someone told me about you and told me to send you to hell."

Ren was silent for a couple seconds, then he moved away from Raphael and sat back down on his boulder chair, crossed his arms, and said, "Make it quick."

One week before all of this even started, in heaven, or, to be more exact, in a fighting dojo, there were many voices moaning and crying in pain. Inside the dojo, many angels were laying on the ground with various weapons in their hands and in agonizing pain. In the middle of the room, surrounded by hurt angels, was Raphael, sitting on the floor with his face leaning on his hand with a clear expression of boredom.

Raphael sighed and said, "Okay, that's enough for today. Once again, not one of you made me move from this spot." Raphael got up and just left the dojo, not even trying to help the injured angels.

Raphael thought, "Goddamnit, I am so bored. I can't fight any of my brothers or we might damage heaven and make a natural disaster in the world of the living. But all of these weak angels are so pathetic. The same can be said about the demons on earth. I guess that's what happens when you were created by God himself first."

The lights in the hallway he was walking in started to flicker and Raphael sensed someone behind him. He turned around to see an angel that he didn't recognize (he must have been from a different archangel army), but something was off with this one. He was swinging back and forth like he was drunk, but angels couldn't get drunk. Not even when they were in a vessel. And his eyes had no pupils and there was a weird aura surrounding this angel.

Raphael said, "Who are you and why are you mind-controlling an angel? You are not another angel and you are certainly not a demon, so who are you and why are you here?"

The angel spoke but his voice was mixed with another voice. "Who I am is not your concern, and why I am here is because I want to ask you a simple question."

Raphael, a hint of annoyance in his voice, said, "Oh, and what will that be?"

"Are you bored? If so, I can help you fix that."

Raphael had no expression, but a little smile came onto his face. "Go on."

Raphael was still stabbed into the ground, telling his story. "And so he told me about you and said to send you to hell so you may become a demon and start this war. So please, there you go. I didn't know you even existed, so this is all whoever mind controlled that angel—he's to blame. I mean, yeah, I did do what he said, but you know I only did it because I was bored." Raphael said it like it was the most reasonable excuse.

Ren was looking down so hard that you couldn't even see his eyes or what expression he was making. He just got up, turned away from Raphael, and said, "I don't want to see you, your clones, or any of the angels you command again. Got that?!"

Raphael nodded his head really fast and said, "Yes, yes, of course I will."

Ren didn't turn around; he just snapped his fingers and teleported away. The blades that were in Raphael fully disappeared and Raphael's wounds slowly closed. Raphael rubbed his arms and legs really fast. When he was done, he got up and heaved a long sigh.

Raphael said with a weak smile on his face, "Well, that's it. It's over. I lost."

Then a gush of blood came flying in the air and a big "Augg!" could be heard. Two blades were stabbed through the back of Raphael's head and out of his mouth.

"Did you really think I'd believe that bullshit of a story? Like, come on. That was the biggest lie I've ever heard, and I'm a demon."

Raphael said, "I-I-wns-I..." Raphael was trying to say something but he couldn't because he was choking on his own blood and on the blades through his mouth.

"Goodbye, Raphael, it was nice knowing ya."

Ren put his left hand on Raphael's shoulder and pushed down, and his right hand, which was the one that was stabbed through Raphael, was pushing up. Raphael's entire head came off his body. His spine was dangling from his severed head; his head was still on Ren's blades. Then Raphael's body caught on fire, including his severed head, indicating that Raphael was dead.

Ren watched as Raphael's body burned into ashes and blew away on the wind. Ren gave a big and loud battle scream, "AAAAAAAAAAAA!!"

When Ren stopped and looked down, he took a deep breath and said, "I did it. I actually did it. I killed Raphael, an archangel, the angel that ruined my life." Then he was silent for a while, just staring at the ash burns on the ground, enjoying the scene.

"Now, all that is left is to break his seal and the other seals so I can kill every angel left in heaven." Ren then snapped his fingers, teleporting away from the new landscape he and Raphael had created, never to return again.

WE WON

It had been six months and two days since Ren broke the first seal and started the war on the world of the living, and it had been two months since Ren's fight with Raphael. After the fight and the death of Raphael, the scale had once again tipped over to the demons' side.

Losing Raphael was a major blow on the angels' side, since he was one of their strongest fighters. And thanks to Raphael, Ren got a whole lot stronger, so now the earth has Ren—the twentieth strongest demon in hell—and Azazel—the tenth strongest in hell—breaking seals. And when Raphael died, the spell that was making clones of himself vanished, and the moment it did, the demons came out of hell and charged ahead to break as many seals as they could.

Remember, Raphael had called back all of the angels that were supposed to guard the seals, so the demons saw that as a big opportunity to break seals without angels getting in the way. It was like Black Friday for the demons. And as the days, weeks, and months went by, more seals were broken and more demons got stronger.

Now, in the present day, there was an island in the middle of nowhere. It looked discarded. It had no humans, animals, monsters, angels, or demons. But that was wrong. It only looked discarded because it was being surrounded by a magical barrier. This barrier made the outside of the island look discarded, but on the inside, it was actually a vacation spot for demons that had been participating in the war. Inside, there were many buildings to stay or to party. There were a lot of restaurants around to eat, and the surroundings and temperature was perfect.

Thanks to the barrier, the temperature was always around sixty degrees, and it had a gentle, cold breeze that made you want to take a relaxing nap. The water was crystal clear, the sand was so soft and smooth that you wouldn't find any trash, big rocks, or seashells anywhere, and the greenery was beautiful. It was the perfect vacation spot for anyone. Except for one thing—there were human slaves of various races, age, and gender. These humans were stripped naked just to embarrass them or to sexually attract the demon toward them so they would buy them or rent them.

What did the demon do to the human slaves? Well, when they bought or rented them, they could bring the demons their stuff wherever he or she wants, bring them food (or they could be the food), be their plaything, be their punching bag when they were not in the mood, or just kill them because they could. They had plenty of humans to bring to that island to be slaves.

It was literally a paradise for a demon, including Ren.

Speaking of Ren, he was on the beachside, sitting on a long chair in his human form, underneath an umbrella for shade, a little stool on his left side. The stool had a cup of fancy wine, and to finish it off, Ren was reading a Bleach manga, one he had already read it before, but he just wanted to read it again. Ren was enjoying himself, his manga, and his vacation so much that he didn't mind all the noise coming behind him.

The noises were human slaves getting beaten, screamed at, killed, or forced to have sex, which were not bothering Ren in the slightest. Ren stopped reading for a second to take a sip of his wine when he heard click-clacking, and footsteps on the sand on his right side. It was a girl in her late teens, wearing a chain around her neck. Her long blonde hair was incredibly messy, she was naked, and covered in cuts and bruises.

The slave girl spoke in a damaged and scared voice. "Here's your food, master."

Ren turned to see a plate with a cheeseburger and fries.

Ren smiled and said, "Good. Come here and put it on my stool." Ren put his opened manga on his lap and grabbed his cup so the stool was empty.

The girl nodded her head and tried to walk toward Ren with her badly damaged body. She made it to Ren and leaned over him to put the plate on the stool. Ren moved slightly so that they didn't bump into each other. She slowly put the plate down gently on the stool and when she let go, she also let out a sigh in relief that she didn't mess up. She moved out of the way so Ren could eat, but something happened they both heard a small splat. They both looked down and what they saw was a really big blood drop on top of Ren's manga, which stained it red.

It must have come from one of the girl's cuts on one of her arms.

The girl stumbled back without falling, the chain making lots of noise. She lowered her head and said, "P-p-please forgive me, master. I'm sorry! I didn't mean to bleed on your book. I promise I'll be more careful!"

While she was pleading for her life, Ren turned to the right side of his chair, put the blood-stained manga down on the chair, stood up, and started to walk toward her. When she was done pleading, she could hear Ren walking toward her. With every step, she could feel her heart stopping. Then something touched the right side of her face. She looked up in shock and saw Ren standing in front of her with a calm expression on his face. And what was touching her face was his left hand.

Ren said, "It's okay. These things happen. It's like you said—you were already bleeding." Ren was talking to her smoothly and calmly.

For a second she stopped shaking in fear, thinking she was going to be okay. Until...

Ren said, annoyed and angry, "At least, that is what I would have said if your disgusting blood landed on any other character. But it landed on my number one favorite character in that series."

Her face slowly changed from happy to "I'm dead." Ren slowly put his right hand on either side of her face and slowly both hands moved up on her face until they just stopped. Ren and the girl just stared at each other for a couple seconds. That's when it happened.

The slave girl screamed in total agony, pain, and shock.

Ren put both of his thumbs in both of her eyes, making sure they went into her skull slowly. The same could be said about his other fingers just digging into the back of her skull. When Ren had had enough of her screams, he got a good grip on her skull and ripped it in half. Both halves of her face went flying in different directions, landing hard on the sand. What was left of her head was literally her brain, still connected to her neck, which was still connected to her spine. Her body fell to the ground, lifeless.

Ren looked down at the body in disgust and said dispassionately, "Stupid human. Next time, go around." Then Ren spit on the body, turned away from it, and went back to sit on his seat. Ren looked at his book with a sad look and slowly closed it, like it was a person and shut its eyes.

Ren said, "Yes, what is it?"

There was a pretty muscular guy with a shaved head behind Ren wearing black shorts and a gray tank top.

"Sir Ren, we need your help."

Ren answered with a sarcastic tone, pretending like he didn't know, "With what?"

"With the final seal, sir."

Ren let out a sigh and said, "Why do you need my help?"

The demon was slowly getting scared as the conversation progressed. "Because, sir, the last seal is being guarded by an archangel."

Ren was actually shocked to hear that and said, "An archangel? Wow, I guess the angels aren't playing around anymore, huh? Well... serves them right. Like, seriously, they just keep underestimating us like we're nothing. They don't send any archangels down to stop us, and look what happened—we got sixty-five seals done. One more would end this lowly world."

The demon didn't say anything because he liked what Ren was saying—that the angels got what they deserved. But he still had to give Ren more information. But before he got the chance to say anything, Ren immediately interrupted him.

"But anyway—sorry, but no. I was told I could have a two-week vacation and as you can see, I've still got five more days left. So no. Go ask Azazel to break the last seal."

The demon's voice dropped immensely. "W-w-w-well w-we can't, sir."

Ren turned his head around to look at the demon in confusion and said, "Why not? Is he not in a good mood and doesn't want to be bothered? I mean, I guess so—"

"Azazel is dead!"

Ren didn't say anything. He just sat there, on his seat, completely still for a full minute before he said very quietly, "What did you just say?"

The demon felt like he should stop and teleport away now. But he knew Ren wouldn't let him until he heard everything.

The demon said, "Y-you see, Azazel died four weeks ag—" The demon couldn't say everything. Well, more like he couldn't say anything because Ren moved out of his seat, destroying it from the force, and grabbed the demon by the throat and started to strangle him. Hard.

Ren was looking at the demon with pure anger in his eyes and he slowly transformed into his half-demon form and said, "No. NO! Azazel is the best! No angel can beat him! And I know it wasn't an archangel because they are so arrogant that if they wanted him dead, they would have tried when he was trying to break one of the seals months ago! So I bet you were going to say it was an unknown angel that killed him!"

The demon couldn't say anything since Ren was destroying his windpipe, so all he did was nod.

Ren was breathing heavily out of rage and said, "Where is the unknown angel? I'll kill it!" Ren loosened his grip so he could hear the demon, because he really wanted to know where it was.

The demon said, "We don't know. Ever since he killed Azazel, he hasn't shown his face in the world of the living and our spies can't find him in heaven. He, like, disappeared from existence."

That was the truth, but not the answer Ren wanted to hear, so he broke the demon's neck and slammed him into the sand, sending sand everywhere. The other demons saw Ren was getting heated so they all walked away with their slaves, leaving Ren and the demon alone.

Ren was breathing heavily from his outburst. He stood up properly and walked toward the water. The demon that got slammed into the sand pulled himself out of the sand without much difficulty.

"Look, Ren, sir. I know you and Azazel were close friends, and I know this is very hard for you to accept, but it's the truth. So let me ask you this—how do you think you got that number?"

Ren wasn't facing the demon. His back was turned toward him. But when he asked his question, Ren looked at the number on his chest. It was the number ten. Ren had become one of the ten demon kings.

The demon said, "You don't have to say it because I know you became a demon king two weeks ago. When Lord Azazel died three weeks ago, no one was strong enough to take his place, not even you when you were the number eleven. At the time, you had to be on his level to get the number ten spot. Or, to be more specific, to reach the destructive capacity that could destroy Mexico and Texas. So the number ten spot was blank for a while. Until two world of the living weeks later the ranking system chose you because you finally reached that level."

Ren finally said something "Yeah, so what? That doesn't make sense. The gap between number ten to eleven is kind of big. I should still be number eleven and there should still be an empty spot for number ten!" Ren's voice sounded a little bit sad, like he was about to cry.

"No, sir. Well, yes, there is a big gap between ten and eleven. But you didn't have that much of a gap when you were eleven. You were already so close to having the same power level as Azazel, but the numbering system calculated that Azazel would still be stronger than you. But when he died and you continued to get stronger from your fights with angels, humans, and monsters, you became the number ten."

Ren didn't say anything. He was lost in his own thoughts. "It all makes sense now why I haven't seen or sensed Azazel for so long and why I got his number.

I just thought he was mad at me for taking his spot, like yeah, we were close friends but he really cared about being a part of the ten demon kings. And it bugged him when said that he was the weakest of the ten. So he's actually dead."

Ren slowly inhaled and exhaled, over and over, until he said, "It's at the cathedral—the place where it all started?"

The demon said with a quiet and calmer tone, "Yes."

Ren opened his wings and asked one more question: "Who is the archangel that is guarding the last seal?"

"The third archangel created by God—God's third son Gabriel."

Ren said very quietly, "Gabriel, huh?" And with that, Ren snapped his fingers and teleported away to go and break the final seal.

The demon was all alone on the beach looking off into the distance, a smile slowly growing in his face, thinking they just won the battle.

In front of the cathedral, there were soldiers guarding it from any demons or monsters or even some humans that were trying to steal or break the seal. It was currently seven p.m., the sun was going down, and the soldiers were getting tired of guarding the church.

On the right side of the church, two soldiers were taking a smoke break and talking to each other. But one of the two was furious about something.

The first soldier said, "Seriously, this is bullshit. Like, why do we even need to guard this church? There is a freakin' archangel in there guarding the last seal." He took another hit of his cigarette.

The other soldier that was smoking with him was trying to calm him down, but he did agree with every word. "Just calm down. I get why you are angry, but this is our job. We have to guard this place with what we have left." He moved his hand closer to the first soldier so he could give him the cigarette. The first soldier gave him the cigarette but he was still not happy.

"Don't give me that crap. We can't kill any demons. I mean, yeah, we can kill monsters, but they are not coming—only demons. And like I've been saying, there's a freakin' archangel in there. An archangel! There is nothing that can beat it."

The second soldier lowered his hand with the cigarette and on his face, he had a hint of fear and disappointment. He looked up at the other soldier and said, "I don't know about that. I mean, didn't you hear? That demon Ren, who started all of this, killed an archangel a couple months ago. And I heard that the place that they fought, which I believe is the Himalayas, where Mount Everest is located, is completely destroyed."

A small laugh escaped the first soldier and he said, "You really believe that nonsense? There is no such thing that has that kind of power, because if those things can actually do all that damage then wouldn't we have faced that multiple times?"

The second soldier finished the cigarette, dropped it, and stomped on it and said, "Yeah, I guess you're right."

"Are you sure about that?" Ren was screaming from a far distance.

Every soldier heard him and immediately moved into their battle positions.

The first soldier screamed in fright and anger, "Where are you?! Show yourself?!"

Ren walked out from the side of a badly damaged building. He was still in his half-demon form with both of his hands behind his back and a smile on his face. Every soldier could see Ren was shaking profusely. They had fought many demons before, but the pure sin that was radiating from Ren was scaring all of these grown, trained men.

Ren said, "Hmm, from what I can see, there are fifteen soldiers with hand-held guns. In front of me, three tanks driving closer from both sides of the church. You guys also have two mortars, and finally, I can sense three snipers at three different locations. Presumably aiming at my head. How about it? Am I right?" The way Ren said that was like a kid bragging about something he knew and he knew he was right. Every soldier started to look at each other in shock, and Ren could see that he was right.

The first soldier said, "Who cares that you got our numbers right?! Tell us who you are?!'

"I'm Ren." Ren spoke with a deep tone, pretending he was Batman.

Every soldier there didn't even hesitate when Ren said his name; they all started to shoot at him. Bullets were being fired at Ren from multiple assault rifles, pistols, and snipers, while Ren was getting hit by shells from tanks and bombs from mortars. Every soldier just kept on firing even though they couldn't see him anymore because of the smoke that was currently surrounding him, but they could all still feel his sin, his presence. They fired until everyone ran out of bullets and bombs. So they all stopped and waited to see if they got him.

For a couple seconds there was silence. The only thing that was making noise was the wind until finally the smoke cleared away from Ren and every soldier couldn't believe their eyes. Ren was just standing there yawning.

The first soldier said, "I don't believe it! Damn it, he regenerated!"

Ren stopped yawning and looked at the soldier and said, "Really? You think I regenerated? Haha, sorry to disappoint you, but no, I didn't regenerate. Actually, none of the bullets or bombs even went through me, or hurt me, for that matter."

The first soldier was trying to get some words out, but his throat was dry. But he finally managed to say what he was trying to say. "Liar! You are lying!"

Ren sighed and said, "Okay, fine. Let me show you, since none of you can see any of the bullets because they are mostly under debris."

Ren lifted his head slightly, and when he did that, suddenly all of these pieces of metal rose up from the ground. From a distance they looked like change, but if one looked closer, they were actually all of the bullets that got bent so badly that they looked like coins. Even the tanks' shells got bent into coin shapes. Every soldier was breathless. None could say anything or even think anything. Some even pissed themselves a little bit.

Ren said, "So, I notice that these bullets are a combination of steel, iron, gold, silver, and a hint of salt. The last time I was hit by these types of bullets was from a vampire. So tell me this—did Alucard tell you guys willingly or did you force him to tell you?" Ren was looking at a soldier when he said that.

The soldier that Ren was looking straight at just started to talk. The soldier didn't know if he was talking willingly or if Ren did something to get him to talk, but all he knew was that he just started to talk. The other soldiers immediately tried to stop him but they couldn't say anything or move. Presumably, Ren was using his telekinesis to keep them all quiet and still, except that one soldier that Ren was talking to.

When the second soldier started to talk, he was sweating a lot and his eyes were out of focus. "We forced him to tell us."

"Why?"

"When he told his scum-of-a-kind to not interfere with any demons that tried to break a seal. The government and military were not happy. So we captured him and forced him to tell us why his bullets work on demons so well, because he never showed or told us what his bullets are made of."

Ren closed his eyes and said, "I see. Is he still alive?"

The second soldier said, "I don't know."

Ren didn't say anything. He just stood there, all of the soldiers staring at him.

But then the soldiers couldn't see Ren anymore. In fact, they couldn't see, hear, smell, or think. All that happened was that they moved their necks to the left and that was it. All the bodies fell to the ground, dropping all the guns they were holding. Their bodies were lifeless.

Ren said, "Alucard, I hope you're still alive and doing well."

Ren started to walk toward the church. He was stepping over or on the bodies of the soldiers. If you looked at them and how they were laying on the ground, all of their heads were in a funny position. What happened was that Ren used his telekinesis to snap every soldier's neck. Everyone's neck—all of the fifteen soldiers in front of the church, the soldiers that were in the tanks, the soldiers that were stationed with the mortars, and the three snipers—was snapped.

Ren opened the churched door with no hesitation and quickly shut it. He stopped moving when he took his third step. Ren could sense something extremely powerful in the church, and the power was coming from behind the last chair in the row in front of Ren.

But something was off. The enormous power wasn't moving. In fact, Ren could hear something: "Zzzzzz."

Ren could hear snoring from where the power was coming from.

Ren said, "You can't be serious? Is he asleep?" He put a hand over his eyes and shook his head in disappointment.

He was going to keep on walking forward but thought, "No. It has to be a trap."

Ren lifted up his right hand, and with his pointer finger, summoned a small hellfire. It was so small that the hellfire looked like the size of the fire that comes out of a lighter. Ren flicked the fire toward where the power was and Ren could tell it hit him.

"AAAA! Hot, hot, hot!?!"

SLAM.

Ren heard the body fall on the floor pretty hard, like if someone fell from a bench while taking a nap, which meant Gabriel was asleep. And Ren realized that he just messed up. He could have broken the seal without fighting Gabriel but stupidly woke him up.

Gabriel stood up, still patting his stomach where the fire hit him, and said, "That was rude! You don't just hit someone with hellfire while that person is taking a nap. Didn't anybody teach you any manners?" From the tone he was giving Ren, he was being serious.

When he finally stopped moving around, Gabriel looked straight at Ren, and Ren could finally see what Gabriel's vessel looked like.

He looked like a man in his late twenties, and he was wearing blue jeans, a leather jacket, black Nike shoes, a black shirt that had the Superman symbol on it, and his facial features looked pretty normal. He had small curly brown hair and blue eyes. All in all, he looked like a regular guy that you might walk by anywhere.

With a small smile, Gabriel said, "Well hello, Ren. It's good to see you."

"I'm supposing you're Gabriel, right?"

"The one and only."

Ren's eyes moved toward the left to see where the final seal was. It took a while, but Ren could see it directly behind Gabriel. It was Jesus Christ's skull and it was on a table in between two white candles with blue flames.

Ren said, "Okay, I have to ask—why is it that when I try to break a seal, it's already out of the statue and on a table? Like, I can't even count how many times that this has happened to me." Ren sounded

But all Gabriel did was shrug his shoulders and say, "Mhm, I guess it just puts more attention on your fights."

Ren gave a little chuckle and said, "Maybe you're right. Okay, okay. Before we try to kill each other, I just have just two questions for you. One that i thought off on the way here and one just now"

Gabriel said, "Okay, go right ahead. I'll try my best to answer them just for you." He said it with a childish tone and gave Ren a wink.

Ren put his right hand on his chin, fully ignoring Gabriel's tone and said, "Which one should I ask first? Hmm. Okay, I guess I'll start with: why are you working with heaven? Like, didn't they kick you out of heaven and send you to earth? Because, if I'm remembering this correctly, you made Islam and its religion, right? Like I said—if I'm remembering this correctly?"

Gabriel's eyes suddenly widened and a big smile appeared on his face. Then he said, "You know, you're the first person that has asked me that question. It's funny really—when this war started and when I joined heaven's side, all the humans I met never asked me that question, they just said, 'Yes! We got Gabriel! We're saved!" Or when I faced a demon, they just ran from me, shit themselves, or insulted me. Don't get the wrong idea—I wasn't getting upset, I was just getting annoyed because I would assume that so many people would ask me that question but they never do. But you're the first, so thank you."

Ren stayed quiet. He just nodded because he could tell Gabriel was happy.

"Sorry, I didn't actually answer your question. Well, to be honest, I didn't have many options. It was either join the demon side that is mostly composed of demons, some monsters, and some humans. Or I could join heaven, which has mostly angels, humans, and some monsters. So I choose heaven. Don't get me wrong—I still have a grudge against them—but heaven's side has more humans and what can I say? I kind of like humans, and even though they did kick me out of heaven, they are still my family and I don't actually hate them." Gabriel was calm. There was no emotion in his voice. It was just the truth, and he gave that truth to Ren.

Ren gave Gabriel a look of satisfaction because he could absolutely respect that. Gabriel didn't have a choice. He had to choose to join a side or die, kind of like Ren when he first became a demon—he had to choose to start the war for vengeance or go to the world of the living and live his normal life.

Gabriel said, "Okay, so what is your second question?"

When Gabriel asked his question, Ren was lost in thought, so when Gabriel spoke, it snapped Ren out of his thoughts and reminded him that he did have another question.

"Okay, my next question is: are you a nerd as well, because I noticed that Superman shirt and I just have to know? Are you a nerd or is it just your vessel?" Ren generally sounded curious.

Gabriel was a little shocked by Ren's question because either he wasn't expecting that question or he was shocked because he should have expected it.

"Yes, I am a nerd. I am mostly into comics, then video games, and when it comes to anime, I like it, but I prefer the other two way more."

Ren got a little excited, like a kid who just met someone at school or at a park that liked that same stuff he did.

"That is so awesome! Finally, I've meet an angel that likes the things I like! Even though I prefer anime more than comics—oh well, I'll take it."

Gabriel gave a small smile and chuckled a little and said, "Same! Every angel I meet doesn't even know what a nerd is! Gosh, I wish we could be friends and not enemies! But unfortunately, that's not the case."

Ren smirked a little, like he was about to tell a joke. Then he said, "Well, we can. All you have to do is to let me break that seal."

"Sorry, not going to happen. But how about you just turn around and walk away?"

"Sorry, but nice try. You have your reasons and I have mine."

They both didn't say anything after that; they just stood there for a couple seconds with smiles on their faces.

Gabriel said, sounding disappointed, "Okay, even though I would like to keep talking to you about this stuff—like, I can seriously tell that you and me could be very close friends—we have to get things started. Unfortunately."

Ren nodded and got into his battle position. Gabriel lifted his right hand up in front of himself and a scroll appeared out of his palm. Ren gave Gabriel a confused look when he summoned the scroll. Ren had seen angels using scrolls plenty of time before their fights for a seal, so why was he shocked? The reason was because from what Ren could sense, that scroll was different from all the other scrolls that Ren had seen. His instincts were telling him to stop Gabriel, but Ren was very curious about what it was.

When Gabriel fully opened the scroll, a huge light burst out and covered the entire inside of the church, blinding Ren in the process. When Ren could tell that the light had finally disappeared, he lowered his arms from blocking the light and opened his eyes. Ren didn't feel like he was in another dimension. In fact, he could tell that he was still in the world of the living. So what happened? That's when Ren noticed it.

Gabriel said, "Well? What do you think? I felt like this would be more fun." Gabriel opened his arms wide like he was showing Ren something really big.

What Ren was seeing was something else. Gabriel didn't send Ren and himself to a different dimension. What he did was make the church bigger. A whole lot bigger.

Ren was hesitant to say anything, but luckily for him, Gabriel answered Ren's question before Ren could even say it.

"Well, as you can see, Ren, this scroll that I invented has expanded the inside of the church by one thousand times its normal size, except for you, me, the furniture, and the seal. And finally the last big kicker is that the walls, floor, and even once again the furniture is one thousand times more durable. But thr spell only worked on the inside. The outside is still the same size and durability. It's kind of like..."

Ren interrupted Gabriel and said, with a choked tone, "The Tardis from Doctor Who."

Gabriel tightened his fist and slowly crouched forward like he was in pain or like he was getting angry over something.

Gabriel said, "Aa, please can you just leave this place? I really don't want to kill you!"

"Sorry, but you know I can't do that. But I have to ask—why are you doing this, instead of sending us to a different dimension?"

"Well, remember—I may be on heaven's side, but I still do have a grudge against them. So instead of sending us to a different dimension so we don't hurt their precious church, I just extended the church to give us more room, and if the church gets damaged, whatever. They can fix it themselves."

Then they both started to laugh, but their laughs were small, quiet, and quick—so quiet that they might not have been able to hear each other's laughter. Gabriel gave a weak smile and looked down. He didn't have anything left to say to Ren to try to change his mind and Ren felt the same way. The time for talk had finally passed. Now it was time to fight.

Ren and Gabriel both summoned their armor at the same time. They both knew that they had to go all out because this fight was literally going to decide the world's fate. When Ren was covered in his armor, he noticed that Gabriel's armor looked exactly like Raphael's. The only difference was that Gabriel's armor had a very shiny bronze color, unlike Raphael's, which was gold.

Gabriel moved his right arm out and summoned his weapon. His weapon was a double-sided katana, unlike Raphael's double-sided Egyptian fan axe. The katana was a little bit taller than he was.

Ren, with his metallic and demonic voice, said, "Hmm, you archangels really like your double-sided weapons."

"Yeah, most of us do, but not all of us." Gabriel's voice was soothing and calm, like an instrument from an opera.

After Gabriel spun it around a couple of times, he rushed toward Ren with great speed and clashed with Ren's weapon. Ren felt the entire impact of the attack. It was very strong but not as strong as Raphael's strength. Ren pushed Gabriel back with his strength and proceeded with his attacks. When Ren got close, he swung from his left side. Gabriel blocked it, but the moment he did, Ren opened his hand and shot hellfire at Gabriel's face. But Gabriel saw Ren open his hand. He shrugged his head up, activating his telekinesis, and moved Ren's arm up so that the hellfire missed his head.

With Gabriel's weapon free, he quickly used the other side of his katana for a thrust toward Ren's stomach. It almost hit Ren's stomach directly, but Ren moved to the side fast enough that the katana only scratched the side of his armor. Ren moved his right leg for a kick, and Gabriel used his left arm to block it. Ren then lowered his left arm, which was still above Gabriel's head, with great speed. Gabriel used his telekinesis to hold it in place. Then Ren, with his free right arm, went for a swing toward the left side of Gabriel's face, but Gabriel blocked the attack with his right free arm and his weapon.

If one looked at these two from afar, it looked like they were tangled up with each other. Finally, with Ren's last free limb—his left leg—he raised it to slice Gabriel from his groin up. But Gabriel was not having this anymore, so with his left arm that was still blocking Ren's right leg, he turned his arm forward so that his hand was pointing toward Ren and shot a big blast of holy water, hitting Ren in the chest and sending him flying back all the way to the end of the church's walls. He was slammed into it while still being pushed back by the holy water.

Ren easily swatted the holy water away to be free from it, then he moved to the left side, completely dodging the down slash that Gabriel did, deeply cutting the wall. Gabriel chased after Ren until, when Gabriel thought he caught up to Ren, Ren suddenly stopped and did a backflip over Gabriel out of nowhere. Then Gabriel felt a sharp pain all over his back.

When Ren flipped over Gabriel, with both of his arms, he slashed Gabriel's back, cutting not too deep but deep enough that a lot of blood squirted out. The cuts would have been way deeper, but Gabriel's armor made sure that didn't happen. When Ren fully landed on his feet, he shot hellfire behind Gabriel and also flew toward him on top of the fire. Gabriel quickly turned and gave a strong kick in the air, sending pressurized air which hit Ren's fire and sent it everywhere while Ren was still going after him.

Gabriel said, "Okay, Ren, I do like that you're spunky and you won't let your opponent get a breather. But personal space!" Gabriel threw his weapon toward Ren.

It was spinning like a deadly buzzsaw. Ren quickly raised both of his arms and blocked the attack. Then, when Ren was blocking the spinning katana, he felt a sharp pain in his back, so he turned to see what it was. And what Ren saw was very shocking. He saw not one, but two Gabriels. Ren could tell they were Gabriels because of the armor and grace. These two new Gabriels cut off Ren's wings.

Ren thought, "What the hell? Two Gabriels?! But how?!" Ren turned his head back forward and he could still see Gabriel in front of him, just standing there.

Before Ren thought how there were three Gabriels, he knew he had to get away from the two Gabriels and the spinning katana quickly. Both Gabriels that were behind Ren spun in sync, one clockwise, the other counterclockwise. They were planning to hit Ren's torso from both sides, cutting Ren in half.

Ren quickly jumped up as fast and hard as he could while the spinning katana was still connected to both of his weapons. And with Ren's wings fully regenerated back, he used them to keep him in the air, and kicked both Gabriels with both of his legs, like a horse. Then Ren lowered his head right under his arms and just turned off the armor on his wings and blades that was holding the weapon in place. With the blades that were holding the katana back now gone, the weapon went past Ren's head, but it cut off his wings with ease.

When the two Gabriels that got kicked by Ren finally got their balance back, they didn't—or couldn't—react to the spinning katana that came toward them, and it decapitated them both. The spinning katana made a U-turn around Ren and landed back in Gabriel's hand. Ren stopped to catch his breath and to look at the two Gabriels that just died. Their bodies were just lying on the ground, with no blood coming out, until they just glowed and vanished. Ren was shocked that the bodies disappeared just like that.

Ren thought, "Okay, by the way how they disappeared, they weren't real angels—or, to be more exact, shapeshifting angels. They were strong, but not as strong as Gabriel, and they just appeared behind me out of nowhere. No, they were here, I just didn't sense them somehow? Was it because I was distracted by the attack and—" Ren's eyes widened, not like Gabriel could see it. "I see. So your power is to make clones of yourself, isn't that right?"

Gabriel didn't say anything. He just made a satisfied grunt, which gave Ren his answer.

Ren said, "Also, I have to ask: how did you know the technique that I used on Raphael?"

What Ren was referring to was that Gabriel's weapon was away from Gabriel for too long and it should have disappeared, but it didn't. The reason was because Gabriel had a very thin blue wire that was connected between the katana's hilt and Gabriel's finger. The wire was very thin holy water that was pumping grace into the katana. It was literally the same trick that Ren created.

Gabriel said, "Well, let's just say that we were watching your final fight with Raphael and that trick was very interesting to me, so I decided to copy it."

"I guess I should be happy that you think it was good and you want to use it. But that's my move, so I don't like an angel using it even if it's you." Ren actually sounded kind of angry.

Gabriel just shrugged his shoulders and got into his battle position again.

And so they were back to fighting.

They both charged toward each other again. Ren was giving a barrage of slashes and jabs from all of his limbs. Gabriel was blocking and dodging pretty much all Ren's attacks, but very few were hitting Gabriel; the same could be said about Ren. Gabriel was making counter attacks at Ren with his weapon and Ren was blocking and dodging most of Gabriel's attacks, but some were hitting him.

They just kept attacking each other over and over again to the point where they couldn't stay in one spot. They were flying everywhere in the church. They just keep on attacking each other with punches, kicks, stabs, slashes, and shots of hellfire and holy water.

So far, it had been evenly matched. At least, that's what Gabriel wanted Ren to think.

Their weapons connected again, but they stayed connected for a long period of time. Ren saw that Gabriel just did something. When Gabriel was connected to Ren, he spread his wings apart and one feather from each wing came off. It fell like a rock, then for some reason, it started to glow, but the glowing was not very bright—in fact, anyone could have missed it if they were not paying attention to it.

The glowing feathers just grew in size, but when it grew, it didn't just grow into a bigger feather. It actually started to grow a torso, then limbs, and then they took what appeared to be the same height as Gabriel, and then finally the two new shapes began to be covered in a shiny bronze colored armor and held a double-sided katana. It all happened within a single second when both feathers fell from Gabriel's wings.

Ren thought, "So that's how he makes clones of himself." Ren gave a little smile because he was glad that now he knew how they were made.

Both of the new Gabriel clones rushed at Ren from both sides. Ren thought he was in a tight spot because the real Gabriel was still connected with Ren's blades to hold him in place while the two new Gabriels were coming toward him. He was stuck. At least that was what he WAS thinking.

Then suddenly, the real Gabriel just quickly moved back, away from Ren to get a great distance from him. Ren couldn't think of why he would do that. Both of the clone Gabriels finally reached Ren and swung at him. But luckily, Ren blocked both attacks with no difficulty.

Ren thought, "What are you pl—"

BOOM BOOM!!!

Two big explosions just appeared in the church where Ren was flying. A big smoke cloud was in the middle of the super-sized church. A small black cloud left the big one still in the air and crashed on the ground. Gabriel took a deep breath and exhaled with great force to blow away the smoke. The smoke went away—from the smoke that was in the middle of the air, to the one that slammed to the ground.

The smoke that was on the ground vanished and it revealed Ren on his knees, shaking from the unexpected explosions. Ren's body had multiple burn wounds all over his body and smoke was coming out of his helmet, which indicated that smoke was coming out of his mouth. The two explosions were so powerful that it almost got rid of Ren's armor. But it wasn't completely gone, it was just badly damaged. At least it was for like a few seconds; the same could be said for the burn wounds because Ren was healed in no time. Ren slowly got up and started to stretch like nothing had happened until he heard Gabriel talking to him.

"Well, what do you think? Pretty devastating, right?" He sounded like a person bragging about something amazing he did.

However, Ren quietly whispered to himself, "So, regular clones and clones can explode with great damage. And, as I could tell, both types of clones had the same strength and level of grace. Pretty annoying and clever."

Gabriel spread his wings again, two more feathers came off, and two more clones formed. Gabriel and his clones charged at Ren. The two clones were ahead of the real one, probably as a distraction. Ren turned with great speed to slash the two incoming angels, but the slashes just went right through the two clones. It was like Ren only hit air.

Then when Ren was still swinging, the real Gabriel appeared in front of Ren and swung his katana sideways, trying to cut Ren's chest deeply, but luckily, Ren used his telekinesis to fling himself back to dodge his attack. A deep sound of metal and bone breaking could be heard.

What happened was that Gabriel's attack did hit Ren's chest, but it only cut Ren's armor, skin, and some of his ribs. The wound immediately closed, Ren regained his balance, and proceeded with his attacks, all while thinking about what Gabriel's power was.

Ren thought, "Okay, so Gabriel's power is to make clones from his feathers. One type is just a regular clone, the other appears to be a regular clone but it can explode, and he can make a clone that is completely intangible. I don't know if he can make other types, but so far, it's just those three. And from what I sensed from the clones, all three have the same grace level, which I managed to calculate is only 70% of Gabriel's already restricted strength."

While Ren was thinking to himself, the fight was not going too well. When Ren was thinking and fighting, Gabriel was just summoning clone after clone after clone at Ren. They were mostly just for distractions or for a shield for any attacks that Ren made that would have hit Gabriel, but the clone got hit instead. The fight wasn't going well for Ren.

The fight had been going on for an hour now and it was still not going well for Ren.

Ren went for an uppercut, but a clone appeared in front of Gabriel and got stabbed in the heart. The clone grabbed Ren's arm tightly to hold him in place while another clone was above Ren, coming down to cut his head in half. Ren quickly raised his free arm to block the attack. It worked, but now Ren was completely stuck again.

The real Gabriel appeared behind Ren and was about to stab his heart, but was stopped by Ren's hellfire that he shot from his feet that hit Gabriel and sent him falling back, which gave Ren enough time to shoot two more hellfire blasts from both of his feet at the two clones, completely killing them both. They both stopped to catch their breath and analyze their next moves.

Gabriel thought, "Okay, calm down. You are getting way too into this fight. Remember that's how Raphael died. So think—you have to find a real opening, and quickly, because from what I heard from my brothers, Ren mostly wins his fights by coming up with a great plan when the fight is prolonged, so I have to finish him off now even though I don't want to."

Ren thought, "Okay, I'm getting nowhere. This entire fight has just been a stalemate. The only new information I've gotten is that he can only summon two clones at a time and the two clones can be the same or not be the same. The most dangerous clones are the explosive ones, but if I stay near the real Gabriel, he won't use them. But soon I have a feeling that won't be the case anymore. So I have no choice. I have to use the Final Attack when his guard is down but..." Ren's eyes wandered around, looking to see what he could use for his advantage. Until he saw something and that gave him a big smile and a plan.

Gabriel spread his wings again and summoned two more clones. They formed and charged at Ren. Ren ran in the other direction, making the two angels follow him, then he turned his head around to see them. With both of his hands extended, he pointed at the clones to shoot small and thin hellfire at them. Both of the clones were too close to Ren, so the two thin hell fires pierced the heads of the clones and then the clones exploded.

Gabriel thought, "Ah, he makes those thin hell fires faster by making them smaller and more compressed. But the damage was weakened, so it wouldn't even work on me, but it would work on my clones since they are weaker than me."

Then Ren appeared out of the smoke and clashed with Gabriel. The impact made him move back a couple of steps, but not that much. Gabriel, with all of his strength, flung Ren back through the smoke again while chasing after him. Gabriel reached Ren and slammed his katana on his weapons, completely breaking the entire floor. Ren moved his right leg with great speed and hit Gabriel on the side, cracking his armor a little bit and sending him flying away. Gabriel stopped himself by slamming his sword on the ground, slowing him down until he was completely stopped. Gabriel raised his head and could see Ren in a stance.

Ren had both knees bent and he moved his arms around, forming a circle. Then, when his arms were in front of his hip, he pulled them back, and with a big thrust forward, sent a huge blast of hellfire toward Gabriel.

Gabriel said, "Ha, okay, so we are pulling an anime style of trying to see if I can stop this big blast that is coming my way. Challenge accepted!"

Gabriel slammed his weapon on the ground and let his weapons disappear while he raised his arms in front of himself to catch the oncoming attack. He grabbed it and held it back.

Gabriel said, "Ha, this blast does have good power, but it doesn't even have enough to hold me in place!" He sounded like he was having the time of his life.

Ren said, "Are you sure you want to move away from that spot?!"

"What do you mean?!"

"Look behind you!"

Gabriel did just that. When he was still holding the fire in place, he turned his head around to see what was behind him. And he couldn't believe it.

What was behind him was the seal—the skull of Jesus Christ. But something was different about it. It had this strange color on it. The color was red, and that's when Gabriel figured out what it was.

The skull was covered in blood—the Pope's blood.

Gabriel thought, "How? When…when did he do it?!"

Ren said, "So you get it—if you move or if even a tiny bit of my hellfire hits that skull, it will catch on fire and I do the chant, and the final seal is broken and I win!"

Gabriel said, "Hm, that is a good strategy, but this fire won't be able to…" Before Gabriel was able to finish his sentence, he sensed Ren disappear from the spot that he was in to directly behind him.

Ren did the same stance and movement as before and sent yet another huge hellfire blast toward Gabriel, but this time it was coming from the opposite side. Gabriel quickly moved his right hand away from the first hellfire and toward the other one to grab it. Now Gabriel was in between two hell fires trying to crush him. But Gabriel wasn't really struggling that hard. Yeah, he was grunting, but he wasn't using that much strength.

"Not bad, Gabriel! Not bad at all!"

"Thanks. But it's going to take more to stop me!"

Ren said with a sadistic tone, "Really?"

Ren then appeared in front of Gabriel, but he was far away from him. Then Ren spread his arms out, bent all his fingers into a clawing position, and moved them close to each other with great speed until they were like a couple of inches away from each other. And that's when Gabriel could feel the two hell fires suddenly get more force in them.

What was happening was that Ren was using his telekinesis to push the hellfire closer toward Gabriel to crush him. But Ren was not done yet. Ren was also sending ten strings of hellfire (one string per finger)—five for the huge hellfire blast on Gabriel's right side, and five for the one on Gabriel's left. Gabriel figured out what Ren was doing.

Gabriel thought, "So he is pumping more and more hellfire into the ones that I'm already holding. Those strings are slowly increasing their damage output. But even though their damage is increasing, the force, or impact, isn't increasing because I already stopped it from moving forward. But then Ren is using his telekinesis to increase the force—impact—of the hellfire already in place. Damn! What can I do?!"

With every second, Gabriel could feel the hellfire getting stronger and getting closer to each other to crush him, and if they touched, they would explore, which would send pieces of hellfire everywhere and no doubt hit the seal. Gabriel was grunting louder and louder. He didn't know how he could hold it much longer. He thought of sending clones, but the feather would just get sucked into the fire. Then Gabriel thought of an idea, and it was the only one he could think of.

When the hellfire got to the point where Gabriel couldn't hold it back anymore, he used his telekinesis to send both pillars of flames up, engulfing himself in the flames, and the fire went up and hit the ceiling of the church. The ceiling was one thousand times stronger than it originally was, but the hellfire was too much; it burned right through the ceiling.

Since the church was smaller on the outside, when the fire came out from the inside, it looked like a mountain that was made of fire just appeared out of nowhere on top of the church. It was so big that it reached all the way up into the thermosphere.

When the fire disappeared, if any living thing was near enough to see the huge hellfire that appeared in the sky, they could also see ashes falling from the sky. The church was covered in smoke. It was so bad that if you were in it, you wouldn't even be able to see your own hand. Ren waved the smoke away with one swing, sending it away from him and the church, and that was when Ren could see Gabriel.

Gabriel looked like a humanoid sculptor that was made of coal. Smoke was coming out of his mouth and noise. Ren walked toward him, thinking he was completely dead, but then he could see Gabriel slowly regenerating. Ren stopped to look at the ever-so-slowly regenerating Gabriel with a humongous look of shock on his face.

"Oh my fucking god! You're still alive?! I swear, you archangels are so amazing, really. I'm just blown away. It must be from your regeneration, natural durability, and your armor durability that kept you somehow alive."

When Ren stopped talking, he thought he could hear Gabriel talking.

"H...h...ow... d...d...id...you..."

It was just painful to hear Gabriel trying to speak. When Ren first met Gabriel, he was so lively and talkative. But now he was in so much pain and was struggling to talk.

Ren said, "I went all out."

Gabriel was still regenerating when Ren said that but Gabriel's eyes were fully regenerated. He turned to look at Ren in confusion.

Ren said, "I went all out with my speed. Don't get me wrong—I was using my full strength with my muscles, telekinesis, and hellfire. Just not my speed." Ren actually sounded sad and concerned for Gabriel.

"W-why?"

"So I could catch you off guard when I went full speed. But you were so strong and your reflexes were so good that I didn't think it would work."

It took a while, but Gabriel regenerated enough to talk normally, even though his body was still really burnt.

"Then when did you put the Pope's blood on the skull?"

"I did it when I killed your two exploding clones. They gave me enough smoke to move, put the Pope's blood on the seal, and move back behind the smoke cloud and rush through it to attack you. But I have to be honest, I wasn't expecting for it to go that smoothly. Were you distracted by something?"

Gabriel's eyes widened because he had been distracted. He distracted himself by thinking to himself about how Ren had killed his clones. Gabriel closed his eyes in disappointment at himself. Then he opened them and asked his final question.

"If you were holding back your speed, then how fast can you truly go?" His voice had no tone nor spirit in it; it was like Ren was talking to a person that was very depressed.

"Well, I was going at you with the same speed that I used on Raphael during our final fight, and you surprised me that you were keeping up with me. Actually, you were a little faster. But not faster than my full speed which is 680 million 500 thousand mile per hour."

Gabriel thought, "Ah, I see. So your speed now is another 50,000 just from going up ten ranks. If you maybe get into the top four, you would be the fastest demon in hell."

Ren said, "But it's like I said, if I had gone full speed right off the bat, you would adapt to it and, unlike Raphael, you would have stayed calm and figured it out quickly. So it was my trump card." Ren walked toward Gabriel until he was in front of him.

Gabriel looked up at Ren. Ren lifted up his right arm above Gabriel's head. Gabriel had no strength to fight back. He didn't even have enough strength to move.

Ren closed his eyes and said softly and quietly, "Sorry and goodbye, Gabriel. I won." Ren lowered his hand to finish Gabriel.

"Sorry, but I won't let you kill another brother of mine."

Ren and Gabriel were shocked to see another person right next to Ren, grabbing his arm. The man was pretty good looking. He wore an entire white suit with white shoes, his eyes were so blue that they look like diamonds, his hair was blond and was combed to the side neatly, and his facial structure was also perfect.

Ren said, "Who are you and where did you come from?"

The man didn't answer but Ren did hear Gabriel talk in a shocked, but mostly scared, tone.

"Brother, what are you doing here?"

The guy looked at Gabriel, concern in his eyes. Then he looked back at Ren with a look of pure rage. He crushed Ren's arm, along with his arm's armor and flung him back all the way to the other side of the room. Ren couldn't stop himself, so he crashed through the wall and ended up outside.

Gabriel started to talk, but his tone sounded like a child that was pouting. "I didn't need your help. I lost, so I should die with dignity."

The man said, "Maybe so, but I won't allow it. I still care about you, little brother, so please don't say stuff like that. It will make me cry." His voice was smooth and caring. Gabriel didn't look in his direction, but he did smile a bit.

Ren appeared in the church, dusting the wood pieces bits off him.

"So, coming from you two keep calling each other brothers, you're an angel, and not just any angel—an archangel."

The man was silent. He just gave Ren a cold look.

Ren said, "So which archangel is it? You called Gabriel little brother and the only two archangels that are older than him are... Lucifer, but he is in hell, so that just leaves Michael."

The man was again silent, but Gabriel gave Ren a nod to answer his question.

Ren thought, "This is just fucking perfect—not only did I have to fight Gabriel, and I almost lost, but now the first and strongest angel ever created by God is here. I doubt he is going to let me leave; even if I do leave, Satan and Lucifer would give me the biggest punishment ever if I didn't break this final seal, and I already took too much damage from Gabriel, so my strength and regeneration is weak. I have to go all out and attack him with all I've got."

Ren tried to move forward but he didn't move. He looked down to see if his feet were stuck, but they weren't, so he tried again. He still didn't move.

Ren was talking to himself quietly: "What's going on? Why am I not moving? Is he using his telekinesis on me? No, he's not. Am I just scared?"

Ren looked down again to see his legs and it was what he thought—his legs were shaking like crazy. And not just his legs—his entire body was shaking. Ren didn't notice it until now, but he could sense Michael's grace and it was huge. It was just like Satan and Lucifer's power. Ren felt like he was being crushed.

Michael said, "What's wrong? Are you scared? Aren't you going to attack me? If not, I'll come to you."

Ren eyes widened and that gave him enough adrenaline to finally move. He went full speed and put all his strength into one big punch. The hit was so strong that the wall that was behind all three of them got completely blown away and destroyed some buildings, too. But Ren's attack didn't hit. His blades weren't even touching Michael. Michael had grabbed Ren's arm before it could reach his face. Then Michael lifted his free arm and gave Ren an air punch to the torso.

Ren's back exploded, sending all of Ren's blood, organs, and bones all over the floor, leaving him a husk just for a couple seconds. Everything that left Ren's body disintegrated and he fully regenerated. But when he did, he gave a big painful scream.

"AAAAAAAAAAAAAAAA!!!"

The pain was so great that Ren couldn't even think about what just happened to him. But Michael wasn't done with Ren. He crushed his arm again and just kept slamming him to the ground over and over again until Ren was just mush on the ground when Michael let go of him. Ren fully regenerated again, and this time, he tried to teleport away. But Ren couldn't snap his fingers. Michael's telekinesis wouldn't let him.

Michael said with a smile, "Okay. Now that I got most of that out of my system, let's get this thing started." He clapped his hands to get the dust off.

Ren said, "S-s-start what?"

Michael didn't turn around. He said, "Fixing everything you did."

Michael stood with his arms and wings spread apart, concentrating. Ren was on the ground, kneeling, not able to move a muscle because Michael was using his telekinesis to hold him in place, while Gabriel was sitting on a chair that he must have gotten from another building.

Slowly, debris that was around was rising and coming close to Michael. The debris started to come together like it was fixing itself, and that's when Ren figured it out—all of the debris that was floating in front of him were pieces of the wall from the church that he broke.

It only took a minute for all the pieces to come together, and slowly but surely, the wall was fixed. But Michael didn't stop there; he somehow fixed all the cracks and holes that were around the church from Ren and Gabriel's battle, practically fixing the entire church except for the ceiling because Ren completely disintegrated that part, but it didn't really matter to Michael. All he wanted was to make that church more presentable for what he was about to do.

Michael walked up to the altar and began his plan.

He had asked Gabriel to clean the skull to get every drop of the Pope's blood off it before he fixed the church. Gabriel finished cleaning it and inspected it to see if he missed a spot, which he didn't. He walked toward Michael, and when he was in front of his big brother, he knelt down and raised the arm that had the skull like a minion giving his boss the thing he was looking for his whole life.

Michael carefully grabbed the skull and said, "Thank you. Now watch that demon and make sure he doesn't interrupt me."

Gabriel nodded his head and walked toward Ren. Ren was still kneeling, not saying anything. It wasn't like he couldn't say anything, it was just that he couldn't say anything. Not even Ren knew why he was just watching Michael doing his thing.

Michael turned toward the altar and gently put the skull on a plate that he had summoned. The plate was made of half gold and half silver. The skull was facing Michael and he put up two candles, both big and white. He put one to the left side of the skull and one to the right. He turned his right hand up and spread each finger apart, and then a bluish-white circle appeared on his palm and a vine with thorns came out of it. The vine moved around, forming a circle. When the circle closed from Michael's palm, the vine wrapped itself in a circle. The circle it formed was small; it looked like only a head could fit in it. And that's when Ren knew what that vine was.

That was a vine from a Hoth Thorne Tree, the same type that was on Jesus Christ's head when he was crucified. So with that, the ritual began and Michael began his chant.

Michael said, "With the bone of the holiest man that has ever existed, with the holiest plant on the earth that he wore when he was crucified..." Michael put the vine on the skull. "With the two purest metals combined that holds the skull, and finally, with the blood of the first being our father ever created..." Michael, with a quick motion, cut his palm and squeezed the blood to drip onto the skull. But the blood wasn't disintegrating; it must be from the ritual.

Michael said, "All of these combined, please, I beg of you—give me the power to reverse all that has happened to humanity, to heaven, and to the earth. Please show us, your children, mercy and forgiveness."

When Michael finished, the candles' tips caught on fire, but this fire was clear, like glass. The flames got bigger and bigger until they started to move on their own. The flames spiraled around each other with grace; it was like the flames were dancing in front of all of them. Then the flames stopped spiraling and fell straight down in the center of all the spirals and hit Jesus Christ's skull, catching it on fire.

Ren said, "What the hell are you doing?! If you were going to catch it on fire, then all you could have done was just let me do it for you!"

Gabriel was supposed to make sure that Ren wouldn't say anything, but he was too focused on the ritual himself. But when they both looked closer, they could see that the skull wasn't melting. Actually, it was like the flames weren't even doing anything to it—it was just there, surrounding it.

As Michael looked up, he could see a figure forming out of the heat, from the flames. Ren and Gabriel couldn't see it because they were further away, but as the figure was becoming more visible, they could.

Ren couldn't believe who the person that figure was taking was. It showed a middle-aged man wearing mostly a white robe, but he also had a brown robe covering his right shoulder. His hands were together in a praying symbol, and finally the man had a brown beard and long brown hair.

Michael, Gabriel, and Ren didn't question who it was. From the energy that this person was giving off and its form, it was actually Jesus himself. The figure was Jesus himself.

Jesus said, "Okay, my son, I'll help you fix everything. Put your dominant hand in the fire." His voice sounded like a saint, like a son from God himself.

Michael bowed his head, stood up, walked toward the flames, and did what Jesus said without hesitating. The flames didn't hurt his hand; in fact, they weren't even hot. Then Jesus put both of his hands on Michael's hand and vanished into the flames. Michael removed his hand from the flames and noticed that some of the flames that were covering the skull were now covering his hand. Without a second to lose, he turned to face Ren and walked toward him. Ren didn't like that Michael, with his burning hand, was walking toward him.

"Hey— Hey— What are you doing? Stay away from me. What are you going to do?!" Ren was very scared. He didn't even have the slightest clue as to what Michael was about to do.

Michael said, "You're the final step to this ritual."

"Huh?"

"One of the pieces for this ritual is the demon that has the most seals broken, which happens to be you."

Ren struggled to break free of Michael's telekinesis but couldn't.

Michael raised his hand up above Ren's head and yelled, "Now repent from all your sins!" He slammed his flaming hand on Ren's head, engulfing Ren's entire head with the flames.

Ren screamed as the flames pierced his head and light came out of his eyes, nose, and mouth. That sent a white, cloud-looking shockwave from Ren, sending out and going around the entire planet and vanishing when it reached the other side of the world. Ren's head was dangling down, spit and snot coming down. His face looked like he was about to pass out.

Ren struggled to say the words, "W-What did y-you just do to me?"

Michael completely ignored Ren's question and asked Gabriel, "Well, did it work?"

Gabriel said, "Let me see." Gabriel closed his eyes for a second, opened them, and said, "Only one third have been fixed."

Michael put his left hand on his chin since his right was still on fire. "Hmm. It must be because of Ren's transformation to a different kind of demon. That might have held the spell back from completing. Damn. Curse that Satan and our dumb brother for creating that spell." He sounded annoyed.

Gabriel said, "Yeah, now that you mention it, what I'm sensing from Ren is that he is not a fallen angel anymore."

Ren eyes widened because he just noticed too that he was not a fallen angel demon anymore. Ren looked at his number and saw that his number was 200.

Ren quietly talked to himself: "I'm a created demon again."

Michael said, "Let me do it again."

Ren said, "No, don—" Ren didn't finish because Michael slammed his hand on Ren's head again and tried to do the ritual again.

"Now repent for all of your sins!"

The same process happened again. Ren's eyes, nose, and mouth glowed, and a cloud-like shockwave came out of him and went around the world until it hit the other side of the planet.

Ren didn't look too good; not only more saliva and snot was coming out, but now blood was coming out from his nose and mouth. But something was off about the blood. It was not disintegrating immediately. It was disintegrating, but not even close to its normal speed. Ren didn't notice because from his facial expression, it looked like he was going back and forth from being conscious and blacking out.

Michael said, "How about that time?"

Gabriel said, "No. Now two thirds of them are fixed. But I've got a feeling one more will do it since Ren is back into his human demon state."

Michael didn't say anything. All he wanted was to get it over with. He put his hand on Ren's head again, but this time he said his chant quieter and smoother.

"Now repent for all of your sins."

And with that, Ren completely blacked out, not knowing what happened.

Ren was unconscious—completely asleep. But even though he was unconscious, he could still feel the pain. At least for a little while. He suddenly felt warm, and the pain was quickly fading away. Ren slowly opened his eyes and he could see Gabriel's hand over Ren, glowing, healing Ren.

Ren slowly got up and put his hand on his head and shook away the light-headedness. He was going to say something to Gabriel, but noticed Michael standing a couple feet away, his back turned away from him, his arms crossed behind his back.

Ren yelled, "Michael!" and tried to shoot hellfire from his hand at him, but nothing came out.

He was going to try again when he noticed that he wasn't in his half-demon form; he was in his human form.

Gabriel said, "It's no use, Ren. You don't have demonic powers anymore. You're not a demon anymore."

Ren looked at Gabriel with a confused and scared look. "No, no, you can't be serious. This is a joke, right?" Ren looked at his hand and tried to transform but he couldn't. He couldn't shoot hellfire, couldn't use telekinesis, couldn't tele-port—hell, he couldn't even sense Gabriel or Michael's energy.

Ren really was not a demon anymore. He was just a human soul.

Ren yelled at Michael, "What the fuck did you do to me?"

Michael didn't even turn around to look at Ren. "The spell that I used on you completely took your demonic powers away and in doing so, it did so many good things to the world."

"What good things?"

Michael finally turned. It might be only his head, but he was now looking at Ren.

He said, "For starters, all of the seals are fixed."

Ren said with a lifeless tone, "What?"

"All the seals you, your new friends, and your kind had broken have all been fixed. All your pain and suffering was for nothing."

Ren couldn't believe what he was hearing. All the fights that he'd been through, all those timess he almost died, all the humans that he sacrificed were for nothing.

Michael said, "But don't worry, there's more."

Ren looked up to stare straight into Michael's eyes.

Michael said, "The gate to hell has been shut forever. Every demonic piece of trash, no matter what number they were, if they even had a number, is now stuck in hell forever."

Ren said, "Which means..."

Michael fully turned around. "Yep. All your new friends that you somehow made in hell—you won't be able to see them ever again."

That was the last straw for Ren. He charged at Michael and tried to punch him. But Michael used his telekinesis to stop Ren and lift him up in the air.

Michael said, "What are you so angry for? We haven't gotten to the best part yet."

Ren was struggling to break free. "What best part?"

Michael took a pause for a second, then out of nowhere, suddenly screamed, "EVERYONE THAT JUST CAME BACK, COME HERE RIGHT NOW!!!"

Ren didn't know why he was yelling but he was going to find out now. A bunch of light appeared around Ren, and not just one or two lights, but multiple lights just kept appearing around him at different times, blinding him until it just stopped and he could finally open his eyes.

A bunch of angels had appeared in the church, and these weren't any angels Ren knew. Every single one of the angels was an angel that Ren had killed. From the last angel that he killed before he went on his vacation to the very first two angels that he killed in front of his parents' house.

Ren was shaking so much that it was like a magnitude ten earthquake was happening, but just to him. Ren was looking around and seeing every angel looking back at him with pure anger toward him. But suddenly in the distance, a very familiar voice started to talk.

"Well, well, look what we have here."

Ren knew that voice. Ren wished he didn't know that voice, but he did. The figure was walking toward him from behind and when he fully walked past Ren into his field of vision, it was him.

Raphael said with a creepy smile, "Did you miss me?"

Ren, with the most scared voice of his life, said, "Raphael, how?"

"Yep, it's me. Let me get right back to you in a second."

Raphael, as much as he wanted to hurt Ren, walked toward Michael and Gabriel and bowed. "Hello, brothers. Nice to see you."

Both Michael and Gabriel said, "Nice to see you too, Raphael."

Raphael lifted up his head, crossed his arms, and said, "Now, I am very happy to be back and all, but I have to ask. How am I—no, how is everyone here alive? I'm pretty sure that we all died because of him over there. And what happened to him?"

Gabriel said, "Michael got a spell from Father to take away Ren's powers, fix all of the seals, shut the gates of hell, and finally bring back to life all the angels that the demon has killed." The way he said it was a little fast and a little bit angry. Maybe because he hated that he had to repeat what the spell did again.

All Raphael said when he heard all that was, "Father gave you that spell, Michael?"

Then every other angel in the room started to talk.

"Father."

"Father."

"Father."

Ren didn't need to know who they were all talking about. But that made Ren even more angry. Ren screamed in pure rage, surprising every angel, even Michael, Gabriel, and Raphael.

"GOD GAVE YOU THAT SPELL? BULLSHIT! DON'T LIE TO ME! YOU CREATED THAT SPELL AND WAITED FOR THIS FINAL MOMENT JUST TO BE A DICK! GOD DOESN'T GIVE A FUCK ABOUT ANY OF US. IF HE DID, HE WOULD HAVE STOPPED THIS WAR A WHILE AGO! OR BETTER YET, HE COULD HAVE STOPPED RAPHAEL FROM SENDING ME TO HELL AND SENT ME TO HEAVEN SO NONE OF THIS WOULD HAVE EVER HAPPENED!!" Ren screamed so loud that blood came out of his mouth while he was screaming. He was slowly losing his voice.

Gabriel chuckled a little and said, "Wow. That was— Wow." He couldn't say anything. He was just shocked by what a human had just said about God and in front of Michael and every angel.

Every angel got furious with Ren; even Raphael got mad. When every angel was about to say something, Michael raised his hand up in the air, saying, "Don't say a word." Every angel, including Raphael, stayed silent.

Michael, surprisingly, wasn't mad. He knew Ren would have this reaction. So he said, "No. God did give me the spell."

Ren, with his damaged voice, said, "Then why did he wait so long? Why did he wait until there was one seal left?"

Michael said, "Because he had faith in us. In humans and in angels. He didn't think he had to step in for his children's problems. He thought that since Raphael started all of this, he would fix it. But when Raphael died by your hands, that's when God decided to make the spell with all of those benefits."

Ren didn't say anything else, not because his throat hurt, but because he couldn't think of anything to say.

Michael said, "Now, since we are done talking, let's go into your punishment."

"Punishment?"

"Yes, your punishment. You will go to heaven, and before you say anything—no, it's not what it sounds like. You will go to heaven in heaven's prison, where you will be crucified to a wall. And there you will bleed to death for all eternity, starve for all eternity, be dehydrated for all eternity, and be in complete darkness. You won't be able to see a single light for eternity, and for the best part—you'll the only prisoner in heaven's prison. For the first time, you'll be all alone. No one to talk to. Not even a rat or insect soul will be in there to great you. You'll go in and you will rot."

All the color on Ren's face—no, his entire body—was gone. He was as white as paper. Then Ren managed to get some more words to say to Michael.

"But that's not fair. What about Raphael? He did this—he caused all of this."

Michael said, "Raphael will get no punishment because he is an archangel. My brother— I'm not going to punish him. If I had to choose which one to hurt—my brother or one lowly human soul—I'll pick the human soul anytime."

"But that's not fair! This is his fault! You said this is his fault!"

Michael gave Ren a cold and evil look and said, "Yeah, but I don't care. The entire world doesn't know that Raphael, an archangel caused this war upon humanity. Forever, they will only know that a demon, a random demon named Ren, caused this war for the sake of Satan and Lucifer."

Michael finally let Ren go from his telekinesis. Since the release was so sudden for Ren, he fell on his butt. Michael walked toward Ren. He squatted down to look Ren in the eye and smiled.

Michael said, "But I do have to thank you, Ren. Because of your whole revenge quest, you benefited our religion and the whole world so much."

"What do you mean?"

"Well, for starters, humans won't see a single demon from now on. The human population went down greatly—like, it only has two fifths of humans left on earth, and finally, the only religion that exists now is Christianity. There is no more Taoism, Judaism, Buddhism, et cetera—only our religion. So now, before we all go back to heaven, we are going to hunt down all monsters, Satanists, and satanic items on this world and destroy them. So thank you, Ren."

Ren just stared at Michael. He couldn't believe that they had all of these benefits thanks to him. Michael stood up, turned around, and walked away from Ren slowly, but before Michael left, he had to say one more thing.

"Oh, yeah. We can't have all of you go to heaven with all of that hate in you." Michael was talking to every angel including Raphael. "So, before you all go back to heaven, you can all take your time beating the shit out of Ren here."

Ren quickly looked up at the back of Michael's head in shock, but he wasn't the only one—even Gabriel looked at Michael in shock.

But every other angel looked at Michael with excitement and happiness.

Michael said, "That's right, brothers and sisters. We can't have all that sin in heaven, so take it out on him. Take your time, make sure he feels every punch and kick or whatever you're going to do to him. Make sure it's not from any of your weapons or powers; remember, I want him alive so we can put him in prison. And if he is about to pass out from the pain, heal him so he stays awake. If he gets too used to the pain, heal him so he doesn't get to used to it. If you are not satisfied, just keep healing him until you are satisfied. Just keep going until your heart is satisfied."

Every angel screamed with excitement like it was a party.

Michael said, "Come on, Gabriel, we have to tell Father about our report."

Gabriel, however, was looking at Ren and saw the pure terror on his face. Gabriel wanted to say something to Michael to change his mind. But he didn't because he knew Michael wouldn't listen.

Michael said, "Oh, and if you help him, I'll kill you myself."

That settled it; Gabriel walked toward Michael and was ready to teleport away.

Gabriel looked at Ren in his eyes one more time and said, "I'm sorry, Ren." A tear came from his eye. Showing that he was sorry and that he did like Ren.

With that, Michael and Gabriel teleported away.

Ren was shaking. He couldn't stop the tears from coming out of his eyes, and looking around to see every angel laughing sadistically and cracking their knuckles and walking slowly toward Ren made him more scared.

Ren thought, "No, no, this isn't fair. Why is this happening to me? This is Raphael's fault, not mine. I don't deserve this. I had a good life, a good family, amazing friends, I was going to be a doctor. Why did it all change so much? No! NO, STAY AWAY FROM ME!"

Ren screamed, with all his might, and in fright, "NNNNNN-NOOOOOOOOOO!"

END

The religious war ended.

Or had it?

Stabbed.

Ren screamed in pain.

An angel said, "Phew! That was the last one."

Another angel said, "Yeah."

Ren had a spike through each palm and a spike that went through both his feet, crucifying him. Ren's blood was seeping profusely out of the wound.

"Okay, let's go. We have to help find a pack of werewolves."

"Yeah, but hold on just a second. I want to do one thing."

The angel, without warning, punched Ren in the face. Blood went flying and Ren spit three teeth out.

"Okay, you got a hit. Now come on. I don't want to be yelled at for being late."

Both angels closed Ren's door and locked it. Then they both left the room, turning off the lights, making it completely dark just like Michael said.

Ren was still crying and quietly said to himself, "Why? Why, why me?"

"Hello?"

Now, the end.

About the Author

Bradley Hall was born in California with his twin sister in 1999. Bradley spent his life in Rising Sun, Maryland, going to school, playing with friends, playing video games, watching anime, going for walks, and helping his family with chores.

Bradley didn't do anything outstanding in his life and was content having a normal life, but he did feel like something was missing, so after many years, he realized that he loved reading and making stories in his head. One day, he decided to make his new dream a reality, so he picked one of the stories that he thought of that he liked the most and made it into this book, called *Religious Wars*.